A Hymn for the Dying

The Kelk Conflict: Annihilation

Book 1 of *The Blacksword Regiment*

by

J. L. Doty

TELEMACHUS PRESS

This book or eBook is a work of fiction. Names, characters, places and incidents are either the product of the author's imagination or are used fictitiously. Any resemblance to actual persons, living or dead, or to actual events or locales is entirely coincidental.

A Hymn for the Dying, Book 1 of *The Blacksword Regiment*
This book or eBook is licensed for your personal enjoyment only. This book or eBook may not be re-sold or given away to other people. If you're reading this book or eBook and did not purchase it, or it was not purchased for your use only, then you should return it and purchase your own copy. Thank you for respecting the hard work of the author.

The publisher does not have any control over and does not assume any responsibility for author or third-party websites or their content.

Cover designed by J. L. Doty.

Published by Telemachus Press, LLC
http://www.telemachuspress.com

Visit the author's website:
http://www.jldoty.com

ISBN: 978–1–951744–19–9 (eBook)
ISBN: 978–1–951744–20–5 (paperback)
ISBN: 978–1–953757–19–7 (hardback)

Version 2023.03.26

KEpuz!po!KJNEFTLUPQ:
Formatted using eTools for Writers 3.8.8, Mar 28 2023, 12:49:58
Copyright © 2013–2016 by J. L. Doty

Printed in the United States of America

10 9 8 7 6 5 4 3 2 1

A Hymn for the Dying

The Kelk Conflict: Annihilation

Book 1 of *The Blacksword Regiment*

For many, the dying part is hard.
For some, the living part is harder.

1

Taken

NEAR MID-AFTERNOON Mathius approached the street where he, his sister, and their parents lived in a small apartment. So far the area had been spared the bombing that had turned most of the city into rubble, perhaps because one of the government factions occupied their district. The regime's soldiers were not kind, but Mathius had heard the rebels were worse.

As their neighborhood came into view, some instinct warned him something had changed while he'd been out. He paused, stepped into the shadow of a nearby building, and scanned the deserted street. He waited, watched, and listened—nothing but silence punctuated by the occasional pop of a distant gun shot, then more silence, too much silence.

Mathius had started the day like any other by going out to scrounge for food and water. Every day it had become more difficult to find the tiniest morsel to alleviate the gnawing emptiness in his gut. Even water had become scarce, so much so that they had stopped bathing. Today his scrounging had not been successful, and if his father's luck had been no better, then he, his sister and their parents would go without dinner that evening. Of late, they'd gone without dinner quite frequently, and hunger had become a constant companion.

He watched the street for several minutes, but saw nothing to warrant his caution. Nevertheless, when he stepped out of his shadow he moved in a crouch, then stopped in another shadow. He held his breath and scanned the street in both directions—nothing. Skipping from shadow to shadow, stopping in each for several seconds and waiting, he reached their building without incident. As he approached it the door swung open, revealing his father, who must have been watching for him.

"Get inside quickly," his father said. But his eyes suddenly widened, and he looked past Mathius.

Behind Mathius, a gravelly voice said, "Ain't you a cautious one!"

Mathius jumped at the sound of the man's voice and spun about. Two rebels dressed in faded, dirty military uniforms stood across the street. Both held rifles aimed at Mathius and his father. One of them had a smooth chin and appeared to be a bit younger than Mathius's sixteen standard years. The other appeared to be middle aged, with several days of prickly stubble blanketing his jaw.

The older man said, "Guess we know which building to search first."

Looking down the barrels of the rebels' rifles, Mathius and his father stood un-moving as more rebels emerged from hiding. Their leader barked orders, pointing and waving his hands, and four of them slung their weapons over their shoulders. Two of the four pinned Mathius's arms painfully behind his back, and the other two did the same to his father. One of the soldiers slammed the butt of his rifle into Mathius's gut, and pain forced him to double over and gasp for air. The men holding his arms didn't let him fall to the ground, and thankfully he hadn't had anything to eat that day, so he didn't vomit.

Their leader demanded, "Which apartment is yours?"

Mathius's father pleaded, "Don't hurt the boy. I'll show you. I'll show you."

Mathius still couldn't breathe and continued to gulp for air as the two men dragged him up the stairs to the second floor, then into the living room of their small apartment. One of them slapped Mathius's face hard and said, "Stand, god damn it."

Mathius managed to get his feet beneath him, still struggling to breathe. One of the rebels restraining his father grimaced with effort, and his father cried out, pain dis-torting his face.

The rebels searched the apartment, emptying drawers onto the floor and overturn-ing furniture. One of them emerged from a back bedroom holding a dress. "Women's clothes," he said. "Other women's stuff too. They got women."

The rebel leader grinned, reached down to a holster on his hip and pulled a grav gun. He pressed the muzzle of the pistol against the side of Mathius's father's head and demanded, "Where are the women?"

The rebels' wary eyes darted continuously about the room. The boy about Mathi-us's age had the same hard, unyielding look of the older men. Smudges of dirt on their faces and arms gave them a filthy, hungry look.

One of the rebels said, "Mercier, just kill the old man and get it over with."

Mathius had just learned the name of the rebel leader, though he wasn't sure how that would help him and his father.

"Where are the fucking women?" the man named Mercier snarled. "Where did you hide them?"

Mathius's father grimaced as one of the men behind him twisted his arm upward. Hissing his words through clenched teeth, his father said, "I don't know . . . where they are."

With the government split into two opposing forces, and the rebels split into three, and all five vying to annihilate each other, the civilian population had learned to live with whoever gained control of a piece of the city on any given day. That morning their district had been under the thumb of the more benign of the two government factions. While Mathius had been out scrounging, a rebel faction must have swept into the west side and met little resistance from their previous masters.

Mercier pressed the muzzle of his gun harder against his father's head and shouted, "You're lying." Mathius's father cringed as bits of spittle erupted from the rebel's mouth and spattered his face.

His father shook his head. "I sent them away and didn't ask where they were going. That way I wouldn't know and couldn't tell."

The rebel leader must realize any smart man would have done the same to protect his wife and daughter. Mathius's father had nothing to reveal, so killing him would be useless, senseless, a complete waste of a human life. Mathius hoped Mercier would realize that and lower his gun. He and his father would get away with just an unpleasant beating. During the last year they'd endured far worse; they could survive a beating.

Mercier nodded, and Mathius stifled a sigh of relief as the man did lower his gun. But then, in one quick motion, the fellow pressed the muzzle against Mathius's father's knee, and pulled the trigger. The grav pistol roared with the characteristic sound of a giant spring uncoiling, followed by a blast of supersonic shock as the projectile exited the barrel. It disintegrated his father's knee in a cloud of meat, bone and blood, spattering bits of it across the room. His father screamed and collapsed, but the two soldiers holding him kept him upright, and he dangled by his arms from their iron-like grips.

Mercier snarled in his father's ear, "Don't lie to me again, asshole."

With tears streaming down his face, his father gasped, "I really . . . don't know . . . where . . . they are. I . . . swear . . . I don't."

"You *swear* you don't," Mercier said. "Well that makes all the difference in the world."

The rebel leader straightened, lowered the gun and nodded thoughtfully, rubbing at the stubble on his chin. With the exception of the boy standing near the door, all of the soldiers exhibited several days' growth of beard.

"Yah," Mercier said. "Come to think of it, you probably are telling the truth."

Mathius's thoughts raced. After the rebels released them, he'd have to get his father to a hospital, if he could find one still functioning. His father would probably lose the leg, but at least he'd live.

"Yah," the rebel leader said. "So you're of no use to me." He raised the grav pistol and pressed it against the side of Mathius's father's head.

For the rest of his life Mathius would always wish he had had the foresight to look away. But with nothing to gain from a senseless killing, he'd assumed Mercier would let them go, and he stupidly looked on as he again heard the roar of the grav gun. His father's head exploded, showering the men holding him with bits of bone and blood and gray matter, pieces of it sticking to the wall behind them.

"No," Mathius shouted, struggling against the men holding him.

Mercier turned at the shout, looked Mathius in the eyes and said, "But you're young enough we can use you."

He looked over Mathius's head at one of the men holding him. "He's your responsibility, Cranoch. See to it he learns to shoot what he's supposed to shoot."

"You killed him for no reason," Mathius shouted, tears streaming down his cheeks.

Mercier shrugged, swung the heavy grav pistol out and slapped Mathius in the face.

••••

The rumble of the big transition ship's drive vibrated through the deck as Cadet Nikaela Vreekande stopped outside the office of the ship's commanding officer, Command Eagle Kristdokar. She wanted to make a good impression, so she took a brief second to check her Kelk uniform, made sure there were no wrinkles, and that every emblem and insignia had been positioned properly. Some of the most powerful members of the Larscom—the highest ranking officers and ruling elite of the Kelk Supremacy—were known to seek Kristdokar's advice upon occasion. And rumor had it that the command eagle might someday occupy a seat on the Larscom Executive Council. Such a sponsor could be enormously beneficial to Nikaela's nascent career.

Nikaela rapped once on the office door, and spoke through her implants, "Cadet Vreekande requesting permission to enter."

A harsh female voice answered. "Enter."

Nikaela pressed the door switch and it dilated, revealing a small room with an older woman seated behind a compact desk, the flash of brass eagles glinting on her collars. Her salt-and-pepper gray hair had aged to mostly salt with just a hint of pepper, and like all Kelk men and women, she wore her hair long. Kristdokar had opted for the shorter style of shoulder length, which was about as short as any Kelk would allow, but not uncommon among the military because of its functionality aboard ship, or beneath the helmet of combat armor. The slight bluish tint to her chalk-white skin had faded somewhat, but the bright red irises of her eyes pinned Nikaela to the spot with a piercing stare.

Nikaela stepped through the door, eyes locked rigidly forward, and heard it contract behind her. She snapped to attention, raised her right hand and held it flat just above her left breast. "Cadet Nikaela Vreekande reporting as ordered, mistress."

Mistress Kristdokar raised her hand and returned the salute as crisply as any of Nikaela's instructors back at the academy. "Ease," she said.

Nikaela put her fists on her hips and spread her feet to shoulder width, standing as rigidly as she had while at attention.

The command eagle leaned back in her chair and eyed Nikaela with that piercing stare. The moment drew out into an uncomfortable silence, and when she finally spoke, Nikaela almost flinched.

"Your mother vied for a career in service to the Supremacy, but proved to be a rather mediocre officer, and never advanced beyond the rank of command superior. Did she blame us that she never rose to the same stature as your grandmother, that she was never invited to join the Larscom?"

Nikaela's grandmother, Major Skalde Adeska Vreekande was a woman who intimidated everyone. Nikaela didn't want this conversation to be about her mother's regrets, or about her grandmother's successes. "No, mistress," she said, "my mother blamed only herself."

Kristdokar nodded. "Did she now?"

"Yes, mistress," Nikaela said. "She told me I should always accept responsibility for my failures, as she did. I think she wanted to set an example."

Kristdokar gave her an unpleasant smile and leaned forward. "But you don't seem to have too many failures for which you must accept responsibility. You've just finished your second year at the academy at the top of your class. Keep that up, and in two more years you'll graduate with honors. Why are you so different from your mother, Mistress Vreekande?"

Nikaela wasn't about to reveal that her mother had done everything possible to ensure her daughter succeeded where she had failed, or that Nikaela had always resented the cold discipline her mother had inflicted on her family. But she thought it might not be a bad thing to reveal that her mother had successfully ignited the flame of ambition in her daughter. "I'm more ambitious than my mother, mistress."

Kristdokar's smile softened. "Good. Ambition is not a bad thing, and it certainly seems to have done well for you. But be careful that you don't let it cloud your judgement on a critical issue."

Nikaela nodded. "I'll try not to, mistress."

Kristdokar leaned back in her chair and regarded Nikaela for a moment. "Did you know that your grandmother sponsored me when I was a very junior officer fresh out of the academy?"

That came as a complete surprise to Nikaela. By custom, a woman could not sponsor her own daughter, but her mother had always resented the fact that her grandmother had not used her considerable influence among the elite of the Larscom to find an appropriate sponsor for her. "No, mistress, I did not know that."

Kristdokar smiled as if she had expected that answer. "Your performance at the academy has brought you to my attention. I and others are watching you closely. Don't disappoint us."

Nikaela said, "I don't intend to, mistress."

It came out more brashly than she had intended, but the command eagle seemed to approve of her boldness.

Kristdokar abruptly stood. "Your third year at the academy begins in a little under a hundred days. I have you until then, and I intend to push you to your limits. We'll see if you can do better than your mother."

To Nikaela, that sounded like a challenge, one she would be happy to meet.

••••

Mathius didn't lose consciousness, but lay on the floor for several seconds while his head swam. Two of the rebels secured his hands behind his back with plast manacles. His face throbbed where Mercier had struck him, and he tasted blood.

Cranoch stood over him, kicked him in the ribs and said, "Get up. If you can't walk I'm not going to waste the effort carrying you. You'll get the same as your father, so get up, shit-for-brains."

Mathius lay there, and as his mind kept replaying the image of his father's head exploding, he didn't care if they killed him. But something inside him made him roll onto his side and struggle to rise, though with his hands manacled behind his back his efforts proved futile. Cranoch and Mercier laughed at his unsuccessful exertions, then Cranoch hooked a hand under one of Mathius's armpits and yanked him to his feet.

They left his father lying on the threadbare carpet in a pool of blood. Using their rifle butts for encouragement, they marched Mathius out onto the street, and forced him to sit there while they searched the other apartments, houses and buildings.

After Cranoch emerged from one, Mathius heard him say to Mercier. "Another empty house. They must have heard we was coming."

Somehow the neighborhood had been forewarned and fled. Mathius assumed that his father had stayed behind to wait for him, and had died because of him. He tried not to think of it that way, but in his heart he knew that to be the truth.

The rebels searched all the houses and buildings on the street and collected whatever they found useful, which wasn't much. Mathius's neighbors had started the day with little in the way of food, and they would end the day with even less. They marched Mathius away, forcing him to follow Mercier and his men, with Cranoch walking behind him, encouraging him with kicks and slaps.

Mathius struggled on, reliving again and again his father's death. He shook his head and tried to flush that memory from his mind. He stumbled, and Cranoch cuffed him in the side of the head. Mathius staggered and fell to his knees. Cranoch cuffed him again and he cried out in pain. The older man leaned over him and said, "Nothing but silence from you, asshole. Got it?"

Mathius nodded, eager to avoid the older man's fist.

"You're learning," Cranoch said. "And you'd better keep learning. Now get up, and show me you can catch up with the rest."

Mathius struggled back onto his feet and rushed to catch up with the other rebels, Cranoch dogging his heels, kicking and cuffing him even when he did keep up. They walked for a couple of kilometers and led him to a walled compound with a gate that had been constructed by slapping together random sheets of metal. Mercier stopped outside the gate and exchanged words with two guards. The gate screeched with an unholy racket as the guards swung it open, and they walked onto the grounds of an old mansion hidden behind a stone wall on a large lot. About fifty rebels moved about, all wearing a mismatched mix of cobbled-together uniforms.

The grounds inside the wall were mostly bare dirt, but well maintained, without the debris that littered the streets. The mansion stood two stories high in the middle of the compound, its walls pocked with holes from weapons fire. It had a flat roof, on which Mathius spotted several snipers, the barrels of their guns aimed out toward the city surrounding them. On a balcony on the second floor a woman leaned on a stone balustrade, her billowing dress exposing copious amounts of cleavage. Behind her stood a young girl that appeared to be about Mathius's age. She wore a dress made of some sort of sheer fabric, and in the bright sunlight the dark areolas of her small breasts produced faint shadows behind the thin material. Their eyes met, and he saw nothing in hers but a haunted emptiness. He wondered if soon he would look out at the world through eyes like hers, lifeless and devoid of hope.

The older woman called down to Cranoch, "Got a newbie, eh? A little old, isn't he?"

"He's young enough to learn," Cranoch said. "It just may take a little longer to teach him what he needs to learn."

Mercier added, "And he'll have a stronger back than the rest. We'll make good use of him."

To Cranoch, Mercier said, "I have to report in." He nodded toward Mathius. "Get him settled."

Mercier climbed the steps at the front of the mansion while Cranoch pointed to a couple of the men and said, "You and you. Come with me"

Cranoch grabbed Mathius by the back of his neck, and with a mix of kicks and slaps he guided him to a building at the back of the walled compound. Two boys sat on the ground in the shade of one of the building's walls, their hands cuffed in front of them. They appeared to be about eight or nine years old, their faces covered with smudges of dirt, and in their eyes Mathius saw stark and unremitting fear.

Cranoch stopped in front of the seated boys, then spun Mathius to face him. "What's your name, kid?"

Mathius thought about giving him a false name, but Cranoch saw something in his face and raised a hand to cuff him. Mathius cringed and said, "Mathius. My name's Mathius."

Cranoch gave him an unpleasant grin. "Well then, Mathius,"—he waved a hand at the two seated boys—"meet Timor and Phillan. You three are going to get to know each other real good."

Without warning Cranoch spun Mathius about. The two men accompanying them each grabbed one of Mathius's arms, and held them while Cranoch removed the manacles binding his hands behind his back. Then they pressed Mathius's back against the outer wall of the building. They lifted his hands above his head to a set of manacles that had been bolted to the wall a few meters from the two younger boys. Mathius didn't resist as they locked his wrists into the manacles, knowing such an effort would be futile. The two men walked away while Cranoch took a step back, put his hands on his hips and looked Mathius over carefully.

Standing there with his arms held above his head, Mathius looked into the older man's eyes, and again the image of his father's last moment of life returned to him. It kept coming back no matter how hard he tried to suppress it.

Cranoch raised his fist and held it in front of Mathius's nose. "Look at this, boy, and tell me what you see."

The threat of the older man standing in front of him forced his attention back to the moment. "A fist," he said.

Cranoch shook his head sadly. "No, Mathius. It's not a fist. It's your teacher."

The older man lowered the fist and drew it back, doing so slowly and methodically as if he wanted Mathius to know what was coming. Then he punched Mathius in the ribs. Mathius cried out, but with his hands locked in the manacles bolted to the wall above his head, he couldn't double over.

Cranoch hit him again and his legs buckled, tears streaming down his cheeks. The manacles cut into his wrists as he hung there with his knees dangling just above the ground.

Cranoch said, "That was your first lesson, kid. We'll continue the lessons in the morning."

The older man turned and walked away. Mathius watched his back recede as he crossed the compound, and any hope he might have had of escaping left him in that instant.

2

Hanging, Leaning, Hanging, Leaning

WHILE THE COMMONWEALTH Senate Intelligence Committee heatedly debated the situation on Novalis III, Lieutenant Colonel Katrine Primatov stood near the back of the room and tried to tune out the noise. Like everyone on Trafalgar, the capital planet of the Commonwealth, they all had their own opinion on how to handle an unpleasant civil war on a minor planet for which they had no official responsibility. Since they had convened in closed session, the politicians spoke with more candor than they might have otherwise. As a senior Blacksword officer, Katrine frequently sat in on their discussions, and might be called upon to advise the politicians.

Her implants chimed and her AI said, *Colonel Blacksword wishes to speak with you, but if you can't break away, she said it's not urgent.*

She subvocalized, "Please put her through."

The colonel's image appeared superimposed onto her visual cortex. Fran Thealone, also known as Colonel Blacksword, was a small, wiry woman with thin cheeks, blue eyes and short white hair. "Katrine," she said. "Any progress?"

As long as Katrine didn't actually vocalize her words, the conversation would remain fully encrypted. "Some," she said. "By and large, they'd like to intervene on humanitarian grounds. But the legal issues we'll run into if we interfere in the internal strife of an independent planet have them stymied. At least they're being pragmatic."

"Any way we can use the Kelk as an excuse?"

Katrine shrugged. "That's why they're in closed session. We know the Kelk are involved. For the most part they're providing humanitarian aid to one of the factions, and maybe we can prove they're shipping in some small arms and ammunition. But that's just not enough."

The colonel shook her head, "Yah, we'd end up with all the independent systems on our back."

Katrine said, "And you can bet the Kelk would have their fingers in that pie."

"You've got people on the ground?" Thealone asked.

"Yes," Katrine said. "If they come up with anything even remotely actionable, I'll let you know."

The colonel signed out.

Katrine returned to listening to a discussion that had digressed into a tedious repetition of an argument that had gone around once already, and come back again.

••••

Mathius had learned that the manacles bolted to the wall were too high up for him to kneel on the ground. He struggled to his feet after Cranoch left, and tried to catch his breath. His fears darted from one thought to another, but thirst quickly surfaced and demanded his attention. He desperately wanted to wash away the salty taste of his own tears.

Dusk had settled over the city, with night not far off. He glanced around the compound, then looked down at the two boys seated on the ground nearby. They stared back at him with wide eyes, but when he looked their way, they lowered their eyes to the ground and quickly bowed their heads.

He said, "My name is Mathius."

The younger of the two boys had short-cropped, brown hair light enough to be almost blond, and a fair complexion. As Mathius waited, the boy slowly raised his head, but refused to look him in the eyes.

"I'm Timor," he said.

The older boy was his opposite, with olive skin and black hair that would probably glisten in the sunlight were it not for a powdering of dust in the dark strands. At the sound of the younger boy's voice, he looked up and said, "I'm Phillan."

Mathius said, "I'm really thirsty. Can you get me some water?"

Both boys shook their heads frantically. Timor said, "We're not allowed to move without permission. We have to be good boys, or Cranoch will teach us a lesson."

Mathius understood such fear, and it occurred to him he would probably come to understand it even more in the days to come.

Shortly before sunset, a rebel guard looped a chain through the manacled arms of the two boys, then locked both ends of it to a metal spike driven into the ground. The guard also delivered a bowl of food for each, but nothing for Mathius.

Mathius hadn't eaten in more than a day and his stomach growled. He asked, "Do I get something to eat?"

The guard looked at him and grinned, but said nothing.

Mathius pleaded, "Can I at least have some water?"

The guard grinned again, and walked away.

From his position standing above the two seated boys, Mathius saw that the food in Phillan's bowl contained a watery gruel, while Timor's contained a thicker and more substantial slop, with bits and pieces of something to chew on. Phillan looked at the gruel in his bowl, his eyes blank and uncaring. He lifted it to his lips and swallowed some of it, then lowered it and looked at the better food in Timor's bowl with undisguised envy. He turned to Mathius and said, "If you're a good boy, you get better food. They start you on the bad stuff, and you have to prove you can be good."

Mathius hadn't been far off about the ages of the two boys. Timor was eight, and Phillan ten. Both tended to avert their gaze whenever he looked their way, though he sometimes caught them watching him when they thought he had turned his attention elsewhere. The two young boys had been captives of the rebels for about three months, so apparently Phillan had not been good enough. Phillan looked at the empty bowl in his hands and said, "I'll learn to be good, real good. I will."

That night Mathius never did find a way to sleep. The height of the manacles wouldn't allow him to sit or kneel, so he tried leaning against the wall and dozing lightly, but weariness crept up on him and he scraped his face as he slid a few centimeters down the wall, then jerked awake. He tried putting one foot about half a step out from wall, and locking his knee so that his leg could act as a rigid brace. But as he started to drift off his knee buckled, and when he snapped to a stop hanging from the manacles with his knees just above the ground, he wrenched his shoulder painfully. He dozed briefly, suspended from the manacles, but his shoulders began to ache, and hanging from his wrists limited his breathing to shallow gasps. The night passed in an agonizingly slow dance of hanging by his wrists, then standing and leaning on the wall, hanging, then standing, hanging, standing, hanging . . .

Mathius heard the slap as a distant noise that seemed to have nothing to do with him. But a fraction of an instant after his mind registered the sound, his head rocked to one side and his face lit up with fire. He didn't have the strength to climb to his feet, but two men lifted him by his armpits and stood him up facing Cranoch, supporting him between them. The night had ended and the early morning sun lit the grounds of the compound with long shadows.

Cranoch leaned close to him hand spoke softly. "You almost weren't breathing. Can't have you dying on me before I know if you can be a good boy. What have you got to say for yourself, shit-head?"

Mathius smelled some sort of food on the older man's breath. But his throat had gone so dry he couldn't speak, couldn't even swallow, could only think of something to wet his lips and throat. He managed to croak, "Water."

"Water," Cranoch said as if addressing a large audience. "He wants water. We rescue him from the streets, and he wants us to give him some of our precious water."

Cranoch looked at Timor and Phillan who still sat on the ground nearby. "You two, stand up."

The two boys jumped to their feet, but with the chain tethering them to the spike in the ground they could only stand in a crouch.

Cranoch asked them, "Should we give him some of our precious water?"

Timor said, "I don't know."

Phillan said, "Sure, why not?"

Cranoch nodded carefully as if he agreed with the boy, then his hand lashed out with blinding speed and he backhanded Phillan. The boy slammed to the ground, and because of the chain connecting him to Timor, he dragged the smaller boy down with him.

Timor lay still like a small animal in the presence of a large predator, his eyes wide and focused on Cranoch. Phillan struggled up onto his elbows, his eyes rolling about and his head rocking from side to side.

"Wrong answer," Cranoch said. "We can't give him water if he doesn't ask politely like a good little boy, can we?"

Timor shook his head frantically. Phillan's eyes continued to roll about without focusing.

Cranoch leaned close to Mathius and said, "You have to ask me real nice-like, like a good little boy."

Mathius said, "Water. Please."

Cranoch rubbed his chin and considered Mathius thoughtfully. "That's better, but still not good enough. For such an impolitely worded request, I shouldn't give you any water at all. But I'm feeling generous. And in any case, it would be a shame if you died, and I do want to keep you alive for a bit."

While the two men continued to support Mathius, Cranoch removed Timor and Phillan's manacles. Then to Timor he said, "Go get Mathius a cup of water."

Mathius breathed a sigh of relief as Timor scurried away across the grounds of the compound. While they waited Mathius couldn't keep his eyes open, and though he tried to fight it, sleep pressed at him and his chin bobbed toward his chest. Fire lit up the side of his face as another open-handed blow rocked his head to one side, and he cried out.

The older man said, "You're not paying attention to your elders, Mathius, and that's very rude."

Cranoch slapped him again, lighting up the other cheek with a fiery burn.

Mathius saw Timor coming their way from across the yard, carrying a small metal cup filled to the brim with water sloshing over its sides. The boy stopped in front of Mathius and extended the cup, but Cranoch said, "Timor, did I give you permission to give the cup to Mathius?"

Timor's eyes widened, and he jerked the cup away from Mathius toward Cranoch, spilling some of the water. He held it up to the older man and said, "I'm sorry. I'm sorry."

Cranoch reached out and took the cup from the boy, smiling and speaking kindheartedly. "You're forgiven this time, Timor." He shook a finger at the boy in a kindly, parental way. "But don't make that mistake again."

The older man looked at the water in the cup and shook his head sadly. "Now that's just too much water for our boy Mathius here. He hasn't yet asked politely enough to get that much water."

Cranoch held the cup out at arm's length, then slowly tilted it to one side. Mathius's world centered on that cup, and as the water cleared the edge and drizzled out of it, he cried out, "No, please no."

The older man smiled and righted the cup, halting the stream of water. He had dripped a small puddle onto the dust of the dry ground, and Mathius watched longingly as the soil slowly absorbed it, leaving nothing but a darkened spot of dirt.

Looking into the cup, Cranoch said, "Now that's the right amount for our boy Mathius."

He extended the cup toward Mathius, who tried to reach for it, but the manacles kept his hands above his head and stopped them far short of the cup. Cranoch pressed the cup to Mathius's lips and upended it in one quick motion. Mathius gulped and got one, small, blessed mouth-full, the rest of it splashing across his face and down his neck. He marveled at the glorious, cleansing taste of it.

"One hour," Cranoch said. "You get one hour to sleep. I want you rested so you can work hard for us."

They released Mathius from the manacles bolted to the wall, locked him in another set of cuffs, tethered him to the spike in the ground, and left him there.

••••

Something crashed into Mathius's ribs, sending a shock of pain through his chest and waking him. He cried out and sat up, squinting at the bright sun now just a bit higher on the horizon. His one hour of sleep had come and gone all too quickly.

Cranoch and another rebel stood over him. The other fellow was younger than Cranoch, but considerably older than Mathius. He said, "He's a pathetic piece of shit."

"Yah," Cranoch said. "But he's got a strong back, or at least he'd better have. Time for him to earn his room and board."

Cranoch leaned down and unlocked Mathius's manacles, then straightened and said, "Put him to work."

With that, Cranoch turned and walked away, leaving the younger man in charge of Mathius. The fellow lifted a boot to kick him again, but he jumped to his feet and backed away from the man. "Follow me," the rebel said.

The man led Mathius across the back of the compound, handed him a pick and shovel, pointed to a spot on the ground and said, "Dig."

Mathius asked, "How deep, and how big?"

"Just dig," he said. "I'll tell you when to stop."

A covered porch had been built onto the back of the mansion at the center of the compound. The rebel left Mathius with his pick and shovel, walked to the porch and sat down in a chair in the shade. He shouted to Mathius, "I told you to dig, god damn it. So get to work."

Mathius sweated under the hot sun, digging holes he learned would be used to anchor fence posts for some sort of enclosure. His brief hour of sleep had reenergized him a little, but he quickly weakened and grew light-headed. Only then did his supervisor allow him the smallest amount of water, and he seemed to begrudge Mathius every drop he consumed.

About mid-day the man fell asleep seated in his chair. Mathius snuck over to the water barrel, quickly drank his fill, and returned to the half-finished post hole he'd been working on. He sat down to rest for a moment, and fell asleep there. The rebel slapped him awake.

At the end of the day Cranoch escorted him back to the manacles bolted high on the outer wall of the outbuilding and locked him there. That night they used a longer chain to tether Timor and Phillan to the spike in the ground. It allowed them to stand up straight and reach Mathius.

Cranoch told the two younger boys. "When Mathius hangs there by his wrists, it looks like he slowly stops breathing. I don't want him to die yet, so you two boys take turns making sure he doesn't. Because if he does die, I'm going to be real unhappy with you two."

Mathius spent another night hanging by his wrists, leaning against the wall, hanging, leaning, hanging, leaning. At one point Timor and Phillan had a heated argument over whose turn it was to get up and wake him, and their raised voices did the job. And because he'd stolen extra water that day, that night he had to pee. With his hands locked above his head, he couldn't think of any other way of accomplishing the task, so he simply pissed his pants.

The next morning Cranoch again granted Mathius one hour of sleep, then turned him over to the other rebel to dig more post holes. And again he managed to steal a little extra water, and a little extra sleep, as long as he didn't mind being slapped awake by the man supervising him.

By the third day in the rebel compound Mathius was starving, and desperately wanted food as well as water. When he asked for some of the gruel they fed Phillan,

Cranoch said, "He wants food now. That is rather presumptuous of you, Mathius. You don't even earn the water we give you, let alone some of our precious food. What are you going to do to convince me I should give you food? Tell me that, Mathius."

Mathius said, "I'll do anything, anything, please." In that moment the realization struck him that he meant every word. He would do anything to make Cranoch happy. "Just tell me what I have to do."

"If we give you food," Cranoch said, "then you have to work that much harder. And someday soon, you're going to have to show me you can be a good boy."

"Anything," Mathius said. "Anything."

That night Cranoch allowed Mathius to drink one small bowl of the watery gruel. Mathius thought that after starving for several days, anything would taste wonderful, but not that gruel. It truly had no taste at all, though it did fill the void in his gut, even if only just a little.

••••

Each day turned into each night, and each night turned into the next day. Mathius lost count of the nights, always locked in the manacles bolted to the wall of the outbuilding, standing, leaning, hanging, standing, leaning, hanging. He learned that if he stood close to the wall, it produced a little slack in the plast tether between the manacles. When he started to drift off to sleep and fell away from the wall, the tether snapped tautly, waking him before he dropped completely. In that way he stood for hour after hour after hour. But even then, exhaustion always won out, and Timor or Phillan woke him, hanging from the manacles, his knees just off the ground.

He lost count of the days digging post holes and occasionally stealing extra water when the man supervising him drifted off to sleep. He coasted through the days and nights in a semiconscious state of delirium, and no longer cared if he lived or died. He swallowed his bowl of gruel, suffered through the night manacled to the wall, and worked through the next day. He didn't think of the days and nights ahead; in the evening his future consisted of merely that one night, and in the morning it consisted of merely that one day. He was always careful to beg for his food and water, and learned that making Cranoch happy was the only thing that mattered in his universe.

Then one night, when he returned from digging post holes, instead of locking him in the manacles bolted into the wall, Cranoch manacled his hands in front of him.

"I'm being nice to you," Cranoch said. "Hands cuffed in front so you can eat and hold your dick when you piss; god knows you stink like piss. But step out of line, and that'll change. Now sit down."

Mathius lowered himself to the ground next to the two boys, and like them sat with his legs crossed.

Cranoch leaned over him and pointed a finger at his nose. "Don't move until I tell you to. In fact, don't even think about moving, because I'll know what you're thinking even before you think it."

That night the guard looped the chain through the manacled arms of all three boys, then locked both ends of it to the metal spike driven into the ground. Mathius tried to count the days since he'd been kidnapped by the rebels; certainly more than one tenday, probably less than two, but he couldn't be certain.

He slept on the ground next to Timor and Phillan. The air had a light chill to it, so they huddled closely to keep warm, though Phillan did object a bit to the smell of urine that permeated Mathius's clothing. Relieved that his ordeal had come to an end, Mathius fell asleep quickly, vowing he would make Cranoch happy.

3

Never Forget

CRANOCH AWOKE THEM in the morning, and for the first time in a long time, Mathius could again think with a little clarity. The older man removed their manacles, and another rebel led Timor and Phillan away. Standing there alone with Mathius, Cranoch said, "Now we start your training, kid."

Mathius had no desire to learn to be a rebel, but knew he had no choice. "Okay," he said, "what do we do?"

"This," Cranoch said, and without warning, the fellow punched Mathius in the nose.

A lance of pain brought tears to Mathius's eyes. He cried out and staggered back as blood streamed out of his nose and dripped from his chin. "Why did you do that? I didn't do anything."

"Training," Cranoch said. "And you didn't go down. That's good. Phillan laid on the ground and cried like a baby when I started his training."

Cranoch drew his fist back, Mathius cringed and covered his face with his hands, so Cranoch hit him in the gut.

Mathius doubled over as the air rushed out of his lungs.

"Don't fall over," Cranoch said. "Show me how long you can stay on your feet." Cranoch raised his fists. "And show me you can fight."

Mathius raised his fists.

Cranoch danced lightly on the balls of his feet, then stepped in for a jab. Mathius tried to block it, but Cranoch dropped into a crouch, spun, swung his leg out and swept Mathius's feet out from beneath him. Mathius hit the ground hard on his back and again the air whooshed out of his lungs.

While he lay there trying to breathe, Cranoch stood over him and shook his head sadly. "And don't ever fight fair." Cranoch kicked him in the ribs. "Remember, only cheaters win."

Cranoch stepped back a pace and said, "Now get on your feet and raise your fists, because the longer you stay down, the harder I'm going to be on you."

Still gasping and trying to catch his breath, Mathius struggled to his feet and raised his fists. Cranoch danced around him and hit him again and again. Mathius staggered about trying to block the blows, but the older man seemed to anticipate each move he made, and all the punches connected painfully. Cranoch beat him until he fell to his knees, his head spinning, and tears streaming down his cheeks.

"And I don't like slobbering and crying," the older man said, then cuffed Mathius in the side of the head, knocking him down onto his shoulder.

"When you cry like some baby, you get even worse."

Cranoch kicked him in the ribs a few times. Mathius lay there, clutching at his sides, hoping the kicking had stopped, wishing the man would be more explicit about what he needed to do to make him happy.

"Get up," Cranoch said, a hard, angry edge to his voice. "If you don't get up now, I'll continue kicking you until you do, or until you're dead. I got no problem kicking you to death, you little turd."

Mathius struggled to his feet and could barely stand. The rebel who had supervised him while he dug post holes joined Cranoch and stood beside him shaking his head sadly. He grinned and said, "He's still a pathetic piece of shit."

That day they put him to work unloading crates from a truck. He spotted a young girl on a balcony on the second floor of the mansion, and he thought he'd seen her before. He paused for a moment and struggled to recall where and when, and he might not have been able to do so had he not remembered the look in her eyes. More than anything, the vacant, empty desolation through which she viewed her surroundings brought the memory back to him. She had stood on that same balcony that first time he'd walked onto the grounds of the compound. The look on her face had not changed since that day.

Every morning Cranoch started Mathius's training with a beating. Mathius suspected the older man pulled his punches to some degree, and not because of any kindness or sympathy; they needed Mathius fit and able to work through the day. He dug holes, scrubbed floors, and sweated over a tub of water to launder the clothing of whoever lived in the mansion. One day they had him unload heavy crates of supplies from a truck. The boxes were marked with words in some foreign language that he couldn't read, but he recognized a graphic symbol stamped on each as the mark of the Kelk Supremacy. On another day he unloaded crates that bore the starburst insignia of the Commonwealth, and those he could read. The Commonwealth supplied them with food and medicine, while the Kelk supplied them with something else.

Mathius had never seen a Kelk, but as a child had heard stories of strange beings with dark-blue skin and demonic red eyes. The tales told of blue-skinned monsters with forked tongues and scaled lizard tails. They stole children in the night, and cooked them for dinner. But as he had grown older, before the unrest on Novalis III had begun and he was still attending school, he had read that they were actually a different race of human.

Mathius recalled the days he'd spent in class with some fondness. His teachers had told him that the Kelk had been isolated on a single planet during an interstellar contraction, and some sort of disaster had produced societal and technological deterioration. Then five hundred years later they reemerged as an interstellar civilization. But centuries of insulated evolution had produced a race adapted to the local planetary and climatological conditions. The Kelk were human, not a separate species, and could interbreed with other races of humankind. But they exhibited exceedingly pale white skin that had a slightly bluish cast to it, salt-and-pepper gray hair, and bright red irises. Mathius had seen a few pictures, and now knew that their eyes did not appear demonic, as the childhood stories had portrayed them, though he didn't know which other parts of the stories to believe.

At random intervals Cranoch marched the three boys down to the river, and made them wade into the water fully dressed to clean their clothes and their bodies at the same time. They were then forced to wear their clothing while it dried out, and on cold days that meant a lot of shivering and chattering teeth. Occasionally, Mathius spotted the young girl on one of the second floor balconies of the mansion, usually in the company of one or more scantily clad women. The women talked with each other, laughed and smoked tobac sticks. The girl just stood at the balcony rail and stared out over the city with those vacant eyes. The days turned into tendays of mind-numbing toil, and each night he returned to the chain to drink his gruel and sleep.

Slowly, through trial and error, each morning during the beating administered by Cranoch, Mathius learned to block many of the older man's punches, but not all of them. Then one day he blocked a punch, and out of sheer frustration he threw a punch of his own. Cranoch side stepped it easily and hit Mathius in the gut. As his abdominal muscles spasmed, Mathius fell to his knees gasping.

"Good," Cranoch said. "Good. You're learning. It took you a while, but at least you finally figured it out."

Mathius didn't understand what was good about that, but that night his bowl of gruel contained a few bits of meat. He savored them, and to make them last as long as he could he tried to chew them slowly. When he finished, hunger still gnawed at his gut.

One day, after his morning beating, the guard overseeing him marched him to the mansion and into the front door. The man showed him to a room where three men were busy at some sort of construction, then he led Mathius to a pile of lumber behind the mansion. Mathius spent the day carrying the lumber to the room under construction and piling it there. He could only lift three or four boards at a time, so the stack of lumber in the back yard dwindled slowly as the day wore on.

On one trip, after he dumped his load of boards in the room, when he stepped into the yard behind the house, he found the young girl standing near the pile of lumber. She stood unmoving and staring at it with her vacant, empty eyes. But as he approached she looked his way, and a tiny spark of life appeared in her face. She had pretty gray eyes, light-brown hair that hung past her shoulders, and he smelled some sort of sweet perfume in the air. She wore that sheer gown he'd seen that first day when entering the compound, and he tried not to stare at her small breasts and the dark shadows of her nipples.

"They make you work hard," she said, her voice a flat monotone.

He shrugged. "I don't have much choice, do I?"

"No," she said. "No choices here. I used to have choices, a long time ago, but not anymore. There was once this—"

The back door of the mansion slammed open with a loud bang, and they both started and looked that way. One of the rebel leaders marched toward them. "There you are," he said. "I've been looking all over for you."

The rebel stepped between Mathius and the girl, and cuffed Mathius in the side of the head, knocking him back a step. "Stay away from her, kid. She ain't for the likes of you. She's mine. All you get is your hand."

Mathius lowered his eyes and bent to pick up more lumber.

The rebel took the girl's wrist, pulled her tightly against him, groped at one of her breasts and kissed her. She looked past the man at Mathius, their eyes met, and the small spark of life he had seen disappeared. In her eyes he now saw nothing, emptiness so complete he thought her humanity had abandoned her.

"You're just what I need right now," the man said. Then he turned, and holding her wrist he marched back into the mansion, with her stepping quickly to keep up.

••••

As the days passed, the beatings grew less brutal and less painful. Mathius never came away from them unbruised, but he slowly learned to live with the pain. And he found he wanted to make Cranoch happy, because the beatings grew less frequent when Mathius did even the simplest of things to prove he could be a good boy.

Phillan had apparently learned to be good, because like Timor, the food in his bowl improved every day. Mathius's gruel also became less watery and more substantial, but not at the same rate as Phillan's.

One evening Phillan told Mathius, "They're teaching us how to use guns so we can help fight the enemy."

"Who are you going to fight," Mathius asked, "government forces, or another rebel faction?"

Timor gave him an odd look, as if the question completely baffled him. Phillan shrugged and said, "I don't know. Just the enemy. Does it matter?"

That night Mathius had trouble falling asleep. He kept replaying that conversation, recalling the look on Timor's face and Phillan's words. Phillan had started out not being good, and had graduated to being good. And now both Phillan and Timor wanted to make their captors happy, would do whatever they asked of them just to get the rewards that came with being a good boy.

Mathius saw that in himself, saw how he had begun to learn the same lesson as the younger boys. Make their captors happy, a simple requirement. Do what they wanted and don't ask questions. First, want to be a good boy, then, learn to be a good boy, and finally, be a good boy.

While Timor's and Phillan's breathing settled into the slow, steady rhythm of deep sleep, Mathius lay awake for some time considering his options. He had no way of determining how deep they had buried the spike that anchored their chain, or if he could pull it out of the ground with sheer brute strength. But that would only free him to move about. With the chain looped through the arms of all three boys and both ends locked to the spike, he'd be tethered to the two younger children. And he still had to get over the wall of the compound, which was well lit at night and carefully patrolled, so he saw no way of gaining his freedom. He'd have to bide his time.

Mathius recalled the image of Mercier murdering his father, and he remembered that the rebel leader had wanted to find his mother and sister. He knew what the rebels would have done to them had they found them. He recalled his encounter with the young girl near the pile of lumber behind the mansion; the momentary spark of life he'd seen in her face haunted his thoughts, the dead eyes in her living face haunted his soul. He imagined his sister wearing that same look of desolation. He resolved then and there that he would survive and make his captors happy, but he would not do so willingly. He would pretend to be everything they wanted him to be, but he would never forget the image of his father's head disappearing in a cloud of blood and brains, nor would he ever forget the young girl's dead eyes. He would be the good little boy they wanted, but someday he would escape. And when he did, maybe he would also call Mercier and Cranoch to account for his father and the girl.

••••

Every night, before Mathius fell asleep, he purposefully lay awake for a while and recalled his father's murder, and that young girl's eyes. He tried to replay his memories like vids on a screen, tried to remember every nuance of every frame. He became adept at freezing an image in his mind so he could examine it carefully, much the way they froze important plays in a sporting event, though he probably wasn't remembering it exactly as it had happened. But it gave him comfort to think that he had the grosser details correct.

Most importantly, he recalled his feelings: the sudden shock of realizing his father had been murdered and nothing could bring him back; the pain he'd felt when he'd looked into that young girl's eyes and knew she would probably never smile again; the fear that his sister might someday find herself in the same situation, if she still lived. He took no pleasure from those images, but at the end of each day, as he lay down tired and hungry and filthy, he wanted to make the rebels happy, wanted to prove he could be a good boy. He came to understand that he must constantly replay those memories to keep from becoming the good boy his masters wanted, though each day he found it more difficult to maintain his resolve. Day after day, Mathius tried to demonstrate outwardly that he could be a good boy, and each evening he struggled to resist the temptation to become what they wanted.

Three months after his forced enlistment in the rebels, Cranoch started his day with the usual beating. They squared off, raised their fists and circled cautiously. Under the older man's harsh tutelage Mathius had learned how to defend himself. He had even gone on the offensive a few times, and Cranoch now moved with a certain wariness.

Mathius threw a quick jab. Cranoch side stepped it and countered with a jab of his own. Mathius blocked it and caught the rebel with a glancing blow on the side of his head. Cranoch danced back a few steps and grinned, rubbing his temple with his fingers.

"Not bad, kid," he said. He wagged a finger at Mathius, like an adult scolding a misbehaving child. "I can see it in your eyes, kid. You're starting to think you can take me, ain't you?"

Mathius didn't say anything to that while he and the older man circled, both looking for an opening. Cranoch threw a punch. Mathius blocked it, crouched and swung around in a leg sweep. But instead of dodging out of the way, the rebel leapt forward above the sweep and landed on top of Mathius, sending him sprawling onto his back with the older man on top. Cranoch raised a fist and Mathius saw something on his hand glisten in the sunlight. Then the fist descended and slammed into Mathius's ribs.

Mathius couldn't count the number of times Cranoch had hit him in the ribs. It had always hurt before, but nothing like this. That day it felt as if he'd been hit with a hammer. Mathius cried out as Cranoch hit him again, and again, and each time he raised his fist Mathius saw that glint in the sunlight. Mathius could only lay there and whimper as the man beat him senseless.

At some point the blows stopped, and only after some unknown stretch of time could Mathius think clearly again. He lay on his side, clutching his ribs and groaning.

"Get him to his feet," Cranoch said.

Two rebels gripped Mathius by his armpits and hoisted him to his feet facing Cranoch. He wouldn't have been able to remain standing if the two men hadn't held him tightly between them. Cranoch slowly lifted his fist and held it in front of Mathius's eyes. He opened his hand so Mathius saw the metal structure on his fist. It had four holes into which he'd inserted his fingers, and a metal brace that rested in the palm of his hand. He slowly closed his fist, and when he did so, that left four metal studs protruding above his knuckles.

"They're called knucks, kid," he said. "Metal knuckles, brass knuckles, lots of names for 'em. It ain't hard to kill a man with these, if you keep beating on him. I told you this once before. Only cheaters win, and I always win. That's a lesson you need to learn right now."

He looked at the two men supporting Mathius. "He ain't going to be no good for a couple of days, so let him sleep it off."

He leaned close to Mathius. "You ain't no good for no work for a while, and I'm holding that against you. You need to show us you can be good for something other than eating, sleeping and shitting, or we got no reason to keep you around, and you'll end up just like your old man."

Cranoch raised his hand, thumb up like the hammer on a gun, index finger pointed forward like the muzzle. He pressed the tip of the index finger hard between Mathius's eyes, rocked the thumb forward as if firing a gun, and said, "Kablooie."

••••

A tiny spot on the handle of an arms locker caught Nikaela's attention. She scrubbed at it carefully with a cloth and cleaning solvent, vowing that she would make the locker shine, all the while resenting that she must do so. A cleaning bot could have accomplished the task more quickly and efficiently than a young cadet officer.

She caught a glimpse of her own reflection in the surface of the locker. She wore a pair of shipboard overalls covered in smudges of dirt, with a large and rather prominent stain smeared across her right breast where she had brushed against something. She had tied her salt-and-pepper hair into an unattractive ponytail, and a streak of some oily substance had darkened the chalk-white skin of her cheek. She didn't bother to wipe it away.

Three months under Command Eagle Kristdokar had proved to be exhausting. The older woman had been true to her word in every regard, and had pushed Nikaela to her limits of sanity and tolerance. Nikaela had scrubbed decks, cleaned latrines, performed every menial task the big ship had to offer, and had been allowed to spend only a few hours each day working at a station, gaining experience that might augment her training as an officer. The older woman had found her wanting in every regard, and Nikaela had long ago abandoned any hope of a sponsorship. She had resolved to return to the academy, fight tooth and nail to graduate at the top of her class, and pray that Command Eagle Kristdokar would not actively hinder her advancement as an officer.

A loud clang echoed through the hull of the ship as it settled into the docks on Viktorkinde Prime. Soon her ordeal would be over, and she looked forward to returning to her third year at the academy.

Her implants said, *Mistress Vreekande, you are ordered to report to the captain's office immediately.*

She looked down at the filthy overalls she wore and said, "I'm not properly attired, and I'm filthy. May I take a few minutes to change?"

Negative. You are ordered to report immediately.

Nikaela assumed the woman wanted one last opportunity to give her a good dressing down. She stowed the cloth and container of cleaning solvent, then hurried to Kristdokar's office. She followed the standard formula. She knocked, requested permission to enter, was granted permission, stepped into the office, saluted and reported.

"Ease," Kristdokar said, just like the first time Nikaela had met the woman. But then she spoke kindly and added. "And relax. The ordeal is over."

Nikaela had been about to place her fists on her hips as required, but now she hesitated, stunned by the older woman's almost motherly demeanor. She said, "Uhhh! Ordeal?"

Kristdokar smiled and said, "Do you think I'm not aware that I just put you through three months of hellish drudgery?"

Nikaela could only say, "I . . . uhhh . . . I suppose . . ."

Kristdokar spoke with an edge of irritation to her voice. "Stop stammering, Mistress Vreekande. You sound like a cadet in the first tenday of your first year."

Nikaela clamped her lips shut. Better to say nothing, than to bungle about like an idiot.

Kristdokar's eyes narrowed and she turned serious. "Do you know what prevented your mother from advancing?"

Nikaela considered that for a moment. Her mother had always been quite reticent, and rarely spoke of her unfulfilled career. "No, mistress, I don't think I do."

Kristdokar spoke as if lecturing a first year cadet. "A Kelk officer must do whatever is required to complete the mission successfully. And if there's no one else available to get down on their hands and knees and scrub decks, then an officer will do that as well."

Not sure where this was going, Nikaela said, "Of course, mistress."

"Of course," Kristdokar said. "But your mother had a difficult time accepting that premise. When given a menial task she resisted, and performed it rather poorly. That alone would not have hindered her career—she did have other failings—but she made that one stand out. Your grandmother once confided in me that she thought she had spoiled your mother, and I concluded long ago that probably prevented her from advancing to the higher ranks."

Nikaela had never heard that about her mother, and didn't know how to respond.

"On the other hand," Kristdokar said, "you made the latrine shine. My officers were quite impressed. And I noticed you also sought out opportunities to study other more important shipboard functions. You performed nicely at every task we gave you, no matter how demeaning. So go back to the academy, continue the good work, and you and I will meet again under more pleasant circumstances. You're dismissed."

Stunned and unable to utter an intelligible thought, Nikaela saluted and turned around to leave.

Kristdokar stopped her by saying, "Mistress Vreekande."

Nikaela turned back to face the woman.

Kristdokar smiled and said, "Before you pack up your gear and return to the academy, be sure to finish cleaning those arms lockers."

4

Without Hope

"YOU'RE WELL ENOUGH to work. Get on your feet."

The toe of a boot nudged Mathius in the ribs, rekindling the pain of Cranoch's knucks lesson. He opened his eyes and sat up groggily as one of the rebels removed his manacles. It appeared to be mid-morning; no sign of Timor or Phillan. He'd slept on and off for two days, and as they released him from the chain he probed his ribs delicately. They hurt like hell, and his sides and chest were a mass of black and blue bruises slowly fading to yellow, but from the look on the face of the soldier standing over him, he knew he must get up now or he'd suffer even worse. He climbed to his feet and stood there unsteadily facing the man.

The fellow looked him up and down, clearly didn't like what he saw and shook his head sadly. "Come with me."

The rebel soldier led Mathius across the yard of the compound to a door in the back of the mansion. Just inside the fellow handed him a bucket of steaming water and a sponge. He pointed up a stairway. "Second floor," he said. "Third room on the left."

Mathius climbed up the stairs, still moving slowly because of his bruised ribs. At the top he found a long hallway with doors on both sides spaced evenly down its length. At the third door on the left two soldiers struggled with a long, thin bundle rolled up in sheets and a blanket. One of the older women he'd seen on the balcony stood in an open door on the right watching them, her breasts clearly visible through the thin fabric of her nightgown, the look on her face mournful and sad. She looked Mathius's way, and a tear rolled down her cheek. She quickly wiped it away, did so almost fearfully as if to hide it.

As Mathius advanced down the hallway, one of the soldiers dropped his end of the bundle and swore. "God damn it. She wasn't that big. Why's she so hard to carry?"

While the fellow struggled to lift his end of the bundle off the floor, the bedding unraveled a little, and Mathius caught a glimpse of light-brown hair caked with a dark, reddish stain. The men grunted with effort as they moved down the hallway toward

Mathius, and he was forced to press his back to the wall to allow them to pass. At that moment he caught a whiff of sweet perfume that he recognized, and he thought he recognized the light-brown hair as well. And his nose also caught a strong hint of shit and urine.

When Mathius stepped into the third room on the left the scent of shit and urine struck him harder than one of Cranoch's blows. He gagged and managed not to vomit only because he hadn't yet had anything to eat that morning. Two soldiers struggled to lift the mattress off a bed, its material darkened by the same reddish-brown stain he'd seen caked in the light-brown hair. A third soldier supervising them growled, "Waste of a good mattress. Boss is gonna be pissed."

One of the soldiers said, "Boss is gonna be more pissed she ain't around no more."

The man supervising the operation spotted Mathius as the two soldiers muscled the mattress out of the room. "There you are," he said. He pointed to a dark-red stain on the wooden floor. "Clean this fucking mess up."

Mathius lowered himself to his hands and knees, dipped the sponge in the bucket and began scrubbing the floor. Satisfied that Mathius was hard at work, the third soldier followed the other two out of the room.

Alone in the room, he scrubbed at the stain and didn't want to believe the evidence in front of his eyes, didn't want to connect the dots and come to the obvious conclusion. The stain resisted his efforts, even though he scrubbed furiously at it, and the water in the bucket slowly darkened as he dipped the sponge into it.

A sniff and a sharp intake of breath startled him. He looked up to see the older woman standing in the doorway, tears streaming down her cheeks.

She sniffed again and said, "She killed herself."

Mathius didn't say anything.

She blew her nose on a handkerchief and said, "Just killed herself," then turned and walked away.

Mathius continued to scrub at the stain, tears streaming down his cheeks, anger growing like a twisted knot in his heart.

●●●●

After Mathius's lesson with the knucks, the beatings ended and they began his training with weapons. They gave him a semi-automatic rifle, not a grav gun or modern weapon, just an old-fashioned, chemically-powered slug thrower. They told him it wouldn't pierce fully-powered, plast combat armor, but their rebel enemies were limited to non-powered, light body armor, and with rare exception, almost all of the government troops were not much better equipped.

"If you do come up against powered armor," Cranoch told him, "run like hell. You're probably fucked anyway, but it don't hurt to run."

He learned to strip the rifle, clean it and reassemble it. For a good month he did nothing but dry-fire the weapon at targets in the distance, then strip and clean it again. Then one day Cranoch handed him one, single round of ammunition, saying, "It's live-fire time, kid."

Not even for the briefest instant did Mathius consider turning his gun on Cranoch. The man wore a sidearm, and rather conspicuously kept his hand always resting on the butt of the pistol. And if Mathius did shoot the rebel, a number of Cranoch's friends stood nearby watching. They also wore sidearms or carried rifles, and Mathius had no doubt their weapons were fully loaded.

Mathius removed the rifle's magazine and loaded the single round into it. He jammed the magazine back into place, pulled the breechblock back and released it. It slid into place with a loud, mechanical snap and the momentary, high-pitched ring of metal against metal. He raised the rifle to his shoulder, took careful aim at the target, and pulled the trigger. The kick of the weapon against his shoulder startled him more than the loud explosion and burst of smoke that erupted from the muzzle. During the last two years he'd grown accustomed to the pop of gunfire both near and far.

Cranoch lifted a pair of binoculars to his eyes and examined the target. He lowered the binoculars and said, "Complete miss."

He handed Mathius another round and said, "Try again, kid."

It took Mathius three tries to even hit the target, and he didn't come anywhere close to a bullseye. Firing one round at a time, a few rounds a day, he eventually proved to be a reasonably good marksman. And slowly, little by little, Cranoch stopped resting his hand on the butt of his sidearm. About a month after he'd fired his first live round, Cranoch handed him a full magazine. Holding the magazine in his hand, Mathius looked at the older man and raised an eyebrow.

Cranoch grinned. "We joined forces with one of the government factions, and they're supplying us now; more ammo, better rations and medicine, everything."

Mathius recalled the boxes he'd unloaded stamped with the symbol of the Kelk Supremacy, but he kept that thought to himself.

Six months after joining the rebels they gave Mathius a camouflage jacket with his name crudely stenciled above the left breast pocket, and he went out on his first patrol. By that time Timor and Phillan had become experienced old-hands at live-fire patrols. As a rookie, Mathius stayed close to them while they stayed close to Cranoch, all of them part of his squad, which was part of Mercier's platoon. Mathius noticed that Timor now carried his rifle and walked with a swagger he hadn't displayed before. Thankfully, Phillan didn't exhibit the same bravado.

They swept through a neighborhood that had been reasonably prosperous before the rebellion. Under Mercier's and Cranoch's tutelage, Mathius had practiced door-to-door sweeps with the other rebels in the squad, but they didn't exercise any of that kind of caution now. Mercier split the platoon up by squad and sent each to search a house.

Mathius, Timor and two other rebels followed Cranoch to the front door of one residence. Cranoch hammered on the door with the butt of his rifle. He turned to Mathius and said, "If they don't answer quick-like, we kick the door down and it goes even worse for them."

When the owner of the property answered the door, Cranoch elbowed him out of the way and walked past him. Mathius and the rest followed into a small living room.

"Spread out," Cranoch said. "Search everywhere. Take anything of use. Anyone gives you trouble, bring 'em to me."

Mathius accompanied one of the older soldiers. They searched several rooms and Mathius noticed that his comrade damaged or destroyed almost anything not of use to the rebels. They slowly accumulated a small pile of goods near the front door, things like food, batteries, tools, and medicine.

The owner pleaded with Cranoch, "Please, that's all the food we have. Leave us something or we'll starve."

Cranoch grabbed the man and slammed him against a wall. The man froze, his eyes wide with fear. Cranoch looked over his shoulder and said, "Timor, come here."

The young boy crossed the room warily and stopped, facing Cranoch and the civilian. Cranoch stepped away from the man, looked at Timor and said, "Well, soldier, do your duty."

Timor's eyes blinked rapidly. He looked at Cranoch, then at the civilian, then at Cranoch.

Cranoch grinned, and quite visibly focused his eyes on Timor's rifle, nodding his head as if giving the boy permission. "Be a good boy, and you'll get a special reward for dinner tonight."

Timor's eyes stopped blinking, and the corners of his mouth slowly turned upward until he too grinned. Then he giggled and glanced down at his rifle, a look of wonder on his face. His head swiveled as he examined it from end to end, muzzle to stock. He giggled again, raised his rifle and shot the man in the face. The fellow dropped like a sack of rocks and flopped onto his side. Timor leaned over him, looked at the ruin of his head, then looked at Mathius and grinned.

Cranoch said, "Now that's a good boy."

The older man looked at Mathius. "See that, kid? Timor knows how to be a good boy."

Mathius gulped and struggled to hold down his meager breakfast.

During their return to the compound, Timor hiccoughed frequently, then emitted that strange, shy giggle.

That night Mathius followed his usual routine of recalling the young girl's empty eyes and her light-brown hair caked with half-dried blood. He recalled the grimace of pain on his father's face when Mercier had destroyed his knee, and the way his head had exploded when the rebel had killed him. To that he added the look in Timor's eyes as he stood over the man he had murdered: joy at taking a life, and fear, and wonder. But worst of all, nothing remained of the little boy Mathius had first met sitting in the shade of the outbuilding. Mercier, Cranoch and the rebels had turned him into something inhuman and uncaring, a maniacal little soldier carrying a loaded gun, with no understanding of what he'd done. Mathius added that to the list of accounts they must reconcile, though he'd probably never have a chance to collect.

••••

Nikaela's third year at the academy had gone well, and she finished it still at the top of her class. All academy cadets spent the gap between their third and fourth year on active duty, many in dangerous situations, a form of live training from which some did not return. Nikaela's orders instructed her to report to the hunter-killer *Skuldev*, docked at Viktorkinde Prime. Her orders said nothing about her mission or responsibilities, which struck her as rather vague, and sparked her curiosity all the more.

Before taking a shuttle up to the space station orbiting Viktorkinde, she reviewed *Skuldev*'s specifications. The ship had a complement of sixty-four men and women. It was all power plant, drive, and transition torpedoes. It had half a dozen defensive pods, but its primary means of protecting itself were speed and stealth. If it must depend on the pods for anything more than the occasional defensive shot, the ship would be in serious trouble.

When she reported to the OOD aboard *Skuldev*, she asked the fellow what her assignment would be. He looked at a small hand terminal for a moment, frowned and said, "You're not assigned to the crew. We're merely transporting your team."

Her curiosity piqued, she asked, "Where are we going?"

He shrugged and said, "I don't know. After you stow your gear, find Command Superior Eindride. You'll be reporting to him, and he may be able to tell you more."

They assigned her to a bunk in a cabin she shared with three other junior officers. She stowed her kit, then found Eindride seated alone at a table in the officer's mess, a steaming cup of hot tea in front of him. He was quite handsome, with sparkling red irises, and a wonderfully bluish tint to his skin.

She approached him, saluted and said, "Maestra Eindride, I am Cadet Nikaela Vreekande. I was told to report to you."

He returned the salute casually and said, "Relax, Cadet Vreekande. Sit down. If you want, get some tea or something."

She sat down across from him. She opened her mouth to say something, but he raised a hand, silencing her.

"I know," he said. "Your orders are quite vague, and that has aroused your curiosity. But curiosity isn't always a good thing."

That sounded odd. She said, "May I ask where we're going?"

He gave her a slight grin. "You may ask, but I can't tell you. Only the captain and I know our final destination, and that will remain sealed until we're well under way."

She asked, "Some sort of covert operation?"

He leaned back in his chair and stared at her, saying only, "You tell me." Apparently, he wanted to see how much she could glean from those purposefully vague orders.

"A hunter-killer," she said. "The perfect vessel to help us get somewhere without being detected."

He didn't move a muscle, but continued to stare at her in silence.

She continued, "So something clandestine. But I'm too junior, and not trained in Special Forces combat, so I doubt it will be some sort of covert assault or combat operation. More like surveillance, or something of that nature."

His grin broadened, exposing white teeth. "Good. You are smart, though you've managed to draw the same conclusions as the rest of the crew. What I can tell you is that it's more of a liaison operation, not surveillance. The Commonwealth has their hands full with a certain situation I'm not at liberty to discuss at this time. It's generating a lot of disagreement within their government and in the highest echelons of ComSecCorps. Our job is to irritate the wound as much as possible without being caught at it."

Nikaela had a hundred questions, but she knew Eindride would not answer them, at least not at the moment. Late that afternoon, a senior noncom and two riflewomen joined their team, and over the next three days, Nikaela learned that all three of them were quite taciturn. None of them exhibited any curiosity about their orders or destination, and she decided she would be wise to put the guesswork aside.

Once *Skuldev* launched and they up-transited out of the Viktorkinde system, Nikaela learned that they would be in transit for eighteen days. At *Skuldev*'s maximum transition drive of four thousand lights, they would cross almost two-hundred light-years. And that would put them quite close to Commonwealth space, though still well outside of it.

With no duties aboard ship, boredom quickly set in. She begged the XO to assign her as a spacer apprentice to some sort of station so she could at least spend the time training in shipboard functions. She also considered taking Eindride as a lover. He was quite handsome and very attractive, and a pleasant tryst would help occupy her time. But rumor had it that he had seen his last promotion, and she didn't want to saddle herself with a relationship that might prove disadvantageous to her own career.

Nine days into the journey, Eindride revealed their destination. Nikaela looked up what she could find on their target, a little known planet in a system claimed by neither the Kelk nor the Commonwealth. It had a single continent in the midst of a vast ocean, and in the past had boasted a strong agricultural base supported by modern technology. But most importantly, its population of twenty million residents had a difficult time getting along with one another. It was also located in the neighborhood of several other independent star systems: Norandyne, the Tollman Protectorate, the Mikotian Republic, Sarkovie, and the Heraclean Hegemony. They all stood directly in the path of recent Commonwealth expansion, and news feeds had reported some unrest and dissatisfaction at the possibility of forceful annexation.

Eighteen days after leaving Viktorkinde, *Skuldev* down-transited at the edge of the Novalis system. Nikaela and the rest of Eindride's small team were then transported in the middle of the night to the surface of Novalis III in a heavily stealthed drop boat.

5

A Good Boy

DURING THAT YEAR Mathius started shaving, though he only needed to do so two or three times a tenday. They also sent him out on patrol into the city quite regularly. Some excursions were just a boring walk through the streets, some a shameful act of taxing the civilian population for the *protection* the rebels supposedly provided, and some turned into lively firefights against opposing factions, though Mathius never knew who they were fighting. During a heated fight, he usually fired blindly over a wall or some other cover, and he tried to always aim a little high. He had no vested interest in helping his faction defeat the enemy, whoever that enemy might be, and in any case the city had been divided up into districts controlled by the warlords leading the various factions. None of them really wanted to conquer more ground, and when the shooting started it usually proved to be nothing more than a skirmish at one of the borders between districts.

On one such patrol they cornered a man and woman in a small house. "Please," the man said. "We haven't done anything. Let us go."

Cranoch shook his head sadly. "But you probably will do something. And I can't appear weak in front of my people."

He looked at Phillan and grinned, and only then did Mathius realize Phillan had yet to murder his first helpless civilian. Phillan's eyes widened and he looked at Cranoch for a long moment. Then he looked toward Mathius, fear written in the lines of his face. They both knew what Cranoch expected of Phillan, and Mathius couldn't help him.

Phillan's eyes glazed over, and he gulped desperately for air, as if trying to hold the contents of his stomach down.

"You can do it," Cranoch said. "Just be a good boy. It's only hard the first time, then it gets easy."

Phillan looked again at Cranoch, then at Mathius, then at the man and woman. He blinked rapidly, his eyes wide, his lips puckered into a tight slash. Then his eyes glazed over and appeared to focus in the far distance. His breathing calmed, and in one quick motion he raised his rifle and shot the man.

The fellow grimaced, clutched his stomach and doubled over, falling to the floor. He lay on his side curled up in a fetal position, groaning piteously.

Cranoch folded his arms across his chest and waited like an impatient school teacher, staring at Phillan and tapping his foot. Mathius couldn't take his eyes off the older man, and he wasn't looking Phillan's way when the blast from the young boy's gun startled him. The woman dropped to her knees, then toppled forward and landed on her face.

"That's a good boy," Cranoch said. He walked over to the groaning man and looked down at him. He shook his head. "But it's a waste of good ammo if you don't kill 'em in one shot." He turned to Phillan and said, "Be careful to do better the next time. Now finish the job."

Phillan stood frozen in place for the longest moment, swallowing and gulping at air. Then he took a step forward and staggered across the room like a drunkard. He stood over the groaning man and stared at him for several seconds. Then he suddenly calmed, placed the muzzle of his rifle against the man's head, and pulled the trigger. The fellow's head exploded much the way Mathius's father's head had exploded.

Phillan dropped his rifle, then fell to his hands and knees, and gagged and choked as he spewed the contents of his stomach on the floor.

Cranoch leaned over him, patted him on the back and said, "Yah, like I said, it's hard the first time, isn't it? At least for some of you." He glanced at Timor. "But it'll get easier. Trust me."

Timor hiccoughed and giggled.

The older man looked away from the young boy and locked eyes with Mathius, and the look on the man's face told him his turn would soon come, and he too would have to be a good boy.

••••

Five days after Phillan proved he could be a good boy, one of the government factions ambushed Mercier's platoon while out on night patrol. The firefight lasted about an hour, then the government forces withdrew. The rebels lost two men and Mercier took a bullet in his right calf. Mathius, Phillan and Timor looked on as a medic examined the wound.

"Nice and clean," the medic declared. "In one side and out the other, as clean as can be. We don't have to go digging for the slug, which always turns out ugly."

Mercier grimaced and snarled, "Fucking hurts like hell."

"Yah," the medic said, "but I can do something about that." He pressed some sort of tool to the side of Mercier's neck, and a moment later Mercier leaned back, breathed a long sigh and said, "I love that shit." His words came out mushy.

They quickly assembled a stretcher, and put the younger boys to work carrying Mercier back to the compound. Under the influence of whatever they had given him, Mercier babbled nonsense and had difficulty remaining silent. As they trudged along, Phillan asked Cranoch, "What did they give Captain Mercier?"

"Pain killers," Cranoch said. "Biotech, antibiotics, accelerated healing, that kind of stuff. Without that he'd probably end up dying from a nasty infection."

Cranoch looked Mathius's way as he spoke to Phillan. "You see, Phillan, now that you're a good boy, you can count on that kind of treatment too, if you get hurt. Much better chance of surviving when you're a good boy. The world's a lot more dangerous place for boys who can't be good."

Mathius lived in fear of the day he'd be required to be a good boy. He couldn't simply murder a helpless civilian, so he'd fail, and Cranoch would probably kill him. But he also knew he was not strong enough to resist the older man, and he feared even more that he would capitulate when the time came. Little Timor giggled and grinned every time he murdered someone, and occasionally Cranoch had to stop him from overdoing it and killing indiscriminately. Mathius didn't want to become a Timor, but he saw no way of avoiding it.

A tenday later, during an afternoon patrol, they found a middle aged couple and the woman's elderly mother hiding in the back bedroom of a partially demolished house. Cranoch questioned them, and they claimed to be alone. But one of the rebels found a young girl's clothing neatly folded up in a dresser in another bedroom.

"Where is she?" Cranoch demanded of the three. The incident reminded Mathius of the day they had killed his father.

"There is no girl," the younger of the two women said. "That's just old clothing we kept around."

"Bullshit," Cranoch said and slapped her, a heavy blow that knocked her to the floor. Her mother cringed and pressed her back against the wall behind her, as if by doing so she could hide from the predators in the room.

The man pleaded, "Please, don't hurt us. You have no right to do this."

"No right?" Cranoch said, laughing. He slammed the butt of his rifle into the man's stomach and the poor fellow doubled over. "That gives me all the right I need."

He straightened and looked at Mathius. "They're not going to talk. We'll find the girl without their help." He finished by giving Mathius that grin. "Do your duty, soldier."

Mathius tried to pretend he didn't know what was expected of him. He looked away from Cranoch to Phillan, and recalled the day he'd been unable to help the younger boy when his turn had come to be a good boy. He looked at Timor, who simply shrugged and giggled. "I'll do it," the young boy said.

"No," Cranoch said, shaking his head and still looking at Mathius. "It's Mathius's turn. Come on, Mathius. Prove to me you're a good boy. Just do it the first time and it'll be easy after that."

Mathius considered throwing his rifle down and running, but Mercier's platoon had spread out through the neighborhood. They'd catch him in short order, and if they didn't kill him outright, he'd be back to eating watery gruel, beatings, and hard labor in the compound. He still slept on the ground with his wrists cuffed in plast manacles, but it had been quite some time since Cranoch had last beaten him senseless. If he wanted to survive he had no choice, and as he raised his rifle and aimed it at the three people huddled against the wall, all staring at him, their eyes wide with fear, his heart pounded in his chest and threatened to climb up into his throat. He couldn't breathe, and then he recalled that young girl's dead eyes, and that defeated him. He lowered his gun without firing it and bowed his head. "I can't," he said, and couldn't hold back the tears that streamed down his cheeks.

"Not a good boy," Cranoch said. He looked at Phillan. "Come here."

The young boy rushed across the room. Cranoch said, "You're a good boy, Phillan. But Mathius thinks he's better than the rest of us. So you're going to help him learn he can be a good boy too, aren't you?"

Phillan nodded eagerly.

Cranoch said, "Put the muzzle of your rifle against the back of Mathius's head."

Phillan's eyes widened and he hesitated.

Cranoch asked, "Are you no longer a good boy, Phillan?"

"No," Phillan said, desperately shaking his head. "I mean yes, I am." He raised his rifle, and Mathius felt the muzzle press against his neck.

Cranoch turned to Timor. "I'm not so sure Phillan is still a good boy. Put the muzzle of your rifle against the back of Phillan's head."

Phillan's eyes widened even further as Timor giggled and raised his rifle.

"Now Mathius," Cranoch said, "It's time to be a good boy. Either that, or you get to be a dead boy. And maybe Phillan gets to be a dead boy with you. Make your choice. Now."

Mathius's tears flowed even more freely than they had a moment ago, and he gulped to get air into his lungs.

Cranoch grinned. "Come on, Mathius. You can do it. I know it's hard the first time, but you can do it. Just be a good boy."

Mathius didn't want to be a good boy, but he didn't want to die either. He thought he could find it in himself to kill someone, but not these helpless people. Did he have the courage to stand up to Cranoch, to die right there and then, rather than needlessly murder defenseless victims? He hoped he did.

Cranoch said, "Raise your rifle, Mathius."

Mathius obeyed, lifted the weapon, aimed it at the man and looked in the fellow's eyes. They were not unlike his father's eyes.

Mathius glanced at Cranoch and the rebel grinned. "I'm going to count down from ten to zero. Before I reach zero, you had better show me you can be a good boy. If you do, I'll stop counting. If you don't, then when I reach zero, Phillan is going to blow your head off, because if Phillan doesn't blow your head off, Timor is going to blow his head off. Won't you Timor?"

Timor said, "Yes. I'm a good boy." He giggled.

"I thought so," Cranoch said. "Timor's a good boy, a very good boy. I can count on Timor."

"You can count on me," Timor said. "You can count on me."

Cranoch made a dramatic show of taking a deep breath, then said, "Ten."

Mathius closed his eyes and swallowed hard to hold his breakfast down.

"It's not that hard, Mathius," Cranoch said. "You've already got the gun aimed at him, so just pull the trigger."

Cranoch hesitated for a second, then took another breath and said, "Nine."

Mathius decided he would not pull the trigger, he would not kill these people. He would let Phillan kill him. He would not become a good boy. Mathius kept his eyes closed, choosing death instead.

"Eight."

Phillan shouted. "Pull the trigger, Mathius."

Cranoch said, "Don't jump the gun, Phillan. Don't blow Mathius's head off until I get to zero."

Phillan said, "I won't. I won't."

"Good boy," Cranoch said, then he added, "Seven."

"It's not that hard," Phillan said. "Just pull the trigger."

"Six."

"Please, Mathius, pull the trigger. Please."

"Five."

Phillan cried like a child, big gulping sobs. "Please, please, please."

"Four."

Timor giggled and hiccoughed.

"Three."

Mathius could never really recall pulling the trigger. Standing there with his eyes closed, determined to resist Cranoch, the muzzle flash lit up the back of his eyelids, the gun roared with an earsplitting boom, bucked in his hands and kicked his shoulder.

Mathius opened his eyes, lowered the rifle and looked carefully at the weapon. To his surprise, no other finger but his rested on the trigger.

The man had slumped to the floor, a small round dot just beneath his left eye leaking a faint trickle of blood down his cheek. His eyes remained open and unseeing, a strange look of surprise on his dead face. His blood and brains had spattered the two women huddled near the wall behind him.

"That's a good boy," Cranoch said. Mathius looked his way, the older man grinned and nodded toward the two women. "I knew you had it in you. Now finish the job."

One of the other rebels leaned in through the open doorway. "Cranoch, what's taking so long? Mercier wants you right now. On the double."

Cranoch looked Timor's way. "You come with me."

To Phillan he said, "You stay here and watch Mathius, make sure he finishes this right."

He leaned close to Mathius's ear. "And you can think about what your life is going to be like if you can't be a good boy. And Phillan can think about what his life will be like if Mathius can't be a good boy. This had better be done when I get back, or we'll exercise the dead-boy option." He looked at Phillan. "And that includes you too."

Mathius closed his eyes and lowered his head. He heard Cranoch and Timor march out of the room. After they'd gone, Phillan hissed. "You have to do it."

Mathius opened his eyes and looked at the boy. "I can't."

Phillan said, "You have to. If you don't, he won't trust you, and he'll make it bad for all of us, if he doesn't have Timor kill us first."

Mathius shook his head. "I can't."

Phillan stared at him for several seconds. Then he put the butt of his rifle on the floor and leaned it against a wall. He turned to Mathius and said, "Then I will."

Before Mathius realized what he intended, the younger boy reached out and ripped the rifle out of his hands, raised it and aimed it at the two women. He glanced at Mathius once, a look filled with fear and loss, then he pulled the trigger. The gun roared, and he pulled the trigger again, and again and again and again. He didn't stop until he'd emptied it into the two women, who lay bloodied and still, their eyes open and glazed over in death.

Phillan turned to Mathius and shoved the rifle at him, slamming it against his chest. Mathius gripped it as Phillan spun away from him and retrieved his own rifle where it rested against the wall.

Cranoch rushed through the door and stopped just within the room, breathing heavily. He hesitated, looked about carefully, looked at Mathius, then at the two dead women. He nodded and crossed the room slowly, reached out, pulled Mathius's rifle out of his hands and sniffed once at the end of the barrel. Then he popped the empty magazine and examined it. He nodded, looked at Mathius and grinned. "That's a good boy. I knew if you had a chance to think about it you'd come round. But next time, don't waste so much ammunition. A couple of clean head shots would have done the job nicely."

Mathius leaned over, put his hands on his knees and spewed the contents of his stomach all over his boots.

••••

The residents of Novalis III used a mix of grav vehicles and old-tech internal combustion transport, probably because fossil fuels were cheap to produce in a nascent economy. Nikaela reminded herself that the word *nascent* no longer applied. The planet's entire socio-economic structure had come to a standstill with the onset of the five-way civil war they politely called an insurgency. Then it had collapsed completely as the violence continued year after year. What little modern tech they still possessed came from off-planet.

She pulled a hooded coat over her dirty and unwashed civilian clothes—they had orders to blend in. The coat nicely hid the grav gun in the holster strapped to her waist. She pulled the sidearm and checked its charge, then the magazine that contained the flechettes it could accelerate up to Mach five. She returned it to its holster.

She looked in a mirror and checked the makeup that hid the bluish-white of her skin, and the contacts that changed the bright red of her irises to a pale blue. The residents of Novalis III came in all sizes and colors, but the unusual hue of Kelk skin and eyes would draw the kind of attention her superiors abhorred.

She walked out of her quarters and into the warehouse where she found the noncom and the two riflewomen waiting beside two trucks. They looked each other over, double checking their appearance to ensure that none of them had missed anything.

Ten minutes later the door to the warehouse office opened and Eindride emerged, accompanied by two fellows wearing tattered rebel uniforms, though for them the word uniform needed a very broad interpretation. Both of them had not shaved for several days, and unsightly stubble had sprouted from their faces. One of the men walked straight to a car parked near the large warehouse doors, while the other accompanied Eindride as he approached Nikaela and her comrades.

Eindride introduced the man. "This is Captain Caster, one of their leaders."

Caster glanced at each of them in turn, and his eyes settled on the swell of Nikaela's breasts hidden by the material of the filthy man's shirt she wore. The Kelk women had been warned to keep their collars tightly closed, and not to expose any skin below their necks. Now that the rebel was close enough, his smell told Nikaela he needed to bathe as well as shave.

Eindride said to Caster, "We'll follow you."

The man's eyes lingered on Nikaela's breasts for a moment, then he turned and walked across the warehouse to join the other rebel in the car near the doors.

Eindride said in Kelk, "Mistress Vreekande, you ride with me."

He climbed into the cab of the larger of the two trucks and sat behind the wheel. Nikaela opened the passenger door and climbed in beside him. He started the truck's engine, and it spewed an obnoxious cloud of gray smoke. As an added measure to hide their racial identities, both of them pulled the hoods of their coats over their heads, hiding their faces in shadow.

They didn't have far to drive, and by design they pulled into the rebel compound as dusk settled over the city. Caster instructed Eindride to park the truck at the back of the compound near a small outbuilding that served as a warehouse.

As Nikaela climbed out of the truck she saw a rebel patrol returning to the compound. Among the armed men were three boys, one perhaps only a few years younger than her, and two even younger than him. All three had the gaunt faces and skeletal cheek bones that came with extended periods of hunger. The older boy stood a little taller than average, and she wondered if he had completed his growth yet. He had brown hair, but she couldn't see the color of his eyes from that distance. The variation in eye color among the common-faces fascinated her, and she thought he would be rather handsome if he filled out and lost the emaciated appearance of starvation. As they got closer she saw that his eyes were red and puffy as if he had been crying. She wondered if he had lost a friend while out on patrol.

The leader of the returning patrol approached them. "What do we have here?" he said to Caster. He spoke as if asking about Nikaela, not the goods they'd brought on the trucks.

"Supplies," Caster said. He introduced the other rebel leader as Captain Mercier.

Caster said to Eindride, "My people will unload the truck. Come, you can relax inside while they sweat. And bring your woman."

Nikaela's face grew hot as she flushed with anger. Eindride saw the look in her eyes, and shook his head ever so faintly from side to side. She took the hint, took a deep breath and reminded herself that she was a soldier with a duty to perform. She squared her shoulders, Eindride gave her a nod of approval, and they followed Caster into the mansion with Mercier walking behind them. Nikaela did not like having the rebel behind her where she couldn't keep an eye on him.

Caster led them through the back entrance of the house to a dusty sitting room decorated with worn and threadbare furniture. He introduced them to his warlord, a chubby fellow with a large gut hanging over his belt, who clearly had not suffered from any lack of food like the three boys she had seen. And like Caster and Mercier he needed to bathe and shave.

While the four men chatted, Nikaela wandered over to a window. She edged a curtain aside and looked out into the back yard of the compound. The three boys had been put to work unloading the two trucks, with two older men overseeing them. She couldn't take her eyes off the older of the three boys. While he worked his eyes appeared focused at some point far across the galaxy, and his posture spoke of desolation and despair.

The boys removed the boxes and crates from the back of the truck and carried them into the outbuilding. Nikaela saw more supplies visible just within the warehouse doors. They were clearly not of Kelk origin, and she wondered at that.

When the boys finished unloading the trucks, the older men led them into the shade at the side of the warehouse. They locked their wrists in manacles, forced them to sit down in the dirt, then threaded a chain between their arms and attached it to a metal stake in the ground. Only then did Nikaela understand.

"Come, Mistress Vreekande," Eindride said behind her. "It is time for us to leave."

Caster and Mercier accompanied them out of the mansion to the truck. Their path took them near the open doors of the warehouse, and Nikaela caught a glimpse of an inked stamp on the outside of one of the boxes. She had assumed that anything not of Kelk origin would have come from the hated Commonwealth, but she didn't recognize anything about the label, and that bothered her.

As they walked to the truck Caster's eyes kept glancing at her breasts, and with great relief she climbed up into the cab and closed the door. When Eindride climbed behind the wheel and they were alone, she said, "Maestra Eindride, I noticed several crates in that warehouse that are of neither Kelk nor Commonwealth origin."

He looked at her pointedly and said, "Are you surprised?"

"Should I be?"

"No," he said, and she detected a note of weariness in his voice. "Everyone is involved, even the small players like the Sarkovites and the Heracleans. Everyone. Probably Norandyne and the Mikotians as well. They're circling like vultures, and playing us all against one another."

6

Escape

ONCE CRANOCH WAS satisfied Mathius would be a good boy, he took the pressure off, and Mathius didn't have to prove himself again. He continued pretending to be a soldier, continued firing a little high to maintain the image that he was a contributing member of the platoon. For several days Mathius feared Phillan would reveal the truth of how the two women had died. But the younger boy probably realized that doing so would go badly for him as well. And after a tenday had passed without any mention of the matter, Mathius's worries dissipated.

There didn't seem to be any purpose to the fighting. Each warlord had a certain territory to call his turf, and none appeared to care about conquering more, as if only concerned with maintaining the status quo. They still went out on patrols, more to *tax* the civilian population than anything else, though there wasn't much left to tax. And they now had a small warehouse stocked with relief supplies from the Commonwealth and the Supremacy, so Mathius wondered why they even bothered to harass the poor people starving in their homes. They fought the occasional firefight.

One night, while out on patrol, they turned down a broad avenue at the edge of their territory, and in the middle of the street they came upon a squad from the one of the rival factions. With no cover, Mathius and the entire platoon dropped to one knee and raised their rifles. The enemy soldiers did the same, but Mercier lifted a hand over his head and shouted, "Hold fire."

The opposing force consisted of no more than a single squad, and Mercier's platoon had them badly outnumbered. Probably because of that, the enemy held their fire as well.

Mercier shouted, "Who's your leader?"

One of the rival soldiers shouted, "I am."

Mercier straightened and shouted, "Then let's talk. You and me. No need to go shooting each other up, is there?"

As Mercier and the other man converged on a spot half way between the two opposing forces, Cranoch hissed to the three boys, "Don't move. But pick a single target, aim carefully, and be ready to fire if I give the order. And the gods help you if you fire before I say."

When the unrest had started it had been easy to distinguish one faction from another, especially government soldiers whose uniforms had been relatively clean and consistent, not the mish-mash of cobbled together outfits the rebels wore. But with time and lack of supply, that had quickly changed, and Mathius had no idea who they now faced. With all of them fully exposed out in the middle of the street, he decided that if he wanted to live, he had better pick a target and aim carefully this time, and be prepared to kill for real.

Mercier and the other leader were about ten paces apart and approaching one another when someone fired his rifle. All of them reacted the same and fired their weapons, and the street filled with the staccato pops of dozens of rifle shots. Mathius pulled the trigger, not really sure what he aimed at. He kept pulling it and pulling it until the bolt on his rifle locked back on an empty magazine.

"Cease fire," Cranoch shouted. "Cease fire, you idiots."

A strange silence settled on the street, smoke from the expended ammunition drifting about them in the dim light. Mercier lay curled up in a fetal position about twenty paces in front of them. All of the enemy soldiers lay still and unmoving.

Cranoch bellowed, "Reload, you morons."

Mathius quickly replaced his empty magazine, and the street filled with the sound of his rebel comrades doing the same.

Again, silence descended. And again, none of the enemy soldiers moved.

Cranoch shouted, "Mercier, you hit?"

Mercier raised a hand and waved. Then he slowly climbed to his feet, holding his sidearm aimed at the unmoving enemy soldiers. He back-stepped carefully, and they all waited for a shot to ring out from the enemy, but nothing happened.

Behind Mathius someone groaned piteously. He looked over his shoulder and saw one of their older platoon mates lying on his back, his arms spread, his eyes open and unmoving. Phillan lay near him on his side clutching his stomach and moaning.

The enemy soldiers had been so badly outnumbered most were dead, and they finished off those who weren't with a head shot. Mercier lost only the one man, with two others wounded. One fellow had a nasty hole in his upper arm, while Phillan had suffered a stomach wound.

Under Cranoch's orders Timor and Mathius handed their rifles to other members of their platoon, then lifted Phillan to his feet, supporting him between them. They half dragged, half carried the boy back to the compound and placed him on a cot in a tent that served as their hospital.

As Mathius turned to leave, Phillan reached out and gripped his hand. His voice sounded weak and distant. "Don't leave me. Please."

Mathius found a stool and sat down beside the boy's cot.

"It hurts," Phillan said. "It hurts so bad, and I don't want to die."

"You won't," Mathius said. "They have those drugs, and pain killers, and all that stuff they gave Mercier when he got shot in the leg. You'll be okay." Mathius reiterated those assurances over and over again while they waited.

One of the medics showed up and examined Phillan. He shook his head and said, "Gut wound. Not good."

He turned to leave but Mathius said, "Wait."

The man hesitated and looked at him warily.

"The drugs," Mathius said. "And medicines. What about those?"

"Yah," the fellow said. "The drugs. Yah. I'll see to it right away."

He turned and left.

Mathius sat down, took Phillan's hand in his and said, "It'll be all right. Just wait and see. They'll take care of you. That's what Cranoch said." Mathius hoped that he spoke the truth.

Mathius never saw the medic again, nor any other medic for that matter. After two days the hole in Phillan's gut oozed a sickly, yellowish ichor, and he laid in bed groaning constantly, his skin covered in a sheen of oily sweat. Cranoch checked in on him every now and then, and he never brought any of those medicines and pain-killers Phillan had earned by being a good boy. Cranoch told Mathius that Phillan had peritonitis, that his guts were slowly rotting away, and still, they gave him nothing for the pain. Apparently, Phillan wasn't a good enough boy for that, and that made Mathius wonder how good enough they had to be. It took Phillan eight days to die, and Mathius added the memories of his long, slow, painful demise to the litany of images he recalled each night before finding sleep.

••••

"Lieutenant Colonel Primatov," Senator Manifort Gascoigne said, "you have people on the ground there, do you not?"

As another closed session of the Foreign Relations Committee wound down, Katrine had been expecting something of that nature. With only one or two exceptions, the men and women on the committee were all sincere. And while party lines often dictated that they not agree on many things, they did all want to see the suffering on Novalis III brought to an end.

Katrine straightened and stepped forward. "Yes, Senator Gascoigne, we do."

Gascoigne had dark hair with an attractive touch of gray at the temples. He could have used a little gene therapy to remove the gray, but that might have detracted from the distinguished-elder-statesman look he so carefully cultivated. In any case, he was old enough, and senior enough, that he could play the maverick politician, even cross party lines with a fair amount of impunity, as long as he did so carefully. But interestingly enough, he never threw his weight around, which Katrine had always thought was one reason he had become one of the most powerful men in the Commonwealth government. He asked, "How many people do you have there?"

Gascoigne's inquiries were really just a show for the rest of the committee. He already knew the answer to each and every question he asked her.

She said, "About a dozen." She glanced briefly at each of the senators on the committee. "Please keep in mind that that information is highly classified."

"Of course," Gascoigne said. "Regarding the Kelk, has anything changed since your last report?"

She shook her head and said, "No. They're supplying some small arms and ammunition, but nothing big, and nothing serious."

A few hardliners on the committee, and in other parts of the government, would love an excuse to have a nice little war with the Kelk. They believed they could eliminate the blue-skinned demons once and for all, though Katrine and many of her military colleagues disagreed with them on that, and would counsel a more cautious approach if the hardliners ever asked, which they didn't.

She continued, "Beyond that, they're supplying mostly food and medical supplies, as are we. Unfortunately, the factions are intercepting most of that, leaving the civilian population to suffer and starve. We—"

Senator Jenine Catarvin interrupted her. "Exactly. We're just prolonging the suffering."

A heated argument erupted, and with no need to fear looking bad in front of the news hypes, several of the distinguished senators shouted with considerable volume. The committee had chewed on that same argument for months. Their humanitarian efforts weren't helping the people for whom they were intended, but were instead keeping the government and rebel factions healthy and supplied, which allowed them to continue to prey on the innocents. Many argued that the Commonwealth's aid actually prolonged the suffering, and that discontinuing such assistance might finally starve the factions into submission. After several minutes of raised voices, Gascoigne adjourned the meeting and it broke up.

As the committee members and their aides filed out of the room, Gascoigne leaned close to Katrine and said, "If you don't mind, I'd like to have a private word with you."

She smiled. They had had many private words on this subject. "Certainly," she said.

Walking side by side, they chatted congenially as they made their way to his private office. Once inside he closed the door, offered her a comfortable chair and a drink.

She declined the drink, but took the chair and placed her briefcase on the floor beside it. Gascoigne poured himself a drink and sat down behind his desk.

He took a healthy belt of the drink, then said, "Computer, full privacy screen."

The computer said, "The room has been cleared and swept of all listening devices."

He said, "And terminate all monitoring services."

The computer said, "Since I'll not be monitoring, you'll have to manually reactivate. Disengaging in three . . . two . . . one . . ."

He smiled at her and said, "Now we can speak candidly."

Gascoigne had earned her trust through years of collaboration, but it never hurt to be cautious. She smiled back at him and said, "You don't mind if I do my own scan, do you?"

"Of course not," he said. "Because we wouldn't have a really candid conversation if I did mind."

Her implants were senior-command, military grade, but emitting signals strong enough to detect listening devices and jam them would not be good for the tissues of her brain. She did use them to communicate with the instrument in her briefcase, and a few seconds later it said, "Privacy screen complete, one questionable device detected and temporarily disabled."

"So," she said. "What can I do for you, senator?"

They had had too many of these conversations before to waste time beating around the bush. He lifted an eyebrow and said, "Last time we spoke you said something to the effect that you'd be more comfortable if we had some reliable assets in the Novalis system, but I vetoed that. What did you have in mind?"

He had just surprised her, which didn't happen often. "I was thinking of crack troops and serious fire power to back them up."

"Serious fire power?" he said, his brows narrowing. "You mean like a big cruiser or two."

She shook her head. "We can't get big ships in there without everyone knowing about it. If you can think of a way to make that happen without committing political suicide, let me know." She hesitated, waiting to see if he had a trick or two up his sleeve she wasn't aware of. He shook his head at her implied question, so she continued. "I was thinking more along the lines of a few assault teams on hunter-killers. It'll take a couple months to set up stealth approaches, but they can sneak into the system and be on hand if anything breaks, be down on the planet's surface in a matter of hours. With the hunter-killers in orbit to back them up with conventional missile strikes if needed, the assault teams could secure sensitive facilities and protect critical officials."

She paused, then added, "Though I'd still like to figure out a way of getting some really heavy firepower into the neighborhood." She let that hang.

Gascoigne leaned back in his chair and steepled his fingers in front of him. He sat there silently for several seconds, his eyes focused in a thousand-yard stare, his head nodding up and down almost imperceptibly. Then he leaned forward, focused his eyes on Katrine and said, "We need to improve our relations with some of those independent systems near Novalis. I'll have to cut a few back-room deals and pull in a favor or two, but it seems to me it might be a good time to send a couple of really big warships on a goodwill tour in that neighborhood. They'll have to visit several ports, spend some time in each, and then move on to the next. It wouldn't surprise me if they were out there for the better part of a year."

Now he had really surprised her. She perked up and didn't try to hide the genuine smile on her face. "I'll have to confirm this, but I think Norandyne is less than thirty light-years from Novalis, and Sarkovie isn't much farther, but in a different direction. From either of those systems, one of our fastest cruisers could be in Novalis nearspace in three or four days."

"Yes," he said, grinning like a schoolboy who had just gotten a big date with one of the hottest girls in his class. "The advance troops can hold the fort, with heavy firepower not far behind to back them up."

She stood. "I'll speak immediately with Colonel Blacksword. I would be very surprised if she doesn't support us fully on this. And I'd bet good money she'll have a creative idea or two to throw into the game."

••••

The rebels finally stopped locking Mathius to a chain at night, but he quickly learned that that did not allow for any opportunity to escape. At night they kept the compound reasonably well lit, and patrolled the wall that surrounded it with a fair number of men and considerable diligence. He reluctantly came to the realization he could only watch, and wait, and hope an opportunity would arise. Each night he revisited the litany of wrongs the rebels had committed, and knew that the longer he remained with them, the closer he came to truly becoming the good boy Cranoch wanted.

One morning they received a report of an incursion into their district by one of the rival factions. Their warlord turned the problem over to Mercier, who took two squads out to investigate, one of them Cranoch's, and this time they moved cautiously.

They paused on a low hillside overlooking the neighborhood in question. Mercier and Cranoch both peered through binoculars over a low stone wall and were silent for several seconds. Then they lowered the binoculars and squatted down behind the wall to confer.

"What do you think?" Mercier asked.

Cranoch shrugged. "Didn't see anything, but that don't mean nothing."

"Yah," Mercier said. "Won't hurt to be careful."

They worked their way into the neighborhood leapfrogging: two men rushed forward to a position of cover, then waited and covered the field of fire while two more men rushed past them. They moved from door to door, checking each house carefully before moving on to the next.

Cranoch had teamed Mathius up with Timor and two soldiers with more experience. The four of them had just finished searching a house where they'd found only frightened civilians, and nothing worth stealing. As they stepped out of the front door of the house, thinking the report of an incursion might have been a false alarm, a small round dot appeared in the middle of Timor's forehead and the back of his skull erupted. An instant later the loud bark of a rifle reached their ears and Timor slumped to the ground.

Mathius dove behind a bush even before someone shouted, "Hit the deck."

The quiet afternoon erupted with the sound of automatic weapons fire, and a strange, screaming, mechanical whine that tore at Mathius's ears. With his heart pounding in his chest, he stared at Timor's lifeless, unseeing eyes and hugged dirt as tracers skimmed over his head. One of the older soldiers lying near him jabbed the muzzle of his rifle under Mathius's chin and shouted, "Get up and run, you asshole, or we're both dead."

Mathius scrambled to his feet along with the two remaining men on his team. He ran, blind fear his only guide, bullets kicking up dirt at his feet. The soldier running next to him grunted and dropped, tumbling head over heels. Mathius crashed through the closed door of a house into a living room, stumbled over a small stool and sprawled in a heap of arms and legs onto a threadbare carpet. Bullets made a strange popping sound as they punched through the thin walls of the house and shredded the furniture around him, and the screaming whine continued to fill the silence between individual shots.

Mathius stayed low and belly-crawled toward the back of the house. On his way there he saw a young girl in a bedroom huddled over a small child, her eyes stark with fear. "Stay low," he snarled at her, thinking of the bullets popping through the walls of the house. "Whatever you do, don't get up." He crawled onward.

The back of the house opened into a small garden and patio, shaded from the sun by tall, leafy trees. Mathius crawled across the patio, around the side of the house and took cover behind a low stone wall about waist high. There he stopped and checked his ammunition: he had two twenty-round magazines.

He quickly glanced over the wall, then dropped back down behind it. No bullets chipped at the stone above him, but that didn't mean no one had spotted him. They might simply be waiting for him to expose himself again, and they'd take his head off when he did.

He recalled the image he'd captured during his momentary glimpse. He had a view of the street where several of his comrades lay unmoving in crumpled heaps, and several more lay pinned down by enemy fire. He couldn't stop wondering what made that strange, screaming wail that filled his ears and drowned out the sounds of almost everything else.

He crawled the length of the wall, crouched and jumped over it into the neighboring yard. Again, no weapons fire peppered the wall near him. He crawled along the back of that house, and found another low wall separating it from the next property. Apparently, before the rebellion had begun, they'd built a cookie-cutter development with all the houses separated from each other by identical stone walls. He jumped over that one, crawled the length of that property and jumped over another.

Again, he chanced a quick look over the wall at the street, then dropped back down behind it. Through sheer luck he'd flanked an enemy machine gun emplacement. They had an advanced weapon he'd heard of but never seen, a rotary that spit armor-piercing flechettes at an amazing rate of fire, and now he knew the source of the irritating whine that dominated the sounds of the fight. He'd spotted five enemy soldiers in the emplacement, and none of them had been paying him the least bit of attention.

He took several deep breaths, trying not to hyperventilate, then rose up, rested his rifle on the wall, fired ten rounds at them in rapid succession, then dropped back down. It was the second time he'd ever really fired a weapon at another human being, and again he didn't think he had actually hit anyone.

He peeked over the wall quickly, long enough to see them swinging the rotary around his way. He dropped down behind the wall again, and as the weapon screamed with its high-pitched whine, he learned that the flechettes pierced the stone. He hugged dirt beneath their line of fire, belly crawled a few meters down the length of the wall, rose up and fired five more rounds, then dropped back down.

He rolled away from the wall as the flechettes tore through it. But a moment later his ears popped and he heard a loud whomp. The characteristic whine of the rotary went silent, though the pop and crack of other weapons continued. Another explosion, and another, then all went still.

He lay there breathing heavily. The rotary had torn away a good piece of the wall, pulverizing it and covering him in a layer of fine rock dust. He patted his arms and legs and torso, and found no wounds beyond a few bruises.

He heard Cranoch shout, "We got 'em. It's all clear."

••••

Mathius rose up slowly until he could just see over the top of the wall. Mercier and three of his men stood among dead and wounded enemy soldiers in the machine gun nest. One of the enemy soldiers raised a hand in a weak gesture of submission. Mercier shot him in the face.

Mathius rose to his feet. Mercier and one of his men started fearfully and aimed their rifles at him.

Mathius shouted, "It's just me. Mathius."

When they lowered their weapons Mathius walked forward.

"You gotta be more careful," Mercier said. "Friendly fire will get you just as dead as enemy fire."

Mathius looked around and saw no sign of Cranoch. He asked, "Where are the rest?"

Mercier grimaced. "We're it, plus Cranoch."

Of the two squads they'd begun with, only six men had come out of the firefight alive and unwounded: Mercier, his three men, Cranoch, and Mathius.

"Good job," Mercier said. "If you hadn't flanked them, none of us would have made it."

Mathius didn't tell him that he'd flanked the enemy through sheer, stupid luck. Maybe they'd give him something a little better to eat that night.

"Where's Cranoch?" he asked.

Mercier pointed to a low, single story building and the dark shadow of an open doorway. Mathius turned and walked toward it, his mind numb. He didn't really care about any of the dead rebels, but the aftereffects of a sustained adrenaline rush weighed heavily on him, and he wanted to sit down and sleep.

The building Mercier pointed him to had been some sort of small government storage facility, constructed with concrete walls and a steel roof. The only light inside it came from the glare that spilled through the open doorway. There he found Cranoch crouched over the body of an enemy officer, rifling through his pockets.

When Mathius stepped through the open doorway, Cranoch looked up and said, "Good job, kid. I knew you had it in you."

"What are you doing?" Mathius asked.

Cranoch raised both hands, holding a dark, round cylinder in each. "Look what I got off this asshole. Micro-nukes, two of them."

The older man looked around. "Won't take out one of these concrete walls, but they'll sure blow the fuck out of anyone inside them. They'll come in real handy some time if we gotta clear a building."

He turned to another dead body. "Let's see if this asshole's got anything."

Mathius's mind raced, Cranoch's words drumming through his thoughts over and over again, *Won't take out one of these concrete walls, but they'll sure blow the fuck out of anyone inside them.*

An image flashed through his mind: his father's head exploding as Mercier's bullet slammed into it. The young girl's dead eyes came next followed by her blood-caked hair, the blood soaked mattress and floor, the smell of shit and urine in her room. He thought of Timor, laying only a short distance away, a little boy destroyed long before he met his own death. And he didn't want to forget Phillan, a friend who'd saved his life by helping him pretend to be a good boy. He recalled now the sickly sheen of sweat on Phillan's face as he lay dying. Without consciously trying to make it happen, in an instant his mind formed a plan.

To make it sound right there would have to be a shot, a momentary pause, then three or four shots in rapid succession. Mathius raised his rifle, didn't really have to aim because he stood only a meter behind Cranoch. He flicked the safety off and said, "Cranoch, this is for the girl."

Cranoch straightened and looked over his shoulder. "The girl? What girl?"

"The girl," Mathius said. "And for Timor, and my father, and Phillan."

Mathius felt no hesitation when it came to killing Cranoch. The man deserved killing, and the world would be a better place without him. Cranoch's eyes widened as he had a tiny fraction of a second to realize he was about to die, then Mathius pulled the trigger.

In the darkened room the bullet thundered from the barrel with a blinding flash. It punched a hole in Cranoch's temple, and his head snapped to one side as he fell in a heap over the body of the enemy officer. Mercier and his men would have heard that shot, so Mathius quickly fired three rounds into the concrete wall as part of his cover story. Then he retrieved the two micro-nukes—he'd never used one before but Cranoch had seen to it he knew how. He set one of them to a two-second delay, then hid them both in his camouflage jacket. He rushed to the open doorway and shouted, "Captain Mercier, one of them was still alive. He shot Cranoch. I think he's dead."

Mercier and his three men broke into a run. They elbowed Mathius out of the way and crowded past him into the room. Mercier bent down to examine Cranoch.

Mathius said, "I shot the bastard after he killed Cranoch." As he spoke he retrieved the micro-nuke he had set to a two second delay, and backed out through the doorway into the sunlight. He stepped to one side, armed the cylinder, hit the firing stud and tossed it into the room, quietly saying, "This is for my father."

He pressed his back against the outside wall of the concrete structure and covered his ears. He heard a muffled shout an instant before the ground shook and a gout of flame and smoke erupted from the open doorway. The silence that followed frightened him more than anything else.

He let the dust and smoke settle for a few seconds, then walked into the room carrying his rifle. He wasn't sure if the men were dead, though no one groaned or moved in the slightest. Interestingly enough, Mercier's grav pistol appeared to be undamaged.

Mathius decided not to leave anything to chance, and he thought it rather poetic when he used the gun that had killed his father to blow Mercier's head off. And as further insurance, he used his rifle to put a bullet in the head of each of the other rebels, just to be sure.

He kept the grav pistol and scrounged more ammunition for his rifle off several of the bodies out in the street. One of the dead soldiers had a military trench knife strapped to his side. It had a twenty centimeter blade, and a steel knuckled grip, much like the knucks Cranoch had beaten Mathius with. He strapped it around his waist along with the grav gun.

He needed to disappear, and wasn't sure if Mercier's comrades could do a body count and realize little Mathius had gone missing. If they did, they might come looking for him. So for good measure he armed the remaining micro-nuke, triggered it and tossed it into the concrete building. It would make the bodies even harder to identify. He took no satisfaction from the sound of the explosion.

It was time to return to his old apartment, to see if he could find his mother and sister. He didn't try to stop the tears that streamed down his cheeks as he walked away.

7

A Friend

MATHIUS MOVED CAUTIOUSLY from shadow to shadow. He had a reasonable understanding of the lay of the city, but he'd been a captive of the rebels for more than a year, and a lot had changed. More often than not he traveled under the cover of darkness and slept through the day. But day or night, when he approached another street, he always stopped in a shadow from which he could see down its length, and waited for several minutes. If the street showed any signs of life, he detoured around it. It slowed his progress considerably, but he wasn't willing to sacrifice safety for speed.

Many of the city's inhabitants had no love for any of the factions, so he considered discarding the camouflage jacket because it marked him as a combatant. But to complete the transformation to civilian he'd have to dump the rifle he carried and the grav pistol holstered on his hip, and he wasn't about to give up his only means of protection. In any case, he didn't have an alternative to the jacket, so he decided to hold onto it until he found something better.

Some sections of the city had been pounded into rubble, and yet others remained completely intact, as if the rebellion had been nothing more than a childish nightmare. In a recently bombed neighborhood he spotted a number of people in the distance and slipped into a shadow. From afar he couldn't make out any details, and chided himself for not having the forethought to steal Mercier's binoculars. His smartest move would be to detour around them, but he needed to cross the river, and they were near the approach to one of the few bridges that remained intact. He decided to move closer and observe, see if he could get around them to the bridge. He moved carefully from shadow to shadow, stopping in each to watch and listen for a time. But no one spotted him, and no one raised an outcry.

They didn't act like soldiers, seemed to be focused on one collapsed building, crawled all over it, and occasionally called out to each other. Curious, he moved to another shadow closer in, and soon he saw that they weren't wearing uniforms of any kind.

"I found one," one of them shouted, and several of them converged on the fellow. They grunted and groaned and struggled to lift a slab of concrete, and Mathius realized they were a group of civilians digging victims out of the rubble of a collapsed building.

He couldn't say what prompted him to stand out into the open and walk their way. No one noticed him at first, but as he got closer a woman pointed at him and said, "Oh no!"

They all looked his way and froze, and he saw the fear on their faces he himself had felt so many times. It bothered him that he could be the source of their fear. They eyed him warily, and he wasn't sure what to say to ease their anxiety. But then he realized there was nothing he could say, because his appearance said it all: a filthy man in a camo jacket carrying a rifle with a sidearm strapped to his hip. He looked like one of the predators they feared.

He stopped at the base of the pile of rubble that had once been a building. Without saying anything he leaned the rifle against a large chunk of broken concrete, pulled off the camo jacket, rolled up his sleeves, and climbed up to the men who'd been grunting over the heavy block of masonry. They'd stopped trying to move it and stood there staring at him dumbly. He bent, put his shoulder against the chunk of concrete and grunted as he tried unsuccessfully to move it by himself. They watched him and didn't move to help. He tried again, and grunted again as he did so. Then slowly, one by one, without saying anything, they joined him, and together they pushed the masonry aside. He sensed that they tacitly accepted his presence, though the wariness remained.

By his estimate his parent's old apartment remained on the other side of the river about a two-kilometer walk from the collapsed building, though the city had changed during his year with the rebels so he couldn't be certain of that. Oddly enough, he felt no great urgency to return to his old home. As he struggled to help pull the lifeless body of a small girl from the rubble, he examined his own feelings about that, and realized he feared the end of the journey. He knew his hopes were unrealistic, and he dreaded returning to their apartment only to learn he would never again see his mother and sister. He almost wished that he would find them dead, rather than not find them at all and never know their fate.

"Would you like something to eat?"

Mathius's thoughts returned to the moment. He'd been wrestling with a block of concrete, and hadn't noticed the older woman approach him. She stood over him, holding out a piece of bread wrapped around a few slices of some sort of meat. She had dark hair cut shoulder length, and though concrete dust caked her face, shoulders, head and hair, he found her quite pretty, and even her sad eyes didn't lessen that impression. She looked at him with compassion and kindness, something he hadn't seen in a long time.

"We don't have a lot of food," she said, "but you've earned it, and we appreciate your help."

He reached out and took the offered sandwich, used his sleeve to wipe the sweat off his face and sat down. She sat down beside him and handed him a canteen of water.

"Were you with the rebels?" she asked.

He shrugged. "Not by choice. They kidnapped me and forced me to be one of them." And he had become one of them. It had been his finger, and his alone, on the trigger of his rifle the day he'd killed that defenseless man.

"How long?"

He grimaced. "About a year, maybe longer. It took that long to find an opportunity to escape."

"Will they come looking for you?"

"No," he said, recalling the way the first micro-nuke had shredded the bodies in the small building. If Mercier's warlord sent someone to investigate, after the second micro-nuke, at best they'd be counting body parts, and Mathius didn't think they'd be that thorough. They would assume he had died with the rest.

"What's your name?"

"Mathius," he said.

"Well, Mathius," she said, extending her hand, "I'm Dr. Tevala."

He shook her hand. It was callused and rough, but small and delicate. "Doctor?" he asked.

"Yes," she said, smiling. "I work in the hospital, trying to put these people back together after they blow them apart."

"Hospital?" he asked. "Where?"

"About a kilometer from here." She pointed west, the same direction he needed to go to find his parents' old apartment building. "It's still intact. The factions have been careful not to bomb it, at least so far." The resignation in her voice implied she wasn't sure how long that would last.

Doctor, Mathius thought. That appealed to him. He'd much rather be among those who put people back together, than those who blew them apart.

"Do you think I could be a doctor?" he asked.

She shrugged. "You seem like a smart boy, why not?"

Someone shouted, "We've got a live one."

Tevala jumped to her feet and scrambled over the rubble. Mathius followed, wolfing down the last of his sandwich.

They had found a woman completely buried by dirt and masonry, but still alive. It took more than an hour to carefully extract her without hurting her further, though they discovered she had a broken leg with a bloody bit of bone protruding from the skin just above her ankle. Tevala splinted and field-prepped it, then stood and said, "We've got to get her to the hospital."

Mathius helped them lift the woman onto a stretcher, retrieved his camo jacket, then slung his rifle over his shoulder and reached down to heft the front end of the stretcher. Tevala gave him a curious look, so he said, "I've got to go that way anyway. Might as well help carry her on my way."

She smiled and extended a hand. "Give me the rifle."

He looked at her warily, and couldn't hide his distrust.

She grimaced. "You don't want to carry it openly." She pointed at the holstered grav pistol and the trench knife strapped to his side. "Or those either. And you don't want to be seen wearing that camouflage jacket. We have to pass a checkpoint, and you'll either end up dead, or forced to join them again."

He handed her the rifle and the jacket, then unbuckled the holster and sheath, and gave her those too. She placed them on the stretcher beside the injured woman, then extended the blanket to cover the weapons and coat as well. Mathius doubted that would work, but Tevala had given him food, and he wasn't going to abandon her now.

Mathius and one of the men lifted the stretcher and they marched toward the river, Tevala in the lead. At the bridge they encountered a government check-point, and passed through it without incident, which surprised Mathius.

Tevala said, "I treat government soldiers as well as everyone else, and I also treat the occasional rebel officer, so they've all adopted a hands-off attitude regarding the hospital and my staff."

She winked and leaned close to Mathius. "If anyone asks, you're part of my staff, one of my assistants."

The hospital stood at the center of a swath of city occupied by one of the government factions. Tevala conducted surgery in a small room on the first floor of the three-story building. Mathius helped them lift the woman onto the operating table, retrieved the holstered grav gun, trench knife, rifle and his jacket, then stepped to one side to watch.

Tevala moved skillfully, and spoke kindly to her patient as she worked. From the makeshift nature of almost everything in the hospital, Mathius guessed they didn't have much by way of medications, nothing like the stuff the medic had used to treat Mercier's wound. With an open wound like that, the woman would probably die of infection. He could do nothing about that, but he consoled himself knowing Mercier and Cranoch would no longer harm anyone.

Tevala finished working on the woman near sunset, and Mathius wanted to take advantage of the darkness to travel. As she cleaned up he thanked her for the sandwich, and told her he had to leave.

She smiled and said, "Whether you find your mother and sister or not, come back if you can. You can help here, and I'll teach you a bit about medicine. Maybe you will become a doctor someday."

Mathius shook her hand, slipped into the darkness and turned west.

••••

Some landmarks that Mathius had depended upon no longer existed, and he dodged several government patrols. It took most of the night to find the street where he had lived with his parents in their apartment. Shortly before dawn he settled into a shadow on the second floor of a building that had been under construction two years ago. The work had been quickly abandoned when the rebellion began. He had a good view of the entire street, so he sat down to watch and wait.

About an hour later a troop of government soldiers walked down the street. The casual way they moved, without taking anything more than the most rudimentary precautions, told him they didn't fear ambush or a firefight. That suggested he had little to fear, as long as he remained diligent and didn't expose himself. He knew exactly what would happen if a squad of government troops spotted a rebel on their turf.

He watched a few pedestrians walk up and down the street, though it was by no means a busy thoroughfare. And while they moved cautiously, they did so without the rapid, furtive movements and overt signs of fear that came with imminent danger. He spent another hour carefully mapping out the route he'd take to their old apartment, selecting each shadow he'd stop in. And to be sure he couldn't be cornered, he rejected any that didn't offer more than one means of escape. Nothing untoward happened during that time, so he climbed down to the ground floor of the half-constructed building.

The sun burned brightly in the sky, but remained low enough to cast deep shadows on the south side of the street. He moved from shadow to shadow along his preselected path, worked his way down the street and stopped in the shade of a building across from their old apartment. The street looked as if nothing had changed, but he knew not to trust in that.

He glanced up and down the street, confirmed that he had it to himself, then sprinted across to the other side, where he slipped into a shadow and waited. There came no uproar, no shouted cries of excitement or fear. Had a rebel or government soldier stepped out of hiding, this time he had a rifle and would not hesitate to use it.

He worked his way around to the back of the building to a door he remembered. Its lock had long ago been jimmied, so he opened it carefully and stepped into a dark hallway. Inside, he found nothing but silence. He hesitated, not sure what had given him pause, then realized the hard wooden floor should have been covered in a fine sheen of dust. Instead he saw faint streaks as if it had been swept. The building had at least one occupant.

He climbed the stairs to the second floor, halted about four steps short of the top, crouched down and peeked down the hallway with his eyes at floor level. He had a moment where it all seemed as if the intervening years had not happened, that he had just returned home from school. All he needed to do was march down the hall to the fourth door on the left, step into the apartment and call out to his mother that he was home. His sister would only be a few minutes behind him, and his father would return from work a few hours later. They'd sit down, have dinner, and chat while they searched the vids to see if they found anything worth watching.

He shook himself, forcing his thoughts back to the unpleasant reality in which he now lived. He climbed the last few steps and walked on tiptoe down the hallway.

The fourth door on the left stood slightly ajar. His mother used to do that on hot days to allow a little cross-breeze through the apartment, but in his heart he knew it hung open because the place had been abandoned long ago. He stopped in the half-open doorway and listened, glanced only briefly at the blood stain in the carpet where Mercier had killed his father. And that was when he heard her humming the way she always had when busy with some task.

It couldn't be her. He must be hallucinating, letting his imagination and desires create sounds that didn't really exist. He pushed the door open all the way and stepped into their living room. When he looked more closely, it appeared that someone had made an attempt to clean away the dark stain in the carpet.

A gasp drew his attention away from the old blood stain, and he looked up to find his mother standing in the entrance to their small kitchen, drying her hands with a towel. Her hair had turned grayer than it had been a year ago, and the crow's feet around her eyes had deepened, but other than that she remained unchanged. She remained alive.

She raised a hand to her mouth and her eyes widened with fear. And only then did he realize she faced an unshaven man in dirty clothing, wearing a camo jacket and holding a rifle.

"Mother," he said. "It's me, Mathius."

Her eyes narrowed with uncertainty, she dropped the towel to the floor and squinted at him. When recognition came, she gasped again and her eyes widened even further. Then she crossed the distance between them in an instant, wrapped her arms around him and almost lifted him off his feet. "My son," she said, tears streaming down her cheeks.

He remembered her being taller, and thought she had shrunk during the intervening year. But it was he who had grown by several centimeters.

He cried with her, holding her in his arms.

••••

Later that evening his sister, Selna, came home and they all shared in another tearful reunion.

She told him, "I've applied for a Commonwealth refugee visa. If they approve it, I can move off-planet and take mother with me. You should apply too . . ."

She hesitated, then added. "But don't tell them you were a rebel."

"I wasn't a rebel," he said. "They kidnapped me and forced me to join them." He tried not to think of the innocent man he had murdered.

She shook her head. "I don't think that'll matter to them."

He learned that a year ago they had hidden from the rebels in the basement of an abandoned building about a half kilometer away. They'd moved from hideout to hideout for six months and nearly starved, but eventually the government faction under which they now lived had swept the rebels out of the district.

His mother said, "We found what was left of your father still lying in the middle of the floor."

Selna added, "There wasn't much left, just bones and hair. We recognized him because of his clothing, though it wasn't in much better shape."

"We buried him out back," his mother said. "Do you know how he died?"

Mathius couldn't lie to them, but he wasn't about to give them the gory details, so he told them an edited version of the truth.

Selna asked, "You were taken by the rebels?"

"Yes," he said.

His mother nodded. "We wondered about that."

They asked him about his time with the rebels and he gave them an edited version of that as well. He enjoyed telling them about Dr. Tevala, but when he said, "I want to become a doctor someday too, like her," hearing the words spoken aloud that way, he realized how foolish they sounded.

8

Scrounging

MATHIUS THOUGHT THAT if he helped save a life or two, it might make up in some small way for the innocent man he had murdered. He returned to the hospital in the hope of helping Tevala as much as he could. She put him to work, saying, "I'm sorry. I can't pay you."

He said, "I don't need any pay."

He didn't mind because it felt good to help someone like Tevala. She did give him a replacement for the camo jacket, a simple coat, used and threadbare, but still functional. "Wear this," she said, "so you don't look like one of those thugs."

He donned the new coat with a certain amount of pride, and considered that full and just compensation for his limited and unskilled services. He almost tossed out the camo jacket, but considered it a terrible waste to simply throw out a perfectly good piece of clothing. So he bundled it up and hid it away in his bedroom. And conscious of Tevala's words about looking like *one of those thugs*, he stored the rifle with the jacket, and stopped carrying it, at least in the hospital. He did continue to wear the grav gun on his hip, though he had no way of properly charging it, so once he used it, he'd have to throw it away. At least the new jacket hid both it and the trench knife nicely.

Tevala gave him some food every day. He always brought it home to his mother and Selna. They shared all their food that way, and they shared their hunger as well.

One day Dr. Tevala seemed preoccupied with worry.

"What's wrong?" he asked.

She closed her eyes and rubbed her temples. "We've been cut off from the relief supplies sent by the Commonwealth. We never got much, but now we don't get any."

"Why?" he asked.

She shook her head with disgust. "The factions are taking it all for themselves. And I think the Kelk have something to do with it."

Mathius recalled the Kelk and Commonwealth symbols he'd seen on the boxes he'd unloaded for his rebel captors. "What do you need?"

"Medication," she said, "antibiotics, biotech, regrowth drugs, rapid healing stims, food, supplies, bandages, anything."

Mathius nodded and said nothing, but he thought he might be able to help. And as he considered the situation carefully he formed a plan that would most likely get him killed. But if not, it would help Tevala. He'd do anything to help Tevala in her tireless efforts to save lives, including murder. He didn't care that anyone else might consider his reasoning somewhat twisted.

He went home and slept through the rest of the afternoon so he'd be fresh; the only good thing he'd learned from Cranoch was to take advantage of the opportunity to sleep when it came. When he awoke, he pulled on the camo jacket and hefted the rifle. He checked his appearance in an old, cracked, full-length mirror to confirm that he once again looked like *one of those thugs*; the dim light of early evening would help in that respect.

Moving with the old caution he'd used when he first escaped his rebel captors, he slowly worked his way into a rebel occupied district, arriving there about an hour before dusk. And there, he went hunting.

The first evening he came up empty handed, but on the second he spotted a patrol of six soldiers out collecting *taxes* from the citizenry for *protection*. They had split up into two teams of three, with each team working a different side of the street.

Mathius hid in a shadow, and from a distance watched a team approach a residence. One of the three snuck around back to ensure that none of the occupants slipped out that way, while the other two approached the front and rapped on the door with the butts of their rifles. Mathius knew the drill well, had learned it under Cranoch's tutelage.

The residents admitted them reluctantly, and after a quarter of an hour the rebels emerged with their loot. One of them walked around to the back of the house to retrieve the third member of their team, and they moved on to the next house. The fellow who'd covered the back never entered the place.

Mathius watched them strong-arm a few more residences, and since each man got a cut of the take, they took turns covering the back. Sometimes the two soldiers kicked the door down and forced their way in. Once, Mathius heard the crack of a gunshot muffled by the walls of the building, and he thought of the way his father had died. But they followed a set pattern, a fact Mathius could use to his advantage. It helped that the soldiers were casual and relaxed on their home turf.

The rebels always sent a medic with a patrol, though after watching Tevala work, Mathius understood they used the term *medic* rather loosely. In fact, the fellow was just another soldier, and was required to perform the same duties as the rest of the combatants. But they had equipped him with a satchel of emergency medications, and would have trained him to some limited extent in their use. Mathius spotted the medic and followed that team, moving closer to them each time they entered a residence. The sky had darkened to deep dusk when it came the medic's turn to cover the back of a house. Full night was not far off.

Mathius waited until a few minutes after the two out front had entered the residence, then edged his way along the side of the house to the back. He stopped at the corner of the building, slung his rifle over his shoulder and pulled the trench knife. He stuck his left hand casually in the pocket of his pants and held the trench knife in his right hand close to his side with his elbow cocked slightly. In the oncoming darkness it would appear as if he had shoved both hands into the pockets of his pants. He wasn't sure if he'd use the knife's blade, or its steel-knuckled grip.

He hunched his shoulders and walked around the corner of the building casually. The medic stood near the back door, leaning against the wall of the house and smoking something that didn't smell like tobacco. He had put his pack on the ground at his feet. At the sound of footsteps, he glanced Mathius's way and asked, "Why so fast?"

Mathius coughed and spit a mouth full of saliva to one side. Growling in a hoarse voice, he said, "Empty."

The medic said, "Abandoned, huh?"

"Yah."

The medic bent to retrieve his pack just as Mathius reached him, a wonderful stroke of luck. With the fellow bent over and unsuspecting, Mathius clubbed him as hard as he could in the back of the head with the butt of his trench knife. The man staggered. Mathius hit him again, the soldier collapsed in a heap, rolled over onto his back and groaned. Mathius stabbed the point of the blade up under the fellow's solar plexus and sliced to one side. The soldier jerked once then laid still, his lips opening and closing spasmodically, blood welling out of his mouth accompanied by a faint gurgle.

Mathius withdrew the knife and wiped the blade on the man's jacket. He grabbed the fellow's pack and tensed to run, but he heard someone inside the house cry out and realized he might do better than simply run. The man he'd just killed was smaller than him, though he never entertained the thought of trying to lift the fellow. And the next property had been bombed into rubble, so Mathius grabbed the man by his ankles and dragged him toward it—adrenaline helped quite a bit. He hid the body behind a pile of broken masonry, then rushed back, retrieved the rebel's pack and rifle, and returned to the body. For good measure he slit the fellow's throat, then backed away and hid behind the remains of a broken stone wall. He quietly chambered a round in his rifle and waited in the dark.

Some minutes later one of the rebels stepped into the back yard. He'd stuffed his hands into his pockets and walked casually with his rifle slung over his shoulder, much the way Mathius had walked when he'd approached the medic. The fellow stopped and looked around, then said, "Tark, where are you?"

He waited, and when no reply came, he called out again, "Tark, god damn it, time to go. Where the fuck are you?"

The third member of their team joined him, saying, "What the hell are you shouting about?"

"Tark," the first said. "He ain't here."

"Well where the fuck is he?"

Had the two decided to search around, Mathius would have first tried to slip away into the darkness, firing his rifle only as a last resort, but his luck held.

The first one said, "Looks like he took off."

The other said, "Shit! Probably plans on selling the meds. Fucking asshole."

The two turned and walked back toward the street at the front of the house.

Mathius waited for over an hour to be sure they were long gone, then quietly emerged from his hiding place. He searched the body carefully, retrieved a compact pair of binoculars that might be of use, and also found some additional ammunition. He didn't want them to find the body and realize someone had targeted their medics, so he piled loose stones and masonry on top of the dead rebel, and covered that with dried brush. They thought the fellow had decided to disappear on his own, apparently a not uncommon occurrence, and he didn't want them to learn otherwise.

••••

The next morning, when Mathius handed Dr. Tevala the satchel, she frowned, considered it for a moment, then gave Mathius an uncertain look. "What's this?"

He shrugged, and hoping she wouldn't detect the lie in his words, he said, "I went out scrounging yesterday evening and found it. Pure luck. Looks like there's some stuff in it you might be able to use."

Her lips pursed, her frown deepened, and he feared she had come to distrust him in some way. She crossed the room and placed the satchel on a table, then took hold of the metal buckle keeping it shut. When she twisted the buckle it snapped with a loud click, and she started. She pulled the satchel's flap back and opened it carefully, leaning away from it ever so slightly, the way one might fearfully open a package containing something dangerous. She looked into its interior for a long moment before reaching into it and retrieving one of the packets of medicine. She held it up and examined it carefully, her eyes slowly widening, her mouth opening into a round O.

It had the same Kelk symbol stamped on the side of it that Mathius had seen on the other packages. Last night he had purposefully targeted a rebel faction different from the one that had kidnapped him. That meant the Kelk were supplying one of the two government factions, and at least two of the three rebel factions. Supplying everyone with medical supplies seemed to be a very humanitarian thing to do.

Dr. Tevala's full-hearted whoop startled Mathius and brought him out of his reverie. She laid the packet on the counter, then rapidly, almost desperately, retrieved another. "Oh dear boy!" she said.

As she pulled each packet out of the satchel, she carefully lined them up on the table. When she'd emptied the pack, she adjusted the position of each packet, looking at them the way a starving man might covet the first food he had seen in months. Then she spun about, and before Mathius realized what she intended to do, she crossed the room, wrapped her arms around him and actually managed to lift him off his feet a few centimeters.

"You sweet, dear boy," she said, planting a kiss on his cheek. Standing with his arms pinned to his sides by her embrace, he thought she smelled rather nice and liked being hugged by this kind woman who put people back together after men like Mathius blew them apart.

She released him, and held him at arm's length. Tears trickled down her cheeks as she said, "You don't know what this means, how many lives it might save."

He didn't really care about the lives his scrounging would save. To get that reaction from Dr. Tevala, he would happily kill any number of soldiers from any and all of the factions.

Mathius went out at night whenever possible. Each faction maintained four or five strongholds in the district they controlled. He shifted targets constantly, never hit the same one twice, and proved to be quite adept at scrounging, though many nights he came up empty handed. But he succeeded frequently enough that Tevala once told him his efforts had saved many lives. He swelled with pride the day she told him that.

One morning Mathius decided to go out during the day to scout one of the government compounds. In broad daylight he had to move carefully, but on their home turf, the patrols the factions sent out didn't move with any stealth, and in fact moved with confidence. Standing in a shadow and considering his next move, he heard a gruff voice say, "My dick's itching like hell. I think that bitch gave me the clap."

Another voice said, "You were born with the clap. Probably gave it to her first. Now she just gave it back to you."

Mathius had learned to choose his hiding places so that he always had more than one means of escape. Standing in the shadow of a partially collapsed wall, he slipped through the jagged hole of what had once been a doorway. The back wall of the room he stepped into had long ago disintegrated into a long, low pile of broken masonry, and he had no trouble slipping out the rear of the building into an old alley choked with rubble. But he didn't go far.

He'd learned through experimentation that he could move with reasonable freedom during daylight hours by following on the heels of a patrol sent out by the local faction. They didn't monitor their back trail with anything more than the occasional glance over a shoulder. And their presence swept the streets clear in front of them. He waited in the alley at the back of the building and listened.

"Boss is gonna be pissed we came up with so little, and most of it close to useless."

"Yah, but he's gotta understand the pickings are getting slimmer and slimmer every day."

"You be sure to tell him that when he's all pissed off and stoned on that stuff he takes."

Good, Mathius thought. They were headed back to their compound, which was exactly where he wanted to go.

He reminded himself not to get overconfident. *Always assume the worst*, he told himself. He had adopted that mantra long ago, and always considered his next move before taking action. He never entered an alley or building if he didn't know for certain he had an alternate escape route. The armed patrols marched down the middle of the rubble strewn streets, while Mathius kept to the shadows and darkness.

He followed the patrol for six city blocks, then peeled off and held back about five hundred meters from their compound. He found a collapsed building with a second floor still partially intact. It took quite a bit of poking around to find a way up, but once he'd gained the high ground he sat down to watch and wait.

The factions never sent anyone out beyond the walls of their compounds except in well-armed patrols. But to assume they never made an exception could be a fatal mistake. If they had stationed a lone sniper out in the streets, Mathius hoped that with enough patience and diligence, the man would eventually give his position away by moving.

He used the binoculars he'd taken off that dead medic to scan the streets in front of the compound. After an hour and no sign of danger, he climbed back down to the street and moved to within two hundred yards of its outer wall. The binoculars turned out to be quite amazing. Though they were compact and light-weight, they could zoom in to incredible magnification.

After an hour he hadn't learned anything and was about to give up, when a flatbed truck pulled up to the gate of the compound. A heavy tarp secured tightly around the edges concealed its cargo. The truck's driver spoke briefly with the guards at the gate, they opened the gate, and the truck pulled into the yard in front of the compound's mansion.

The driver and three men removed the tarp to reveal a number of heavy crates. Mathius dialed the magnification on the binoculars up to maximum and watched the men unload the truck. From that distance, even the binoculars weren't good enough for him to read the stamps on the sides of the crates, but he saw that Kelk symbol, blurry and ill defined, yet easily recognizable. He'd unloaded similar crates while a captive of Cranoch and his comrades, and recognized an ammunition crate when he saw one.

Over the next two months he confirmed that the Kelk Supremacy was supplying both government factions and all three rebel factions with arms and ammunition. It was one thing to supply medical supplies to everyone, but weapons too? That seemed to mean that they didn't side with anyone, and he didn't understand why they would do that.

9

An Unconventional Secret

WHEN NIKAELA'S IMPLANTS woke her, she climbed out of bed and put on the cleanest clothing she possessed, which was filthy by any normal standard. She drew her one-cup ration of bathing water and returned to the mirror on the wall near her bed. She splashed a few grams of water on a cloth and tried to remove the grime from beneath her eyes. The makeup intended to hide her bluish-white flesh compounded the situation by attracting dust and helping it stick to her skin.

She had looked forward to her training mission with considerable excitement, had thought it would be wonderful to be part of the crew of one of the big transition ships. Now, she longed for the day when it ended. Their water ration on Novalis III made shipboard rationing seem lavish in the extreme. Unlike the general population they didn't want for food or drinking water, but she fantasized about the day she could take a full shower, or even the incredible luxury of a hot bath. She finished cleaning up and joined her comrades in their makeshift mess hall for breakfast.

Across the table Eindride asked her, "Think you can get through that new shipment today?"

The previous night a hunter-killer had down-transited into the Novalis system and delivered several tonnes of supplies. A heavily stealthed grav boat brought the goods down to the surface. Such operations always increased the danger of discovery, and everyone's nerves had been on edge until the boat had returned to its rendezvous with the hunter-killer.

"Yes," she said, "it shouldn't be a problem. Worst case scenario is that I might need a few hours tomorrow morning."

"Good enough," Eindride said. "I don't need to make any deliveries until late tomorrow."

They finished breakfast, Nikaela grabbed an inventory terminal and went out to the main warehouse floor. Over the past few months she had learned that inventory days were the most exciting she could hope for. The nature of their racial characteristics confined them to the warehouse and its immediate environs. She'd lost about half her pay to the two riflewomen playing cards, though that didn't really matter since none of them had any place they could go to spend it.

She started with the smaller crates, logging their serial numbers and scanning their inventory details into the terminal. Sometimes she had to break open a pallet and separate the individual crates to get to the labels and scan them. It proved to be physically demanding work and she enjoyed the exercise.

She climbed to the top of a pallet, and could barely see the label she needed to get to on one crate because another blocked it, hiding the serial number she needed to scan. She cut the strapping tying the crates to the pallet, and as she edged one crate to the side, it tumbled off and smashed to the warehouse floor, landing on a corner and popping one of the latches that held it closed.

"By my ancestors!" she said, and climbed down to the floor, hoping she hadn't damaged anything.

The crate proved to be quite heavy, and it took all her strength to muscle it back upright. The popped latch was bent and twisted. She disengaged the other latch and opened the crate to make sure she hadn't damaged any of its contents . . . and froze at what she saw.

The crate she'd popped open appeared to be a simple box of plast and wood. Inside she found another crate—an ammunition crate.

She scanned the label on the outer crate: food, medical supplies, and some small-arms ammunition, all benign stuff. Something warned her she should reseal the crate and forget the whole incident, but she couldn't leave it at that. When she popped the latches on the interior crate and opened it, she found large-bore mortar rounds. But not just ordinary explosive or fragmentation shells; these were meant for something else, something she didn't recognize, something unconventional. She resealed the container and did what she could to repair the broken latch.

After that she sampled every tenth crate, carefully opening it, looking at its contents, then resealing it. The labels on the exterior containers specified all sorts of rather mundane supplies, with nothing more deadly than small arms and ammunition when it came to weapons. But many of the crates actually contained something she suspected might be far more lethal, though she couldn't be certain of that from simply the appearance of the unusual ammunition itself.

She finished late the next morning, then hunted down Eindride. She found him alone in the mess hall seated at a table with a cup of tea in front of him, reviewing something on a small access terminal. Had he not been alone, she would have waited for another opportunity. He didn't look away from the terminal as she stopped in front of him and remained standing.

"Command Superior Eindride," she said. "May I speak with you in confidence?"

He finally looked away from the terminal, one eyebrow rising sharply. "So very formal," he said, a tone of caution in his words. With a hand gesture he indicated the seat across from him. "Please sit down."

She pulled the chair out and sat down, resting her forearms on the table in front of her.

He said, "What's on your mind, Mistress Vreekande?"

Now that she sat there facing him, her confidence faltered. "I found something unusual while running inventory yesterday, something that . . . bothers me."

His brow furrowed and he stiffened, giving her the impression the information she was about to impart might not surprise him. "Something unusual?" he asked, emphasizing her words carefully. "In what way did it bother you?"

Slowly, haltingly, wondering if speaking up would prove to be a horrible mistake, she told him of the crate she'd accidentally damaged, and the discovery she had made about its actual contents.

He shrugged it off. "One crate mislabeled. It happens. Isolate that one and make sure it doesn't go anywhere. We'll dispose of it later." He sounded like a man who didn't believe his own words.

"I sampled several others," she said, "and found a consistent pattern of mislabeling."

He sat up straight and stiffened further, his face devoid of any expression. "What are you saying?"

She had gone too far to stop now. "It appears we are transporting . . . unconventional weapons that I believe may be illegal—"

He leaned forward and hissed. "Shut up."

Nikaela wasn't about to allow herself to be drawn into something like this. "But the Larscom would—"

"Dammit, I said shut up. Don't say another word. Nothing. Do you hear me?"

A painful knot formed in her gut.

He stood, crossed the room to the door and glanced quickly into the hallway beyond. He returned, stopped behind her, leaned down and snarled in her ear, "Forget you ever saw that. And if you kept any records, destroy them. Keep nothing that can be held against you."

She turned to face him, his face uncomfortably close to hers. "But—"

"By your ancestors," he hissed. "Do you want your career to come to an end the way mine has. You all know I'm never going to see another promotion, but this could end far worse than that. Forget the whole thing and never say another word about it. It never happened, you never saw that stuff, and we never had this conversation."

He turned and marched out of the room, leaving his cup of tea and the terminal behind.

Nikaela took his advice and looked the other way, and they never spoke of it again. Eindride still had her conduct physical inventory, but she never again looked beyond the label on the exterior crate. A month later, while reconciling the physical inventory she'd taken with the records in their database, the air raid sirens interrupted her.

••••

Complete darkness, not even the faintest trace of light. Eyes open, lying flat on his back on a hard floor, Mathius lifted a hand and waved it in front of his nose; blackness so complete he wondered if he might be blind. He swallowed and tasted the acrid tang of concrete dust, and when he put his teeth together they ground on sandy grit. He touched his cheek and found a dusting of the same grit plastered there by a sheen of perspiration.

But where was he? How had he gotten there?

He sat up cautiously, but not cautiously enough because he banged his head on something unyielding and hard, producing a flash of pain. He cursed and lay back down.

He reached up and found a cut on his forehead where it had collided with something. His fingers came away from it sticky with what felt like blood. Fear told him he must think this through carefully.

He reached up and felt the dusty edges of broken stone above him, with a spike of metal protruding from it. No, not stone; broken concrete with twisted rebar exposed. With his fingertips he explored its dimensions. A massive slab of concrete rested at an odd angle just above his head.

Memories flooded through his mind in a strange play of images and recollections that came in reverse order. There had been a massive thump, his ears had popped and the floor beneath his feet had jumped as if a giant god had stomped an enormous foot on the ground nearby. Before that there had been the roar of fighters and the whine of an attack ship's grav drive—loyal government forces or one of the rebel factions, it really didn't matter. And only a second before that the muffled scream of the air-raid sirens had sounded in the distance; just an instant of warning, though probably not enough to save anyone.

Where was he now? How had he gotten there?

He'd been in the hospital's basement—he recalled that now—on an errand to scavenge bandages for Dr. Tevala. He thought momentarily of his desire to become a doctor, but knew there was little chance that dream would ever come true. Clearly, Tevala's parole had expired and one of the factions had bombed the hospital.

There must be rescuers working through the rubble. "Help," he cried out. "Can anyone hear me? I'm in the basement."

He held his breath and listened. Nothing! Utter silence, a stillness so complete it stoked his fear. There should be some sounds, someone moving about somewhere. The hospital had been overcrowded, and if he now lay beneath a massive pile of rubble, there should be someone searching for survivors.

He didn't hurt, no pain anywhere at all. He wiggled his toes, moved his legs a little, flexed his hands and arms, patted down his torso—nothing. No pain, injuries or wounds, other than the bump and cut on his head from sitting up carelessly. But over him lay some unknown amount of broken hospital. He'd seen it before, victims completely unhurt, protected within a hidden pocket beneath a mountain of debris. Unhurt at first, but they sometimes starved to death before anyone found them, or they or the searchers caused the rubble to collapse further, completing what it had failed to do on the first try.

He tried again. "Help! Help! I'm in the basement."

Again, there came no response.

As an experiment he lifted one leg and didn't bang it against anything, so there must be more headroom over the lower half of his body. He reached up to grasp the slab of concrete above him, thinking to use it as an anchor to slide out from beneath it. But he'd learned through experience that large pieces of collapsed buildings could be precariously balanced, and applying any force to it might dislodge it, which would not be good for him while he lay beneath it. So he eased his way out from under it using his elbows and heels to scrabble forward centimeter by centimeter.

When he thought he'd slipped clear of the slab he sat up slowly and didn't again bang his head on anything. Cautiously, he reached up and waved his arms above his head. He didn't encounter any obstructions, so moving slowly, he rolled over onto his stomach, then gradually rose up probing the space above him with his hands so he didn't crack his head again. He rose all the way to his knees without encountering another obstruction. Still no impediments blocking his way, so he climbed to his feet. Raising his hands above his head he encountered the concrete slab of the ceiling. He shouldn't be able to touch the ceiling without climbing a ladder.

If he wanted to live he needed to find the stairway that led out of the basement, if it still existed. He prayed that it still existed.

Moving like a blind man with his hands extended out in front of him, he didn't step forward because he might trip over some obstacle. Instead, he slowly slid one foot out, scraping it along a floor littered with concrete dust and small chips of masonry. When he didn't encounter anything he slid the other foot forward in the same fashion, one scraping step, then another, then another. On his third shuffling step he encountered some sort of obstruction. He reached out and carefully touched it, and cut his finger on a sharp edge of twisted metal, but ignored that. Slowly, by feel, he determined that he stood before the warped remains of a set of metal shelves. He recalled them, and if they hadn't been badly displaced from their original position, the stairway out of the basement would be to his right.

He'd been carrying his rifle when he'd descended into the basement, so it must be somewhere nearby. But it could easily be buried, so he decided he'd be foolish to attempt a search in the dark. And he still had the grav pistol and trench knife strapped to his hip.

As he turned toward where he thought the stairway should be, the building groaned and something snapped with a loud crack, though the sound came through muffled by the basement walls enclosing him. Dust settled down into his hair and on his shoulders, and as he imagined a massive slab of building crushing him, he fought the urge to rush toward the stairs.

He resumed the slow, steady pace, shuffling forward one sliding step at a time, his hands extended out in front of him, careful not to wave them about wildly because of the possibility of more torn metal, and sharp edges that could mangle his fingers and hands. He found the steel rail to the stairway, twisted and bent by a massive block of masonry resting on the stairs. He probed it carefully with his hands to determine its outlines, and again cut his fingers on something sharp. He found some space on one side, though too narrow for him to squeeze through. But there appeared to be plenty of room above the chunk of stonework.

He discovered that broken masonry provided lots of jagged edges that he could grasp rather securely. He thought again of the danger of dislodging a precariously balanced piece of the building, but he had no choice so he ignored his fears and climbed upward. He scraped his knees and elbows, cut his forearm on something sharp, tore his clothing in several places, but he managed to climb over the block of concrete with nothing but minor wounds to show for his efforts.

On the other side, the stairway appeared to be intact, though like the floor, dust and debris littered the steps. He moved cautiously upward, again testing the space before him with every step.

The door at the top of the stairway remained intact. He turned the knob and pushed, but it only moved a few centimeters. It wouldn't open, no doubt because of debris lodged against the other side of it, probably more broken concrete and steel. He put his shoulder against it and heaved with every bit of strength he possessed. It moved a few more centimeters.

He saw movement, and to his surprise realized he'd opened the door enough of a crack to let in a tiny flicker of firelight, though he barely had enough illumination to make out the shape of his hand. Outside, night had descended while he'd been unconscious, and something burned somewhere beyond the door.

He put his shoulder to the door and heaved again; grunt and heave, grunt and heave. Again the building groaned with the sound of steel girders twisting. This time, with the door partially open, the snap of breaking concrete sounded more like a gunshot. He stopped to catch his breath, and wondered if pushing on the door might dislodge a landslide of broken building that would crush him.

He called out, "Help, is anyone there? I'm trapped in the basement."

He listened and heard only the crackle of flames, no sirens from emergency vehicles, no cries of pain or sorrow. In the middle of a large city there should be rescuers, even in a derelict and war-torn city such as this. He'd been through it before, had helped dig victims out from beneath the rubble of collapsed buildings on more than one occasion, had seen with his own eyes the crushed bodies of those who didn't make it, and the crushed limbs of those who did. The sounds of the city were bereft of all the noise its occupants should be making.

He put his shoulder to the door and again leaned into it, grunting with the effort. He eventually reverted to backing up and slamming into it. And bit by bit the door opened a fraction of a centimeter each time, until it would go no further. But he'd opened it enough that he might be able to squeeze through. It still bothered him that he had heard no response from anyone outside. The night remained eerily still, the only sound the crackle and pop of a fire burning nearby.

Debris about chest high blocked the gap he'd opened in the door. He climbed it and turned his head sideways to make it fit through the opening, scraping his ears painfully in doing so. With his head above the top of the door he now saw more flickering firelight. He had no idea of the time of night, be it late, or the wee hours of the morning. The hospital that had once been a building three stories high now lay in a ruin of twisted steel and broken concrete.

He pushed upward, but his chest wouldn't fit. He discovered that by exhaling and forcing every bit of air out of his lungs, he could just barely squeeze his chest into the gap. But he got stuck half way there, with all the air expelled from his lungs, and the narrow gap of the doorway preventing him from inhaling. He tried to retreat back into the basement, but a sharp edge of metal cut into his ribs and he couldn't go back. If he didn't figure out something, and quickly, he'd suffocate there, hanging half way out of the door. That thought gave him a spurt of energy, and ignoring cuts and scrapes and sharp edges, he pushed upward and cleared his chest, then his hips, legs and feet.

He tumbled out onto the debris, and something stabbed him in the left arm just below his shoulder. He froze, realizing that the rubble beneath him could be a death trap if he moved incautiously. With his right hand he carefully probed the wound in his left arm. A small spike of metal protruded from the fabric of his shirt. He grasped it, gritted his teeth, closed his eyes and yanked.

"Ahhh," he cried out at the pain, but he had pulled the spike free. He tossed it aside, cursing and holding back tears.

He paused to look around. A number of fires broke the darkness of the night, though one seemed closer than the others. He cautiously made his way toward it, climbing over twisted steel girders and broken concrete. At one point he stepped on something soft, and when he reached down he discovered a woman's leg. He spoke softly. "Are you alive?"

He got no response, and in any case, the leg was cool to the touch, and stiff. He hoped it wasn't Dr. Tevala.

Moving in that way, he made it out onto the street. From the light of the flickering fires, he saw that not a single building remained whole. And most strangely, there were no sounds of life, no rescue parties, no cries of pain in the night. He waited and listened for several minutes, and for the first time in years, he didn't hear the muffled pop of gunfire in the distance.

10

Retreat

WHEN THE AIR raid sirens first sounded, Eindride ordered them all to don chemo-bio nullification suits. He then instructed them to trigger the suits for class-null extreme negation. Nikaela's suit responded by injecting certain compounds into the atmosphere it fed her, agents that would protect her even if her suit were breached. As she breathed them in, she experienced a heady sensation, and found herself grinning a lot, a reaction she struggled to control. It occurred to her that Eindride knew exactly what level of protection they needed, so he knew exactly the dangers they faced.

Throughout her months on the surface of Novalis III, she had not met or seen another Kelk beyond the five members of Eindride's team, and had subconsciously assumed they were the sole representatives of the Supremacy on the planet. But as the nightmare of that night progressed, Kelk compatriots streamed in in small groups, most carrying with them dead comrades. One fellow arrived in a small grav transport, and with him he brought five companions, all dead. None of them wore uniforms, nor did they display any rank or insignia, but they all had the grim look of soldiers performing their duty; her guess would be Special Forces of some kind. She noticed that many of those still alive had a reaction to the chemical cocktail they breathed similar to hers, and tended to grin even when standing over the bodies of their dead comrades, a macabre sight she would always remember.

They piled the bodies among the crates in the warehouse, and Nikaela noticed that the dead Kelk considerably outnumbered the living.

Eindride gathered his small team to one side and said, "We're one of three bases of operations on this planet and each has a hunter-killer in orbit assigned to it. Ours is sending its boat down to evacuate us."

Nikaela couldn't see his face through the head-gear of the nullification suit. His head swiveled slowly, obviously scanning the entire warehouse. "Including us, I count thirty-one still alive. It's going to be cramped. Don't worry about food; we can live for a long time without eating. But bring all the water you can carry."

He looked at Nikaela, and she saw the red glint of his eyes behind the visor of his suit. "Vreekande, follow the same procedure as when taking a delivery. Only this time, once the boat is loaded, get aboard immediately, then I'll close the doors and join you."

She said, "Yes, Maestra Eindride."

Nikaela trotted across the floor of the warehouse to the big doors and took her usual station near its controls. This time, however, several of the Kelk who had come in from unknown locations in the city took up positions around the doors, all carrying heavy assault grav rifles.

Through her implants she monitored the boat's descent, and at an altitude of two hundred meters, she hit the switch on the doors and they slowly slid aside on hardened plast tracks. The armed Kelk around her all leveled their rifles on the opening that appeared and the deserted street beyond, a precautionary measure she fully understood.

The boat dropped down to street level, then floating on its grav fields eased its way through the doors and into the warehouse, its cargo hatch already open. Even before it had come to a stop, her Kelk comrades began climbing into it.

Eindride trotted across the warehouse to join her. "I've got the doors," he said. "Get on that boat."

She turned toward it, but he stopped her by saying, "One more thing."

She turned back to face him.

"Remember," he said, "you never saw what you saw, and we never had that conversation. There's going to be hell to pay for this. Keep your nose clean and mouth shut, and you are junior enough that no one is going to pull you into it. At least, I hope no one will."

She glanced over her shoulder at the dead Kelk piled near the crates. "What about the bodies?"

"They'll be taken care of," he said. "We've made arrangements for that. Now get on that boat."

Nikaela trotted to the open hatch of the boat. One of the Special Forces people leaned out and gave her a hand climbing into it. With the cargo hatch still open, the boat glided slowly through the doors and hovered a meter above the street, the doors of the warehouse closing before it came to a stop. Eindride ran the short distance to the boat, Nikaela leaned out and extended her arm. He gripped it and climbed aboard.

Nikaela had a giddy view of the street below as the boat lifted, its cargo hatch cycling slowly shut while it rapidly gained altitude. They'd reached about two hundred meters when the warehouse exploded in a massive ball of fire. The detonation so encompassed the entire building that she realized the structure had been prepped with charges long ago in anticipation of the need to erase the evidence of Kelk involvement.

Secondary explosions followed, the heavy arms that weren't supposed to be there detonating in a staccato sequence of blasts. Nikaela reminded herself that those arms didn't exist, that she had never seen them and didn't know anything about that.

She now understood what Eindride had meant when he said the bodies of their comrades would be taken care of.

••••

Mathius had only one thought: he must return to the apartment he shared with his mother and sister, and make sure they were all right. Initially, he moved cautiously from shadow to shadow, fearful he might encounter whoever had done this. But he came across any number of crumpled heaps lying on the ground unmoving. Finding only death and destroyed buildings, he quickly abandoned all caution and walked down the middle of the street where the debris and bodies were the fewest.

Near one of the bodies he spotted the familiar shape of an automatic weapon. He retrieved it, then rifled the body for any extra ammo.

To his great relief, just a few streets from the hospital, he came upon buildings that had not been bombed and remained whole. So they hadn't destroyed the entire city, they hadn't murdered everyone. He would again find his mother and sister alive and healthy, and together they'd grieve the loss of so many people. But block after block, street after street, he encountered only death. Most of the bodies were surrounded by the smell of bowels that had emptied upon death, the same smell he'd encountered when the young girl had killed herself. It was a smell he would never forget.

Dawn broke as Mathius reached the district where he lived, and he had yet to encounter another living person. Even there, a deathly stillness hung over everything. He stopped before turning down the street that contained their small apartment building, and peered around the edge of a structure on the corner. He spotted a body lying on the sidewalk a few doors from his building. He stepped out into the middle of the street and ran.

He found his mother lying in a pool of blood on the floor near where his father had died. She appeared to have bled out through her eyes, ears, nose and mouth. He stood there staring at her, noting with an edge of hysteria to his thoughts that the threadbare carpet now contained matching blood stains from his mother and father.

He searched the apartment carefully, but found no sign of Selna. Hopefully, she had escaped the death that had turned the city into an enormous graveyard.

He returned to the small living room, laid the automatic on the floor, unstrapped the belts for the trench knife and grav gun, and laid them next to it. He sat down on the floor and held his mother's stiff and lifeless body in his arms as tears streamed down his cheeks. He sobbed like a child and fell asleep there, sitting in her blood.

He awoke to the sound of someone in the hallway just beyond their apartment door. Sharp, bright light spilled through the windows, telling him that full daylight had come while he slept. In his arms, his mother's body remained stiff and unyielding.

The apartment door creaked, drawing his attention. It opened slowly to reveal a strange figure standing in the hallway, human in shape but completely covered in mottled gray-black plast, its face and eyes hidden by an opaque visor. And though he'd never before seen powered combat armor, he recognized it instantly. In its hand the figure held a weapon of some sort, like, and yet not like, any pistol Mathius had ever seen before.

He looked to where he had dropped the automatic weapon, grav gun and trench knife. They lay just out of reach, but as he looked at them, the armored figure spoke in a metallic voice. "Don't try it, kid. Just stay calm. We're here to help."

Mathius lunged for the weapons. Something made an odd crackling sound and his muscles went limp. He shit and pissed his pants.

••••

The boat carrying Eindride's team barely made it out of atmosphere before the Commonwealth sealed off access to the planet. The boat's pilot shut down all but the most essential systems, then they went free and coasted toward a rendezvous with *Skuldev*, counting on a considerably reduced emissions profile and the boat's stealth capabilities to evade capture. Nikaela didn't need to be told that there were no guarantees.

As the most junior member on the boat, her sources of information were limited to Eindride and what filtered down to her through the rumor mill. The Special Forces people were by nature taciturn, so word-of-mouth provided only the most limited details. Thankfully, Eindride made a concerted effort to keep the members of his team informed. That first day on the boat he told them, "The Commonwealth has been sneaking assets into the system for several months now."

"Assets?" Nikaela asked.

She learned that *assets* meant two heavy cruisers and three destroyers, plus the infamous Blacksword regiment. As a child she had heard stories of the bloodthirsty Blackswords. As an adult she had long ago concluded that the tales had been embellished and exaggerated by the telling from one child to the next. Or perhaps it had been adults who had provided the embellishments; there certainly were enough hardliners among her Kelk superiors who believed Commonwealth interests fundamentally conflicted with those of the Supremacy. The propaganda arm of the Larscom made considerable effort to propagate the stories. There seemed to be a general consensus that all Kelk should despise the Commonwealth, and especially the Blacksword.

Eindride continued speaking, "They got a lot of press coverage out of some sort of goodwill tour, used that as an excuse to get them into the vicinity, then quietly kept a couple of them parked one light-year out so they could get them in here quickly."

Eindride's eyes focused far away for a moment. "If only they had been more pro-active."

Nikaela tried not to think about that, and none of them spoke for several seconds. Then Eindride snapped out of his reverie. "*Skuldev* is running silent about two AUs out. We've got enough velocity to get there, but coasting like this will take close to twenty days. We don't have food and water for that, but we're going to push it to the limit then make a run for it."

Most everyone on board had brought some water with them, and they pooled that resource. If Nikaela had considered the food and water ration on Novalis III extreme, five days later she thought she had come to understand the true meaning of hunger. But then she recalled the gaunt cheeks of that young boy she'd seen in the rebel compound that day, and realized she had no grasp of what real hunger felt like.

Without gravity, and with no bunks and only a few seats, they tended to float about the cargo hold while sleeping. She tried hooking her arm around a brace and locking her fingers, but that worked only while she remained awake. Once asleep her arm and fingers relaxed and she floated about with all the rest. She found it disconcerting to wake with her nose in the crotch or armpit of someone who hadn't bathed in several days, though she had to admit that anyone who awoke with their nose in her armpit would experience the same unpleasantness.

By the twelfth day, with water rations limited strictly to consumption, the atmosphere in the boat reeked of unwashed bodies, and the water from the overwhelmed recyclers exhibited a decidedly sharp tang. At that point *Skuldev* fired up it sublight drive and raced toward them at close to ten thousand gravities. The hunter-killer's power plant lit up the Novalis system for all to see, and they spent a tense half-hour while the ship accelerated to the half-way point, then decelerated and desperately tried to match the boat's velocity.

One of the Commonwealth cruisers tried a few long shots with its transition batteries, and a destroyer fired up its drive and accelerated toward them. But the ComSec ships had been caught off guard in a parking orbit, and *Skuldev* scooped up her boat without incident, then raced out of the system.

The journey back to Viktorkinde proved somber and uneventful, though Nikaela finally got to take that hot shower. And even with standard shipboard rationing, it proved to be luxurious in the extreme. Just before they docked at Viktorkinde Prime, Eindride said to her, "Remember what I told you. You're junior enough you'll get a pass on this one—as long as you didn't know anything. You did as you were told by your superiors, and beyond that, you must plead complete ignorance."

As Nikaela stepped out through the hunter-killer's personnel hatch and onto the docks, she found herself facing a squad of Larscom Military Constables. Behind them two MCs escorted Eindride off the docks, his hands cuffed behind his back in manacles. A tall woman, rank of senior command superior, with the name SKARSDAG stenciled on the chest of her uniform, stepped out from among the MCs and approached her. Nikaela snapped to attention and saluted.

The woman returned the salute and asked, "You are fourth year cadet, Mistress Nikaela Vreekande?"

With a heavy lump forming in her throat, Nikaela managed to squeak out, "I am."

The woman's eyes bored into Nikaela as she raised a hand and signaled to the MCs behind her. A tall, burley fellow stepped forward, and without asking permission reached out and took Nikaela's duffel.

Skarsdag said, "You are not under arrest. But you are being confined for questioning by orders of the Larscom Executive Council. Please turn around and place your hands behind your back."

Nikaela did as instructed, felt the cold of hard, plast manacles clamped around her wrists. It sure didn't feel like she wasn't under arrest, but she decided to keep her mouth shut about that.

They locked her alone in a cell, a plast room with a bunk, a toilet, a hardened plast door, and no windows. She sat there for two days, her gut churning with fear. The only other person she saw during that time was an orderly who brought her meals: institutional food on a tray. The woman always smiled at her when she left the tray, but said nothing. And she smiled again an hour later when she came to retrieve it. Each morning she also came and escorted Nikaela to a large communal shower, though she bathed alone and in silence, with her companion looking on. She wondered what they thought she might do, squeeze down through the drain. At least she no longer had to ration, and each day dallied under the hot spray until the orderly told her to end it.

Nikaela spent much of the third day lying on her bunk, resigned to the fact that her career had come to a most undramatic end. Without warning the door to her cell opened, and Command Eagle Kristdokar marched in, her eyes hard and angry.

Nikaela jumped up from the bunk and snapped to attention.

Kristdokar waved her salute aside impatiently and said, "Sit down and shut up."

Nikaela killed the salute and sat down on the edge of the bunk, her hands shaking, while Kristdokar paced back and forth rapidly in front of her. The older woman spit words at her angrily. "I'm here to see to it you don't get sentenced to a low gravity gallows. And if we're really lucky, you'll get to keep your career."

She stopped pacing, put her hands on her hips, leaned forward and put her nose a few centimeters from Nikaela's. "What do you know of what happened on Novalis III?"

Nikaela said, "I . . ."

Kristdokar interrupted her, "Think very carefully before you answer."

Nikaela tried again. "I . . . don't really know . . . what happened. Some sort of bombing and a lot of deaths, I think. We were forced to evacuate rather quickly. I never really learned what happened, just rumors."

Kristdokar straightened and her breathing slowed. She nodded and spoke more calmly. "That's a good start."

She considered Nikaela for a long moment, then asked, "Do you know *how* it happened."

She had placed considerable emphasis on the word *how*, and Nikaela recalled Eindride's last words to her. "No," she said. "Like I said, there were air raid sirens, a quick evacuation, then a lot of rumors running through *Skuldev*'s crew, many of which contradicted one another."

At that point Kristdokar questioned Nikaela for over two hours. Nikaela stuck to her story and pleaded ignorance. Kristdokar finished by saying, "Okay, this just might work. You'll be released shortly. Return immediately to the academy and resume your studies. At some point you'll probably be called to testify at a tribunal, or one or more courts-martial."

She spun toward Nikaela and pointed an angry, shaking finger at her. "And don't you dare change a single word of what I just heard."

••••

Katrine sat at a table in the officer's wardroom of the hunter-killer *Harkness*. She had one hand wrapped around a cup of caff, while the fingertips of the other drummed a staccato beat of impatience on the tabletop. The caff had gone cold, but she lifted the cup to her lips and sipped at it anyway.

Purely through happenstance, when the shit hit the fan on Novalis III, she'd been on Norandyne getting a situational update from the COs of three of their warships. They had rushed to the Novalis system and been on the scene in just a few days; a few days too late as it turned out.

Once she had grasped the magnitude of the incident, she realized there wasn't anything she could personally contribute to the situation, and that she must get word back to Trafalgar immediately. Any officer wearing the rank of a Naval Ops captain officially outranked her, but the Blacksword patches on her sleeves lent her a certain amount of added authority. And it didn't hurt that they knew she advised some very powerful people in the capital. She didn't have to push too hard to get them to agree to give her their fastest hunter-killer.

Her implants chimed. "Colonel Primatov, this is Commander Sallman. We're six light-years out, and really pushing the range of our transition com, but we've been able to establish the three-way link with Trafalgar that you requested."

She glanced around the wardroom. A young lieutenant j. g. sat nearby, his attention wholly focused on the screen of a reader.

She really needed to speak candidly, so she said to Sallman, "I'll take it in my stateroom. Give me a few seconds to get there."

She left the half-empty cup of caff sitting there—a small breach of mess etiquette, but one she could live with. She rushed to her stateroom, closed the door, sat down and keyed her implants. She triggered an encryption algorithm that not even the ship's systems were privy to, and a split image of Senator Gascoigne and Fran Thealone appeared, superimposed on her visual cortex. Gascoigne had a serious case of bed-hair, while Thealone showed no such signs of having just been awakened. Her short-cropped white hair probably gave her some immunity to that.

Even though they were on a three-way com link and weren't in the same room, Gascoigne nodded toward Thealone and said, "Colonel Blacksword."

Without preamble, Thealone gave Katrine a piercing look and demanded, "What?"

Katrine had told *Harkness*'s CO to tell them she needed to speak to them on a matter of *utmost urgency and the highest priority*. She and Fran had long ago agreed she would never use exactly those words for anything short of monumental proportions.

Katrine took a deep breath to calm her racing heart, then said, "Someone supplied some of the factions on Novalis III with unconventional weapons, mostly artillery and mortar deliverable bio toxins, with some nerve agents thrown in for good measure."

Gascoigne closed his eyes, lowered his head and rubbed his temples. Thealone simply continued to stare at her with those pale-blue eyes.

Katrine continued. "We're certain the Kelk supplied some of it, but we suspect others did as well. I've got several teams working on the ground trying to do a forensic analysis of the origin of the weapons."

Gascoigne opened his eyes, gave her a pained look and said, "How bad?"

Katrine had tried not to practice how she would say these words, but she'd had nothing to do but think about them over and over again for several days now. "Apparently, those factions receiving such weapons had been stockpiling them for quite some time now. They had all held back, limiting themselves to conventional weapons, and fearing the consequences if any one of them started something they couldn't stop. But one of them must have panicked for some reason, and once one crossed that line, they all did. It all happened in a single night."

Gascoigne simply again said, "How bad?"

Katrine wanted to close her eyes and look away, but she didn't. "We won't know the actual tally for quite a while, but of the twenty million residents of Novalis III, I doubt more than a few thousand survived."

Thealone's eyes widened and she took a deep, involuntary breath. She said, "Someone is going to want to use this as an excuse to start a war with the Kelk."

Gascoigne added, "Yah, a lot of someones."

"Mani," Thealone said. "Can you meet me in your office in one hour?"

"Of course," he said. "And before I get there I'll alert the senate leadership."

Thealone turned her attention back to Katrine. "Katrine, I'm sorry to do this to you, but we need you to turn right around and go back there. I want you riding herd on those forensic teams. And make sure no one hides anything from us."

Gascoigne leaned forward and asked, "It'll take you several hours to turn that ship around, right?"

Katrine said, "I would guess no less than six or seven, maybe more."

Gascoigne nodded. "Good. We need to make sure you don't run into any egos out there. So long before you're out of transition com range, I'm going to have orders cut for you that'll give you the authority to rip anyone a new asshole, including the highest ranking admiral I've ever met."

11

The Proud, the Many

"WHEN I SAY 'shit,' you shit. Do you understand me?"

Over four thousand voices shouted in unison at the top of their lungs, "Sir, yes, sir."

"I don't mean you pull down your pants and shit, you just start shitting, pants up or down. Do you understand me?"

"Sir, yes, sir."

It took John a moment to realize that he was one of those shouting. Exhaustion weighed heavily on him, and he tried not to sway drunkenly as he stood there beneath the hot sun, his arms rigidly braced at his sides, his shoulders aching from the weight of his backpack, the butt of his rifle resting on the ground beside him.

"If your pants happen to be down when I tell you to shit, then you get to shit on the ground. But if they happen to be up, then you produce a full-on pant-load right then and there. Do you understand me?"

"Sir, yes, sir."

John just wanted to lie down and sleep. He didn't even care about eating. The final march for recruit training had been three days of limited rations, almost a hundred kilometers of marching in full combat kit, and no more than a few hours of sleep each day. The recruits had returned thinking they'd completed the last ordeal of boot camp, only to learn that they must now stand under the hot sun and listen to a lecture on shit, though if John had been asked, he would have to admit he had learned a few new and creative ways of shitting his pants.

"When I tell you to shit I want to see gobs of it running down your leg. I want to hear it squishing in your boots . . ."

It occurred to John that it would never squish in his boots, because the bottoms of his khakis were tucked into the tops of his boots, so it would all just pile up there. But that was probably a fine point the DI didn't really care about.

A female recruit standing three rows in front of him and two positions to the left began to sway a bit, at first side-to-side then back and forth. John wasn't fool enough to be obvious about watching her. He kept his eyes locked rigidly forward, but he could see her nevertheless.

". . . big gobs of it piling up in your pant legs just above your boots. Do you understand me?"

"Sir, yes, sir."

Good, John thought. The DI understood those fine points as well.

The female recruit's swaying grew more pronounced. One of the assistant DIs noticed and marched her way. He stopped directly in front of her, leaned forward and shouted, "Are you going to be the first, you weak-willed piece of shit?"

In the glare of the hot sun, John noticed drops of spittle erupting from the DI's mouth as he shouted at her, probably spattering her face and cheeks with it. "Are you going to shame your comrades, give up while the rest of them remain standing, show them that you're not fit to wipe their asses after they shit their pants? Are you?"

She managed to keep on her feet and settled into a steady rhythm swaying back and forth, no more side-to-side. When she swayed forward she went far enough that the DI standing in front of her had to lean back a little. He did so several times as he swayed with her, then he grinned and stepped back a pace to give her more room. Her head rocked as she swayed, then finally the DI stepped to one side and extended a hand out as if politely inviting her to precede him through an open doorway. She didn't stumble or lurch but toppled forward, and as she did so the DI shouted, "Timberrrrrrr!"

She remained stiff and rigidly at attention all the way to the ground, falling like a tree axed down in the middle of a forest. She hit the dirt face down and bounced once, raising a small cloud of dust. With the weight of her backpack on top of her, it must have hurt like hell, but then again she probably wasn't feeling anything at the moment. John envied her that.

"Because if I say 'shit,' and you don't shit, then I'm going to beat the shit out of you. Do you understand me?"

"Sir, yes, sir."

Two med-techs guided a grav stretcher down the rows of recruits. They carefully checked the unconscious young woman, then lifted her onto the grav stretcher and carried her away.

John lost track of time as the senior DI continued his tirade on the subject of shit. The fellow demonstrated a very creative vocabulary when it came to the emission of fecal matter from the human body, and John suspected he could go on for hours without ever really repeating himself.

". . . Do you understand me?"

John couldn't recall what the senior DI had been saying, though it certainly must have had something to do with shit. But even though his throat hurt and he now sounded a bit hoarse, and he really needed a drink of water, he shouted back with all the rest, "Sir, yes, sir."

Nearby another recruit slumped to the ground. He didn't topple like the first, but merely collapsed where he stood, falling into a heap of backpack, khakis, rifle and gear. A DI bent over him, pressed a small med unit to the side of his neck and stared at the display for a moment. Another med-tech with another grav stretcher joined the DI. The tech lowered the stretcher to the ground, they rolled the unconscious recruit onto it, then the tech reactivated the stretcher's grav fields and carried him away. Only then did John notice that the ranks of recruits had thinned considerably. By his estimate, less than a quarter of Echo Company remained standing.

••••

Colonel Stephen Brightlaw's implants chimed and said, *Colonel, there's an incoming call from Major Hershman.*

Brightlaw glanced at his watch: mid-afternoon. The recruits would have long ago returned from their three-day final march, greatly relieved that they'd finished basic training, and thinking that the next step would be graduation from boot camp and a ten-day leave. The DIs took a certain sadistic pleasure in the looks on their faces when they learned they still must endure the privilege of listening to Senior DI Prescott's traditional lecture on shitting their pants. Hershman would be out on the parade ground overseeing the exercise.

Brightlaw decided to take the call on his terminal instead of directly through his implants. "Computer," he said, "take the call, terminal feed."

The image of Hershman that coalesced on the screen in front of him appeared lifelike in every respect, but Brightlaw knew it to be an avatar generated by the major's implants.

"Ted," Brightlaw said. "How goes the shit lecture? Prescott come up with anything new this time around?"

"Nah," Hershman said, giving him a cheesy grin, "just the same old shit." It was an old joke they had shared for many years now, and both men always got a little chuckle out of it.

Brightlaw glanced again at his watch. "Should be winding down about now."

"That's why I called, sir," Hershman said. "Prescott's had to repeat himself. It looks like we're going into overtime."

"Nothing we didn't anticipate, though, right?"

Hershman lifted an eyebrow. "Actually, we may have a rather unusual development on our hands. We've still got a dozen left standing, and most of them are those we predicted would be the last."

"Most?" Brightlaw asked, his curiosity piqued.

"Yes, sir," Hershman said, grinning. "It appears we might have a darkhorse among them. I think you'll want to see this for yourself."

In one motion Brightlaw stood, said, "I'll be right there," and killed the feed on his terminal.

••••

John considered faking it. He could slump down and pretend to pass out, lay there with his eyes closed and finally get some rest. But the damn DIs probably had some way of identifying a faker. They could be absolutely fiendish when it came to detecting a recruit's attempts at deceit, and then they'd make his life even more hellish than they had already. They might actually make him shit his pants and walk around for a few hours with a full-on pant-load. And of course, they'd have his platoon mates heckle the hell out of him. Then the DIs would invent a new name for him, something to do with shit.

He caught himself swaying and straightened.

A female DI noticed, her head snapping toward him like a dangerous predator eyeing its next meal. She marched his way, descending upon him with a cold, hard look on her face. She stopped in front of him, and because he had several centimeters on her she craned her neck to put her nose a finger's breadth from his, but she managed nicely.

"I saw that," she shouted, "you piece of decomposed brack shit."

John didn't know what a brack was, probably some animal on some planet somewhere. And of course, since the subject of the day was shit, it had to be the animal's shit that she wanted to discuss.

"That was absolutely sloppy," she shouted. "Are you going to be next? Are you going to show us all how worthless you are?"

Behind her, John noticed that out of the entire company, there were only a few of them still standing. Their comrades had been carried away one by one, and as he looked on another one fell. They'd reached the point where there were few enough of them still standing that the assistant DIs could give each remaining recruit the pleasure of personalized treatment. John would have preferred to remain just another anonymous recruit.

"Look at me," John's DI shouted. "Pay attention to me when I'm speaking to you."

John tried to look her in the eyes, but she'd put her face so close to his he couldn't, and his eyes crossed and focused on nothing. As she shouted at him he was struck by the odd thought that she smelled rather nice, like flowers or something. And perspiration. He could smell sweat on her as well, not a bad or overpowering smell, but a very female one. She smelled of flowers and sweat. She smelled good.

He couldn't really see her face, not with his eyes crossed, but while she continued to shout at him he wondered if she was pretty. He tried to recall each of the female DIs, but at that moment he couldn't put two thoughts together into a coherent sequence. And in any case, thinking of one of the DIs that way was an absolute betrayal of his squad mates. But she smelled like an old memory, a good memory, though try as he might he couldn't recall it.

Behind his DI, one of the few recruits still standing toppled over sideways and landed on his shoulder. As the med-techs carried him away, John hoped the fellow wasn't hurt.

"Look at me," his DI shouted.

Again he looked down into her face, his eyes crossed and uncrossed, and she swayed back and forth. He thought it cruel of her to tease him by swaying back and forth like that, another nasty DI trick, and that angered him—back and forth, back and forth. The DIs were sneaky that way, and he resolved not to succumb to her tricks— back and forth, back and forth. *Sneaky bitch*, he thought. Her swaying only made him dizzy, and he'd be damned if he would let that affect him—back and forth, back and forth.

Something slammed into his back, and he wondered for a moment if one of the other DIs had hit him from behind; that would be so unfair of them, but so DI of them. It took him a few seconds to realize he was staring straight up into a bright, clear sky, and that the planet hadn't suddenly shifted on its axis and slammed into his back.

The DI leaned over him and shook her head sadly. "You pathetic piece of shit."

He didn't have to fake it when he passed out, and then he dreamed of the day he enlisted.

••••

Mathius awoke in a comfortable bed, completely unable to move anything but his eyeballs, not a muscle. He felt no pain, could breathe again and felt better than he had in a long time, was in fact quite relaxed, and drifted off to sleep.

When he awoke the second time a man stood over him wearing a white coat and looking very much like a doctor. "Well, young fellow," the man said. "You've decided to rejoin the living."

Mathius discovered he could now move his lips and vocal cords. "Where am I?"

The doctor smiled. "You're in a hospital ward in a Commonwealth rehabilitation center. By the way, how'd you break your nose so badly?"

Mathius opened his mouth to make up some lie that didn't involve Cranoch's fist, but the doctor didn't really care for an answer, and continued speaking. "We fixed it, since you were already out. Only took ten minutes."

Mathius opened his mouth to ask a question, but the doctor said, "Don't worry, you won't feel anything. It's been a full day, so it should be completely healed by now."

The doctor was apparently one of those people who didn't wait to hear a question, but instead answered the one he thought you were about to ask. Mathius quickly learned the fellow usually answered the wrong question. He again tried to ask a question, but the doctor spoke before he could do so.

"No, you're not paralyzed. We've got you on a selective whole-body nerve block. And from what we can tell, you haven't suffered any injuries, just a few bruises and some nasty scars here and there."

Thankfully, he had guessed the right question that time. He continued. "We're going to remove the nerve block now, and you'll feel a little unsteady on your feet, but that'll pass in a matter of minutes."

Another fellow stepped into Mathius's field of view. This one looked more like a professional athlete than a doctor, though he wore surgical scrubs much like the doctor. The doctor said, "This gentleman is one of our orderlies, and he's going to help you take your first few steps."

Mathius's legs wobbled a bit at first, but as the doctor had promised, in a matter of minutes, and with the orderly's help, he was able to walk on his own. It felt good to be up and walking about, and he had the strangest feeling, as if he'd just eaten a full meal, a feeling he hadn't had in a long, long time.

They put him in a bunk room with a number of other refugees, all overseen by several athletic, beefy-looking *orderlies*. Mathius thought it quite obvious that *hospital ward* in a *rehabilitation center* were nice euphemisms for a cell block in a prison complex. Later that afternoon Mathius learned why.

One of the beefy orderlies escorted him into an office where a woman in uniform sat behind a desk. She stood as he walked in, extended her hand and said, "I'm Captain Terschon, ComSecCorps, Naval Ops."

Mathius shook her hand as she said, "I have a few questions, so please sit down."

She indicated a chair in front of her desk. She sat down behind the desk, Mathius sat down in the chair, and he thought it quite telling that the beefy orderly remained standing behind him within easy reach. The fellow didn't exactly rest his big paws on Mathius's shoulders, but he easily could have.

She looked at a small screen in front of her and said, "You were found in possession of a number of military type weapons. But you weren't wearing a uniform of any of the government or rebel factions, and you're name isn't on our proscribed list of combatants. Tell me about those weapons."

Mathius knew that if they put him under deep neural probe, they'd learn every-thing. "I picked them up that night on the streets. It seemed wrong that there was no one—not anyone—on the streets, just a lot of dead bodies. So I figured I might need to defend myself."

"And you know how to fire an automatic weapon?"

He shook his head and lied. "No. I figured if I had any trouble, I could just wave it at them and scare them off."

She leaned back, steepled her fingers in front of her, and regarded him carefully.

"What happened?" he asked. "Where is everybody?"

Captain Terschon ignored his question. "You were found holding a dead woman in your arms, and apparently crying over her death. Who was she?"

"My mother."

She leaned forward and her eyes seemed to pierce his soul. "Almost the entire population of Novalis III was wiped out that night, more than twenty million people. There are only a few thousand survivors. I need to know why you survived, so tell me what happened to you that night. Help me understand what to do with you."

Mathius told her he worked for Dr. Tevala, scrounging supplies for her, though he didn't tell her he murdered government and rebel soldiers to acquire them.

She asked him, "Do you know Tevala's first name?"

"No," he said. "I admired her a lot, was hoping I could be a doctor someday."

She grimaced when he said that, and asked him for the location of the hospital. He told her, she hit a switch on her desk and said, "Security, check on one Dr. Tevala." She gave them the location of the hospital, and finished with, "I want a full report on my screen immediately."

She quizzed him thoroughly on Tevala, the hospital and the scrounging responsi-bilities he'd performed for her. He told her how he'd awakened in the basement of the hospital, managed to crawl out from beneath the rubble and make his way back to the apartment. Had she known to ask the right questions, she might have learned that he was just another murdering thug. But it became clear she *wanted* to believe him, and then she finished by looking at her screen and reading intently for a few minutes.

She said, "Your story checks out. Too bad about Tevala."

They moved him out of the *hospital ward* with the beefy *orderlies* and into a bunk room with a lot of other male refugees, no orderlies and just a ComSecCorps officer there to supervise them. Mathius learned that the Commonwealth had intervened, stepped in with overwhelming force with the intent of ending the rebellion on Novalis III. He didn't really care who they had sided with, or if they had sided with anyone at all. The government forces had frequently been just as ruthless as the rebel factions when it came to brutalizing the civilian population, though they didn't *tax* the population; they simply took. And from what Mathius had heard, the Commonwealth authorities themselves weren't sure which side had been the first to release the bio agents. Once one side started the others had retaliated in kind, so it didn't matter. With everyone dead, the rebellion ended before the Commonwealth arrived; twenty-million lives lost.

Mathius had survived only because he'd been buried in a basement, and the bio toxins had decomposed by the time he'd dug his way out. He learned such deadly weapons were engineered that way. After all, if the toxins remained active too long, it would hinder the victors when they took possession of their newly conquered territory. Unfortunately—or maybe fortunately, Mathius thought—the victors had died along with the vanquished.

Mathius learned that they couldn't use deep neural probe on him without a court order, or special circumstances. He decided he would never give them cause for special circumstances.

••••

The Commonwealth evacuated the few thousand survivors of Novalis III to another planet. Mathius was too old to go into foster care, so Commonwealth Refugee Services helped him find an apartment and a job as a clerk in a small office. He didn't really have any skills of real value, and understood that they had given him the job as consolation. They apparently considered the job as some sort of restitution for what had happened.

He worked hard, though without any vigor, and he took no joy or pride in it. He accepted his meager paycheck every tenday, and tried not to grieve for his mother and sister. He coasted through a few months that way with no purpose, no thought to the future. Just get up every day, go to work, do his job, and come home at the end of the day. He ate only when forced to by hunger.

At the end of one particularly ordinary day, as he walked down the street to his apartment he passed by the Commonwealth recruiting office, just as he did every day on the way to and from work. But for some reason he paused that day and looked at the vid screens in the window.

The vids showed proud young hymn and women exercising, training, using instruments and equipment foreign to any of Mathius's experience. He'd applied to get an advanced education, but he didn't have the money, and the entrance exams for the programs funded by the government were highly competitive. They didn't tell anyone their actual scores. Mathius had simply received an electronic form memo informing him that other candidates were *more appropriate for the program.*

He went back to his small apartment, ate dinner, and went to sleep. But he couldn't put that recruiting office out of his thoughts.

The next day, on the way to work, he stopped again and looked at the vids in the window at the recruiting office. That evening he looked up the brochures for all the different jobs and functions in the Commonwealth Security Corps. He read them carefully, ate dinner, and went to sleep.

Each morning for several days he stopped briefly on the way to work and looked at the vids in the window at the recruiting office. And each evening he reread those brochures.

One day, while walking home from work, everything he'd read in those brochures kept fluttering through his thoughts in random bits and pieces. They told of advanced training and education. They told of a future, of the pride one could take as a member of ComSecCorps. They didn't tell of stopping or preventing atrocities like Novalis III, but that seemed to be implied in the literature. The brochures and vids made it clear that one could take pride in being admitted to ComSecCorps. Mathius thought about becoming one of the proud, one of the few, of doing something that had meaning and consequence. And at that moment, walking home, he came to the recruiting office. He paused, thought about it for a moment, opened the door and walked in.

Just inside a young woman sat behind a desk. She wore a uniform that looked like those he'd seen on the vids and in the brochures. As he walked through the door she smiled at him and said, "What can I do for you, young man?"

Mathius shrugged. "What does it take to enlist? I think I'd like to. Can I qualify?"

"Perhaps," she said, cocking her head slightly to one side. "I'll need to get some basic information before I can answer that."

She turned to a screen on her desk, hit a few keys, then looked at Mathius and said, "What's your name?"

"Mathius," he said.

She hit a few more keys, then said, "What's your given name, Mr. Mathius."

She had misunderstood him, and he almost said, *That is my given name*, but he hesitated before doing so. The people of Novalis III didn't go by two names, so the only name he had was Mathius. And Novalis III didn't exist anymore, and everyone he'd ever known had died there, so he decided it was time for a new start, and for that he needed a new name, a good Commonwealth type of name.

"Johnathon," he said. He liked the sound of that name.

She entered that into the computer, but a search turned up his real name and circumstances. He'd been stupid to think he could get away with that. But all she said was, "Oh, you're one of those people who has only one name. But if you want I can add the given name to your record. Are you sure Johnathon is the name you want to take, because once I do this it'll be permanent?"

He didn't hesitate. "Yes, I'm sure."

So Johnathon Mathius filled out forms, took a number of tests, and sat in front of instruments while they scanned and poked and prodded him. After a couple of hours of that they ushered him into an office where he stood in front of a desk. Behind it sat a man in uniform who appeared to be middle aged. The sleeves of his shirt contained a lot of chevrons and stripes, with a colorful display of little flat, rectangular ribbons of some sort on his chest, and brass emblems on his collars.

"John Mathius," the fellow said. He pointed to a chair. "Have a seat, kid. Relax."

The fellow looked at a computer screen for several seconds, then he looked at John and said, "Why do you want to join the Blacksword Regiment? We don't usually get requests to specifically be a Blacksword."

John thought that, *Because I got nothing else to do*, wouldn't be a good response. He also considered and rejected, *I need something better than my present job*, and for a moment he almost simply shrugged, but caught himself before making such a dumb-shit gesture. He thought of one of the recruiting brochures he'd read. It had intrigued him, and he'd read every word in it several times, had almost memorized it. If they could really fulfill on those promises, he'd finally have purpose to his existence.

"Because they're the best," he said, "and I want to be one of the proud, one of the few."

The recruiting officer leaned forward, put his elbows on the desk, steepled his fingers in front of him and stared at John for a long moment. His lower lip quivered a little, then a moment later his chin joined it, and he burst into laughter.

"That's good," he said, struggling to catch his breath. "That's a lot better than 'I got no job,' or 'I got nothing better to do.' "

The fellow switched to an imitation of a dumb-kid accent. "Then there's 'Gee, I don't know, man.' "

He wiped tears from his eyes and said, "Got that right out of the recruiting vids, did you? You should be in the PR department."

He slowly calmed his laughter. Apparently, the look on John's face prompted him to say, "No, kid, I mean it. Seriously. You should hear the crap I hear. But taking a nice lah-dee-dah statement right out of the recruiting bullshit like that, that shows you got some brains, which, by the way, disqualifies you from ever being an officer. No criminal record, and you did well on the intelligence tests and the cognitive scans, so the Commonwealth can use you." He leaned forward, speaking in a confidential tone. "And we're supposed to give a little priority to survivors of that Novalis mess. You're in, kid. You made it, but don't bullshit an old bullshitter."

John provided a DNA signature and they gave him deadhead passage on a Commonwealth destroyer to a nearby solar system and a planet named Miriteen. He'd been on a starship once before, packed into the hold of the vessel with other survivors as the Commonwealth evacuated them from Novalis III. That first time he had expected there to be some dramatic sense of displacement or change when the starship made transition, but he had felt nothing.

The Commonwealth had everything arranged very neatly. On Miriteen they gave him a ticket on a surface transport to a Security Corps base outside a small city. The sign over the main gate read COMSECCORPS RECRUIT DEPOT, MIRITEEN.

They weighed him again, and poked and prodded him again, then looked carefully into every orifice he had. And after they'd looked into each one of them once, they then looked into them again. After the poking and prodding, he took a series of tests that involved everything he'd learned in school. He also answered a lot of strange questions that didn't seem to have anything to do with anything, and they put some sort of apparatus on his head while a technician looked at a screen and said things like "Hmmm!" and "Ahhh!"

He lined up with a dozen other recruits, both male and female, all naked as the day they were born. They handed each of them a khaki uniform completely devoid of insignia. The recruits dressed under the eyes of two men and a woman wearing uniforms with a lot of chevrons and stripes on their sleeves. The woman stood tall enough to look most men in the eyes. The men appeared tough and hard, the woman even tougher, though still attractive regardless of that.

The woman bellowed at the top of her lungs, "Listen up, you pieces of shit. I'm Master Sergeant Omuglu, Senior Drill Instructor in charge of your training platoon. You're going to spend the next year and change in training. During your basic training, which lasts the first third of a year, you will always address me as *ma'am*. Do you understand?"

John mumbled, "Yes, ma'am," though his words were drowned in a general chorus of mumbling from all the recruits.

John would not have believed the woman could come up with even more volume, but she managed. "You will always respond to such a question from me with 'ma'am, yes, ma'am.' Or, if it's one of these gentlemen,"—she tilted her head toward the two men standing beside her—"then you'll answer with 'sir, yes, sir.' Do you understand?"

She shouted at them and made them shout at her, kept shouting until they were screaming at the tops of their lungs.

"That's better," she said. "Now follow me."

She spun about and marched out the door. The two men followed and the recruits hurried after them. She led them to a line of single-story buildings, stopped in front of one of them, turned and walked in. It contained two rows of over-under bunks with an aisle down the middle.

Recruits who had arrived before them snapped to attention as the tough woman and her two comrades entered the building, and even John saw that they did a rather sloppy job of it, not that he thought he could do any better.

The woman assigned each of them to a bunk; John got a lower.

The woman marched to the door, stopped, turned around and shouted, "You'll be up before dawn tomorrow, so get your beauty sleep, children, because you're going to need it."

She turned and marched out the door.

One of the male recruits who'd arrived earlier stepped out into the aisle between bunks. He stood taller than John by a few centimeters, had broader shoulders, and excelled considerably in the good-looks department. He shouted, "You fuck-ups make sure you toe the line, because we don't want you making us look bad. We're stuck in this platoon with you, and we can't do anything about that, but we damn well intend to make sure you don't pull us down."

A young woman standing next to John whispered, "Asshole."

John looked her way and she grinned. They'd shaved her head like everyone else. She had strong features and eyes that appeared defiant, with rather nice-looking curves she couldn't hide, even in an unattractive uniform. She whispered, "That's Macus DeLeon. And to hear him tell it, us fuck-ups are the only thing standing in the way of him becoming a Blacksword."

She stuck her hand out. "Nigurski's the name. Carla Nigurski. But you can call me Biff."

John shook her hand and said, "Mathius . . . uh, I mean . . . John Mathius."

"Nice to meet you, John Mathius."

That was John's introduction to the Commonwealth Security Corps, and on that day he became one of the proud, and apparently one of the *many*. He learned they didn't let just anyone join the Blacksword Regiment. To be a Blacksword, he had to prove he was better than most, but no one gave him any guidance on how to do that. He soon learned that what the Commonwealth needed him to do was run a lot, exercise a lot, scrub floors a lot, shout "Sir, yes, sir," a lot while listening to Drill Instructors expound at considerable length on shit, and stand in the middle of a dirt parade ground with the other recruits until they all passed out. To John's disappointment, he proved that he was quite adequate at all of that. Good enough to make SecCorps, but not good enough to be a Blacksword.

12

Darkhorse

JOHN MATHIUS AWOKE to the sound of some sort of instrument beeping nearby. He knew immediately that he lay in his bunk, in the barracks, because he'd awakened there so many times before. Most often the DIs shouted them awake in the dark hours of early morning, but when he opened his eyes that day, daylight streamed through the windows. He had no idea if he'd awakened in the morning or afternoon. He recalled only that yesterday he'd passed out on the parade ground while listening to a tirade on shitting his pants. He had to think about it for a moment, but was pretty sure he hadn't shit his pants before or after passing out. He wondered if they'd now make him memorize Senior DI Prescott's litany on walking around with your pants full of shit. They had made him memorize just about everything else.

The instrument beeped at him again, drawing his attention. They'd strapped a small monitor to his arm. A med tech appeared beside his bunk and looked at the readings on its face. "Looks like you'll live," he said. He removed the monitor, adding, "We always keep a close eye on the last few to go down."

"Why?" John asked.

The tech frowned and grinned. "Some of you are so stubborn you hurt yourselves. Then we gotta fix you up."

John recalled someone helping him stagger to his bunk late the previous day. He had a vague memory of dropping his gear on the floor and falling into his bunk. He thought he should feel a lot worse, but he felt rather good and he said so.

"Yah," the tech said. "We juice all of you up pretty good. Do it out in the field right when we load you on the stretcher. Supplements, concentrates, stuff like that, including some regrowth stimulants to repair any tissue degradation. That stuff helps a lot, and most of you just need a good night's sleep, though some of you do have to spend a little time in the infirmary. Anyway, you and your buddies are all okay, so I'm out of here."

As the tech packed up his gear, John sat up and glanced around. Some of his platoon mates had been lounging on a couple of bunks talking quietly, which was odd, because the DIs never allowed them free time like that during the day. That made John very uneasy.

When they saw that John had awakened, they stood and came his way, the young woman he'd met that first day leading them. She had high cheek bones and lips that formed a thin, sharp line, with dark-brown hair cut down to stubble like all SecCorps recruits. Somewhere, Carla Nigurski had gotten the nickname Biff, a name John always thought didn't really fit the rather nice curves she couldn't help but display, and because of that he thought of her as Carla. John had no doubt that every heterosexual man in the room had fantasized about Biff Nigurski at one time or another, maybe even a few of his gay buddies as well. But no one, including Carla, had ever attempted to do anything about it, because the DIs had made it clear from the beginning that during basic, *the only thing you're going to fuck is your hand, or if you run out of ammo, the breech of your rifle.*

John swung his legs off his bunk as Carla and the others gathered around him. Standing over him she planted her fists on her hips and looked at him with dark-brown eyes. "Well, well," she said, "sleeping beauty awakes."

John recalled dropping his gear on the floor, but there was no sign of it now. "Did you guys stow my stuff?"

"Yup," Carla said. "You were pretty wasted when they brought you in, and the rest of us had already gotten a little food and shut-eye. We didn't want to give the DIs an excuse to rip you a new one."

"Thanks," John said.

He looked around the barracks and couldn't hide his unease. He leaned forward and hissed, "What's going on, Carla? Where are all the fucking DIs?"

Roark Checkov sat down next to John on his left and slapped him on the back. "We got the day off, Johnny-boy. After learning all the SecCorps rules about shitting our pants, they're giving us the day off to recover."

Carla sat down next to John on his right. "You were the last recruit standing in Echo Company, you stubborn son of a bitch."

"Yah," Roark said, forcing John to swivel his head around to look him in the face. "Never thought you had it in you."

John recalled standing for hours on end in the rebel compound, his wrists manacled above his head to the wall of the outbuilding. Maybe he'd learned a thing or two from that.

One of the recruits standing over them said, "Watch out for DeLeon. He's pissed he wasn't the last one standing."

Macus DeLeon, the best in the company, he could out-run, out-lift, out-shoot any of them, and he and the recruits of Echo Company had long ago concluded he would always come in first at everything. DeLeon and a few of his friends talked openly about becoming Blackswords, even spoke as if their eventual elevation to such hallowed ranks was a foregone conclusion. They were, after all, the best in Echo Company.

"Not good?" John asked.

"No," Carla said, grimacing. "Watch your back. He's really pissed."

The grimace disappeared and she gave him a devious smile. "But you showed that dick-head he doesn't get to be first at everything." She leaned close to John. "If it wasn't against the rules, I'd fuck your brains out just to say thanks."

One of the other girls named Leeze Caputto looked around carefully and said, "Go ahead, do it. We'll keep a lookout. But make it quick, and we get to watch."

The loud, parade-ground voice that interrupted them was one they all recognized instantly. "Recruit Mathius, front 'n center."

Roark and Carla jumped to their feet and snapped to attention with all the rest. John stood, swayed as a wash of vertigo reminded him it was the first time he'd been on his feet since passing out the day before. But he shrugged it off, pulled out his best parade-ground technique, marched out from between the bunks, made a hard right turn, marched the length of the barracks and stopped in front of DI Omuglu. He snapped to attention. "Recruit John Mathius reporting as ordered, ma'am."

She threw a salute back at him, looked him up and down, and as she did so her brows furrowed. She leaned forward and sniffed. "You stink, you haven't shaved, and your uniform looks like hell. What have you been doing, sleeping in it?"

Unfortunately, John had no choice but to speak truthfully. "Ma'am, yes, ma'am."

Her nose wrinkled. "You've been sleeping in your uniform? Why the hell would you do that?"

"I was unconscious, ma'am. I didn't mean to, ma'am."

She closed her eyes, rubbed her temples, and shook her head. "Explain."

When he told her that he'd just awakened from the previous day's ordeal, she nodded and her anger disappeared. "Get cleaned up. Now."

She looked past him at his friends. "And the rest of you, help him. He's going to see the colonel, so I want the stink gone, the uniform crisp, and that chin of his as smooth as a newborn baby's ass."

She finished at parade-ground volume. "You've got ten minutes. Do it. Now."

For the next ten minutes John's feet didn't touch the floor. His platoon mates stripped him, showered him, shaved him and dried him. The uniform they put him into didn't smell like one of his, and probably came in bits and pieces from several of them. But in under ten minutes they planted him in front of DI Omuglu. She looked him over, then looked past him to his platoon mates. "Well done, people."

To John, she said, "Follow me."

She turned without another word and marched away. He followed.

She led him out into the bright sun, then past the rest of Echo Company's barracks. As she marched him toward the admin building the fact that he was about to face the old man hit him in the gut. Colonel Brightlaw was a man he'd only seen from a great distance, during speeches and addresses to all four battalions of the Recruit Depot. In fact, John had never before spoken a single word to an officer of any rank, and thinking about that, he missed a step. Omuglu glanced over her shoulder and gave him a nasty look, but said nothing.

The sign above the main doors to the building read, COMSECCORPS RECRUIT DEPOT, ADMINISTRATION. She stopped just beneath it and turned around. He stopped in front of her and waited as she looked him over critically. For some reason all he could think of was food, and he realized he hadn't had anything to eat since the field rations he'd wolfed down on the final march.

She said, "This is important, young man. It won't do to merely answer questions correctly. You have to answer them from your gut. They're going to want to know what's inside you, what makes you tick. Be sure to let them see the truth."

She didn't say anything more, but turned and marched through the doors. He followed her down a long hall with office doors on either side, trying to decipher what she'd just told him. She made a turn, called a grav lift and waited. Several seconds later the doors of the lift whooshed open. The two of them stepped in, the doors closed, and the lift shot them upward at more than a hundred Gs, but compensated internally with gravity fields so they felt nothing. An instant later the doors opened on the eighth floor.

She led him down a hall then through an office door. A uniformed clerk seated behind a desk said to Omuglu, "Colonel Brightlaw is expecting you, Sergeant. Please go right in."

Omuglu nodded toward another door and spoke quite softly as she said to John, "Walk through the door behind me, and stop at my left side. You know the drill."

John had never stood in front of the colonel before, so he hoped he knew the drill.

Omuglu opened the door and stepped through it; John followed. The sergeant stepped forward to stop in front of an imposing desk behind which sat an even more imposing man. As she had instructed, John marched forward and stopped half a pace behind her and to one side.

He snapped to attention and kept his eyes locked forward. He focused on an award hung on the wall above and behind the man seated at the desk, though as he'd crossed the room he'd gotten a good look at the fellow. He'd also caught sight of three other people in the room, standing to the sides, but had only managed a fleeting glimpse at them and knew nothing more than that they too wore uniforms, and that one might be a woman, and two of them men.

Omuglu said, "Master Sergeant Omuglu, accompanied by Recruit Mathius, reporting as ordered, sir."

The salute that Brightlaw returned was not in the least sloppy, was in fact every bit as crisp as that of any DI. He said, "At ease and relax, sergeant."

Omuglu relaxed and assumed the proper position. John didn't move, not sure if he was doing the right thing, but the colonel had specifically addressed the sergeant when he'd given *her* permission to relax. He hadn't given that same permission to John, so he remained with his hands rigidly braced at his sides.

Brightlaw had a head shaped like a round ball, without a hair on it and so smooth that he clearly shaved it every morning. When John remained rigidly at attention, the man smiled and said, "You didn't warn him, did you, Sergeant?"

"No, sir," Omuglu said. "You gotta know I wouldn't do that, sir."

Brightlaw smiled. "That, I do, Sergeant."

She added, "And I'm not surprised Recruit Mathius didn't fall for it, sir."

One of the people standing to the sides spoke in the contralto of a woman, "Most of the rest did. And they're supposed to be smarter than him."

John was careful to keep his eyes locked on the wall behind Brightlaw and not look her way.

Omuglu said, "Different kind of smarts, ma'am."

One of the others spoke in the baritone of a man. "I expected that of them. And I expected him to miss it as well."

Brightlaw leaned back in his chair, clasped his hands together and looked over them at John.

Of the three uniformed people standing to the sides, one had yet to speak, and John wondered at that.

Brightlaw leaned forward and said, "Step forward, Recruit Mathius."

With parade ground style John took one step forward.

Brightlaw stood, walked around the desk and stopped, facing John squarely. "Do you know why you're here today, Recruit Mathius?"

John said, "I can only guess, sir."

"Then guess."

"It has something to do with yesterday, with me being the last one standing in Echo Company." When it came to the entire training regiment, no one had told John if he'd been in the last ten, or the last twenty, but he knew it must be something on that order.

Brightlaw nodded and smiled. "In that, you are correct. But it might not be exactly what you think. We've already had a few of the others in here this morning, but you're the last."

Brightlaw glanced to one side, "Major Hershman, please summarize Recruit Mathius's performance to date."

The man who'd spoken earlier said in the same baritone, "He's done well on physical training, but not the best. Good strength, but not the best. Good stamina, but not the best. Good academics, but not the best. Excellent marksmanship; I'll give him that. Can strip and reassemble a weapon as if he's an old hand at it. And his aptitude tests indicate he'll do well with tech, but probably not the best. Overall, a good recruit, with a good future in SecCorps . . . but not the best."

Brightlaw looked past John. "Sergeant Omuglu, does he work hard?"

"Yes, sir. Very hard, sir. Harder than most."

"Not a natural, huh?"

"No, sir, he has to work his butt off for every bit of it."

Major Hershman said, "Sir, there's one more thing that I think might be relevant."

Brightlaw focused on John and didn't look Hershman's way as he said, "And that is?"

"He's one of the survivors of Novalis III."

The contralto said, "Owe! That was an ugly business."

Brightlaw's brow furrowed with anger, and John feared he'd done something to bring on the colonel's wrath. But the man looked toward the contralto as he said, "That was a Commonwealth fuckup. We should have intervened long before we did."

He turned his attention back to John. "Did you lose anyone on Novalis III?"

John wasn't about to discuss his father, mother and sister with a man he barely knew, and the fact that the man asked him to angered him. "Everyone lost someone on Novalis III,"—he almost forgot to add—"sir."

Brightlaw stepped back and sat on the edge of his desk, and from the look on his face he hadn't missed the hesitation. He nodded, looked John in the eyes and said, "Your record is not bad, Private Mathius. But the others who came before you this morning, those who were among the last to drop yesterday, we expected that of them, but not you. Why were you able to surprise us that way, Recruit?"

John didn't know where this was going. "I . . . I don't know, sir. I just . . . had to stay standing as long as I could . . . sir."

Brightlaw rubbed his chin, frowned, and his eyes bored into John for the longest moment. "You're not mediocre—better than most, but not the best. All our measurements, all our scores and testing methods, they tell us you're an excellent SecCorps recruit, but not the best. Certainly not as good as the other recruits we've spoken to this morning, the others who were among the last standing. Those tests and scores tell us that yesterday you should have grouped into something close to the top thirtieth percentile. And yet you did much better than that. Why is that, Recruit Mathius?"

"I don't know, sir," John said. It occurred to him then that there might be a more ominous reason he'd been called to stand before the colonel. "I . . . I swear I didn't cheat, sir,"

To one side the baritone laughed. Brightlaw threw his hands up in frustration and spoke angrily. "I know you damn well didn't cheat. You couldn't, not so that we wouldn't know about it."

Brightlaw took a deep breath and calmed himself. "And we think we know how you did it."

Brightlaw leaned close to John and said, "Those tests and scores and measurements tell us a great deal about you, but they don't tell us everything. You see, Recruit Mathius, there's a certain type of soldier with qualities we can never measure. The kind of soldier we're thinking of can't be weak, or stupid, or vainglorious. They must have developed the proper physical, mental, and technical skills of a good soldier. But even the best soldier, when all is lost, might lie down and weep. When the situation is hopeless, the odds overwhelming, even a soldier who had the highest scores in training might give in to despair. But the soldier I'm thinking of can rise above his own physical and emotional limitations, can rise way above what those measurements tell us he's capable of. He or she is the soldier who finds that last gram of willpower. And when all he has left is one round of ammunition against overwhelming odds, it never occurs to him to put the barrel to his own head and use the last round to escape the pain of defeat. No, he spits in the face of the enemy, fires that last round at the opposing force, looks the devil in the eye no matter how frightened he is, and charges. And while most of the time he ends up dead, sometimes he or she succeeds, because he's just too bloody fucking stubborn to die."

Brightlaw leaned away from John and gave him an unpleasant grin. "Yesterday, out of four battalions—more than four thousand recruits—you were the last recruit standing in the entire training regiment, not just one of the last. None of us would have predicted that. That's what you are, soldier. You're just too stubborn to drop."

Brightlaw looked around the room and asked, "Anyone have any questions?"

Of the three people standing to the sides, John knew one man from his baritone and the woman from her contralto, but he couldn't have described any of them because he'd kept his eyes locked rigidly forward, as protocol demanded. Anything less would have been a horrible breach of discipline. But the one person who had yet to speak, now took a breath, and strangely enough, that act alone made everyone hesitate. The voice that spoke was clearly male, but soft and muted.

"When you enlisted, why did you ask to join the Blacksword Regiment? Not just SecCorps, but specifically the Blacksword Regiment?"

In the last few months, the Blacksword Regiment had come up only when DeLeon had looked down on the rest of the platoon and told them they weren't good enough to make the grade. John realized now how naive he'd been to even think he could qualify for the Blacksword. He didn't know how to answer that, so he said, "The recruiting officer asked me the same question, sir."

The soft voice asked, "And what did you say?"

John tried to think of a lie, because the truth would embarrass him. They'd laugh at him just as the recruiting officer had.

The soft voice didn't alter noticeably, but for the first time John heard steel in the man's words. "I will not be happy with anything less than the truth, young man."

"I, uh . . ." John hesitated, feeling hot and flushed. "I said that . . . the Blacksword is the best. That I want to be one of the proud . . . one of the few."

Brightlaw grinned. The woman with the contralto laughed and said, "Right out of the recruiting brochures."

John couldn't let it stand at that. "But I—"

Omuglu shouted, "As you were, soldier. You will speak only in response to a direct question or order."

The soft voice spoke again, but now his words no longer contained the sharp edge of steel. "Thank you, Sergeant. But I do want to hear what the young man has to say. Please continue, Recruit Mathius."

John swallowed hard before speaking. "The recruiting officer laughed at me too, sir, and said the same thing. 'Right out of the recruiting vids,' he said. He didn't take me seriously either, but what I said was the truth. It really was . . . sir"

The soft voice continued relentlessly, "And why do you want to be one of the proud, one of the few?"

Unfortunately, John didn't really know the answer to that question.

The soft voice said, "It's not a difficult question, not if you don't dig deep to answer it and simply throw out some casual remark. But if you think carefully and look into your heart, really look deep into your soul, it may be the most difficult question you've ever answered."

John struggled to put words to his feelings. They'd never found his sister. He'd always assumed she'd been a nameless body laid to rest in one of the many mass graves, and as John thought about that his gut tightened with fury. "I'm very ordinary," he said, trying to keep the anger out of his voice but doing a poor job of it. If he hadn't been so ordinary, so passive, maybe his sister and parents would be alive today. "I've been ordinary all my life, and being ordinary is all I have to look forward to. I don't like being ordinary, and I don't want to continue being ordinary."

Again, he'd almost forgotten to add, "Sir."

Brightlaw raised an eyebrow. To one side, the contralto said, "Hmmm!"

The soft voice said, "Thank you, Recruit Mathius."

Brightlaw nodded thoughtfully. "After graduation you'll go into advanced training, during which we're going to expose you to everything possible. We'll test all of you to determine the skill sets at which you excel, if any, whether it's Infantry or Naval Ops. Being a soldier isn't just aiming your weapon and hitting the target, though that is a skill we require of you. What do you think you'll excel at, Recruit Mathius?"

John wanted to say, *Killing the bastards who murdered my father*, but he didn't think that would endear him to the colonel. "I don't know, sir."

Brightlaw stared at John for a long moment, as if he understood that John hadn't spoken his mind. "One thing we'll be looking closely at is leadership skills, so after advanced training and a year of active duty, you'll return here to attend Command School and be given temporary assignments of responsibility. No doubt you'll fuck it up, and when you do you'll need to learn from that. Then you'll fuck it up again and you'll need to learn even more. And hopefully, you'll eventually learn enough so you don't fuck things up too much in a live-fire situation. Any questions?"

Even though John had always been ordinary, he had prided himself on not fucking things up, and Brightlaw's assertion that he would, only fueled the anger already sparked by the questions about Novalis III. He tried to keep that out of his voice as he said, "One question, sir."

Brightlaw nodded. "Fire away."

John knew he was taking an awful chance, but he'd worked hard to forget Novalis III, and now that the colonel had reminded him of it, he just didn't care. "Yesterday I got to hear Senior Drill Instructor Prescott's stock lecture on shitting my pants. Did I just hear your stock lecture on fucking things up, sir?"

Behind John Omuglu stepped forward and bellowed in his ear, "What kind of idiot question was that, you moron?"

Brightlaw grinned and said, "As you were, sergeant."

John couldn't turn around to look at Omuglu, but he heard her step back, breathing heavily.

"So you're a smart ass," Brightlaw said. "Good. You just proved me right, because that was your first fuck up."

The colonel's eyes shifted focus to look past John. "Master Sergeant Omuglu. I noticed the parade ground is a little rocky today. But that's not going to be a problem, because Recruit Mathius here has just volunteered to spend his day off picking up rocks."

"Yes, sir," Omuglu said, a decidedly satisfied tone in her voice.

Brightlaw said, "Dismissed."

John saluted, spun and followed Omuglu to the door, but Brightlaw stopped them with, "One more thing."

John spun back to face the colonel, and in doing so he caught a glimpse of the fellow with the soft voice, even if only momentarily. But he dare not take advantage of the instant so he looked Brightlaw in the eyes as the colonel said, "Kid, you may be the kind of soldier I spoke of. Then again you may not. Yesterday you rose above the ordinary, but you might never do so again. And whether or not you do, is up to you. So if you don't, and you remain ordinary for the rest of your life, and that disappoints you, you'll only have yourself to blame. It is you who must make sure you are not ordinary."

Brightlaw saluted and said, "Now you're dismissed."

Again John spun about, and this time Brightlaw didn't stop him as he followed Omuglu out of the office. As he marched behind her to the grav lift, he thought of the glimpse he'd gotten of the fellow with the soft voice. The man wore a SecCorps uniform much like any other, with one exception. On his sleeve he wore a cloth emblem that contained a background of silver thread surrounding a black sword.

13

Party Time

JOHN SPENT THE afternoon walking behind an autonomous grav truck programmed to move at a walking pace and slowly cut a zig-zag pattern across the dirt parade ground. When he saw a rock—and there weren't that many—he bent over, picked it up and tossed it into the bed of the truck. Most of the rocks he found were about the size of the tip of his thumb, or smaller, and as dusk approached, he'd accumulated a small pile of gravel that didn't even come close to challenging the capacity of the truck. As his fatigue grew, and his gait slowed, the grav truck matched his pace. It was a numbing, senseless exercise, and he wanted to kick himself for mouthing off to the colonel. But the man had brought up painful memories that John had struggled hard to lock away and forget, and through the afternoon his thoughts kept returning to that small apartment, and the matching blood stains on the threadbare carpet, in the city that had ceased to exist.

Up ahead John spotted a rock larger than the others, though still not big. He wanted that rock, needed it as if it held some sort of trophy value, a testament to an afternoon of futile effort. He stopped when he reached it, and bent down to pick it up.

"Mathius."

When someone used his old name like that, it confused him, and he had to remind himself that he had left Mathius behind and become John. He paused, still bent over, and stared at the rock, trying to determine if he should respond to the voice, or pick up the rock. He wanted to pick up the rock.

"Recruit Mathius."

That was better. Ignoring the rock, and recognizing Omuglu's voice, he straightened and turned to face her. He threw his shoulders back and swayed a little as he saluted her. "Ma'am."

She spoke in a normal tone of voice, which surprised him. "You dumb shit."

To hear her speak in anything less than parade-ground volume seemed an aberration of monumental proportions. "Yes, ma'am," he said, looking into her eyes, and knowing in some deep down part of his gut that she was right. He should have kept his mouth shut.

She lifted an eyebrow and shook her head. He'd never really looked at her before, not as a human being. He'd never looked beyond the ruthless, diabolical, sadistic, inhuman machine called a Drill Instructor. She had dark-brown eyes in a strong face with skin a deep olive hue. She kept her coal black hair cut short, just covering her ears.

She looked him up and down from head to toe. "You look like hell. You've got twenty minutes before evening mess. Get cleaned up and be there on time."

He stared at her for a moment, his exhaustion clouding his thoughts.

She pulled out the parade-ground volume. "Move. Now."

John tried to double-time it across the parade ground, but all he could manage was something a little bit faster than a walk, and it included a lot of stumbling and staggering. Thankfully, Omuglu didn't follow him to pass judgement on his speed and running style, though doing that would have been so DI of her.

When he reached the barracks he found Carla Nigurski waiting just outside the entrance. "You look like shit," she said.

He bent down and put his hands on his knees to catch his breath. "That's about how I feel."

"Watch out for DeLeon, John."

He straightened. "Why? He still pissed?"

"Yah." She grimaced and gave him a sour look. "He says you cheated, because you're not good enough to beat him. And the fact that you drew punishment detail proves it. I told them you didn't cheat. Tell me I was right, John. Tell me you didn't cheat."

He nodded, looked her in the eyes to emphasize his words, and spoke very carefully. "I didn't cheat."

She grinned. "That's good enough for me."

She hooked her arm around his, like a pretty girl on a date. "Let's piss him off a little more."

John frowned and shook his head. "What? Why?"

She wrinkled her nose in distaste. "He keeps trying to get in my pants, wants me to meet him outside in the middle of the night while everyone else is asleep. Like what? I'm going to let him have at me standing up against the barracks wall? Might be fun for him, but not for me."

"But that could get you both washed out. I can't believe he'd be that stupid."

ComSecCorps could have drugged them to eliminate sexual desire. But they didn't because, according to the DIs, the recruits were supposed to demonstrate that they could obey the rules and exercise self-restraint, or get kicked out. They had already eliminated quite a few that way.

She grinned. "That's not why I keep turning him down."

"Then why?"

She raised one finger. "One, I don't like the asshole." She raised a second finger. "And two, I like to watch him squirm when I turn him down, which has a bit to do with number one." She raised another finger. "And three, I've got my eye on someone else."

John reached over and carefully unhooked her arm from his. "I don't need more trouble."

The grin on her face turned mischievous, and she raised both eyebrows. "Don't tell me you haven't thought about it. I've seen the way you look at me,"—she wiggled her chest at him—"especially in the showers."

He shook his head and turned away from her. He walked through the barracks door with Carla a pace behind him, then started down the aisle that ran between bunks down the middle of the room. Roark and some of his friends stood in a small group talking quietly, but their conversation died when they saw him. Roark's eyes flashed briefly to Macus DeLeon, who lay on his bunk in uniform, his ankles crossed and his hands behind his head, elbows out. The room grew quiet and still.

John didn't hesitate and headed for his bunk, but only made it half way there when DeLeon said, "How did you do it?"

John stopped and said, "Do what? Stay on my feet?"

DeLeon stood and stepped into the aisle in front of John. "No, how did you cheat?"

One of DeLeon's friends, seated on a bunk nearby, said, "Leave him alone, Macus. He's had a bad enough day as it is."

John had to think for a moment to recall the fellow's name: Paul Ackrov. His words came as a surprise, because until that moment, John had counted Ackrov among DeLeon's sycophantic friends. Like DeLeon, Ackrov did everything better, faster and smarter than the rest of them. Everyone assumed he and DeLeon and those like them would get stripes added to their uniforms much faster than the rest.

DeLeon stared John in the eyes and didn't look Ackrov's way as he said, "He's a cheat, Paul. That's the only way he could have lasted longer than us."

Behind John, Carla said, "He didn't cheat."

DeLeon looked past John at her. "They gave him punishment detail. That proves it."

John said, "They gave me punishment detail because I mouthed off to the colonel."

Roark's eyes widened, but he kept his silence.

"Bull shit," DeLeon said. "You cheated."

John turned a little sideways, edged past DeLeon and continued walking. "I wasn't merely the last standing in Echo Company."

"What do you mean?" DeLeon demanded, turning to follow John's progress as he walked to his bunk.

John paused and looked over his shoulder. "They told me I was the last one standing on the entire parade ground. Of all four battalions, I was the last recruit standing—period."

Roark fist-pumped and said, "Yes."

DeLeon's face reddened, and though he kept his hands down and braced against his sides, his fingers curled into fists so tightly his knuckles whitened. John thought it quite possible that DeLeon would have struck him under other circumstances. But with witnesses present, that would get him tossed out of SecCorps.

John knew that goading DeLeon that way would probably prove to be a mistake, but at that moment he didn't care.

••••

Miriteen was one of four recruit depots distributed among the more than twenty solar systems of the Commonwealth. Upon graduation from basic, all recruits were granted a ten-day leave, after which they were required to return and report for advanced training. Like John, all of the recruits in his training battalion had come from planets in the gravity wells of nearby stars. And while the Commonwealth allowed them to travel deadhead if they chose to do so, ten days just wasn't enough time for anything but the shortest of interstellar trips. That separated the recruits into two clearly defined categories: those whose family had both the time and money to travel to Miriteen for the graduation ceremony, and those who didn't, which proved to be quite a few of them.

DeLeon's parents made the trip, which made John aware of a third category: those whose parents could ride deadhead on military transport. Both wore ComSecCorps uniforms, his mother a lieutenant commander in Naval Ops, his father a captain in Infantry Ops. Both wore Blacksword patches on their sleeves.

Some of the recruits without family present pooled their meager earnings to rent cheap places at the beach or other vacation spots, while others simply went into town to party. The DIs warned them, "Coming back to the depot drunk or stoned is a washout offense. So sober up before you do."

The first morning of leave, John, Carla, Roark and several of their platoon mates went into town to join the party crowd. On the way there, seated in the surface transport, Carla asked John, "Family can't afford to come see you?"

None of them knew that John had left his family behind in the mass graves on Novalis III, and he wanted to keep it that way. "Yah," he lied.

"Mine can," she said, "but they don't care."

Something in her voice made him look her way.

"Don't worry," she said. "I don't care that they don't care."

John heard the lie in that and the anger that colored her words. Apparently, Carla Nigurski had something she wanted to keep to herself as well. He had no right to press her on the matter so he said nothing about it.

They checked into a cheap hotel on the edge of town known for being tolerant of recruits who wanted to party, as long as they didn't go too far. The proprietor told them, "Have all the fun you want. But if I get a call or a visit from the cops,"—he hooked a thumb over his shoulder—"you're out on your asses. Pay in advance, and no refunds."

They partied hard that night, danced and sang to a lot of loud music. Someone christened a well-known DI with a crude nickname, and that became a popular trend, so they got inventive regarding each of the DIs. The pseudonyms with which they christened them usually had something to do with an illegal sexual act involving some strange animal on a far-off planet, and were always quite explicit.

At one loud and crowded party he spotted a female recruit from another platoon, a familiar face he had seen a number of times in the mess hall, and on other occasions in the Recruit Depot. Their training had never put them face to face before, but she had always given him a nice smile when she noticed him noticing her, and he did rather enjoy noticing her. She had blue eyes, and from the short stubble on her head and her eyebrows he guessed she had light-brown hair. From across the room she saw him looking her way and gave him that smile again. John eased his way through the crowd toward her, but with recruits packed elbow to elbow, by the time he crossed the room he lost sight of her. He rose onto his tiptoes and scanned the crowd, and even though he stood a little taller than average, he saw no sign of her.

The following night, at a loud party with a lot of loud voices and music, someone tapped on his shoulder and he turned around to find that it was she who had done the tapping. She stuck out her hand, "I'm . . ."

The blast of the party music drowned out her words and he didn't catch her name. On leave they had all dispensed with military uniforms, and she wore pants and a simple blouse open at the neck exposing a bit of cleavage. She stood a little taller than average, and didn't have the curves of a Carla Nigurski, but that in no way lessened his attraction to her.

He shook her hand and needed to shout to be heard above the noise, "I'm John Mathius."

She leaned toward him and shouted back, "I know."

He frowned and asked, "You know?"

"Yes," she shouted. "You were the last man standing."

"You know about that?"

She raised an eyebrow and gave him the look of a parent lecturing a naive child. "Of course I know about that. Everyone knows about that. The DIs made sure we all knew, so that we knew none of us were the last one standing."

She hooked her elbow through his and shouted, "Let's get out of this noise."

They carried their drinks out to another party at the hotel's swimming pool. Quite a number of recruits had decided to do a little swimming, some in their full civilian attire, and some in nothing at all, though even those who started out swimming in full attire, quickly qualified for the nothing-at-all status. It appeared that no one had thought to bring a swimming suit, and no one cared.

Bright lights illuminated the pool area, but she stopped and turned to face him in the shadows beneath a large tree. She reached out, carefully took the drink out of his hand, and placed both their drinks on a nearby table. Then she wrapped her arms around his neck and kissed him. He put his arms around her waist and pulled her tightly against him. The kiss lasted a long time, and was followed by several more.

She whispered in his ear, "This celibacy thing got really old, really quick."

John awoke in the morning lying naked in bed next to her. She lay on her side facing him, still asleep, a rumpled sheet covering her from the waist down. When he sat up, she groaned and opened her eyes.

"John," she said and sat up beside him. Only then did he realize he had never learned her name, and wasn't sure how he would correct that without pissing her off.

"Morning," he said, hoping to cover up his ignorance.

She stretched and groaned, naked from the waist up. They'd all become rather inured to nudity—after all they showered together. And John had come to understand that the mores he had grown up with on Novalis III tended toward a more conservative view on that subject. He decided he liked being a little parochial, didn't take the opportunity for granted, and thoroughly enjoyed looking at her small breasts. Some of his platoon mates who'd grown up in more liberal environs just didn't have a real appreciation for a pretty, young, naked woman. But somehow he did need to learn her name, hopefully without upsetting her.

He tried to recall the way in which they had met. She had introduced herself, but the din of the party had drowned out her words. He had a perfectly good excuse. Surely, she'd understand it wasn't just forgetfulness on his part.

"Last night," he said, "when we first met, and you introduced yourself, the party was really loud, and I . . ." Saying it like that, he realized it wasn't going to sound as clear and straight-forward as he had thought it would a moment ago.

She frowned and looked a question at him. But then her eyes widened and she said, "You forgot my name."

"No," he said. "I didn't forget it. It was just too loud when you—"

She threw her head back and laughed until tears streamed down her cheeks. "Well," she said, "if I'm nothing more than your fuck puppet, you can just call me, Hey-You."

No matter how hard he pressed her on the matter, she refused to tell him her name. Had they gone to her hotel room last night, he'd wait until she went to the bathroom, then quickly search through the closet. If she had a uniform hanging there, he'd get her last name from the stencil above her left breast pocket. But his hotel room had been closer, and they had staggered there, groping at each other.

He gave up and decided to simply enjoy looking at her naked body, though if the name thing had really upset her, looking was now probably all he would get to do. She must have seen the look in his eyes because she leaned over and kissed him on the cheek. "Last night was fun. Let's do that again."

"Tonight?" he asked, thinking this time he'd try to maneuver them to her hotel room.

She grinned and shook her head. "No, right now."

••••

Nikaela arrived a month late for her fourth and final year at the academy, an unforgivable act of tardiness, especially for the cadet who had been at the top of her class the previous three years. They expected her to set an example for the other cadets. As she unpacked her gear in her dorm room, a first year cadet appeared in the doorway, saluted smartly, and said, "Command Eagle Liefjahrl orders you to report immediately to his office."

She had expected such a summons from the Commandant of Cadets, and knew that the dressing down she was about to receive would be at very high volume, and monumental in the extreme. She feared they might expel her, and didn't think she could face her mother if they did. She crossed the campus with a heavy heart, a cold wind blowing out of the north chilling her to the bone.

Nikaela stepped into the commandant's outer office and stopped at the desk of a uniformed clerk. She opened her mouth to identify herself, but before she could speak, the clerk said, "The commandant is expecting you, Cadet Vreekande. Please go right in."

The fact that the clerk knew her name the moment she walked into the room, and the commandant would immediately interrupt whatever he was doing; Nikaela rightfully took that as a bad sign.

She opened the door, stepped into the office, stopped the required two paces before the commandant's desk, snapped to attention and saluted.

Seated behind his desk, Liefjahrl returned the salute casually and said, "Ease, Cadet. Relax. Sit down."

Nikaela said, "I . . . uh . . . ."

Liefjahrl hesitated and one eyebrow rose in disapproval. "Mistress Vreekande, you're stammering like a first-year cadet."

She sat down, not sure what to expect. Liefjahrl didn't question her in any way about her tardiness. He pleasantly outlined one month of accelerated study with special tutors so she could catch up with the rest of the fourth-year class. He then dismissed her by simply saying, "Welcome back, Cadet. We need to get you back at the top of the class."

That set the tone for the entire year: no reprimands or demerits for her tardiness, just get back to her studies and pretend nothing had happened. Kristdokar had told her that if anyone at the academy asked about her training tour, she was to tell them she had served aboard *Skuldev* and honed her shipboard skills. Most importantly, the hunter-killer had never gotten near the Novalis system, or better yet, Nikaela had never heard of the place.

Nikaela paid close attention to the news feeds. The tragedy on Novalis III received considerable coverage, but it was treated by the Commonwealth as a result of the in-fighting among the five factions on the planet, and no mention was made of Kelk or Commonwealth involvement, or of interference by any of the smaller independent governments in nearby star systems. From the Kelk perspective, the incident had been a problem outside the Supremacy's sphere of responsibility. It briefly received headline coverage, then was quickly forgotten. And the courts-martial that Kristdokar had mentioned never happened; no news, no stories, no rumors, nothing.

Three months prior to finishing her final year at the academy, Nikaela had concluded the whole Novalis III incident had been quietly handled behind the scenes. And then she received orders to report immediately to Erikdeg military base, a remote location on the other side of Viktorkinde. The orders contained no information about the length of her stay, or her responsibilities when she got there, or why her studies at the academy were being interrupted so close to final exams.

14

What's in a Name?

APPARENTLY, THE PARTY crowd intended to party through the day and into the night, then through the next day and the next night, and to continue that right through to the end of their leave. John and Hey-You spent several days and nights together, but they tired of the partying. John realized he'd had his fill of drinking, dancing, singing, and shouting crude epithets regarding the parentage of DIs, though by no means had he had his fill of Hey-You. She agreed with him, and they decided to go back to the depot a little early. He still hadn't learned her real name. He had even made sure they ended up in her hotel room one night, but no, when he searched her closet he learned she hadn't brought any uniforms.

Carla and a dozen of their platoon mates had beaten him to it. He found them in the barracks, some of them playing cards, some just sitting on their bunks and talking. He wasn't in the mood for cards, so he sat down among the group that included Carla. She looked at him and said, "Have a good time with your little friend?"

John had specifically avoided Carla for the last few days because he didn't want that kind of complication.

"What's her name?" she asked.

He said, "Hey-You."

Carla frowned, clearly not sure what he meant by that. One of the other female recruits gave John a warning look.

Carla and Leeze Caputto had become good friends, but John saw no sign of Leeze and tried to change the subject. "Where's Leeze?"

Carla gave him a sour look. "You know Leeze. She won't stop partying until she has to. Now about this girl—"

Thankfully, at that moment Sergeant Omuglu rescued him by marching into the barracks, her boots thudding on the planks of the floor. John spotted her first and said, "Attention."

They all jumped to their feet.

"Rest," Omuglu said impatiently as she strode across the room. "Relax. Sit down."

John still found it disconcerting to hear her speak in a normal tone of voice, and from the look on Carla's face, he guessed she did too. They did relax, but none of them sat down.

Omuglu stopped in their midst and planted her fists on her hips. "Not out partying with the rest, huh?" She looked at John. "Why not?"

He shrugged. "I did for a while . . . but the partying got old." He added, "Ma'am."

She shook her head. "You don't call me ma'am now. You graduated. You're soldiers now. You call me sergeant."

"Yes, ma'am," he said. "I mean sergeant."

She ignored him. "Bored, huh? All of you?"

They mumbled their general agreement.

Omuglu grimaced and shook her head. "Don't mumble. You're supposed to be soldiers now, so stop sounding like a bunch of green recruits."

She scanned their faces and took an instant to make eye contact with each of them. "Boredom is bad. Bored soldiers get into trouble, and if they can't find trouble, they make it, so I gotta make sure that don't happen."

She looked at Carla and John. "Nigurski and Mathius. You two tested well on tech, reflexes and spatial orientation. Let's see how well you do in a flight simulator. Report to Sim-Tech. Tell them I've authorized you to spend the afternoon learning how to be pilots. Tell them to start you on small craft like gunboats, and if you do well, work you up slowly to the bigger stuff."

She looked at the rest of them. "And the rest of you—"

She singled them out two or three at a time and gave them orders to report to one of the advanced training facilities on base. "We'll get you all a little jump-start on the rest of your platoon when it comes to advanced."

One of the young soldiers said. "But aren't we on leave, sergeant?"

"That you are," she said, nodding her head and grinning. "That means you get to do whatever you want to do." She leaned toward the soldier so that her nose almost touched his. His eyes widened as she growled, "And I'm telling you what you want to do. Got it?"

"Yes, Sergeant," he said.

"But you're right," she continued. "You are on leave. So I'm going to let you be lazy, let you get a little extra shut-eye, let you sleep in each morning."

They relaxed a little, and she added, "I'm not going to wake you up until dawn."

John thought that the looks on the other soldiers' faces probably mirrored his own.

Omuglu pulled out the parade-ground volume and bellowed, "I gave you all orders. Move."

After several days of intense training in the simulators, while John did well, Carla proved to be the better gunboat pilot. On the last day of their ten-day leave both were given the opportunity to do some rudimentary maneuvering in actual gunboats out on the landing field: simple stuff, like a vertical lift on the boat's grav fields, then put the thing back down on its landing skids. John knew full well that the automated stability systems in the boat helped considerably.

When their leave ended, they officially began their year of advanced training.

••••

John had come to suspect that the purpose of basic wasn't really to teach them how to fight like soldiers, but to break down their old civilian reflexes and turn them into a team. In basic they'd trained with old-fashioned, chemically-powered, slug-throwing rifles, old tech that wouldn't stand a chance against modern weapons. John had excelled because he'd trained under Cranoch with such weapons for more than a year. Whenever John had made a mistake, the older man had beaten him mercilessly, which provided considerable incentive to learn his lessons quickly.

Phase one of advanced training consisted of exposure to much more sophisticated technical systems in a combination of classroom, simulator and field exercises. He learned to operate a wide range of weapons: mortars, rotary emplacements, energy weapons, grav launchers. They also trained on command and communication systems, field logistics, emergency medical prep, just about everything.

When they introduced them to grav guns John learned why Mercier's grav pistol had had such a devastating effect on his father's knee and head. Its gravity field accelerated a small flechette up to something over Mach five. The shell would puncture armor, or flesh, then fragment into hundreds of tiny pieces. It frequently caused more damage than an explosive round.

SecCorps appeared to be throwing everything possible at them, just as Brightlaw had said they would. John noticed that when he did well at something, they scheduled him for more training on that, so he tried to do well at everything. He recalled Brightlaw saying how all their testing procedures couldn't tell them everything about a soldier, and he suspected that by exposing them to a wealth of experiences, SecCorps hoped to uncover a pleasant surprise or two. John also hoped to prove he could do better than the category into which their measurements and tests had put him. At some point they would assign him permanently to either Naval or Infantry Ops. And rumor had it that if one excelled at a wide range of skills, he might be allowed to choose. He liked having choices, because that meant he had more opportunity to determine his own fate, to maybe not be so ordinary.

At the end of the first month of advanced, they fitted all of the new soldiers with neural implants. It took a full month for the neural circuitry to grow inside their skulls, and another to become fully active, during which time the medical staff carefully monitored them all. The learning curve for thought triggers and mental initiation sequences proved difficult, and they were told that the better part of a year would pass before they developed the skills needed to make full use of the implants. For those few who couldn't master it, their implants were degraded to civilian status, then they were released from the corps with honorable discharges. At that point ComSecCorps didn't use the term *washout*, but all of the young soldiers knew that calling it anything else amounted to nothing more than a polite euphemism.

••••

John made a concerted effort to learn Hey-You's real name. He knew the barracks she bunked in, so he knew her platoon. He went there one day during a short period of free time, hoping to corner one of her squad mates. He encountered a female soldier just outside the barracks door.

"Hi," he said. "I'm looking for someone, but I don't know her name."

She grinned. "You're what's his name, right? You must be looking for Hey-You."

He grimaced. "What's her real name?"

Her grin broadened, she turned, opened the barracks door and stuck her head inside. She shouted, "Hey-You, What's-His-Name is here to see you."

Apparently, she had enlisted the aid of her platoon mates to help her keep John in the dark, and they'd dubbed him What's-His-Name in retaliation. He figured he could at least get her last name from the cloth stencil on her uniform, but when she stepped out of the barracks, she had it covered with black tape.

She flashed him a white-toothed grin and said, "Hi, What's-His-Name."

He shook his head. "I'm sorry about the name thing. Just tell me your real name. Please."

She ignored the request and said, "Have you got leave this ten-end?"

"Yah," he said. "Why?"

She turned away from him and opened the barracks door, but looked over her shoulder before stepping through it. "So do I. Let's go into town and get a room. Who knows, in the throes of ecstasy I might inadvertently reveal my real name." She gave him a calculating smile. "So it's your responsibility to get me to the throes-of-ecstasy part. That's an order, soldier."

Resigned to the fact it could be quite a while before he learned her name, he said, "I take all my responsibilities very seriously."

"I know," she said, then stepped through the door and closed it.

As he turned to walk away, he noticed several female soldiers looking at him through the windows of the barracks, all displaying that same white-toothed grin.

By the time they shared a hotel room on their two-day leave at the end of the tenday, he still hadn't learned her name. But he did learn that she didn't seem to care too much about that, and she called him John, not What's-His-Name. He did fulfill his responsibilities, but she didn't shout out her name.

She couldn't wear the black tape over the stencil on her uniform in front of any of their superiors, so he surprised her one day in the mess hall, and learned her family name was Teleman. That evening during the study hours before lights out, he logged into the base comp system and looked her up. In the computer, her first name was listed as Hey-You. He decided to look up his own record, and learned that he was now officially listed as What's-His-Name.

They shared a room on their next leave, and he asked, "How the hell did you do that?"

She flashed him that satisfied, white-toothed grin and said, "Friend of mine in cyber, changed a few lines of code so that every time you log on, if you try to look up certain people, you get a special response."

The next time he got leave, he didn't get to share a room with her. The powers-that-be had discovered the lines of code her friend in cyber had altered, and she and her friend spent their leave removing unsightly rocks from the parade ground. John looked her up again, and learned that the lines of code had been corrected; she'd been given the name Tamith. He asked one of her friends and was told that she went by Tam. But the next time they went on leave together, she refused to answer to Tam, and insisted he call her Hey-You.

••••

Three months into their advanced training, Omuglu woke them up one morning and announced, "Now we separate the whores from the virgins. Pack it up, children. You're all going to spend the next month on an orbital weapons platform."

Towed by heavy grav tugs into orbit around a planet or its primary, the big weapons platforms were strictly defensive installations. They had only the most rudimentary sublight grav drives to provide for orbital adjustments when needed, but they bristled with massive power plants, transition batteries and transition launchers. A heavy cruiser or destroyer would think twice before taking one on, especially since the platforms were always positioned to backup and support one another.

Too deep within the Commonwealth to fear attack or invasion, Miriteen's best defense had always been its location. But as a major Recruit Depot for ComSecCorps it boasted three platforms for training purposes. Their month on a platform would also provide the opportunity to train for the first time in vacuum, where they would practice boarding and other space combat drills in heavy combat armor, putting into practice a lot of the classroom stuff they'd studied. John, Carla, Roark and the rest of their squad were assigned to Platform II.

They hefted their gear and boarded one of several gunboats resting on its skids in the middle of the parade ground.

"I've been looking forward to this," Carla said as they settled into their seats. "This is when it gets real."

The ride up to the platform took a couple of hours. Roark slept like a baby. Carla fidgeted with nervous energy. John grew bored.

When they arrived, the gunboat mated to a personnel hatch on the platform, they muscled their gear through it, and the senior chief of the platform showed them to their bunks. That reminded John that they'd have to be conscious of naval etiquette.

While stowing their gear, an irritatingly loud klaxon sounded, a continuous alarm blared, the gravity in the bunk room went to zero, the hatch they'd just come through cycled shut, and a voice blared over a speaker, "Vacuum integrity breach. All hands, standard breach procedures."

John's training kicked in. To make sure he didn't float off in an uncontrolled fashion he pushed off lightly with his toes and drifted toward the ceiling. They'd practiced this repeatedly in a zero-G room back at the depot, but Roark, Leeze and one other member of their squad missed a beat and flailed their arms as they floated upward. John reached the ceiling and caught a handhold, steadied himself and said, "Stop flailing and float free."

Roark obeyed immediately.

Carla had reacted like John and held tightly to a handhold. John said, "Carla, I'll get Roark, you get one of the others."

John kicked off toward Roark, caught one of his outstretched hands, and they both tumbled lazily as they drifted back to the floor. When they bumped against the deck, John parked Roark at a handhold, then turned and saw Carla had nicely snagged Leeze. He repeated the maneuver to snag the third, and in a matter of seconds all eight members of their squad were stable and hanging onto something to keep from drifting about.

A few seconds later the alarm stopped blaring, the hatch cycled open, the senior chief stuck his head in, looked around and said, "Well I'll be. We don't usually get a squad where everyone passes our little test. Usually end up with at least one or two floaters. You did all react properly, didn't you?"

"Yes, Chief," John said. "We did."

The grin on the chief's face told John he suspected the truth, but he didn't call them on it. And of course, none of them were going to enlighten him on the matter. It occurred to John that they could have been under visual observation the entire time, and the senior chief knew exactly what had happened. John gave the room a quick scan, but couldn't see any obvious pickups.

During that month they learned that when slamming big shells into transition, the transition batteries sent stray gravity waves rolling through the platform, and they all found it difficult to keep the food in their stomachs. Roark proved to be especially susceptible to that problem and spent the first tenday on his hands and knees in the head, blowing chow. But with a little help from medical, he recovered nicely by the second tenday. John and Carla both managed to keep their lunch down without the drugs. John even pre-qualified as a targeting specialist for the big transition batteries.

15

Guilt by Association

DEAD-HEAD PASSAGE to Erikdeg base had been arranged for Nikaela on military transport. The remote location of the facility meant she couldn't get direct passage, but had to change transport twice at other military installations. With delays and layovers, the journey took more than three days.

When she stepped off the shuttle at Erikdeg, Kristdokar stood waiting for her on the tarmac; the former command eagle had been promoted to brigadier skalde. The older woman led Nikaela to a small room furnished with a table and two chairs. Nikaela wasn't even allowed a chance to unpack. Kristdokar simply waved a hand and said, "Toss your duffel in the corner there, and sit down."

The brigadier skalde then repeated her interrogation of several months earlier, questioning Nikaela for more than two hours. She finished by saying. "Good. When you're called to witness, don't deviate one iota from anything you just said."

Nikaela had one serious concern. "Will I be required to testify under neural probe?"

Kristdokar shook her head. "Legally, they would need some indication of wrong-doing on your part to force that. And at this point they have no such evidence. But when a mistake results in twenty million deaths, rules can be bent. Don't give them a reason to bend anything."

Nikaela had the impression that they were dealing with people who didn't have to worry about doing things legally.

As if reading her thoughts, Kristdokar said, "And they don't want this to blossom into anything larger than it already is."

Nikaela had access to all her text books through the base's comp system. She quickly learned she was not allowed to leave the base, so she exercised in the gym, and studied what she thought she might be missing during her stay at Erikdeg, though that was purely guesswork on her part since they did not allow her to communicate in any way with the academy. In fact, they did not allow her to communicate in any way with anyone outside of Erikdeg. It proved to be a very lonely time.

Twenty-two days after setting foot on the tarmac at Erikdeg, she received a message from Kristdokar to put on her best uniform and be ready, though the message didn't say ready for what. Two hours later Kristdokar took her in hand and led her to an isolated building on the edge of the base. Two armed MCs waited at the doors, and she noted others stationed at regular intervals around the structure.

Kristdokar led her down a hallway, then through a door guarded by two more armed MCs. At one end of the room, seated behind a table were one brigadier skalde, the only man, three female major skaldes, and one female vice skalde. As the ranking officer, the vice skalde would be in charge of the tribunal.

At the other end of the room five prisoners sat at five tables with their hands manacled in front of them, the plast chain between their wrists bolted to the top of each table. She recognized one of the prisoners: Eindride. Two others, like Eindride, wore the rank of command superior, one man and one woman. The remaining two were a command eagle and a command hawk, both female. Behind each prisoner stood an armed MC, and next to each sat a command eagle with his or her hands free and unrestrained. Those would be their advocates.

No introductions were made. Nikaela was instructed to sit in a simple chair near the table containing the five skaldes. The skaldes and the advocate command eagles then grilled her for the next five hours. It came to an end when the vice skalde leaned back in her chair, steepled her fingers in front of her and stared at Nikaela for several seconds. Then, without shifting her eyes away from Nikaela, she said, "Brigadier Kristdokar, please approach."

Exhausted and frightened, Nikaela had forgotten about Kristdokar, who had remained seated near the back of the room and silent through the entire afternoon. Kristdokar stood and walked forward, stopping in front of the table containing the five skaldes. She leaned forward and bent down, lowering her head to the same level as the vice skalde, who never took her eyes off Nikaela. The other four skaldes seated at the table leaned in close to listen, and the vice skalde said something Nikaela couldn't hear. Kristdokar answered, and like the vice skalde's voice, hers remained too low for anyone else in the room to hear. The vice skalde never took her eyes off Nikaela while they conversed quietly for about five minutes, and no one needed to tell Nikaela that, like the prisoners, she too was on trial here. She knew with absolute certainty that her future was now being decided by that woman.

Kristdokar straightened, turned and crossed the room to Nikaela. She simply said, "Come with me, Mistress Vreekande."

Kristdokar led her back to her quarters in silence. Before the older woman left, Nikaela asked, "What will happen to them?"

Kristdokar shrugged and said, "The eagle and the hawk will probably be executed in a low gravity gallows. The command superiors will likely receive life sentences without the possibility of parole, though your man, Eindride, did try to alert his superiors, but was warned off by the eagle with a beating and a nasty threat. He'll probably be shown some mercy, maybe only ten years at hard labor, then dishonorable discharge."

Nikaela wondered exactly what charges had been levied against the five prisoners. But the whole situation, the structure of the tribunal and Kristdokar's demeanor, warned her that asking too many questions could be dangerous.

It occurred to Nikaela that the tribunal hadn't needed her testimony, especially since she had claimed ignorance of the entire operation and offered no evidence that might aid the prosecution. Her superiors had most likely questioned all five prisoners under deep neural probe, and with twenty million lives lost she didn't think they had spent much time debating the legalities of doing so.

From Eindride they would have learned of her discovery of the mislabeling of the crates, and her knowledge of the unconventional weapons being supplied to the five factions. She had to think long and hard to understand why they had bothered to call her out to a remote base to testify, and concluded they wanted to teach a harsh and severe lesson to a promising, but very junior, cadet. And the last part of that lesson had been Kristdokar's candor regarding the unforgiving punishments the five defendants would receive.

When Nikaela returned to the academy, out of curiosity she looked up her own record. It contained no mention of either absence during her fourth year, as if she had been present the full year without interruption. But because of the additional month of absence so close to the end of the year, she had fallen considerably behind. She crammed, got very little sleep, but she quickly came to realize that there just wasn't enough time. She didn't think she was going to do as well on her final exams as she would have, and probably wouldn't graduate at the top of her class. She concluded once more that any chance at sponsorship by Kristdokar had died along with the twenty million lives lost on Novalis III. Perhaps that too was part of the lesson.

••••

"My dear Colonel Primatov!"

Katrine recognized the voice of Senator Jenine Catarvin and turned about. Katrine stood taller than most women and many men, so she easily spotted the plump little woman as she edged her way through the crowded room toward her. The senator carried an empty champagne glass in one hand, but spotted one of their host's waiters with a tray of full glasses, and momentarily diverted her course. She exchanged her empty glass for a full one, then completed the journey to Katrine.

"Where have you been?" Catarvin asked. "We haven't seen your lovely face here in the capital for months."

Katrine smiled and said, "I've been assisting with that horrible tragedy in the Novalis system."

"Oh yes," Catarvin said. "Twenty million people. I do hope you and your military colleagues can make those Kelk monsters pay for that."

Catarvin had never struck her as an anti-Kelk hardliner, but perhaps sentiment had shifted during Katrine's absence.

Catarvin leaned close and said, "Did you learn anything especially interesting all the way out there?"

"No," Katrine lied. "My responsibilities were limited to a few Blacksword teams doing investigative work on the ground. There were quite a number of military personnel with a lot more rank than me in charge of the investigation."

That had been one of the distinct advantages of Gascoigne's orders: they had given her the authority without the rank. And since her orders hadn't been made public, and she only occasionally needed to flash them in front of some stubborn officer who outranked her, the press and everyone else had naturally focused on all the people with lots of stripes on their sleeves, or stars on their shoulders. That had allowed her a fairly free hand.

Behind Catarvin Colonel Blacksword approached them. Thealone rescued her by touching Catarvin's arm, leaning close to the woman's ear, and softly saying, "Jenine, dear, let me steal the good colonel for a few minutes."

The senator said, "I suppose you military people have something hush-hush to discuss."

"Not really," Thealone lied. "But it's something that even I find horribly boring, and I don't want to bother you with it."

Thealone took Katrine by the arm and led her away. They said nothing as they crossed the large room full of people, and no one hindered them with an attempt at trite conversation. Perhaps the sight of two very senior Blacksword officers walking side by side proved a bit intimidating. Thealone led her down a long hallway, then stopped at a door much like many others. The older woman opened it, and indicated Katrine should precede her. She knew what to expect.

Within waited Manifort Gascoigne and Tarsik Obradour, two of the most powerful men in the Commonwealth. Obradour, their host for the evening, stood several centimeters shorter than Katrine, which normally didn't make her uncomfortable, but with him it did. His pale-gray hair had been clipped quite short, and he wore a suit that probably cost a year of Katrine's salary. He held no official position in the government, but as a wealthy and influential fundraiser, he frequently played king-maker. Katrine had met him a few times before, but had never spoken with him at any length, and remained wary of him because he had a reputation as an adamant hardliner.

"Colonel Primatov," he said, crossing the room. He shook her hand gently. "Thank you for joining us. I noticed Fran had to rescue you from Jenine Catarvin."

The only way he would know that is if they were all under surveillance. Then again, he wasn't the type of man to unintentionally give away a piece of information like that, so he wanted her to understand the situation fully.

He continued. "I do thank you for agreeing to meet with me this way. They briefed me on your findings on Novalis III, but I wanted to hear it directly from you."

She smiled, and knew she did a poor job of hiding her discomfort. "I wouldn't be here if you didn't have the proper clearances." She had checked that out carefully.

He gave her a predatory smile. "Yes, I do have those clearances, don't I?"

Gascoigne said, "Drinks, everyone. I'll do the honors."

He didn't wait for Katrine to accept or decline, and in short order he handed her a small glass of something. She sniffed at it: her favorite whiskey—of course they knew everything about her.

Obradour said, "So, what did you learn out there, Colonel?"

She shrugged. "It wasn't hard to trace the chemo, bio and DNA signatures of the agents that were used. Many were clearly Kelk."

"Many?" Obradour asked, one eyebrow rising. "I thought the Kelk were wholly responsible for that tragedy."

Fran Thealone had warned her that Obradour was quite good. She and Gascoigne had already briefed him on her findings, and yet he did an excellent job of maintaining the pretense that this was the first time he had heard the details.

She spoke carefully. "We're quite certain the Kelk also believe they were wholly responsible for it."

"Ahhh!" he said, brightening. He looked at Thealone, then at Gascoigne, and waved a finger at the senator. "You forgot to tell me that. You see, that's why I wanted to hear it directly."

He turned back to Katrine. "So, please continue."

"Many of the agents did carry Kelk signatures," she said, "but some had indicators that led us to believe they might have been of Commonwealth origin. We found some remnants of shell casings that pointed to certain commercial interests in a few of the independent systems near Novalis. But when we tried to backtrack the evidence, they were long gone and the trail cold."

Katrine hesitated. "I'm not sure what else to tell you. I can provide you with the intimate details, if you wish."

He casually dismissed that thought with a wave of his hand. "No, that won't be necessary. If at some point, I do need them, I'll let you know."

He stared into his drink for a long moment. Then he perked up, looked at Gascoigne and said, "Okay, Mani. I'm convinced."

To Katrine he said, "We're going to squash a lot of this. We'll let you know what you can actually put in your report. Right now we don't need an interstellar war."

Katrine probably did a poor job of concealing her surprise. It was not Obradour's style to be an outspoken firebrand, but his views on the Kelk were well known.

"Well, Colonel," he said, "I do thank you for indulging me."

He politely took her drink from her hand and put it on a table. He took her by the arm, and she towered over the little man as he escorted her to the door like a kindly father. He stopped at the door, and before he opened it, he turned to her and said, "I know I'm considered a hardliner regarding the Kelk, but I want you to know more about me than what a single word can convey. Understand that if the Kelk want to start a war, then I'll be happy to give them their damn war and get the thing over with. But if it's not the Kelk who are trying to start a war, then I want to know who we're really fighting, and the reason for the war, before we start throwing warheads at someone. I don't like being manipulated, and I hope you'll continue to help me find the truth."

Katrine, Gascoigne and Thealone stepped out into the hall. Obradour remained in the room and closed the door softly. Katrine wasn't sure what had just happened.

••••

That year consisted of intensive advanced training for John and all of his comrades. He did well on all of the classroom stuff, including planetary and interstellar navigation, and several classes on engineering in the big interstellar transition ships. And their instructors made them study naval customs, rank and insignia until they knew it as well as infantry. Carla and he also qualified as pilots on everything from small grav lifts to drop boats, and that included the large boats able to carry two platoons in full kit and heavy combat armor from orbit to a planetside drop zone. John wasn't sure he wanted to specialize as a pilot, and when he asked Omuglu about that, she said, "Qualifying doesn't necessarily mean you'll get assigned to that specialty. We like to make sure we've got extra people in every specialty, so if you've got the skills, we get you qualified. Never know when a particular skillset might save an entire platoon, or even a battalion."

John and Carla were not alone in getting the extra training. John learned that while everyone had to qualify with basic weapons, his friends were also qualifying in several specialties. And none of them yet knew to which specialty they would ultimately be assigned.

Everyone also needed to qualify in combat armor as well. The heavy combat armor had plast plates thick enough to stop many types of rounds on its own, but when powered, could withstand punishment that might easily rip a soldier in two. They trained extensively in both heavy and light combat armor. To qualify in the heavy stuff, they executed a free orbital drop to the surface of Miriteen from one-hundred kilometers up, using the gravity field generators in their armor to moderate their speed and set down without injury. Sergeant Major Prescott told them, "Regardless of where you end up, you ain't ComSecCorps unless you can put on plast and do boots-on-the-ground with the rest of us. Everyone's a grunt when the bullets start flying. Some grunts get to give orders, and some take 'em. That's ComSecCorps."

He gave them that little speech repeatedly at any offhand moment that suited him, and it never varied by a single word. He had spit those words at them so often that when he spontaneously broke into that mantra, many of the young soldiers rolled their eyes, looked at each other and mimicked him by quietly mouthing the words along with him. Occasionally, he caught them doing it, and several hours later the parade ground had been deprived of more unsightly rocks. John suspected the NCOs snuck out at night and dumped the rocks back onto the field, just so they had plenty of rocks to be picked up by recruits stupid enough to do something worthy of rock detail.

John and his platoon mates also spent time training on Naval systems, and he learned that even those in Naval Ops had gone through standard ComSecCorps basic, then the mandatory year of advanced training in technical systems and infantry combat. Even an admiral could ". . . put on plast and do boots-on-the-ground . . ." though John wondered if someone like that might be a little rusty when the time came.

During the last few months of that first year, with their implants now fully mature, the med-techs taught them how to develop a personal encryption key so their implants couldn't be subverted by an external signal.

"Think of something permanently etched in your memory," their instructor told them. "It can be a really good or a really bad memory, but something you've never been able to forget. We'll have you concentrate on that when we set the key, and after that no one will be able to tamper with your implants unless you use that key to grant them access. You can even describe it in detail to an enemy, but that won't replicate the image you recall. They might blow your brains out, but they won't be able to reprogram your neural circuitry. You've got five days to think on it and choose the right memory sequence."

There were a lot of questions from the young soldiers. If they took a head wound and ended up with whole or partial amnesia regarding that memory, the med people would have to scrub their implants completely and regenerate them. And the Corps would regularly require them to use that key to grant access for programming modifications. John wondered if the Corps had inserted a back door so they could get access without his permission. One of the other young soldiers had the same thought and asked that question.

Their instructor said, "No, we don't do that. If someone leaked that information and the methodology, the entire Corps would be at risk. I will confess the subject comes up now and then, and is debated rather hotly, but nothing ever comes of it."

Then the man grinned unpleasantly and added, "But if we did do that, I'd simply lie to you and tell you the same thing I just said, wouldn't I?"

Five days later John had them set his encryption key to the memory of his father's head exploding when Mercier shot him, a memory he couldn't forget no matter how hard he tried. Then a few days later SecCorps made them open their implants for reprogramming so they could insert temporary code to provide virtual effects during combat simulations. The code for virtualization would be removed before they went on active duty. At least that was what they were told.

At that point, SecCorps added virtualized combat training to the curriculum.

••••

The graduation ceremony proved to be rather anticlimactic. Under ordinary circumstances, Nikaela's instructors would have been absolutely furious with her, dropping from first to tenth place in her class. They all knew she had been absent, and yet they all pretended she hadn't, as if she'd been in tenth place all along, as if there had been no sudden fall from grace. One of them told her, "You'll do well. Tenth place in a class your size is admirable."

Her classmates gave her sly looks and the occasional frown, and none of them, not even close friends, asked her outright what had happened. The undercurrent of furtiveness surrounding her unusual and unexplained absences had damped any inquisitiveness. They all probably suspected that their careers could be damaged just like hers. No, it was clear to all that they should feign uncaring ignorance, stay out of Nikaela's shadow, and not ask the questions that everyone wanted to ask. That applied to everyone but her mother.

When they met after the graduation ceremony, her mother took her by the arm, and without saying a word forcefully pulled her up to her quarters. Two of Nikaela's roommates started and froze as the woman dragged Nikaela into the room. Her mother gave them both a furious look, then hooked a thumb over her shoulder pointing toward the door. "Out," she said. "Now."

Nikaela had known the two girls for four years, and both had proven time and again they were not easily intimidated. But at that moment they scurried out of the room like frightened children.

Her mother slammed the door, then turned to Nikaela and demanded, "What in the name of our ancestors happened?"

For a single, strange moment, Nikaela looked at her mother as another woman, not just as a mother. Still attractive and a little taller than her daughter, her hair hadn't yet begun to gray, still remained mostly pepper and only a little salt. Nikaela had heard she had taken a new lover recently.

"I asked you a question," she demanded, her voice cracking with anger.

Nikaela didn't have any answers for her, or rather, the answers she could give might get her court-martialed and her mother arrested on some vague charge—or quite possibly, they'd just quietly disappear. And Nikaela couldn't come up with a plausible lie, so she decided to feign the uncaring ignorance of her classmates and instructors.

"I graduated," she said. "Did quite well, in fact, near the top of my class."

"Near the top of your class," her mother said. She crossed the small room in one, long stride, and stopped with her nose inches from Nikaela's. All Nikaela could think was that her mother had the prettiest, blood-red irises, and she felt a pang of jealousy.

Her mother shouted, "Near the top. *Near* is not where you were only a few months ago. What . . . happened . . . to . . . you?"

Nikaela's heart pounded as if it might burst out of her chest. She tried not to let that show, tried to maintain that uncaring ignorance as she said, "Tenth out of more than five hundred. One of my instructors said that's quite admirable."

Her mother's face had started to darken, had shifted toward the blueish side of white, as it did with any Kelk pushed to the limit of endurance. "I didn't raise you to be *quite admirable*. I raised you to be the best."

Frustrated that she couldn't speak openly and tell the truth, Nikaela's exasperation chose her words for her. "No, you raised me to better than you. And at that, I did succeed . . . quite admirably."

Her mother started and her eyes blinked rapidly. She stepped back from Nikaela and put an arm's length of empty space between them. Nikaela watched her struggle to speak, but she said only, "I . . . I . . ."

She had hurt her mother and she regretted her words, but she wasn't about to retract them. Nikaela spoke softly, "I still intend to have a career in service to the Supremacy." She couldn't say anything outright, but she could at least drop a hint. She added, "Regardless of what obstacles the Larscom might put in my way."

The look of incredulity on her mother's face disappeared, and she frowned in thought. She lowered her eyes and stood there Din silence for several seconds, then seemed to come to some conclusion. She stepped back another pace and looked Nikaela in the eyes. When she spoke, the outright anger had completely disappeared, and her words came out soft and intimate. "Beware of those old women. They can be quite dangerous."

Nikaela would never have thought to hear such words from her mother. She had always expressed only admiration and praise for the elite of the Kelk Supremacy, and now, to call them dangerous?

At that moment, it occurred to Nikaela that if she hadn't been shielded from the consequences of the tragedy on Novalis III, she would have ended up much like her mother. If Kristdokar hadn't intervened and coached her, Nikaela might have spent a few years in uniform, then, after the promotions ceased, looked for something else to occupy her time—perhaps a daughter. Could something similar have happened to her mother, something that had ended her career, but about which she could not speak?

Her mother spoke softly, "Come, daughter. You look like you need a drink, and I could use one as well. And from the look on your face, I think we'd both be wise to never discuss this again."

She took Nikaela's arm, but not forcefully as she had done before. They walked out of the room, arm in arm, the way Nikaela might walk with one of her classmates.

••••

"Incoming," someone shouted over the command grid. John hugged dirt behind the remnants of a chest-high stone wall. The helmet speakers in his light combat armor cut out and the ground shook as the incoming mortar round exploded nearby, pelting them with a rain of rocks, sod and clumps of dirt. When the deluge ended, he climbed up onto his knees, muscled his grav rifle up over the top of the wall, and blindly fired a burst at the enemy.

Several of his comrades did the same, but the scream of a rotary answered them, and they all ducked back behind the wall. Firing over five hundred tiny flechettes per second, it could easily cut a soldier in two. Chipping away at the rock and mortar of the wall, the rotary showered them with dust, sand, and small shards of stone. If the enemy soldiers decided to concentrate their fire on a single spot, they could probably punch through the wall, so John and the rest of his platoon kept them honest by spraying rounds at them. He didn't think they hit anything.

"Corporal Mathius," the lieutenant commanding their platoon shouted. "Move out to the right with your squad and try to flank that rotary."

John looked at what was left of his squad, six soldiers all huddled behind the protection of the wall, Carla and Leeze crouched on the right just short of where the wall ended. Beyond that, only a line of rubble remained to mark where the wall had once stood, extending all the way to the corner of a building. They'd have to sprint through about twenty paces of open space with no cover.

"Taklo," John shouted, "Nigurski, Bershma, Caputto, you heard the lieutenant. You four first, and don't cluster, don't make it easy for them. The rest of you provide cover fire. On my count: three, two, one—go."

Carla, Leeze and the two others broke into a run, while John and the rest, including the other squads, sprayed rounds at the enemy. They kept it up until all four of them made it across the open space where they took cover behind the corner of the building. That left John and two others, one of them Roark Checkov.

John looked at each of them quickly, saw the fear written on their faces, thought they probably saw the same in his. "It's our turn," he said. "Ready?"

They each gave him a sharp nod.

He shouted over the command circuit, "Three, two, one—go."

John literally ran for his life. About half way across the open gap, he glanced over his shoulder and saw that only one soldier followed him. Back behind the wall Roark remained unmoving, still and silent. John dug in his heels, reversed direction and sprinted back. The rotary opened up just as he dove behind the cover of the wall. He rolled over and got to his knees breathing heavily.

Roark remained crouched, his eyes wide, not really focused on anything—a thousand-yard stare. His hands trembled, and his jaw fluttered up and down in an almost imperceptible quiver.

"Roark," John shouted. "You gotta do this."

His eyes focused on John's face. He struggled to speak, and finally said, "Okay." He gulped hard. "Okay. I can . . . do it."

"Ready?" John asked.

"Okay," Roark said, though it came out almost like a question.

"We'll be all right," John said. "Let's do it. Three, two, one—go."

John got up and sprinted again through the open gap. This time he heard Roark's boots thudding on the dirt behind him, could hear him grunting with the effort.

The rotary opened up, screaming with its characteristic, high-pitched whine, reminding John of the day he'd first faced one as part of Cranoch's squad. Just as John reached the safety of the building, Roark grunted and collapsed in a tumble behind him. John skidded to a halt, turned and looked back. Roark lay on the dirt, his rifle tossed to one side. He sat up and extended a hand toward John, a pathetic pleading gesture. John ran out into the open again, and when he reached Roark he hooked one hand under an armpit. But when he tugged, the arm came away without the rest of Roark, ending in a stump of shredded meat and bone.

The rotary screamed again. It cut a line through Dygh Roark's chest, then through John's thighs. He screamed as a flood of agony washed through his legs, and he collapsed in the dirt next to Roark. His light-combat harness sensed the loss of blood pressure and engaged tourniquets in his thighs. It flooded his system with pain killers and initiated a nerve block. It must have determined that his injuries were so grave, he could no longer function as a combatant.

He lay there, unable to move, looking into Roark's face. More rounds slammed into Roark's body, and his eyes stared back at John with the blank, empty look of death.

Oddly enough, John realized that in his dying moments, his friend's body provided protective cover for him.

John's orders had gotten his friend killed. He tried to tell himself that it wasn't his fault, that they had both only been following the dictates of their duty, but he had trouble believing that.

••••

Conscious thought returned slowly, and John lay on his bunk for quite some time with his eyes closed.

Someone in the barracks spoke in a strangled whisper, "Fuck! Fuck! Fuck!"

John opened his eyes and sat up slowly. It came as no surprise that Roark sat on the edge of his bunk a few rows down, his elbows on his knees, clearly lost in thought. John glanced at his own sleeves; the corporal's stripes had also been part of the simulation.

The medics were always careful to bring them out of the virtualized combat simulations slowly. If they snapped awake suddenly to find that they and their friends weren't maimed or killed, and the medics repeated that too many times, it could produce certain psychological instabilities. They had never left their bunks, not through the entire exercise, and by allowing them time to recognize in a dream-like state that their memories were not real, the transition back to reality proved less jarring. At least that was the theory. John thought it likely the people who had made up that theory had never experienced a VCS, not like the one he and Roark had just been through.

The simulations were supposed to expose them to their first real combat experience, to help them overcome their fears before they actually needed to put their new skills to use. John had his doubts about that.

16

A Question of Guilt

AT THE KNOCK on the door, Stephen Brightlaw said, "Enter."

The door to his office opened and Major Hershman stepped in. The look on his face immediately got Brightlaw's attention. They'd known each other too long for him to miss such obvious unease.

Hershman saluted.

Brightlaw returned the salute, then said, "What is it?"

Hershman grimaced. "That obvious, huh?"

Brightlaw pointed him to a chair and Hershman sat down. Brightlaw said, "I can tell I'm not going to like it, so just spit it out."

Still grimacing, Hershman asked, "Have you reviewed the VCSs?"

"Yes," Brightlaw said tentatively, concluding he must have missed something. "I saw nothing unusual."

"Neither did I," Hershman said. "But the psych people brought something to my attention. We put our new soldiers through five simulations of first-time combat, and the physio-psychological responses of our darkhorse were not consistent with someone who's never been in battle before."

Brightlaw leaned back in his chair. "We get plenty of those, people who were previously police officers, or served in the military of an affiliate system, or other high-stress professions. Life on Novalis III must have been a pretty high-stress existence, don't you think?"

Hershman clearly did not like the news he had to impart. "And when we see one of those, we tweak the sims to fine-tune our understanding of their responses. We can distinguish quite accurately between actual combat and just a high-stress history. Private Mathius has been in combat before, and not just a time or two. But there is nothing about that in his record."

"Okay," Brightlaw said, making no attempt to hide his skepticism. "He's had a taste of battle. I think there was plenty of combat to go around on that planet."

"Stephen," Hershman said quietly, "think it through carefully. Who might he have served under in combat, and what might he have done while doing so? And who might he have harmed?"

Realization hit Brightlaw like a punch in the gut. "Oh shit!" he said. He closed his eyes and rubbed his temples. "The kid did so well in the sims I was thinking of giving him a promotion. But now we're going to have to get the legal people involved, aren't we?"

"Yes," Hershman said. "We can't have even a hint of war crimes or human-rights violations in the corps."

With his eyes still closed, Brightlaw said, "Is it possible Private Mathius could face prison time?"

"Yes, quite possible," Hershman said, "though, if my worst fears are realized, even a low gravity gallows is not out of the question."

••••

Since they had not left their bunks and got no real exercise during the virtual combat simulations, the VCSs were interspersed with intense workouts in the gym. John and several of his comrades had spent the morning exercising, then finished with a five kilometer run. When they returned to their barracks they all crowded into the showers.

John had made reasonable progress in overcoming the conservative values he'd grown up with on Novalis III, but still found it difficult to shower next to a very naked Carla Nigurski. Thankfully, he'd also developed the ability to not have an obvious reaction to her very curvaceous curves. He suspected he would never become truly complacent about showering with a mixed crowd of men and woman. Thankfully, Hey-You wasn't one of his barracks mates. Given their history, he thought that if he showered with her and his squad mates, he'd have a reaction he couldn't hide, which would prove to be quite embarrassing.

They were just finishing up in the showers when Sergeant Omuglu stuck her head in and said, "Private Mathius, finish up on the double, get dressed and come with me." She didn't say anything about where they were going, and she spoke softly, which scared them all.

John toweled off quickly and wasted no time getting into uniform, though, given the last time she'd escorted him out of the barracks, he took an extra few seconds to make sure he had everything right and proper. As he carefully checked his appearance in the mirror, Carla stepped up beside him and said, "Did you do something?"

The answer to that was a whole history of lives lost and lives taken, but he wasn't about to go into that with her. And in any case, he felt confident he'd finally left Novalis III behind.

"No," he said, thinking that whatever this was about, it wouldn't be that. Probably something minor.

When John stepped out of the head, Omuglu looked him over carefully and nodded, then led him out of the barracks where two armed Military Constables waited for them. John couldn't hide the look of surprise on his face when he saw them. He glanced Omuglu's way, but she didn't respond and still remained silent. The two MCs took up positions walking on either side of John, and the three of them followed the sergeant.

She led them to the administration building, and into a rather Spartan room that contained a bank of instruments on one wall, a simple bare table, and several chairs. They sat John down at the table, and Omuglu walked out of the room, closing the door behind her and leaving him with the two MCs. The two men stood stiffly at ease near the door, staring straight ahead and not looking at John. This didn't appear to be something minor, and his heart quickened.

As he waited his nervousness grew, and he tried to think of what he might have done wrong, but drew a blank. After an hour the door opened, and an officer in a ComSecCorps naval uniform walked into the room carrying a small comp interface tucked under one arm. John stood and snapped to attention. He had to think for a moment to recall the rank insignia of Naval Ops: a full commander.

"At ease," the man said.

He turned to the two MCs. "Please wait outside."

The two men said, "Yes, sir," saluted, turned and walked out of the room.

After the door closed, the naval officer said to John, "We have to talk." He extended his hand and John shook it.

"I'm Commander Micklaczek. I'm your advocate. Sit down and relax."

John did not relax, and as he sat down he asked, "Advocate?"

"Yes," Micklaczek said. "I'll be representing you. We're in the investigatory stages of an inquiry, and if you're lucky, it won't go beyond that."

John's head spun and his thoughts raced. "And if I'm not lucky?"

Micklaczek's eyes narrowed and he shook his head. "Let's don't go there, not unless we have to."

John asked, "Did I do something wrong?"

Micklaczek ignored him. "Now under ordinary circumstances you could not be forced to testify under deep neural probe without a court order. But the enlistment documents you signed do relax those strictures if certain special circumstances apply."

John asked, "What special circumstances?"

The commander gave John a pained look. "War crimes and human rights violations."

John let that sink in and tried to calm his racing heart. Any fool could look at John's short life and figure out that this wasn't about mouthing off to the colonel.

Deep down inside he'd always known his actions would catch up with him, and understood now he'd been lying to himself when he thought he'd put Novalis III behind him. His voice came out rough and edgy as he said, "This is about Novalis III, isn't it?"

Micklaczek nodded tiredly. "Unfortunately, yes. You're going to be questioned under deep neural probe. Don't attempt to lie in any way. If you do, the probe technician will catch it, and you'll look even more guilty. On the other hand, you can refuse to answer a question on the grounds that doing so may incriminate you, and the technician will not probe you for the answer. However, I must warn you that if you do exercise that right, the nature of the incident on Novalis III is of such sensitivity, that it is likely they'll have no problem getting a court order and forcing you to answer under probe at a later date."

John considered the commander's words carefully and said, "So I might as well just answer all their questions today and get it over with?"

The commander closed his eyes and rubbed his temples. "Yes."

John said, "They've already convicted me, haven't they?"

Micklaczek opened his eyes, and in them John saw sad resignation. He lied, "I don't know."

John leaned forward and said, "The *incident* on Novalis III! Is that all it was to you people, an incident?"

The man's eyes widened. He hesitated and opened his mouth to say something, but the only door in the room opened before he could.

Brightlaw, Hershman, the soft-spoken man with the Blacksword patch on his uniform, and a tall woman entered the room. They all wore ComSecCorps infantry uniforms, the woman a bird-colonel with the name PLETH stenciled above the breast pocket of her uniform, the Blacksword fellow a major named Teal.

As John stood and snapped to attention, a female lieutenant followed the others in and sat down at the bank of instruments.

Brightlaw spoke with a sharp edge of anger in his voice. "At ease. Sit down. Relax."

John sat down, but he sensed in them all a dour mood, which spoke volumes for the gravity of the situation, and he couldn't relax.

When previously standing at rigid attention in the Colonel's office because he'd been the last recruit standing, he had only gotten a brief glimpse of the Blacksword major, and seeing him clearly now, the fellow's appearance surprised him. In all respects he seemed quite ordinary. He stood average height with a normal stature, had neatly trimmed dark hair, no facial hair, and ordinary brown eyes. John had expected a Blacksword officer to appear superhuman in some way, and chided himself for being so naive.

Colonel Pleth had light-brown hair cut chin length, piercing gray-blue eyes, and a thin figure without a lot of curves. She stared at John with a determined and no-nonsense look. He saw no sympathy or compassion in her eyes.

Brightlaw introduced Pleth as the corps' advocate. John didn't need to be told that any future he might have would be decided by her. Brightlaw introduced Teal without giving a reason for his presence, and John wondered at that.

Colonel Pleth took over and spoke to John. "We're going to be questioning you under deep neural probe. If I ask a question, the answer to which might incriminate you, you may refuse to answer on those grounds, and the technician will not probe you for the answer." She didn't warn him that if he did exercise that option, they'd simply get a court order and force him to answer later.

The female lieutenant placed a small harness shaped like a set of earphones over John's head, but instead of cupping his ears, two small electrodes the size of the tip of his thumb rested on his temples. She said, "These will communicate directly with your implants. You won't feel a thing." She returned to the bank of instruments.

Colonel Pleth took a breath, and her first question made John's gut tighten. "Private Mathius, have you ever murdered anyone?"

John thought of the man he'd killed for Cranoch so he could be a good boy. And of course he'd killed Cranoch and Mercier—that was probably murder as well. He thought of the many soldiers he'd killed to acquire drugs, medicines and supplies for Dr. Tevala. And he recalled Micklaczek's warnings. He said, "Yes."

"How many did you murder?"

He shrugged. "Too many to count."

The young lieutenant operating the probe inhaled sharply. Pleth looked her way, and she nodded. Apparently, that meant John had told the truth. Brightlaw and Hershman both frowned unhappily. Micklaczek squeezed his eyes tightly shut and grimaced. Teal did not react in the slightest.

Pleth said, "Do you remember the first person you killed?"

"Yes," John said, surprised at how flat and emotionless he could sound at that moment.

Pleth's face remained completely impassive, her lips pressed into a thin, flat line. "Who was it?"

"A civilian man."

"Why did you kill him?"

John had to think for a moment to recall the incident. "We thought he'd hidden a young girl from us, and he wouldn't tell us where she was."

Even Teal reacted to that, his eyebrows lifting. Micklaczek clearly thought that his client had chosen to get himself hung.

"Why a young girl?" Pleth asked.

John saw by the look on her face that she already knew the answer, but she wanted him to say it. "They were kept in rooms upstairs in the mansion."

"Why?" she demanded again.

"For the officers."

"Why?"

"For sex."

Pleth looked at John with obvious distaste as she said, "Please describe in detail the incident in which you murdered the civilian man."

John told them of the man, his wife and her mother. He told them how he'd killed the man on Cranoch's orders, and Phillan had killed the two women, then allowed Cranoch to believe that John had done it so they could both be good boys instead of dead boys.

Major Teal said, "Colonel, may I ask a question?"

She smiled politely and nodded. "Certainly, Major."

"Private Mathius," Teal said. "Tell us how you first met this man Cranoch."

John gave them an edited version of how Mercier and Cranoch had killed his father, then kidnapped him. When he finished Teal nodded for several seconds, and his eyes didn't seem to focus on any particular target in the room, the characteristic sign of a person communicating through his implants. Then he looked sharply at Pleth and said, "Cranoch and Mercier were known to the Blacksword."

Micklaczek said, "I have a question as well, if you don't mind, Colonel?"

She nodded, and at that point John's advocate, the corps' advocate, and the Blacksword questioned him for four solid hours. They were not harsh or unkind, but they kept at him relentlessly and made him remember things he'd completely forgotten. They even made him relate the minutiae of his day-to-day existence as a prisoner of the rebels: scrubbing floors, digging holes, moving lumber and unloading trucks. He told them about the girl, and how he had scrubbed her blood off the floor in her bedroom after she'd taken her own life. At one point, when describing how he had unloaded heavy crates of supplies from a truck, he mentioned that the boxes were stamped with a graphic symbol containing the mark of the Kelk Supremacy.

Apparently, thinking nothing of that, Pleth opened her mouth to ask her next question, but the Blacksword major interrupted her, "Colonel, a moment please."

She frowned, but said, "Certainly, Major."

Teal then carefully questioned John about the crates, their size, shape, and the way they were packed on the truck. It didn't take John long to understand what the major hoped to learn, so he blurted out. "They were ammunition crates, Major. I know what an ammunition crate looks like. I even helped unpack some of them, so there's no question what they contained."

Teal frowned and his thoughts turned inward for a moment. Then he said, "That is surprising information, young man. We didn't know the Kelk were supplying arms to Cranoch and Mercier's faction."

John shrugged and said, "They were supplying arms to both government factions, and all three rebel factions. They were supplying all of them."

Brightlaw leaned forward and spoke for the first time, his voice hard and irate. "And you know this how?"

The room held to an unpleasant silence as everyone waited for John to speak. Each of them had a different look on their face: Pleth calculating; Brightlaw angry; Teal curious; Hershman with a frown that John could not read. Of them all, only Micklaczek remained completely expressionless.

John described how he'd scouted many of the compounds during the daylight hours to determine how best to get at their medicines and supplies, and how best to ambush their night patrols. He told them how he'd used the binoculars to watch men unload ammunition crates stamped with that Kelk symbol. He finished by saying, "I saw something similar in more than one compound in each of the five different factions."

Hershman said, "Shit!"

John's superiors then broke into a heated argument about the evidence he had just given them. They said something about it reenergizing an inquiry by some commission in the Commonwealth senate.

Pleth ended the disagreement by saying, "Enough. We've drifted badly off topic. This is a discussion best taken off-line."

They returned to questioning John, and made him relive every second from his first sight of Cranoch and Mercier, right up to the moment when he'd awakened sitting on the floor of his parents' apartment with his mother's blood soaked corpse in his lap, awakened to find a ComSecCorps soldier in full combat armor standing in the doorway of their apartment. When they finished, sweat stains darkened the armpits and back of his tunic, and exhaustion weighed heavily on him.

Brightlaw said, "Let's adjourn to my office to discuss what we've learned here."

The officers filed out of the room. The MCs returned and took up their positions on either side of the door, standing at ease, but still as rigid as any DI standing at attention.

••••

Stephen Brightlaw sat down behind his desk, the position of power, though he didn't feel terribly powerful at that moment. Teal chose to stand, leaning casually against one wall. Hershman and Micklaczek both sat down in chairs, while Pleth paced back and forth in the middle of the room. Brightlaw didn't envy her the decision she must make, though he hoped to help her make the right one.

"Okay," she said. "The kid's a killer, but not a sociopathic, homicidal murderer. Nor is he a sadist or a rapist."

Hershman said, "If he'd been sociopathic, homicidal or sadistic, our psych people would have uncovered that easily."

Pleth dismissed his comment with an impatient wave of her hand. "Unfortunately, he did commit murder on more than one occasion. The first incident we can put to rest, the one where Cranoch made the other kid hold a gun to Private Mathius's head. That's more than enough coercion to give the boy a pass on that one."

She stopped in the middle of the room, looked at each of them and said, "So, Cranoch and Mercier!"

Brightlaw hoped to convince her not to imprison the kid. "I found it interesting the way he built up that mantra of all the wrongs they'd committed."

"Yah," she said, "and he recited it back to himself every night to keep from turning into a . . . *good boy*, was the term he used. That took a lot of discipline."

In his usual soft-spoken voice, Teal added, "And maturity."

She spun toward him and put her fists on her hips. "Help me with Cranoch and Mercier, Major. You said you knew of them. I get the impression we don't mind hearing that those two low-lives took one for the team."

Teal nodded and thought for a moment, then he spoke carefully. "About a year before the factions deployed the bio weapons and turned the fighting on Novalis III into a tragedy of monumental proportions, a certain agency in the government asked the Blacksword to prepare an intervention scenario to end the mess—it's a shame they waited too long to let us implement it. We had people on the ground from the beginning of the troubles there, monitoring the situation and keeping us informed. As part of the scenario we came up with a list of names, basically people who were to be arrested so they could stand trial for some very unpleasant acts. Among them we had a special list of those who were not to be taken alive, regardless of the circumstances; best for all concerned if we made sure they chose to fight to the death—save us the time and trouble of long, drawn-out trials and executions. Cranoch and Mercier were at the top of that list."

Pleth considered Teals words for several seconds. "All right, he gets a pass on that one too. I can write up a legal justification for that with a clear conscience. What about the others? He was not a combatant when he killed the medics and the other soldiers to steal supplies."

Hershman stood. "But he was. He fought for the only faction that deserved anything descent out of that mess: that doctor and her patients. Damn it, the men he killed weren't soldiers, they were predators."

Micklaczek stood and faced him, shaking his head. "They were soldiers. Don't even imply anything otherwise. They were combatants and he was a combatant who killed the enemy. Let's keep it simple and straight forward."

Everyone looked to Pleth. She closed her eyes and rubbed her temples as she said, "I think I can make that work. I'll write it up that way, though the justification for letting him walk away clean is a little thin."

She opened her eyes and grinned. "I'll just have to be creative. But it might come back to bite him some day, so let's document everything and get all the probe results on record. If they probe him again some years from now, it won't be as clear."

Major Teal stepped forward and said, "If it helps any, I've discussed this with Colonel Blacksword, and she tells me she would like to attach her personal signature to that document."

Pleth's grin broadened. "Thank you, Major. And then I'm going to bury it in the sealed records of that horrendous incident so it'll take a congressional mandate to open them."

After Micklaczek and Pleth left the room, Hershman said, "That was a close one."

Brightlaw thought of Pleth's words, ". . . might come back and bite him some day . . ." and he wondered if young Mathius would ever be free of the taint of Novalis III.

17

Cat and Mouse

WITH THE COMPLETION of their year of advanced training, ComSecCorps as-signed John's squad to the marine contingent aboard CSC *Defiant*, a destroyer docked at Miriteen Prime. They assigned Hey-You's squad to similar duties aboard the heavy cruiser *Wicked Fury*, which would down-transit into the Miriteen system twelve days hence. John and Hey-You spent one last night together.

"I'm going to miss you," he told her.

She kissed him on the cheek. "And I'm going to miss you. But no regrets. It was fun while it lasted. And maybe some time we'll get to do it again."

They parted with a kiss, and no regrets. In a year they'd both return to Miriteen for Command School, and John decided he would try to rekindle their relationship then.

ComSecCorps gave John and his squad mates two-day passes and commercial tickets for transit up to the big space station orbiting the planet. They could do what-ever they chose while on leave, as long as they reported to the ship on time, and sober. It pleased John that he, Carla, Leeze and Roark could remain a team, and also that he didn't have to put up with DeLeon any more, at least not until they returned for Command School.

Carla discovered that ComSec maintained transient accommodations on the big space station. The four of them could get bunks in a large barracks with a communal shower, and a place to securely stow their gear, all on the cheap. And since none of them had ever spent any real time on a station, they decided to spend their leave there and do a little sight-seeing. They took the first available shuttle off planet, and when they stepped onto the massive station, John's implants automatically connected to ComSecCorps Operations Command. They checked into the barracks, dumped their gear, then went out to explore.

They strolled down an avenue wide enough for their recruit battalion to parade in full dress, and tried not to gawk like bumpkins. An advertisement flashed into the vir-tual overlay of John's vision, then another, and another.

Carla stopped in the middle of the sidewalk and shook her head. "This is ridiculous. They're trying to sell me all sorts of girlie stuff."

Leeze said, "What's wrong with girlie stuff? I like girlie stuff."

Roark made an obvious point of leaning over and looking at Carla's butt. "You'd look good in girlie stuff. You should try it some time. You and Leeze would make a couple of good looking girlie girls."

Carla turned on him angrily. "Not the stuff they're trying to sell me—negligées and bedroom crap—I'd look like a hooker."

Roark said, "But you'd be a damn good looking hooker."

She looked at John and stuck her chest out as she said, "I would, wouldn't I?"

He ignored her.

Leeze grinned. "I don't care what I look like, as long as the guys are looking."

They quickly learned to set up reception filters in their implants to shut out most of the pitches the stores pushed their way.

They found a concourse filled with shops, bars and restaurants, and ate a meal in a relatively inexpensive place. Unfortunately, everything up there but their bunks proved to be more than they could afford. They spent one night in the transient barracks, then decided to report a day early for duty aboard *Defiant*; on ship they could at least get free room and board. John keyed up a map of the station, and his implants projected a virtual overlay with directions for the most direct route to *Defiant*'s mooring.

The docks on Miriteen Prime bustled with activity, the whine of large grav lifts a constant background din as stevedores loaded and unloaded supplies through gaping cargo hatches. As they headed for the military docks, Roark got in the way of a heavily loaded lift and had to skip quickly to one side. The dockworker driving it raised a fist and shouted, "Out of the way, shit head."

With their implants guiding them they found *Defiant*'s aft personnel hatch. John walked through a passageway about three meters long with expansion joints that provided a flexible coupling to the station. Recalling the lessons he'd learned regarding naval etiquette, when he stepped into the big transition ship, his duffel over one shoulder, he turned to the Commonwealth ensign draped from a bulkhead, and saluted it. He turned to the officer of the deck, a female lieutenant j. g. with a name tag that read SHERSON. He saluted, saying, "Private First Class John Mathius reporting for duty. Permission to come aboard, ma'am."

Sherson appeared to be several years older than John, and while slight of stature she looked at him with an air of confidence through dark brown eyes. She returned the salute. "At ease, Private Mathius, and welcome aboard. You're a day early."

John grimaced. "We didn't realize the station was so expensive, ma'am."

She smiled. "You'll get used to that. Please report to Staff Sergeant Nomal Parma. I've notified him you're now on board."

New directions appeared superimposed over John's vision.

••••

Carla said, "I thought we were done with training." She sounded a little petulant, which was so uncharacteristic of her.

John looked at the powered combat armor partially disassembled in front of them. He, Carla, Leeze and Roark had taken it apart and put it back together twice already.

Roark said, "I wouldn't call this training."

Sergeant Parma must have overheard them. He turned away from another group sweating over the reassembly of a suit of armor. "Private, you live and die by your armor, its reserves, and the weapons you carry. You're going to take it apart and reassemble it until you can do so in the dark, with one hand tied behind your back."

Parma clearly didn't see Leeze roll her eyes, because if he had, she'd probably find herself cleaning latrines.

When they had first reported to Parma, he had put the four of them to work immediately. And when the rest of their squad reported in the next day, he put them to work as well. They'd been disassembling and reassembling combat armor for three days now.

Parma continued, "Tomorrow, we fit all of you newbies with your own personal suit, and then you're going to take it apart, and reassemble it all by your lonesome. Your one and only love will always be your armor and your weapon."

John noticed a slight vibration in the deck beneath his feet that hadn't been there before. As they worked on the armor, he checked the ship's schedule in his implants and confirmed that they were about to launch. He keyed up a ship-wide status overlay, and confirmed that the ship's crew had brought its main power plant and engines online. An hour later they'd just finished reassembling the armor when the docking gantries gave the big transition ship a soft push, and a clang echoed through *Defiant*'s hull. *Defiant* drifted free, then engaged its grav drive, and slowly pulled away from the massive station. Six hours later they up-transited out of the Miriteen system.

After a tenday, the new privates knew every seam and seal in their armor, though they couldn't actually reassemble it in the dark with one hand tied behind their backs. Once each soldier passed the Staff-Sergeant-Nomal-Parma test on armor, they went on to other duties, like scrubbing decks. John learned that scrubbing decks had been a time-honored tradition throughout the history of Naval Ops.

Parma told them, "It would be a damn shame if you newbies didn't get to experience firsthand the tradition and honor of scrubbing decks. It is a real honor, you know? Naval traditions are wonderful, ain't they?"

Parma dispersed the newbies among the squads of *Defiant*'s platoon of marines, pairing each of them with a more experienced soldier. Parma assigned John to a squad led by Corporal Umthaller, a woman of sharp angles and straight, rigid lines. She paired him up with a soldier named Sidewinder, a fellow with a buzz-cut of light-brown hair and a perpetual grin on his lips. For some reason, no one told John the man's real name, and the fellow had even replaced the stencil above his left breast pocket so it read SIDEWINDER. They even addressed him as "Private Sidewinder."

"We'll get you settled away," Sidewinder told John.

Ten days after they up-transited out of the Miriteen system, John received orders to report to the XO's office. His implants directed him up several decks to a stateroom door in officer's country. He knocked and was told to enter. He put on his best parade-ground technique, stepped through the door, snapped to attention and said, "Private First Class Mathius reporting as ordered, sir."

Commander Straus sat behind a small, fold down desk barely large enough to hold the terminal in front of him. He casually returned the salute and said, "At ease, Private."

John assumed the proper position, but he didn't feel at ease.

Straus looked at the terminal for several seconds, then looked John's way. "I've been doing this a long time," he said, "and when I look at a new soldier's record, I know how to read between the lines."

He nodded toward the terminal. "There's something missing here."

The man had neither asked a question, nor given an order, so John kept his silence.

"Where are you from, soldier?"

John knew he shouldn't lie, so he simply said, "Novalis III, sir."

Straus continued to stare at the screen in front of him as he said, "Got off planet before that atrocious mess happened, eh?"

John simply said, "No, sir."

Straus's eyebrows lifted and he looked away from the screen at John, but he showed no other sign of surprise. He stared at John for a long moment, then said, "I won't press you on the matter. You've got a good record, and good reports from your instructors. Have you decided yet which branch you want to enter?"

Naval Ops or Infantry; John pondered that for only a fraction of a second before saying, "I don't yet know, sir."

Straus pursed his lips and nodded slowly. "Hopefully, you'll know by the end of this year. You did well in the navigation classes, and it looks like you excel at some skills needed in Naval Ops, so we're going to expose you to a lot of stuff to see how you do."

John learned that each of the new soldiers had reported to the XO for a similar interview.

John trained and drilled with the marines, but they also apprenticed him at navigation and helm, though he knew it took years to qualify for a rating as a helmsman on a big transition ship. He learned quite a bit about interstellar navigation from Lieutenant Commander Forcis, a petite, little woman with a commanding personality.

While in transition they were almost completely blind, could detect only stellar masses or another ship in transition nearby, but only if that ship expended a lot of energy with a sharp maneuver. She taught him to take the limited data they could garner as they passed within a few light-years of a star, then compute a correction to keep them on course. She warned him that the error from calculations made while in transition slowly accumulated.

He was assisting Forcis at the navigation console on the bridge when they down-transited at the edge of Commonwealth space for a navigation check. She made him duplicate her efforts; they both separately retrieved nav data from the scan console, then computed a course correction to their desired destination, a relay buoy from which they could check in with Sector Operations Command.

She looked at his computations and frowned. John had a scan summary in the corner of one of his screens. She tapped a finger on the icon representing a nearby star and spoke impatiently, "Your new course would put us right in the middle of that solar mass."

John had learned that her impatient manner was not an indication of disapproval, merely her style. She then patiently walked him through her own calculations, and was in the process of pointing out his errors when the officer at the scan console said, "Skipper, I've got an incoming transition wake about five light-years out."

The bridge went silent. Forcis looked toward *Defiant*'s CO, Captain Franklin Garris, so John did likewise, though he had to lean to one side to see around their console and through the cramped confines of the bridge.

Garris said, "How hard are they driving?"

"About three thousand lights, sir."

Garris asked, "Pushing hard, eh? Kelk?"

The scan officer shook his head. "Too far out to get a good transition profile, sir. But they are coming from that direction."

Forcis leaned close to John and whispered, "Five light-years is about the extreme limit of our detection range for transition phenomena."

Garris said, "Nav?"

Forcis spoke, "About twelve hours out, sir."

Garris sat silent and unmoving for several seconds, then said, "Nav, Helm, cancel that up-transition. We're going to sit tight and see what's coming our way."

On the surface, the atmosphere on the bridge returned to normal, but John sensed an underlying tension. Forcis went back to explaining the errors in John's calculations, but John had trouble concentrating. About an hour later, she said, "That's enough, Private. Go get some shut-eye."

John hesitated. She noticed and her eyes narrowed. He said, "With your permission, ma'am, I'd like to be here when . . . whatever happens happens."

He'd never seen her smile before, but at that moment she gave him a broad grin. "We just might make a spacer out of you yet. Go down to mess, tell them you're on bridge watch and they'll feed you. Tell Parma the same thing, and get that shut-eye, then come back here in eight hours. If anything breaks before then, you'll hear from me."

John went to the galley and ate, then laid down on his bunk, but he had trouble falling asleep. He lay there, suspecting he wouldn't sleep at all, and his implants woke him up six hours later. He shaved, grabbed a quick shower, put on a fresh uniform, and returned to the bridge. The tension there had ratcheted up considerably, and the pretense of normalcy had completely disappeared.

Forcis showed him how the officer at the scan console had identified the transition profile of the incoming wake: an armed Kelk frigate.

"Scan," Captain Garris said, "what's our status?"

"They're a little over four hours out, sir, and they've been holding a steady course the entire time."

"Nav," Garris continued, "can we intercept? Can you get us on their tail about five hundred light-hours behind them?"

Forcis said, "I need a few minutes, sir."

"Granted."

Forcis worked frantically at her console, and didn't waste time trying to turn her efforts into a lesson for a young SecCorps private looking over her shoulder. When she finished, she looked up from her work and said, "It's going to be more like a thousand light-hours, sir, but we can do it. I can have a detailed intercept plan for you in about ten minutes."

Garris's lips curled upward in a grin that looked anything but pleasant. "Very good, Commander. Set it up."

Forcis went back to her frantic efforts, and as promised passed the detailed intercept plan to Garris, XO Straus, and the pertinent duty stations on the bridge and in engineering. Straus suggested a couple of changes, Garris approved, Forcis made them, and five minutes later *Defiant* was pushing her sublight grav drive to the limit on a vector perpendicular to that of the incoming Kelk frigate. The bridge then settled into its routine, and Forcis walked John through the plan and her calculations.

A half hour later they up-transited, though Forcis's intercept plan required them to start out at minimum sustainable transition velocity of fifty lights, and work their way slowly up to match the Kelk's velocity of three thousand lights.

Forcis told John, "That'll minimize our transition flare, make it less likely that Kelk man-of-war can spot us. They're blind right now, but if we maneuver too hard, or make any sudden changes, they'll spot the transition noise."

The Kelk's vector, if they held steady, would take them a little over one light-year to one side of *Defiant*'s original position. During the next three hours, for long stretches of time, not a sound could be heard on *Defiant*'s bridge as they closed that gap, and slowly arced around in a long, slow turn to match the Kelk's vector.

With a half hour to go, Captain Garris said, "Mr. Straus, sound General Quarters, Watch Condition Red."

A loud, irritatingly unpleasant horn burped once, was followed immediately by the steady clang of the alert klaxon. Straus spoke precisely over allship. "Watch Condition Red. All hands, this is not a drill. Repeat: this is not a drill." He repeated the message one more time.

John had seen and heard it all before in practice, but never before for real, and never before from the bridge. "Ma'am," he said to Forcis, "we're not at war, or anything, are we?"

"No," she said, and for once the impatience had left her voice. "But we don't know much about the Kelk, and frequently learn something from one of these maneuvers. This kind of thing goes on all the time and it never hurts to be cautious."

Once all stations had reported in, someone killed the alert klaxon, and the bridge went silent, as if everyone there held their collective breath.

Garris said, "Com, put me on allship."

The captain then carefully explained the situation to *Defiant*'s crew. He finished with, "No one is to fire on that ship without specific orders from Fire Control."

After he had finished on allship, Garris said, "Fire Control, keep a tight rein on your people. We don't need to start an interstellar war."

Forcis spoke softly to John. "We're not at war with the Supremacy, but there are many who don't like the Kelk, and might get a little trigger-happy. We have to be careful."

Ten minutes later, they settled in behind the frigate at a distance of just over nine hundred light hours.

Fire Control reported, "We've got a targeting solution, sir."

"Helm," Garris said. "See if you can close that gap a bit."

It took over two hours, but they slowly closed the gap to five hundred light-hours, then four hundred, with Fire Control constantly computing and recomputing targeting solutions. At that point, with *Defiant* deep within the Kelk's transition wake, gravity waves rolled through the ship on a regular basis, though they weren't yet as bad as John had experienced during training on the weapons platform. But then they cut the gap to three hundred light-hours, then two hundred, and finally one hundred, and John fought to keep from spilling the contents of his stomach all over the nav console. To take his mind off the nausea he did a quick calculation. If the Kelk miraculously came to a complete stop, they'd close that distance in 120 seconds.

The scan officer shouted, "They're maneuvering."

Garris snarled, "Come on Scan, you've got to give me more than that."

"I'm getting nothing but transition noise, sir, a lot of it. No, wait . . . they're decelerating hard."

Garris shouted, "All hands, crash-stop."

John had put summaries from several departments on his screen. In one, he watched the main power plant redline as *Defiant* pushed its systems to the limit, trying to decelerate from maximum transition velocity to down-transition in the shortest possible time.

Scan said, "They just down-transited."

"Helm, Engineering," Garris said, "get us into sublight . . . now."

A heavy gravity wave rolled through the bridge, and had John not been strapped into his seat it would have thrown him to the floor—*deck*, he reminded himself.

Scan said, "We just passed them, sir. They're behind us now and they . . . just up-transited."

Garris said, "Abort crash-stop. Helm, all ahead full. Firewall this boat and keep us ahead of them."

When calm returned to the bridge, *Defiant* and the Kelk frigate had traded places, with the Kelk now chasing *Defiant* some unknown number of light-hours behind them. Over the next six hours they traded places twice more, all the while computing targeting solutions. It proved to be a real lesson in diplomatic interactions with the Kelk Supremacy. It ended when both ships went into crash-stop, pushing their systems to the limit, and they both down-transited in almost the same instant.

"All stop," Garris said calmly. "Rig for silent running."

The hum of the ship's drive disappeared, and when they cut gravity, John's harness kept him strapped in his seat. He expanded the scan summary in the corner of one of his screens. The Kelk had shut down her drive as well, and both ships were coasting about a hundred light-hours apart.

Forcis leaned close to John and spoke softly. "That's their last known position based on transition noise. Now that we're both sublight, our drives are static, and our power plants close to idle, we don't have a transition wake and we're not making any transition noise. We and they are now both limited to velocity-of-light detection, so anything one of us sees of the other will be several hours old, and very hard to spot."

Garris ordered the Helm to accelerate on a vector perpendicular to their previous course. They brought the sublight grav drive up to ten gravities, a mere trickle of what it was capable of. An hour later they upped it to one hundred Gs. A few seconds after that, Scan reported, "I've got 'em, sir. They're pushing their grav drive a bit in sublight, and I'm getting a little transition noise."

Forcis said to John, "The error bars are now probably too large to compute a targeting solution. We're headed away from each other."

A minute later Fire Control confirmed that. "Too noisy to get a targeting solution, sir."

When *Defiant* and the Kelk frigate finally parted ways, John's shirt had more and bigger sweat stains than he'd had when Pleth had interrogated him about Novalis III. And while they and the Supremacy weren't at war, they had just played a very dangerous game, and he thought it quite foolish to toy with their luck that way. He never voiced that thought to anyone.

With the excitement over, they returned to normal shipboard routine, and John and his squad mates once again took up their training. When they entered orbit around a planet, if they stayed for any length of time, the marines took the opportunity to conduct ground exercises to help integrate the newbies. Along with the rest of the platoon, John and his squad mates from Miriteen practiced free orbital drops in nothing but heavy combat armor, air drops in light armor, and drops in which the boat settled into the DZ and they spilled out of it. Parma and the marine CO, Lieutenant Katherine Komisky, threw everything at them they could think of. They quickly integrated with their more experienced comrades and became part of the team.

Eight months after they joined the crew of *Defiant*, the ship down-transited for a nav fix. The bridge contacted a nearby relay buoy and received orders to proceed to the Vischas system. They were to rendezvous with the heavy cruiser *Wicked Fury* and a troopship carrying a company of Blacksword regulars, their mission to provide support to the new government on the planet Reisenar. John wondered if he might run into Hey-You, and thought a lot about her on the way there.

••••

The shuttle dropped down through the outer reaches of Reisenar's atmosphere, then leveled off at about ten thousand meters. Katrine looked out a window and watched the countryside roll past beneath her. She tuned her implants to a pickup in the bow of the shuttle, and saw the city of Helmanport in the distance as a jagged line on the flat horizon. But the shuttle dropped lower as they approached the outskirts of the city, and just at the edge of it the boat settled onto the grounds of the Commonwealth embassy. When the shuttle came to a stop in the embassy garage, a guard in a SecCorps uniform opened the shuttle hatch. As Katrine stepped out of it she almost saluted, but recalled at the last instant that she was playing civilian on this trip.

Inside the embassy, an aide led her immediately into the presence of Ambassador Starkman, a short fellow with close-cropped gray hair. He stood, and walked around from behind his desk. He dismissed the aide, then closed the door and turned to Katrine.

"Ms. Primatov," he said. "It's really Colonel Primatov, isn't it?"

She smiled and said, "To be precise, it's Lieutenant Colonel Primatov. But since I'm really not supposed to be here, we thought it best for me to adopt the guise of a commercial attaché."

Starkman smiled happily. "That was wise."

Only Starkman and the ranking ComSecCorps officer at the embassy were aware of her true identity. There were also some Blacksword assets in the city, but Starkman was wholly unaware of their existence, and she intended to keep it that way. An undercover Blacksword operative had accompanied her down on the shuttle, and he would shortly make contact with those assets. Then they too would know of her true identity, and be prepared to support her if need be.

"Now, Ambassador," she said. "I was given to believe that you have certain misgivings regarding Prime Minister Benkamil's request for our assistance. Can you tell me what it is that troubles you?"

Starkman appeared a bit uncomfortable. "I don't know that I would say it *troubles* me. That is perhaps too strong of a word. Something about the man just doesn't ring true. But it doesn't really matter, does it? We'll shortly have a company of your Blacksword soldiers down here to support us. I can't imagine we'll have any problems with them present."

18

Doesn't Add Up

NIKAELA'S SUPERIORS GAVE her command of a full platoon, one of four assigned to the First Liaison Company under the command of Senior Command Superior Thordahl, a small man with a pleasant smile. She noticed that her platoon had
quite a number of experienced veterans, and as a newly commissioned Command
Boss, Junior Rank, that surprised her. She had failed to graduate at the top of her
class, and had feared there might be other repercussions from the Novalis III tragedy. But if so, they had apparently forgiven her, or possibly they simply absolved her
of any responsibility. Then again, perhaps this was all a reward for keeping her
mouth shut, or maybe it was part of the lesson they wanted to teach her. All the pos-
sibilities made her head spin, so she stopped trying to speculate and decided to simply be grateful for her good fortune.

When she reviewed the records of the men and woman under her command, she
noticed that with the exception of a few rookies, many of them appeared to have blank
little gaps in their files that could be interpreted in any number of ways. Nikaela suspected that the benign name of First Liaison Company did not represent its true responsibilities.

Her platoon also included a very senior noncom, Oberseergent Beksalla Geltkarl,
an imposing woman of both physical stature and commanding demeanor. Nikaela
wanted to make a good impression with her.

When they first met, Nikaela said, "Oberseergent Geltkarl, I am honored to have
such an experienced NCO working with me. I hope you will help me avoid any obvious mistakes."

The woman had served the Supremacy for more than fifteen years. She smiled
pleasantly. "I will help wherever I can. But you would not be in charge of this platoon
if you hadn't demonstrated to our superiors that you are a capable officer, and know
how to lead ... with discretion. First Liaison Company often performs ... unusual
duties for the Larscom."

That statement confirmed Nikaela's suspicions about her new assignment. The next morning First Liaison Company boarded a destroyer on Viktorkinde Prime, and spent fifteen days in transit to a remote outpost near the edge of Supremacy space. From there they boarded *Reguskalde*, a fast heavy cruiser with reasonably good stealth capabilities. They transited to the Vischas system, where the cruiser parked in an orbit around the planet Reisenar while its boats shuttled First Liaison Company down to the surface. Since there were no enemy units in the neighborhood, they didn't have to exercise the stealth capabilities of the cruiser. But at the request of their hosts, they did heavily stealth the boats as they descended to Helmanport, Reisenar's capital city. They landed quietly under the cover of darkness with no fanfare or press coverage. Once they unloaded their gear, the boats returned to *Reguskalde*, and by prior agreement with the planetary government, the large cruiser up-transited out of the system and returned to the Supremacy.

In fact, known only to Thordahl, his officers, and a select few of their NCOs, *Reguskalde* did not leave the system. The cruiser spit out an easily detected burst of transition noise that anyone might reasonably think had been the flare from a ship making up-transition for interstellar transit. It then rigged for silent running, and remained at the edge of the Vischas system. It pleased Nikaela that her superiors demonstrated enough paranoia to allow them some backup.

Thordahl set up his headquarters in a two story building near Parliament House, and not far from the Prime Minister's residence. He stationed the other three platoons of First Liaison Company at strategic points in the city, but kept Nikaela and her platoon close at hand, instructing her to secure their headquarters and get an encrypted transition-com link established with *Reguskalde*. Nikaela suspected that Thordahl wanted to keep a close eye on his newest and most junior officer until she proved herself.

Thordahl had instructions to present himself to Prime Minister Benkamil. While the platoon checked out their equipment and swept their quarters for any monitoring devices, he, his XO, and Nikaela donned crisp, new uniforms, and presented themselves at the Prime Minister's residence. An aide ushered them into a sumptuous office, and as they stepped through the door, Benkamil rose from behind a massive desk.

The man wore a dark, conservatively cut business suit, over which he had donned a colorful and heavily decorated, floor-length robe open in the front; probably some sort of ceremonial attire. He stood quite tall, had piercing dark eyes, black hair and a carefully trimmed goatee. He swept around the desk with a dramatic flourish, the robe billowing out behind him as he crossed the room. He greeted Thordahl first, gripped him enthusiastically by the shoulders, then bobbed an air-kiss to either side of his face. Nikaela thought she detected a slight look of distaste on Benkamil's face, and she wondered if he, like so many, regretted the need to associate with his Kelk allies.

Thordahl introduced his XO, Command Superior Brynjar, and the fellow was forced to suffer the same treatment. This time she didn't detect the look of distaste. Perhaps she had been wrong, or perhaps Benkamil merely hid it well.

Thordahl introduced Nikaela. They had all been briefed on the customs on Reisenar. She braced herself and didn't flinch when Benkamil gripped her shoulders and did the air-kiss thing. She wasn't accustomed to strangers touching her in that way, and was thankful she didn't have to put up with actual cheek-to-cheek contact. The look of distaste had returned to the Prime Minister's face, but still faint and hard to detect, so Nikaela put the thought out of her mind.

With introductions complete, Benkamil had tea brought in, and they all sat down to chat amiably. They spoke for a good hour. Recent elections on the planet Reisenar had failed to anoint a clear winner among six political parties, so they had formed a delicate coalition from three of them. The pro-Congress party favored complete independence, but without a majority they were forced to form an alliance with a pro-Commonwealth and a pro-Kelk party. But a small number of individuals in a hard, right-wing faction had made their discontent known by taking up arms, and the newly elected planetary government had asked for assistance from the Supremacy.

Their orders instructed them to keep a low profile, to advise and support, and provide training to the local armed forces. They included no mention of delivering covert supplies to the locals, which pleased Nikaela greatly. She did not want to go through that again.

When they left, once out on the street and away from any prying ears and listening devices, Brynjar said, "I don't trust that man."

Thordahl said, "I don't trust any of them."

Two days later Geltkarl woke Nikaela at dawn. Their com tech had received an encoded message from *Reguskalde*. Two warships had appeared on the cruiser's screens about one AU from Reisenar. They had clearly been running silent, with all but essential systems shut down and their power plants on standby, making them undetectable at any distance beyond a few hundred thousand kilometers.

Reguskalde had detected them when they powered up and moved into position off Reisenar, settling into distant orbits about ten million kilometers from the planet, easy targeting range for big transition batteries or transition torpedoes. They had then disappeared from *Reguskalde*'s screens, obviously again running silent. Interestingly, they had emitted emission profiles quite like those of Kelk warships. But after careful analysis, *Reguskalde*'s crew concluded they were not Kelk.

Nikaela asked Geltkarl, "What do you think?"

The older woman shook her head. "*Reguskalde*'s crew knows what they're doing. If they say they're fake, then they're fake. And the Larscom would not do that to us. Those warships are not Kelk."

Nikaela had been thinking exactly the same thing.

When they reported the information to Thordahl, as an obvious test he asked Nikaela, "What orders will you give your platoon?"

The barracks to which they'd been assigned was a small two-story building. She said, "Post armed guards at all entrances to this building. Put a couple of lookouts on the roof, and tell everyone to be ready to don full combat armor on a moment's notice. I'd also put some tracking monitors in the second floor windows, along with rocket launcher teams. They can track anything incoming and compute a ballistic trajectory back to its source, then respond with extremely good accuracy. And have a couple of mortar teams ready to set up on the roof quickly if we do take fire."

Thordahl said, "Why not armor up and deploy the mortars now?"

"Those on the roof can be easily spotted," she said, "either by aerial reconnaissance, or from the roofs of buildings taller than this one. No one will pay attention to lookouts, but if they see us setting up fire teams on the roof, they'll know we're getting information we shouldn't be getting. That might tip our hand. Did I miss anything, maestra?"

Geltkarl nodded and smiled, then said, "Until further notice, I recommend we eat only rations we brought with us. No food prepared by anyone else."

"Excellent idea," Nikaela said. "But let's accept the foreign food, pretend we're eating it, but have our people analyze it, then dump it somewhere. If it's supposed to affect us in some way, they'll just think the crazy Kelk monsters are immune to their poisons. No sense in tipping our hand."

Geltkarl smiled. "Mistress Vreekande, somehow I knew you and I would get along quite nicely."

Thordahl nodded his approval and said, "Do it."

Nineteen days later they received another coded message from *Reguskalde*. The Commonwealth had entered the system in force.

••••

With the difficulties on Reisenar, the newly elected planetary government had asked the Commonwealth to step in. Prime Minister Benkamil felt that a show of force, a visible presence with boots on the ground, would quell the unrest without the need for violence. ComSec Command wanted to appease the new government's fears and felt that such a display wouldn't hurt, so with some reservations, they agreed.

Intelligence reports indicated that the insurgents were well equipped, but they didn't have any weaponry that could penetrate powered armor. John and his comrades from *Defiant*, along with the marine contingent from *Wicked Fury*, were given the task of keeping the embassy secure, while the company of Blacksword soldiers from the troopship patrolled the streets. It should be a tenday or two of easy duty; a milk run for the new soldiers' first real drop.

John glanced up and down the row of SecCorps troops seated next to him in the drop boat. They cut gravity on *Defiant*'s Hangar Deck and John's stomach rose up into his throat. A moment later the pilot of their drop boat activated its internal gravity fields, and he felt as if his stomach had been hammered down into his bowels.

Allship blared through his implants, "Orbital stabilization in ten minutes and counting. Drop injection to follow immediately."

Opposite him and a few seats down, Carla sat with her back rigid and straight, her eyes wide and round. Leeze Caputto sat next to her, looking just as frightened. Carla looked at him, gulped fearfully and opened up a private line through her implants. She spoke with a tremble in her voice, "I'm scared. I thought the VCSs were supposed to give me all this fucking confidence and eliminate newbie jitters. I don't feel confident. I feel like shit."

Their first live-fire drop facing an armed enemy, and she should be scared, but John didn't say that. "Me too," he said, though his voice didn't break the way hers had.

Seated next to him, Roark's eyes appeared to focus on some distant point, something much farther away than the opposite wall of the inside of the drop boat. If John had to guess, Roark would be the one to freeze.

"This is a milk-run, people," Parma bellowed. "Or at least that's what intel says. But intel's been wrong before, so if you want to stay alive, keep your eyes and ears open, and assume the worst. It's gonna be a compensated drop all the way down, so no hi-gee necessary."

As part of their training, the young soldiers had been exposed to hi-gee just to see how they handled it. The high-gravity compensation drug affected some people with a slight, euphoric high, and some with a little nausea, but John had felt nothing.

John scanned the row of troopers seated across from them. Their squad leader, Corporal Umthaller, looked bored. He now knew her well enough to know the expression she wore on her face belied the fact that she didn't miss anything.

Roark nudged him with an armored elbow. "Why aren't you scared like all the rest of us?"

John looked into Roark's eyes and tried to speak with confidence, but his voice still came out strained. "I am scared."

That was the truth, though he had to examine his own doubts to understand why. During his first real patrol with the rebels on Novalis III, they had given him an empty rifle, and Cranoch had been behind him ready to blow his head off if he didn't obey every order to the letter. It occurred to John that the bastard had provided a kind of bolster to his courage that got him through that first time. But experience did not lessen the dread, probably because he knew what to expect from the enemy, had witnessed first-hand the pain, and seen the finality of violent death. His gut churned with fear, but he managed to find calm in his thoughts, perhaps because, unlike the rest of them, he knew what to expect of himself. He was no grand hero, but he knew for a certainty that he would not let his comrades down. Possibly, Roark saw past the fear in John's gut to the calm certainty in his thoughts. However, none of them knew of his experiences on Novalis III, and he was not about to enlighten them.

John shrugged. "We'll do okay." He nodded and added, "You'll do okay."

Roark grimaced and spoke through gritted teeth. "They'll do okay." He nodded toward a couple of the more experienced soldiers. "I'm shitting my pants."

John grinned. "Even without Senior DI Prescott's orders to do so?"

Apparently, Carla had been listening to them. She let out a short bark of a laugh.

John's implants chimed with an allship message from the bridge. "Standby for up-transition."

A virtualized telltale near the bottom of John's vision flickered, telling him *Defiant* had up-transited and was maneuvering in-system to a position off Reisenar.

"Visors down," Parma said, "and seal 'em up."

John dropped the visor on his combat armor. His ears popped as the plast suit ran an automatic pressure check.

A small square in the upper-right corner of John's visor blackened and his suit computer displayed a stylized image of a suit of armor colored in green. A readout next to it told him the core of his reactor pack carried a full charge, enough energy to take out several city blocks if released explosively, though failsafes in the reactor pack would prevent that from happening.

"Computer," he said. "Status, physical, execute." The display on the inside of his visor changed to the silhouette of a naked man, all green with blotches of yellow on his left shoulder and thigh.

He said, "Computer, only class-three injuries or worse."

The blotches of yellow disappeared. The suit no longer displayed the minor bruises he'd picked up a few days ago in hand-to-hand combat drills.

John's implants spoke in Parma's voice. "Full pre-combat check, people."

John said, "Computer, status, global, execute."

The inside of his visor flashed a detailed summary of his armor status: reactor pack levels and reserves; seal conditions; minor malfunctions flagged for repair at the next overhaul; maintenance status and schedules; his first-aid reserves, which consisted primarily of drugs. It then began a full systems self-test.

He paid particular attention to his reactor pack reserves. In their initial orientation to powered combat armor, the young soldiers had been warned that without energy from the reactor pack to reinforce it, the plast shell encasing them could protect them only from low velocity projectiles. It required copious amounts of power to deflect high-velocity rounds like those his grav rifle could spit.

His suit finished the pre-combat check with nothing more than a few minor maintenance issues that it flagged for repair at the next overhaul. For a moment he had hoped that it would find something serious and scrub him from the mission, but he would have been ashamed and disappointed at that.

"Down-transition," the bridge said. "Stable orbit in two minutes."

Parma bellowed, "Pawlski," the name of a soldier John barely knew. "Stand down. Your drop status is null."

The trooper's suit must have found something more serious at the last minute and reported it on the command grid. He'd remain in the drop boat while his comrades took up positions on the embassy grounds, then return with it to *Defiant* to enact repairs.

"As I told you," Parma continued. "We drop to the surface, form up and secure the perimeter of the embassy grounds. Keep your armor powered, and do not fire your weapon unless you have absolutely no other choice. We're there purely to protect the embassy and its staff, while our Blacksword friends are going to walk around the city looking real tough and mean."

The Commonwealth embassy had been established on an estate on the outskirts of Helmanport. It consisted of an old mansion with several outbuildings situated on wide open grounds, no wall or enclosure to hinder an attacking force. Hopefully, that wouldn't be a problem.

The pilot said, "Stable orbit and ejection in fifty seconds."

John tapped into an external view from the front of the boat, and thought-keyed it for display on the inside of his visor. It showed the open main hatch on Hangar Deck, a background of black space with just the edge of a reddish-brown globe showing in one corner. In the distance John spotted a glint from something in orbit nearby. An outboard scan summary in the lower right corner of the inside of his visor confirmed that it must have been sunlight reflecting off the troop ship's hull. *Wicked Fury* appeared as another blip on the inside of his visor.

On the scan summary a drop boat emerged from the troop ship, floating for a moment just beyond the ship's hull, drifting away slowly. Then its pilot fired up its grav drive and it sliced diagonally across the inside of John's visor. Another boat appeared and followed it, then two more. A boat also emerged from *Wicked Fury*. John thought about Hey-You.

At that point their boat's hull echoed with a metallic clang and the image in his visor ratcheted sideways as Hangar Deck Crew locked their boat to the ejection boom. A moment of silence and stillness, then their boat rushed forward and the docking boom expelled them into the blackness of space.

Milk run, John told himself. *Milk run.*

19

Milk Run

AS THEIR BOAT dropped through a light cloud cover in the outer reaches of Rei-senar's atmosphere, John felt the tension in Roark seated beside him, and he thought of Carla's earlier words about being scared. Leeze hadn't said anything, but she didn't look all that confident either. He keyed a private circuit to the three of them and said, "Just a milk run, nothing to worry about."

Roark said, "You don't sound like you believe that."

"Yah," Carla said. "I was waiting for you to add a *but* to the end of that sentence."

Leeze held her silence.

"You heard Parma," John said. "He wouldn't lie to us." Even John heard the doubt in his tone. "But do what he said: assume the worst and be ready for it. It never hurts to think that way."

The boat descended rapidly at thirty Gs, the maximum at which the pilot could maintain internal gravity compensation. Above that, John and his platoon mates would feel the jolt and sway as the pilot turned and maneuvered the vessel.

John couldn't see the other boats on visual, so he enlarged the scan summary, which showed the blips of four boats from the troop ship, a full Company, plus the lone blip of *Wicked Fury*'s boat. The troop ship's orbital velocity had strung them out in a line, each boat separated from the next by twenty kilometers. But as they dropped toward Helmanport, the pilots broke that formation to descend toward pre-determined drop zones.

Watching the precision with which the pilots maneuvered their crafts, the strange dance of the blips on his visor mesmerized John and helped him forget his fears. He looked at the blip of Hey-You's drop boat on the inside of his visor. After a year of active duty they'd all return to Miriteen for supplemental command training. He hoped she and he would rekindle their relationship, though a year could be a long time and either of them might have—

"Incoming."

The shout on the command circuit snapped John's attention back to the scan summary. One of the boats blossomed into a bright red smear, telling him it had taken a direct hit from ground fire.

"Where the hell did they get advanced shit like that?" someone shouted.

The pilot of John's boat spoke calmly, "Going to max, evasive maneuvering."

He firewalled the grav drive to forty Gs, and with the boat unable to compensate above the thirty G limit, John felt the differential of ten Gs pressing him into his seat. His suit automatically flooded his system with hi-gee to keep him conscious. Next to him Roark giggled, one of the side effects some troopers felt.

An icon flashed on the inside of John's visor, signaling an incoming message from *Defiant*. "Hostile action, multiple ship engagement, possible Kelk involvement."

"You know what that means, people," Parma said. "They got their hands full up there and we're on our own. Keep it tight and minimize reactor pack drain. Save it so you got something to dish out when the time comes."

One of the boats from the troop ship blossomed into a fireball, but didn't disintegrate like the first, though it skewed heavily to one side and dropped out of formation.

"Fucking milk run my ass," Carla said.

Roark said nothing, but John noticed his hands trembling. Through his implants he heard shouts of, ". . . incoming . . . evasive maneuvering . . ."

By the time they reached the turnover point, their boat sliced through the atmosphere at well over orbital velocity, its hull screaming as it cut an ionization trail toward the ground. John's suit muffled the noise to a faint background growl, but he felt every jerk and bump as the pilot maneuvered the craft toward their designated drop zone.

The scream of the hull suddenly declined to a low-level background; their velocity had dropped below that necessary to form a superhot plasma around the hull of the boat. The pilot cut the acceleration back below the threshold where the boat could compensate, and all sensation of motion disappeared. Then the boat lurched heavily to one side and John's suit muffled the sound of a loud whomp. The boat shook and jerked spasmodically, and the fact that John felt the motion meant it had taken damage and something had gone very wrong.

Their pilot barked over the command circuit, "Initiating abandon ship sequence . . . three . . . two . . . one."

Explosive bolts fired, and the cargo hatch in the aft belly of the boat tumbled away, showing them wispy yellow clouds in a sky with a little too much red in it. The way the clouds moved rapidly through the narrow field of view in the open hatch told John the boat had gone into a tumble. Servos whined, and John felt the sideways push of a gravity field accelerating him and his platoon mates, in their seats, toward the open hatch. Then he flashed through it and into the wide open sky. A staccato sequence of explosive pops disintegrated the clasps on his seat harness, and it fell away from him.

He had inherited the tumble of the boat, but his suit's automated stabilization kicked in and got him into an upright position about three thousand meters off the ground. Then the tumbling boat slammed into him, and the jarring collision sent him to the edge of consciousness. His suit fed him a dose of combat kikker which sent his heart pounding up into his throat, but his thinking cleared.

The sky shot past above, followed by the city, then the sky again, then the city. The back of his combat harness had snagged on a jagged remnant of one of the blown hinges, pinning his backside to the belly of the boat next to the gaping hole of the cargo hatch. Debris sprayed wildly out of the opening, driven by centrifugal force as the craft tumbled and spun and spiraled out of control toward the buildings below.

He gripped the side of the open hatch, tugged and pulled, grunting with the effort, trying to climb along the skin of the boat and dislodge the snagged harness. With the ground rocketing toward him he didn't have time to retrieve a knife or tool and cut it loose, and learned quickly that he didn't have the strength to overcome the forces pinning him to the belly of the boat. Then another surface-to-air rocket disintegrated the boat around him.

Consciousness seemed a distant memory. His suit said, "Initiating nerve jacker hyperdose."

He slammed to full consciousness and screamed as every muscle in his body triggered spasmodically and his nerves lit up like fire. "Fifteen hundred meters to impact," his suit said.

The armor had protected him through the collision with the boat, through the wild ride stuck to its belly, and the second rocket impact, but a series of red emergency warnings flashed across the inside of his visor, and the suit had trouble stabilizing him a second time.

He killed the automated systems and went into freefall, still trying to shake off the effect of the jackers. He spread his arms and legs and used air-drag to stabilize in a flat position. The tumble of the boat had smeared his platoon mates across the open sky, then carried him even farther away from his comrades. He could now only locate them as blips on the inside of his visor. Five hundred meters away, one of them exploded in a fireball. He selfishly hoped it wasn't Roark, Carla, Leeze, or Hey-You.

"Reactor pack cells two and three heavily damaged," his computer said. "Initiating jettison sequence—"

"Abort," he screamed. With his gravity fields gobbling power, he needed those cells regardless of their condition. "Override, override, override."

He tried the suit's stabilization systems one more time, but that sent him into a spin. He killed the automated systems, stabilized again in free-fall, and went to full manual, all the while his suit nagging him with warnings that the fucking reactor pack cells were about to go critical and smear him in little bits and pieces across the sky. He tucked his knees into his chest, got his feet beneath him, and fed power to his suit's gravity field generators.

"Reactor pack cells two and three approaching critical—"

"Shut the fuck up," he screamed as he wobbled on full manual, but they'd practiced this a dozen times and he finally gained control at about a thousand meters.

His suit said, "*Shut the fuck up* is not a recognized command sequence. But . . ."

He ignored it, felt an imbalance in the gravity fields emitted by his suit, so he compensated and stabilized further, steadily decreasing his drop velocity as he rocketed toward an unpleasant meeting with the ground. He got his drop rate under control at about a hundred meters, aimed for the flat roof of a two-story building, and slammed down onto the center of it. Luckily, he didn't punch through the roof and into the floors below, but the force of the landing sent him into a tumble.

"Reactor pack cells are experiencing energy density overload—"

He rolled with the tumble, came up running and shouted, "Now you can jettison the fucking things."

Knowing what to expect, he put everything he had into a sprint across the flat top of the building. Four strides before reaching the edge of the roof, two loud pops told him his suit had dumped the two damaged cells and he'd left them behind. He triggered his gravity fields just as he hit a knee-high facade surrounding the perimeter of the roof, planted one boot on it and leapt, using his gravity fields to keep him from falling to the busy street below, and his momentum to carry him across to the next building.

He had a brief moment in which he looked down upon a busy downtown street jammed with traffic, two accidents blocking a broad avenue and bringing all surface transport to a stop, civilians rushing about in a panic and screaming at each other. And then about ten meters before he finished the long jump to the other building, the reactor pack cells he'd dumped behind him blew, and a wall of smoke, flame and broken concrete slammed into his back.

It actually helped a little by adding to his momentum, though he hit the roof of the building going much too fast. He went down hard, bounced and tumbled, and would have broken his neck had his armor not protected him. He skidded across the roof, slammed up against the knee-high façade surrounding its perimeter and came to a stop as debris from the exploding cells peppered the roof around him. Lying in the shadow of the façade he froze, waited for anyone or anything to react to his presence, but the roof appeared deserted.

He lay there for several seconds listening to the sounds of distant blasts and gunfire in the city surrounding him. He'd lost his assault rifle somewhere between his ejection from the boat and landing on the flat roof of a two story building. But he still had his grav pistol, so he unclipped it from his thigh plate, and rose carefully to his hands and knees, wanting very much to avoid providing a silhouette the Kelk could target on, or whoever had ambushed them.

"Reactor pack reserves badly depleted," his suit said. "Integrity check on remaining cells one and four is positive. Cells are functioning properly, though full maintenance check is recommended."

He almost said, *Fuck the maintenance check*, though he was getting really tired of the way he couldn't piss off the damn computer, no matter what he said, or how he said it. And he knew, *Fuck you*, wouldn't work any better.

He struggled to his knees, still bent over in a crouch and keeping a low profile, and quickly scanned the roof around him. He saw some climate control ducting, and a lone door set in an angular structure that probably opened onto a stairway leading down to the lower floors. The buildings nearby stood the same height as his, and he didn't see anyone on top of them. He glanced up into the sky, saw the last few of his comrades descending toward the ground, the nearest one several hundred meters distant and tumbling badly.

He tried the command circuit but it was overloaded with everyone shouting at once. The inside of his visor should be covered with green blips, giving him the location of his comrades, but all he saw there were sporadic flashes.

He heard sirens and horns blaring all around him, so he rose up slightly and peaked over the façade lining the perimeter of the roof, conscious that even exposing just his helmet above its protection could get him killed. Below him the chaos in the street continued unabated, and it appeared to be blocked by the two accidents, creating a gridlocked jam of surface vehicles for as far as he could see.

A new sun blossomed in the sky overhead, and the street below went silent. "Extra-atmospheric detonation," his suit computer said. "Altitude in excess of three hundred kilometers. Yield strength unknown."

Another sun blossomed well outside the atmosphere. Someone up there was throwing around a lot of big warheads, and he hoped it was *Defiant* and *Wicked Fury* doing the throwing and not the receiving. In any case, he didn't think he could count on any help from the two ships.

He crawled on his hands and knees to about three meters away from the edge of the roof, then, confident that he couldn't be seen from below, stood and crossed to the other side. A few meters from the edge he crouched down again and approached it slowly.

The building across the street where he had jettisoned the two cells had partially collapsed, and a roaring fire billowed out of two windows near the corner on the second floor. Half the second floor had tumbled into the first, and rubble filled the street.

The detonation from the two cells had been dirty and inefficient, with a lot of energy going into heat instead of explosive shock, otherwise the cells might have taken out more than just that one building.

He crawled a few meters away from the edge, stood and trotted in a crouch to the angular structure containing the door to the stairwell. He considered descending to the ground floor, but thought it wise to wait for the chaos in the streets to subside.

Bright sun in the slightly pinkish sky cast a strong shadow on one side of the structure containing the stairwell door. His suit had only the most rudimentary stealth capability, so he sat down in the shade, hoping it would provide some protection from observation if the enemy flew by overhead. He could only hope that *Defiant* and *Wicked Fury* would soon take care of the Kelk and return to provide fire support from orbit.

If it was the Kelk? The message from *Defiant* had said, "*. . . possible* Kelk involvement." He wished he knew for a certainty what enemy they faced, but at that moment he could be sure of nothing.

He took stock of his situation. Gravity field generators gobbled power like there was no tomorrow. Omuglu had warned them, "Don't go jump happy and start hopping around on your gravity fields. You won't have any power left for your armor when you need it most."

For a planned drop of more than a few thousand meters they carried extra cells for the descent and dumped them when they hit dirt. The unplanned emergency drop had badly cut into his reactor pack reserves, and jettisoning the two damaged cells had left him with a bare minimum to function. He'd lost his rifle, but he still had his sidearm, and his combat harness carried a selection of grenades and micro-nukes. But he'd made it down in one piece, and the most important properties of his armor still functioned properly. He'd have to be careful about the damage to his automated stability systems, but he could live with that. He needed to find his platoon mates, if they still lived.

He pulled up the mapping system in his suit comp, but it warned him, "Telemetry feed is sporadic due to possible suit damage. Location services may need dead-reckoning calibration."

Information provided by the locals frequently proved inaccurate or out of date, sometimes by design, so ComSec never depended on such data. Following standard procedure, *Wicked Fury* had topographically mapped the city from orbit and recorded key monuments, bridges, structures and buildings. Then she had dumped a couple dozen mini-satellites into a GPS grid around Reisenar, but his suit was apparently having trouble getting a down-link from them.

He triggered the command circuit and flagged his message for delivery when possible, "This is Private John Mathius, third squad, *Defiant*. I'm somewhere in the city, but suit damage is preventing me from getting a solid coordinate fix. No injuries, but

I'm extremely low on reactor pack reserves. My suit remains unbreached, but I'm experiencing some functional difficulties. Haven't had time to do a full systems check yet, will check in when I do."

He rested his sidearm in his lap, sat back against the wedge-shaped stairwell structure and tried to relax. The sun sat low on the horizon, and with his system still strung out on the jackers and kikkers, he knew he wouldn't sleep.

Could they really be facing some sort of Kelk assault? But the Supremacy had never before assaulted Commonwealth troops head-on. They'd always—

His com came to life. "Mathius, Parma here, do you read?"

"Sergeant," he said. "Good to hear from you."

"I got your message, Private, but we're not getting a telemetry feed from your suit, so we don't have your location. How bad off are your reserves?"

John keyed up a display of his reserves on his visor. "Enough to power my armor and keep me from taking hurt, as long as I don't get into an extended fire fight."

"Then don't fire unless you have to. We can't send a boat out for you. They've got the airspace pretty well blanketed, and we'd just lose another boat. Keep your head low and try to make your way to the embassy. We're reassembling there."

"Will do, Sergeant."

They signed off.

A clock overlaid in the corner of the inside of John's visor told him he had about an hour before nightfall. He decided to wait in his shadow for darkness, and for the chaos in the streets to subside.

20

High Ground

WITH THE COMING of a moonless night, the city had completely shut down. Crouched near the edge of the roof of their building, Nikaela scanned the streets around them. An eerie silence had settled over the city, broken only by the occasional pop of distant gunfire. With four potentially hostile warships dominating Reisenar's nearspace, they had decided not to attempt to get through to *Reguskalde* with their transition com. If one of those ships detected any transmitter splash, it could provide a nice homing beacon for a big transition battery. For all intents and purposes, they were now on their own.

Someone had set up a grid of missile emplacements that completely dominated the airspace over the city, and once the shooting had started there had no longer been any need for Nikaela and her comrades to conceal their distrust and caution. They had all donned full combat armor, then set up the mortars, rocket launchers and tracking monitors on the roof. They had commandeered a couple of police grav cars and a large grav truck from the parliamentary garage. The vehicles weren't really flight worthy, but when pushed they could ascend high enough to float over most of the cars, busses and trucks clogging the streets. They would come in handy to ferry troops around if need be.

As Nikaela scanned the rooftops of the buildings around them, Oberseergent Geltkarl dropped to one knee beside her. "Is there anything to see, mistress?"

"No," Nikaela said. "The city is locked up tight. It's as quiet as a tomb out there."

"If you please, mistress," Geltkarl said. "Thordahl wants us below. Brynjar just got back from Parliament House, and Maestra Thordahl wants to discuss our options."

Nikaela turned to one of the unterseergents in charge of a squad. "Did you hear that, Unterseergent?"

He nodded. "If anything breaks, mistress, you'll hear right away."

Nikaela followed Geltkarl down to a small office on the second floor where Thordahl and Brynjar waited for them in the dark near a window. As they entered the room, Nikaela and the noncom retracted the visors on their helmets, a courtesy for this kind of discussion. The two men turned away from the window and retracted their visors.

Thordahl said to Brynjar. "Tell them what you just told me."

The XO's eyes flashed an angry red as he said, "Parliament House is almost as quiet as the city, only a few clerks and some low-level functionaries about. I did manage to speak with Benkamil's secretary, and she put me in touch with the Prime Minister by land line. He and the rest of the government have gone into hiding outside the city. They're scared, and worried there might be a popular uprising, so he asked that we keep our platoons in place."

Thordahl asked, "Do you trust that man?"

Brynjar grinned. "He and the top people in the government left the city long before the shooting started, which I find suspect."

Thordahl nodded thoughtfully. "I do wish we could get our hands on him."

Brynjar's grin broadened into a sneer. "I left one of our best people there with the secretary. I told her he's there to ensure her safety so she can help us communicate with the Prime Minister again if something urgent comes up. With all the unknown dangers in the streets right now, she was greatly relieved."

Thordahl and Geltkarl both smiled and nodded. Nikaela's confusion must have been visible on her face, because Brynjar added, "She knows his location; I'm sure of it. One word from us, and our man will bring her in so we can question her. Then we'll go and take Prime Minister Benkamil into protective custody. And we'll ask him some very pointed questions."

Nikaela couldn't help but smile, though her thoughts returned to the two warships with emissions profiles faked up to look like Kelk ships. Like Geltkarl and Thordahl, she didn't believe for a minute they were actually Kelk, especially since *Reguskalde*'s crew had determined their profiles had enough discrepancies to eliminate that possibility.

"Those mystery warships," she said, "could they be one of the opposition parties?"

Brynjar frowned uncertainly. "I asked Benkamil that, and he said none of them have the wherewithal to fund warships on their own, that all six parties would have to band together and pool their funds for that. And they can't be in the same room with each other without starting a war, so I doubt it. That does agree with our intelligence reports."

Thordahl said, "What about one of the other nearby independent systems? The Heraclean Hegemony, Sarkovie, someone like that?"

Brynjar frowned uncomfortably. "It's possible, but they too would have to cooperate, and they're no better than the fractured Reisenar political parties. The most obvious candidate is always the most likely."

Geltkarl said what they were all thinking. "The Commonwealth?"

Brynjar sighed heavily. "Benkamil told me the Commonwealth is quite unsettled by their improved relations with us, and has dropped veiled hints that they might intervene if it goes any further. He says they've been rather heavy-handed lately."

Nikaela said, "But would they kill their own people like that? We saw one drop boat completely destroyed."

Thordahl closed his eyes and lowered his head. "That kind of thing has been done before, an empty drop boat with an autonomous AI pilot. No one hurt or killed, but a very dramatic show for everyone to witness."

Nikaela said. "How do you know that? Who would do that?"

Thordahl lifted his chin, opened his eyes and his brow furrowed. Brynjar lifted one eyebrow, while Geltkarl wouldn't meet Nikaela's gaze.

"Oh," Nikaela said. "We have, haven't we?"

Thordahl spoke in a flat monotone. "Look at who has the most to gain from this. Two mysterious Kelk warships attack Reisenar and their Commonwealth allies. They're repelled, and the difficulties on Reisenar are attributed to Kelk aggression, so the Commonwealth steps in to subdue the unrest by taking control of the Vischas system. It prevents the locals from allying with us, and brings another system into the Commonwealth. And it fits with the rather aggressive expansion plans they've exhibited in this sector for the past few years."

Brynjar sounded tired when he said, "And they can claim to their citizenry that they were not the aggressor."

Nikaela's thoughts raced from one possibility to another. The Kelk were not at war with the Commonwealth, though interactions in the field all too often ended up in an exchange of gunfire. And such misunderstandings had occurred more frequently of late. Both sides had made attempts at establishing some sort of diplomatic relationship, but they had failed miserably, and the two powers seemed to be edging their way toward the inevitability of interstellar war. Sadly, the conclusion her superiors had just drawn seemed all too probable.

Thordahl's head nodded up and down almost imperceptibly for several seconds, his eyes focused on a distant thought. "We can't take any chances."

He turned to Nikaela. "Mistress Vreekande, with Oberseergent Geltkarl's assistance, I want you to assemble two squads of our best people. Those Commonwealth troops are scattered all over the city. If we detect any of them in small numbers, be prepared to go after them. Kill if need be, but try to capture if possible. We need information, and I would dearly like to question one of them."

To all of them he said, "We will not fire first, but if we are fired upon, we will respond and defend ourselves with whatever is required, including lethal offensive action, if need be. Spread the word, and let's get a message out to the other platoons."

••••

Lights on the streets below cast enough illumination for John to see reasonably well on the rooftop, and he didn't have to expose himself by using his helmet lamps. He still had trouble getting any data from the GPS grid, so his implants could only guide him by dead-reckoning, estimating that he had about a five-kilometer hike to the embassy on the east side of the city. If he got lucky, he'd come across some of his comrades on the way. The Blacksword soldiers from the troop ship had targeted drop zones more toward the center of the city, so John and the platoons from the two warships were on their own on the east side.

He climbed to his feet next to the angular structure on the roof, and found the door to the stairwell locked. His kit included several micro-nukes, but he never considered using one to blow the door. That kind of noise could attract attention from half way across the city. He could jump off the roof and make a controlled descent on gravity fields, but the damage to his automated stability systems bothered him, and he didn't know what he'd be jumping into. In any case, the damn gravity generators gobbled copious amounts of power that he couldn't afford to expend. No, it would have to be the stairway, but before opening the stairwell door, he needed to recon the streets around him.

He stayed low and walked the perimeter of the roof. The traffic accidents hadn't been cleared away and still blocked the street. It appeared many of the motorists had been forced to abandon their vehicles, leaving them parked haphazardly in the middle of the broad avenue. He considered the possibility that some of the motorists had been stranded there, and might be spending the night in their vehicles.

An alley on one side of the building remained relatively clear. He saw what looked like a couple of large trash receptacles at the far end, and a car parked at the other end near the entrance to the street. Directly beneath him a lamp illuminated the alley, and underneath it he saw a dark, rectangular shadow that must be the recess to a doorway. He'd much rather exit the building into the alley than directly onto the street.

He lay down and watched the alley for any movement, any hint he might step into danger, but all remained silent and still. The city contained a wealth of energy sources and hot spots, masking any IR signature he might pick up with a forest of false positives. But while that might work against him, it could also work in his favor, masking his own signature and reducing the situation to the simple common denominator of who spotted the other's movement first. He had honed those reflexes back on Novalis III, and knew that game well.

After a half hour with no movement or sign of danger in the alley below, he crawled back a few meters from the edge of the roof and rose to a crouch. He crossed to the stairwell door, and there he retrieved a power knife from his kit. He switched it on and it hummed for a second.

He inserted the power knife's blade into the gap between the door and its frame, then sliced downward past the lock. It made a momentary screech as it severed the locking bolt and he cringed at the sound. He stepped to one side, put his back against the structure, and waited. There came no response to the noise, no outcry or any reaction.

As he opened the door it squeaked on its hinges. Safety lighting illuminated the stairway nicely. He crept down the stairs slowly, listening for any sound to indicate he wasn't alone, and reached the ground floor without incident.

The alley he'd spied from above ran along the back of the building, and he found a hallway that led that way. He'd gone only a few paces down its length when he heard the faint sound of muffled voices. He disengaged the safety on his grav pistol and moved forward with more caution.

The voices grew louder as he walked, though still muffled and indistinct. Half way down the hall he stopped at a closed door and listened carefully, heard two or three people talking behind it, but couldn't make out their words. He concluded he had come upon some civilians trapped in the city by the chaos, and would probably run into more as he worked his way toward a rendezvous with his comrades at the embassy. He reengaged the safety on his grav gun and walked past the door.

The hall ended in a sharp right turn beyond which he found another corridor with several doors on the right and one lone doorway on the left. Those on the right were probably offices or storage rooms, while that on the left had an exit sign above it.

It unlocked easily from the inside with the turn of a latch. He opened the door a crack and peered out into the alley. He waited several seconds and saw nothing through the narrow opening, so he opened the door fully, but remained in the shadow of its recess. He leaned out just the faintest bit and looked up and down the alley.

He waited for five minutes and again nothing happened, so he stepped out of the door recess and moved cautiously toward the end of the alley and the automobile parked there. He approached it and glanced inside. To his relief, he found it unoccupied.

He glanced up the street. Any one of the abandoned cars could conceal danger, though his armor would most likely prove invulnerable to anything a civilian might carry. But that was a hazard his instructors had hammered into them repeatedly. Wrapped in powered combat armor, it was all too easy to feel invincible without even realizing it. Omuglu had told them, "And that's when some asshole gives you a nasty surprise. Always assume the worst, and don't get over confident."

A sun blossomed in the night sky lighting up the street, and appearing even brighter than those he'd seen earlier during the day. "Extra-atmospheric detonation," his suit computer said. "Estimated altitude at one thousand kilometers. Yield strength unknown." Whatever they had stumbled into had turned into an extended battle.

"Insurgents, my ass," he said to himself.

John waited for the burst of light to die down, then headed east up the street, moving from shadow to shadow as he'd done on Novalis III.

••••

Whenever the crack of weapons fire broke the stillness of the night, John stopped and listened carefully, hoping to get some idea of the direction from which the sounds had come. He thought it safe to assume that if he located the source of the gunfire, he would find ComSecCorps comrades, or he'd find enemy combatants fighting his comrades. One way or the other he would locate friendlies to team up with. But the buildings around him, while no more than two to four stories high, reflected and echoed the sounds, making it impossible to determine direction, and dashing any hope of using that tactic to join up with his fellow soldiers.

For the most part the streets were deserted, but occasionally he spotted a civilian or two hurrying along a sidewalk. He noted several people sleeping in abandoned cars, and concluded the city had basically been shut down. He had covered about a kilometer when a police officer stepped out of an alley and they came face to face, startling them both. The fellow had some sort of weapon strapped to his side, and his hand shot reflexively toward it, his eyes wide and frightened. John didn't want to hurt the man so he simply froze and stood there shaking his head slowly from side to side, the grav pistol clutched in his hand. Without being obvious he disengaged the gun's safety, but didn't raise it, instead kept it pointed at the ground. John doubted the fellow's weapon could penetrate his armor.

The image of a fully armored ComSecCorps soldier carrying a heavy grav pistol must have had a marked effect on the officer. He didn't draw his weapon, but merely rested his hand on it, and stood there facing John through several seconds of indecision.

John hoped the fellow spoke some Lingua, the de facto standard language for interstellar communications. "I have no reason to hurt you, so don't give me one."

The fellow nodded once, made his decision, then lifted his hand carefully off the weapon. Holding his hands in front of him, palms out, he backed slowly away. Once he had put about twenty paces between them, he turned and ran.

Moving from shadow to shadow John made slow progress. Most of the buildings in that area of the city were two or three stories high, but he spotted one in the next block a little taller than the rest. It was a bit out of his way, but a detour could be worth the effort if it gave him an opportunity to scan the city from higher ground. He turned that way and moved cautiously toward it.

It stood four stories high, and had large windows along the sidewalk in front, behind which he saw a lobby, reception area, and a bank of elevators. If he could get to its roof, or a window on the fourth floor, he could survey the surrounding city and get a better idea of his position. He might even give his implants enough dead-reckoning information to reset its mapping system more accurately.

In an alley along one side of the building he found a window large enough to climb through. Using a light from his kit, he peered through it and saw a desk and chair in what appeared to be a rather Spartan room. Seeing a couple of cleaning bots parked in one corner, he concluded he had found the maintenance supervisor's office.

He used the butt of his pistol to break the glass; no alarm sounded, though a silent message could have been sent to some monitoring station. But if so, he didn't think anyone would respond on that night. Still, he walked out of the alley, crossed the street and waited in the shadows of another alley for half an hour. No police came to answer a silent alarm, no security detail, no reaction whatsoever, not surprising given the dramatic events of that afternoon.

He returned to the alley and climbed through the window into the office. He approached the only door in the room, and waited for several seconds. From outside, the building had appeared deserted, and he heard nothing now to make him think otherwise. He opened the door slowly and found an empty hallway. He stepped out into it, and saw two other doors similar to the one from which he'd just emerged. He walked the length of the hallway slowly, trying to make no sounds whatsoever. It opened into a hallway at the back of the building, and following that he found the main lobby.

He didn't even consider the building's elevators. In the silence surrounding him, if they still functioned they'd likely make enough noise to be heard throughout the entire building; too much chance of stepping out of the lift into an ambush. But exit signs had been posted in both Commonwealth Lingua and the local tongue, so he had no trouble finding a stairwell.

The stairs had an intermediate landing half way between each floor. Low level night lighting provided more than enough illumination, which again meant he didn't have to broadcast his presence with the glare of his suit lights. He climbed the steps carefully, taking them one at a time and listening for any sound that broke the eerie stillness of the building. At each landing he stopped short of it by a few steps and peered around to the stairs that led to the next landing. In that way he slowly made his way to the fourth floor.

The stairwell continued up from there to a metal hatch set flush with the rooftop. The hatch had been thrown wide open, and he saw stars glistening in the night sky high overhead. He had to assume someone had beaten him to the roof, and recalling

Omuglu's words, he would be smart to assume that that someone would not be friendly.

He bent into a crouch and tried not to make even the faintest sound as he took the steps one at a time. Five steps short of the roof, he slowly raised his head until he could just see over the lip of the hatch. A patchwork of large climate control units and ducting turned the otherwise flat roof into a great place for an enemy to hide and ambush him. He turned about slowly, scanning the entire rooftop, doing so with his IR and energy detection on full gain. But as with the rest of the city he saw too much background noise for that to be of any use. He repeated the scan on full visual and still saw nothing, so he slowly climbed up out of the rooftop hatch, staying in a crouch and trying to look in all directions at once.

With his eyes no longer level with the rooftop, he noted that two large climate units were the only structures on the roof large enough to hide any danger. He approached them, and cringed as his boots crunched on some loose gravel. Behind them he found one of his platoon mates sprawled on her back. He recognized the name stenciled on her chest plate: Strelman, a woman he'd known, though not well. Some sort of weapon had shattered her visor and left an unrecognizable mess where there should have been a face behind the visor. Concentrated enemy fire had pitted and scarred her plast where the armor had protected her. The climate control unit next to her had also taken quite a bit of fire, and would probably never work again.

John detached a telemetry line from his suit, and connected it to a port on the dead soldier's reactor pack. It downloaded her identification and told him she had died about three hours ago, which would have been shortly after their disastrous drop. It also confirmed that he could do nothing to help her. His system logged the location so they could recover the body later, if that became possible. The weapon that had penetrated her combat armor was nothing a civilian or police officer might carry.

She also had four, fully functioning reactor pack cells, two with almost a full charge. He removed them and plugged them into the empty ports on his reactor pack. Glancing around, he saw no sign of her assault rifle. But with a bit of searching he found it behind some duct work where it had landed when she had dropped it. He placed it on top of the large climate unit, quickly stripped it and confirmed it had taken no damage. As he reassembled it he wanted to kiss both Omuglu and Parma for making him strip and reassemble his weapons ". . . until you can do so in the dark, with one hand tied behind your back."

With the exception of the damage to his telemetry feed, he now had enough reserves to be fully operational. He had a fully functioning heavy assault rifle, and enough charge in his reactor pack cells to operate his weapons and dish out a little hurt if he needed to. Though he resolved to maintain his caution and not become over confident.

John returned to the stairwell hatch and slowly closed it. Happily, its metal hinges screeched a little, not enough to be heard down on the street below, but enough to warn him if someone else opened it while he focused his attention elsewhere. Then he returned to the climate control unit and hunkered down to plot a route to the embassy.

21

Done With Murder

JOHN CHECKED IN with Parma again. The boat from *Wicked Fury* had made it down in one piece, and the troops from *Defiant* were trickling onto the embassy grounds in twos and threes. It appeared that with the exception of the one boat carrying a platoon of Blackswords, they'd taken very few casualties in the chaotic drop. He almost asked about Carla, Roark, Leeze, and Hey-You, but realized that would be inappropriate. He told the sergeant to put Strelman on the KIA list.

Standing behind the big climate control unit and leaning on it, he ranged on a bridge that crossed a river, and a large monument about a kilometer away, a steel monolith that stood about a hundred meters tall. He fed their coordinates into his implants, they recalibrated, corrected the logged location of Strelman's body, then overlaid a virtual image of the path he should take through the streets of the city to reach the embassy. He decided to carefully reconnoiter the route his implants had chosen for him, so he crossed to the east side of the roof in a crouch and knelt down.

Starting with the street below, he methodically scanned east, increasing his visor's magnification as he did so. Beyond a few city blocks, buildings obscured the streets he would have to walk, so he scanned the rooftops around him. Four hundred meters out he spotted some movement on the roof of a three story building. He dialed the magnification up, but the city's lights left the top of that building heavily shadowed, and he could only make out vague shapes that appeared to be troops in light combat armor. He went to IR and had no trouble confirming that impression. But oddly, they had all squatted down on one side of the building's roof near its edge, and appeared to be gesturing as if pointing to something in the distance. He logged the coordinates of that building, then scanned in the direction they appeared to be watching and pointing.

Three hundred meters from them, and about the same distance from John, he saw an ornate building that stood out quite prominently. His mapping system identified it as Parliament House. Next to that he saw troops in heavy combat armor moving about on the roof of a two story building. The lighting there wasn't so dim, and he saw that they had set up a couple of mortar emplacements and rocketry teams. The first group of combatants in light body armor on the three story building had the advantage of height, and the group in heavy armor on the building near Parliament House appeared to be unaware that they were being observed. He also noticed that on some of them, their heavy armor seemed strangely misshapen, but he couldn't identify exactly what about it bothered him.

He backed away from the edge of the roof and returned to the climate control unit. From there, he carefully scanned the city in all directions, and detected three more groups of combatants in light armor, but no more in heavy armor. And they all appeared to have selected buildings where lights from the city barely lit the roofs they occupied. Could the groups in light armor be observation posts? Their locations and distributions would be ideal for coordinating the targeting of the missile installations that controlled the airspace above the city. And selecting only buildings with dimly lit roofs must have been set up well in advance.

He logged each location, then returned his attention to the only group in heavy armor, the one on the building near Parliament House and under scrutiny by one of the observation posts. Their insignia seemed odd, but the dim illumination of the city's light pollution was too low, and the distance too great, to see well enough to recognize the markings. The mortar emplacements had been deployed near the center of the roof, while observers lay prone near its edges on all four sides. And again something bothered him about the shape of some of the armor they wore.

One of the observers waved an arm, and two suits of armor crossed the roof, dropped down on their hands and knees, and crawled forward to join the trooper. Buildings nearby the armored figures obscured his view of the streets beneath them, but he saw a group of soldiers passing through an intersection. He zoomed in, and didn't need bright lighting to recognize the insignia of ComSecCorps troops. An ambush. He had no time to waste.

He rested his rifle on top of the climate control unit, set it to fire three-round bursts at maximum muzzle velocity, then adjusted his sights for three hundred meters. He took aim at the armored soldiers on the distant rooftop. At that range he didn't expect to hurt them, but he could hopefully alert his comrades in the street below to their presence and break up the ambush. He fired a burst, and another, and another, watched the bullets kicking up chips of masonry near the distant figures. He fired again and again.

They returned fire immediately, much too quickly to have spotted him, especially since his grav rifle didn't spit a muzzle flash. He ducked behind the climate unit as rounds thudded into it. He wondered for an instant how they could have spotted him so quickly, and realized then what a fool he'd been. They had equipment to track his incoming rounds and compute their back-trajectory, probably had him located to within centimeters. Their response would be mortars and rockets, and he had only seconds to live.

He turned and sprinted across the roof. If he had to he would take his chances and jump off the roof, using his gravity fields to descend to the street. But with his damaged stability systems he decided he couldn't chance it unless he had no other choice. As he ran bullets peppered the rooftop around him and pinged off his armor.

He reached the hatch in the roof, grabbed its metal latch and heaved, throwing it to one side with a loud metallic crash. He jumped into the dark opening of the stairwell and took the steps three at a time. Just as he hit the fourth floor, the roof above him exploded, a block of masonry slammed into him and knocked him into a tumble down the stairs. He came to a stop on the landing between the third and fourth floors. Luckily his rifle had come with him. He scooped it up and continued down the stairs, again taking them three at a time.

When he reached the third floor and started down to the second an explosion above him rocked the building, and the entire structure groaned, a sound he had first heard on Novalis and would always remember. The steps turned into a hazy blur as he concentrated on staying on his feet and not turning his desperate rush into a head-over-heels fall.

Exiting through the window in the landlord's office would put him in the middle of that alley, a deadly trap. So when he hit the first floor he charged down the hall to the front lobby. As he sprinted through the lobby he fired a burst from his rifle into one of the large windows at the front of the building. It punched three holes in the window and sent a starburst of cracks radiating outward from them. He hit the cracked window at full charge and crashed through it, large shards of glass slicing down onto him and splintering off his armor. He stumbled out onto the street where he slammed into an abandoned automobile.

Another explosion high above sent blocks of masonry raining down on him, and only his armor kept him alive, a telltale in the corner of his visor telling him his reactor pack was close to red-line as it prevented the stones from breaching the plast. The building groaned, and he thought it might be close to collapsing, so he ran the only direction open to him: north, away from any rendezvous at the embassy.

As he approached the next intersection, he stopped before entering it and slipped into a shadow. He keyed his suit to mask his IR signature, glanced around the corner of a building, saw that the intersection was clear, and sprinted through it. He had put more than a block between him and the four-story building when another shell slammed into it, and the building collapsed with the groan of twisting steel and the gunshot crack of snapping structural supports. A giant cloud of concrete dust and debris billowed up the street toward him.

At the next intersection he stopped again and peered around the corner, exposing as little of himself as possible. He saw movement, heard a shout and jerked his head back just as the pop of several weapons broke the silence of the street. Heavy rounds tore chips of stone out of the corner of the building where his head had been a moment earlier.

He backtracked at a run, sprinting down the sidewalk and trying to stay in the nighttime shadows of the building. They had him pinched between enemy soldiers only a few seconds behind him, and the collapsed building not far in front of him. Up ahead the streets were probably blocked with rubble, and to continue on in that direction might prove to be a fatal trap.

He came to an alley just as he heard rifle shots behind him. He ducked into it and jogged toward the far end, his lungs now burning from the pace he'd kept up since diving from the roof of that building into its stairwell. More shots zinged off the entrance to the alley just as he reached a large, steel trash receptacle parked more than half way down its length. He took cover behind it, and wedged himself into the narrow space between the wall of a building and the dumpster. He set his reactor pack into standby mode, crouched down, and froze.

••••

Nikaela stopped just short of the mouth of an alley. She raised a hand above her head, halting the squad behind her and the squad across the street. With two squads under her command, her Kelk ancestors would frown upon her if she failed to bring down one, lone ComSec soldier, though she had to remember that their first priority was to capture him if at all possible.

Her prey had warned the small group of Commonwealth soldiers they'd been tracking, and they had disappeared into the city. But the lone soldier they now hunted had needed to descend four floors under fire, while she and her two squads had been on the ground floor ready to sortie on a moment's notice.

No sign of him up ahead, but he'd had time to reach the next intersection, so that meant nothing. And the street offered any number of places in which to hide: parked cars, a large construction dumpster, shadowed doorways into which the street lighting did not penetrate.

She leaned forward and peered around the corner of a building into the alley. It too offered a number of hiding places including a large steel trash receptacle. He'd probably gotten far enough ahead of them that they'd lost him, but they could at least sweep the street and this alley to be certain of that.

She keyed her com and contacted Geltkarl, in charge of squad two across the street. "Oberseergent, take your squad and sweep the street up to the next intersection, then hold there. We're going to sweep this alley."

She responded with, "Yes, mistress."

Nikaela pointed to the soldier carrying the squad's multi-barreled, portable rotary. "Move to the other side of the alley," she said, "and be ready to provide cover fire."

She pointed to two riflemen. "You and you, sweep the alley."

As they started down the alley, she raised her rifle and sighted down its length at the dumpster, the nearest location where someone might hide.

••••

John had a slanting view through a narrow slit between the wall of the building and the dumpster, and he saw the street just beyond the mouth of the alley. With his IR signature masked and his reactor pack in standby mode, the cooling system in his armor had shut down and the temperature inside his suit rose steadily.

An armored figure stopped in a crouch near the mouth of the alley. He waved, and another armored figure crossed the mouth of the alley, carrying a rotary. The first one, obviously the officer in charge, pointed down the alley, probably issuing commands over their com. Again, John couldn't clearly make out the insignia stenciled on their armor, but when the officer stood, John understood what bothered him about the shape of their armor: it was tightly fitted to the wearer's body, including a thin waist with slightly broader hips, and a little extra room on the breast plate for a pair of breasts. Commonwealth armor tended toward the androgynous, whereas the Kelk liked theirs tightly fitting. The squads hunting him were Kelk, and the officer in charge of them probably female.

He switched his assault rifle to full automatic as two more armored figures stepped into the alley, both crouched down and carrying assault rifles much like John's. Shutting his reactor pack down was a dangerous gamble, because without power, a round from either of those rifles would punch a hole right through the plast plates of his armor. But he'd be much harder to detect.

They waved hand signals at each other, and one started down the alley, walking slowly toward John's hiding place. When the soldier had advanced about ten paces, the other followed, matching his pace. John waited, his heart pounding in his chest, the interior of his armor growing uncomfortably warm.

The first enemy soldier reached the large trash receptacle and halted on the other side of it. Pinched between the dumpster and the wall, John could no longer see him through the slit between it and the building, but he saw his companion clearly, still about ten paces behind him. He heard the first enemy soldier stop on the other side of the dumpster, and tried not to grip his own rifle with crushing force. The soldier flashed a light briefly up and down the alley, and along the side of the dumpster where he might have hidden, but not behind it where he really hid. Then John heard the crunch of gravel beneath the soldier's feet as the Kelk took one careful step, then another. His companion followed, always maintaining a distance between them of about ten paces.

John sweated profusely as the temperature in his suit climbed to an uncomfortable level and drops of moisture formed on the inside of his visor. The first enemy soldier moved deeper into the alley and came into view on the other side of the dumpster, his back to John. The other stepped out of view as he stopped on the other side of it, just as his companion had done moments ago.

John had a clear view of the back of the first soldier, and now he saw the soldier's insignia clearly. John recalled the briefings they'd been given on adversaries they might face in the field: a Kelk with the equivalent rank of private first class, confirming his earlier conclusion. Without doubt, as soon as the fellow turned around, he'd spot John immediately.

A bright, red warning icon flashed on the inside of his visor, and his suit computer said, "Critical hazard warning. Possible terminal hyperthermia."

John lowered the muzzle of his rifle a few centimeters, aiming it at the back of the enemy soldier. He unclipped a grenade from his kit, and programmed it through his implants for a one second delay. He put his reactor pack back into full combat mode, and stopped masking his IR signature. His reactor pack needed a few precious seconds to fully power up. He watched a virtual readout climb from zero to ten, then twenty, then thirty percent. It had reached fifty percent when the Kelk turned around.

John keyed the grenade and tossed it over the dumpster to the other side of the alley. In the same motion he pulled his grav rifle's trigger and it kicked in his hands, spitting a stream of rounds that pinged off the first enemy soldier's armor.

The grenade blew, lighting up the alley with a blinding flash and rocking the heavy steel dumpster. It slammed the large steel box against him and slapped the Kelk in his sights to the tarmac. He could only hope it had taken out the second Kelk on the other side of the dumpster.

The first staggered to one knee and spun, reflexively firing his rifle and spraying an arc of rounds across the alley. One ricocheted off the stone wall next to John and punched into his armor. Pain shot up his side as his suit computer said, "Torso breach. Vacuum integrity no longer valid."

John fired another burst at the Kelk. The stream of rounds from John's rifle finally overwhelmed the man's armor and he dropped to the tarmac. Ignoring the pain in his side, John charged out from behind the dumpster, hurtled over the fallen Kelk and sprinted up the alley, hoping the Kelk's companion wouldn't put a burst of rounds into his back. He was just short of the street at the far end when the high-pitched whine of the portable rotary opened up behind him. His reactor pack had reached full combat status, and flechettes zinged and popped off his armor. Pain shot through his right thigh and he tumbled to the pavement, skidding out of the alley into the street on his armor plates.

"Thigh breach," his suit computer said. "Penetration wound."

John fired a burst blindly down the alley, then scrambled behind the edge of a building. He slung his rifle around the corner of the building and sprayed rounds blindly into the alley, a move purely intended to make the Kelk hesitate and give him time. The narrow gap between buildings would make a direct assault up the alley a costly move. They'd probably try to flank him, or bring up a shoulder fired rocket launcher.

He unclipped a grenade from his kit, set it for a three second delay and tossed it down the alley as far as he could. A flash of light was followed by the sound of the detonation, then a wall of smoke and debris erupted up the alley. He fired a burst from his rifle into it, then turned and hobbled up the street limping badly, each breath bringing a sharp pain in his side and slowing him.

••••

As John staggered up the street his suit computer said, "Class-three torso wound. Shallow damage from plate splinters is not critical. Full penetration through right thigh plate produced class-two wound."

The flechettes hadn't penetrated his torso armor, but damaged it enough to drive splinters into his side. Class-three meant the suit could handle the wound, and he could go for an indefinite period of time without attention from a medic. It was the class-two thigh wound he worried about most. His suit could only handle it for a limited period of time, and it would hamper him badly.

Running up the street with an uneven gait and breathing heavily sent one stabbing pain after another through his chest and he couldn't keep it up. He stopped in the shadow of a street vendor's stall to catch his breath.

His suit computer said, "Initiating pain block and blood loss suppression."

He gasped involuntarily as the pain blinked out like a light turned off by a switch, and he could breathe fully again. Class-three also meant the suit could probably maintain bleeding suppression even during strenuous activity—probably.

His computer said, "Class-two thigh wound will soon need medical attention."

He keyed his com to the command circuit. He tried to get something through to his comrades. "Mathius here. It's Kelk. I saw Kelk, came across a patrol of them. Almost got wacked in the process."

He killed his com and said, "Computer, combat kikker, execute now."

His suit flooded his system with a strong dose of combat drugs. It didn't lessen any pain, but he suddenly didn't care about it, and felt as if he could do anything with inhuman strength.

The muffled crump of an explosion behind him told him the Kelk were close on his heels. They'd either made a foray up the alley, or circled around the block, and were now only a few hundred meters back, probably less. He limped up the street and took a random turn at the next intersection, just as he heard the thump of a grenade launcher. The corner of the building he'd just rounded exploded, slamming him to the pavement and showering him with broken masonry.

"Reactor pack damage," his suit computer said as he scrambled to his feet and ran. "Deactivating and isolating damaged cells. Reactor pack operating at eighty percent capacity."

Half way up the block he spotted stairs in the middle of the sidewalk, an entrance into Helmanport's subway system. If he could lose his pursuers in the maze of its passageways, he might live through the night. He ran to the stairs and raced down the steps, taking them two at a time.

At the bottom of the stairs the subway corridor branched left and right. With no time to pull up a map of the system and study it, he turned right into a well-lit passageway and froze, listening for any sounds of pursuit.

At that time of night the subway system should have been crowded with early evening traffic, but it remained deserted, confirming his suspicion that the city had truly shut down. He waited in silence. A few seconds passed, then he heard boot-steps on the sidewalk above. More boot-steps followed, then several more. There must be a couple of squads of Kelk up there. John turned away from them and moved as quietly as he could down the subway corridor. He thought it incongruous that he could tip-toe in heavy combat armor.

About twenty paces down the passageway he turned a corner and came upon five civilians seated on the concrete against one wall, all huddled beneath blankets. A woman took one look at him and screamed. That panicked a little boy who started wailing, and John had no doubt their cries had alerted his pursuers to his presence.

He ran past them into a section of corridor where the lighting had failed, providing shadow so dark it forced him to slow, put one hand against the wall and drag his fingers along it. The wall abruptly ended at a turn, down which he saw dim lighting about twenty paces distant. His instincts shouted at him to run and put as much distance as possible between him and his pursuers. But then he thought of the civilians, and he imagined the Kelk repeating Cranoch's and Mercier's atrocities here on Reisenar. He hesitated, fear of dying a sharp knot in his chest, but he'd heard of how bloodthirsty the Kelk could be.

"Fuck!" he said, thinking, *I'm done with murder.*

He turned back, stopped at the turn in the corridor, masked his IR signature, leaned out from the cover of the corner and shouldered his rifle. Protected by the darkness in his stretch of passageway, he had a clear line of fire to the civilians huddled in the lighted section in the distance. The woman had ceased her screams and now tried to calm the young boy, who sobbed quietly. A shout drew everyone's attention to the corridor that led down from the street.

••••

One of Nikaela's soldiers reached the stairs to the subway ahead of her and started down the steps. "Hold," she shouted, and he froze.

She had two people down—one dead and one badly wounded—and had left two more behind in the alley to take care of them. Her prey had proven to be more dangerous than she had anticipated. Some of her less experienced people wanted to even the score, and that could make them sloppy. It could also make them vengeful, which might cloud their judgement. Her Kelk superiors would be unhappy if she let this get out of hand.

She caught up to the soldier at the top of the stairs and dropped into a crouch. She sent Geltkarl with all but two of her soldiers up the street to look for any sign of their lone quarry. To the two that remained she said, "With me, down the stairs."

As they eased their way slowly down the stairs a scream echoed up from below. Both of her soldiers reacted by starting forward. She stuck her arm out, blocking them, and said, "And we move with all caution."

One nodded immediately. The other hesitated for a moment, then nodded slowly as if reluctant to do so. She looked at the stenciled name on his chest plate: BRIIKENDOR. His lover was one of the wounded they'd left behind. She would have to watch this one closely.

At the bottom of the stairs the subway corridors branched left and right. They stood in darkness, but farther along in both directions the passageways appeared lit. To the right she heard sobs and crying, to the left only silence. She pointed to the right, and the three of them moved forward slowly, their weapons held ready.

She halted them at the edge of darkness before stepping into the lighted section of corridor. Five civilians sat on the floor huddled against one wall, a middle-aged woman comforting a sobbing young child. No sign of their prey.

Nikaela switched on her external helmet speaker, pointed forward, and the three of them stepped into the light. Briikendor and the other soldier immediately raised their weapons and aimed them at the civilians.

"Weapons down," she snapped. "They're civilians."

The one soldier obeyed immediately, but Briikendor hesitated.

Nikaela looked at the poor, pathetic civilians, then reached out, doing so slowly. She placed a hand on the muzzle of Briikendor's rifle, and forced it down so it pointed at the floor. He started to say something, but she snapped, "Silence."

••••

When the three Kelk stepped into view, John had to think carefully to recall the rank insignia he'd studied: two enlisted soldiers led by a command boss, junior rank, the lowest rank of Kelk officer, equivalent to a Commonwealth second looie or ensign. Now that John had a clear view of her shape, any question of her gender had been fully resolved. As the two riflemen raised their weapons and aimed them at the civilians, John sighted down the barrel of his rifle at them, took a deep breath, held it, and prepared to fire. But the officer raised a hand and barked a sharp, unintelligible command. The timbre of her voice left no question that she was female.

One soldier obeyed immediately and lowered his rifle, but the other hesitated, as if he might defy his superior. The officer looked at the civilians for a long moment, then reached out, placed a hand on the barrel of the soldier's rifle, and carefully lowered the muzzle so it pointed at the floor.

The soldier started to say something, but the officer silenced him with a harshly barked command.

John waited, ready to pull the trigger at the slightest hint that they would harm the civilians. But the officer leaned down and said something to a male civilian. The man, his eyes wide and fearful, pointed down the corridor in John's direction.

The officer straightened and looked John's way, and he wondered if she could somehow see through the darkness that hid him, even with his IR signature masked. She turned and barked a command at one of the two soldiers. The fellow nodded and raced back the way they'd come. The civilian had confirmed that John had entered the subway system. The officer had clearly sent a runner up to street level where their coms weren't blocked by tonnes of earth and concrete. The runner would call in the rest of her troops.

She snapped out another command to the remaining soldier who nodded, crouched, and moved past the civilians, headed John's way.

Careful to make no sound, John lowered his rifle, turned and moved deeper into the subway system.

22

Battle Kin

NIKAELA ASKED THE civilian man, "Did a soldier come this way?"

The fellow hesitated for only a moment, his eyes wide and fearful. Then he pointed farther down the corridor into darkness. She saw nothing there, but hadn't expected to. Her prey had already proven to be quite dangerous and wouldn't be stupid enough to wait around.

She wasn't sure she could control Briikendor, so she decided to send him up to retrieve Geltkarl and the rest. She said to him, "Go up to street level and tell them he came this way. Tell them to join us."

He nodded and raced back the way they'd come.

She looked again into the darkness of the corridor. She couldn't wait for Geltkarl. Her prey had a head start, and if she delayed even just a little, she'd probably lose him in the maze of passageways in the subway system.

She pointed into the darkness and said to the other soldier, "Let's go."

Only then did she realize she'd left her helmet speaker active. She silenced it and followed the soldier.

••••

The pain suppression for the class-two wound in John's thigh failed little by little as he worked his way deeper into the passageways beneath the city. His limp grew more pronounced and he slowed further, gritting his teeth with each step, pausing frequently to catch his breath.

The corridor he followed branched again. *Good*, he thought. That would force his pursuers to split up.

He went right, a purely random choice, but he heard voices up ahead. He crept forward slowly and stopped at a turn in the corridor. He peered around it and saw a group of about a dozen civilians. The Kelk officer would question them and know that

he went this way, or, if the civilians knew nothing about a lone, armored ComSec soldier, they'd know he went the other, so it really didn't matter. He turned around and
retraced his steps to the branch in the corridor, and going the other way he didn't encounter anyone.

As he rounded a corner he heard boot-steps behind him and guessed the Kelk
were only a few dozen paces back. But it sounded like there were only a few of them,
that the officer hadn't waited for her comrades to join them before following him.

Up ahead he saw an open space lit much more brightly than the passageway. He
staggered toward it, then out onto an elevated subway platform, a wide open concrete
slab about a meter and a half above the grav tracks on either side of it. No place to
hide, his only escape the subway tunnels themselves.

He staggered to the tracks on the right, leaned out and looked up and down their
length. They went straight for a good two hundred meters in either direction before
turning. With the Kelk close on his heels, he wouldn't get far before they spotted him,
and trapped in the narrow confines of the subway tunnel he'd be an easy target. He
staggered to the tracks on the other side of the platform; the same thing. He heard
boot steps in the corridor he'd just emerged from. A steel catwalk extended along the
wall of the tunnel just above the tracks at the same height as the platform. Hoping it
led to someplace he might hide, he stepped onto it, and immediately realized his mistake as the metal grating creaked with every step he took. He pressed his back against
the tunnel wall and froze.

He listened carefully and imagined the subway in the middle of rush hour, filled
with commuters, all pushing and shoving their way through the crowds. The walls of
the passageways would echo with voices and all sorts of sounds, not the eerie silence
that surrounded him now.

He heard the creak of moving armor joints, the soft hiss of a boot heel on the
concrete of the platform. One glance into the subway tunnel where he hid, and
they'd spot him immediately. And he dare not move, not with the creaking catwalk
beneath his feet betraying his location. He quietly unclipped a micro-nuke from his
harness, then set it for its twenty-pound maximum yield and a one-meter proximity
detonation. It would blow when it got within one meter of a non-ComSec reactor
pack.

He needed to get the nuke within range of his target, or it would just clatter across
the concrete. And once it came to rest he doubted the Kelk would be stupid enough to
walk up to it and get their asses blown to hell and back. With the platform to his right
and his back to the subway tunnel wall, it would have to be a quick look, then a left
handed toss in the same instant.

He took a breath, turned slightly, leaned to his right. The metal catwalk creaked
beneath him just as he peered around the corner of the tunnel into the platform, and

as he glimpsed the two armored Kelk he gave the nuke an underhanded toss. But he realized in that instant that they were too close, only a few meters away, and with his arm extended palm out, he could not possibly retract it before the nuke blew. With every muscle in his body straining to pull his head and arm back into the protection of the concrete tunnel, he saw the small canister of the nuke arc toward the enlisted Kelk, the officer several meters to one side.

The micro-nuke exploded and the blast slammed into his arm. It sent a sharp stab of pain knifing through John's hand and spun him in a whirl off the catwalk. A wall of flame and smoke plowed into him, and then he tumbled to the grav tracks below, where he landed hard on his back. He lay there for a moment, his eyes closed, gasping as he almost lost consciousness.

"Hazard warn . . . Initiating turni . . . severed dig . . . Vis . . . breach . . ."

John opened his eyes. His thoughts focused on the pain in his left hand and arm, while his gaze settled on a maze of electrical conduit in the rounded ceiling of the subway tunnel above him. A crack in the left side of his visor drew his attention.

"Hazard warning," his suit said. "Non-critical gauntlet breach. Class-one injury. Tourniquet isolation for damaged hand and severed digits. Initiating pain suppression. Visor breach, no injury detected."

"Computer," he said. "Status, physical, execute."

His suit displayed the silhouette of a naked man on the inside of his visor. It showed a yellow blotch for the plast splinters in his side, red blotches for the torso and thigh injuries, blinking red on his left arm and hand. Thankfully, the damage to his visor hadn't resulted in a head or face injury.

John raised his left hand and looked at it. The blast had shredded the palm of his gauntlet, the weakest part of his armor. His little finger was completely missing, and the two next to it ended in badly foreshortened stumps. A crack in his forearm plate extended from his wrist half way to his elbow. He sat up, looked around and tried to focus his thoughts, tried to think of something other than the pain.

The blast had thrown him down onto the tracks. He heard a scrabbling sound on the subway platform above him, then the clack of plast on concrete, and a strange electronic whine that didn't belong there. No sign of his rifle, so he struggled to his feet, stayed in a crouch and drew his sidearm. Moving slowly, he rose up and peered over the edge of the platform.

The Kelk soldier lay in a sprawl with his arms and legs at odd angles, and he remained still. Near him, the officer lay face down, streams of bluish smoke rising up off her reactor pack. Her right ankle ended in a bloody stump, though he saw no pulsing blood so her suit had pressure-clamped it properly. An electrical discharge arced near the base of her pack and she spasmed, lay still for a moment, then tore frantically at her helmet. The blast had damaged her reactor pack and probably scrambled its failsafes, a rare occurrence, but one his instructors had warned him about. If she didn't get out of her armor in short order, it would probably cook her alive.

Recalling the civilians she had spared, John staggered down the tunnel to the end of the catwalk and found a metal ladder there. With only one working hand, he snapped his sidearm back into the clips on his thigh plate. He pulled himself up onto the catwalk, his left arm clutched to his side. The metal grating creaked beneath his feet as he staggered down its length and out onto the subway platform.

The Kelk officer had rolled onto her back and was pulling and disengaging her armor seals. When she saw John approaching, she hesitated and reached for her sidearm. John crossed the distance between them in a staggering shuffle and kicked her arm aside. He pulled his own sidearm, pressed the muzzle up under her chin and she froze. With a badly damaged reactor pack, a slug from his grav pistol could easily punch through her armor.

She had half unclipped her sidearm from her thigh plate, so he kicked at it and it broke free. He kicked it again and it tumbled off the platform and onto the tracks. Then he clipped his sidearm back onto his thigh plate, reached down and quickly disengaged one of her armor seals. She hesitated for an instant, then frantically tore at her waist seals.

John got her chest plate off, tossed it to one side, saw charred uniform and flesh beneath it. She got her helmet off and tossed it aside as John popped her shoulder seals. Her reactor pack now emitted an unpleasant whine accompanied by more smoke. It popped and clicked, another electrical discharge arced across the top of her pack and she spasmed again, then lay still.

John rolled her over onto her face and popped the last of the seals keeping her back plate in place. With his damaged hand he struggled for a moment, fighting to ignore the pain, but he managed to muscle her back plate and reactor pack off her. The whine turned into a high-pitched scream as he carried the pack to the edge of the platform and tossed it down onto the tracks. Not sure what to expect, he pulled his sidearm, bent into a crouch and returned to the Kelk officer, who lay face down, unmoving.

Her reactor pack emitted a series of pops and crackles as he rolled her over. He thought she might be dead, but then she took a breath and opened her eyes, and for the first time he looked into her face.

He had expected her to appear alien and strange, and there was that, but he found her visage very human and rather attractive. Her salt-and-pepper gray hair was more pepper than salt, telling him she was quite young, and her bright red irises didn't strike him as demonic in any way. The chalk white skin with a bluish cast to it didn't repulse him as he had thought it would, and the sharp lines of her face were not severe as he had expected. She was actually quite pretty, in a Kelk sort of way. He couldn't see her tongue, but he had to believe it wasn't really forked.

Her reactor pack emitted a loud pop, pulling him out of his thoughts. A bolt of lightning arced up to the ceiling of the tunnel with an ear-splitting crack.

He asked, "How bad are you hurt?"

Her eyes blinked rapidly for a moment, then she calmed, still breathing heavily.

"How bad are you hurt?" he asked again.

She appeared to consider the question carefully, then said, "No talkie Lingua."

"Bullshit!" he said. "You're an officer. We know they train you in Commonwealth Lingua. I'm not stupid."

She regarded him for the longest moment, then smiled. After their briefings on the evil and diabolical Kelk, for some reason he had expected her to have pronounced canines, like the teeth of a large predator. Or possibly her teeth would be honed to barbaric, razor sharp points. But they appeared quite normal, and he chided himself for being so naive. He still hadn't seen her tongue.

She spoke in a thick accent. "I know shit word, not bull word. What is shit-of-bull? Is bull an animal?"

"I don't know," he said. "Probably. Maybe. I've never seen one so I don't know."

She grimaced, clearly in pain. "So what is shit-of-bull mean?"

"It means I don't believe you."

Drops of sweat had formed on her cheeks and upper lip. "You now kill me?"

He thought about that for a moment, thought about his motives and recalled that he was done with murder, recalled the civilians she had spared. "No," he said.

Her eyes narrowed. "Shit-of-bull to you."

He shrugged it off. "I'm done with murder. I'm not going to kill you."

She frowned at that and struggled to sit up, grimacing with pain. He glanced about quickly and made sure there were no weapons nearby, then snapped his sidearm back into the clips on his thigh plate. When he stepped behind her and slid his hands beneath her shoulders, she flinched.

He'd forgotten his left hand. His suit had used local anesthetics to turn it into a numb stump, and he got a painful reminder that it was now a shredded mess. He helped her get into a sitting position, and she scrambled backwards on her hands and elbows, placing her back against the wall of the platform.

She looked at him curiously and said, "We are enemies. Why not kill me?"

He recalled the civilians in the passageway. "Why didn't you let your men kill those civilians back there?"

Her frown deepened. "I don't kill if don't have to."

He grinned at her and said, "Neither do I . . . at least not anymore."

Her eyes narrowed with thought. "Not anymore," she said. "Means you once did kill without have to."

"Once," he said. "A long time ago."

She lifted an eyebrow in question, and again it struck him as a very human gesture. He had to remind himself that she was fully human, and in answer to the implied question, he said what he had never acknowledged to his own platoon mates. "Novalis III."

She flinched, as if he'd struck her. Then she grimaced and said, "Bad tragedy. Kelk mistake. No excuse."

He wondered for a moment if she knew something about Novalis III, something more than what the news feeds served up. He thought it interesting that the Kelk considered Novalis III a tragedy, while his own superiors thought of it as merely an incident.

She asked, "Why start war with Kelk here?"

"We didn't start this," he said. "You did when you ambushed us."

"Embush?" she asked.

"Attack without warning," he said. "The missiles that hit our drop boats. The two Kelk ships that hit our ships in orbit."

She shook her head. "Not embushing you. Not Kelk here. Not Kelk in orbit. Fake Kelk ships. Someone else ships."

He thought of the observation posts he'd spotted, and how one of them had been watching this woman and her people. They were clearly not Kelk or Commonwealth, and for that matter not allies of either. And if they had posts like that all over the city, they outnumbered the Kelk and the Commonwealth troops. It didn't add up. Or rather, it did add up if he believed her.

"About three hundred meters from your headquarters," he said. He rattled off the coordinates of the observation post he'd spotted. "You should check out the building there, especially the people on the roof. They've got the high ground on you, and they've been watching you closely."

She gave him a curious uncertain look. "Are you shit-of-bull now?"

"No," he said, shaking his head. "No shit-of-bull. And go armed. I don't think you're going to find friends there."

He straightened and said, "I suppose, if we ever meet again, one of us will have to kill the other." For some reason that thought saddened him.

The look on her face turned sardonic, she shrugged and said something in Kelk. It sounded like "Neertha kaaschmot." She rolled the r's heavily, probably some Kelk saying that meant, *That is inevitable*, or something like that.

He turned away from her and paused for a moment over her chest plate. It still lay where he had tossed it onto the concrete of the platform. He didn't know any Kelk and couldn't read the strange symbols stenciled above her left breast. He thought that if he survived this night, maybe he'd make the effort to learn a little Kelk. He flagged the image of the stenciled name on her chest plate for hard storage in his implants. He could recall it, and maybe he'd start with that.

He staggered to the far side of the platform where he wouldn't have to contend with lightning bolts from her damaged reactor pack. Time to choose right or left. He thought going right might take him east and closer to the rendezvous with his platoon mates at the embassy, so he turned that way. He didn't try to hide his actions because her comrades would soon be on the scene, and he wouldn't get far regardless of the direction he chose. He staggered down the length of the catwalk, then climbed down the ladder and onto the subway's grav tracks.

••••

Seated on the floor of the subway platform with her back against a wall, the ComSec-Corps soldier standing over her, Nikaela tried to ignore the pain from the burns on her back and ribs, and the agony of her missing right foot. This man with the name MATHIUS stenciled on his chest plate had saved her life, and he'd as much as admitted that it had something to do with Novalis III. Had he been one of the soldiers sent in by the Commonwealth to intervene, sent in too late, as it turned out?

No, she thought. She couldn't see his face or anything about his physical appearance, but he seemed too young to have been part of the intervention team, perhaps only a few years younger than her. His rank of private-first-class added some confirmation to that assumption. And most important of all, he wasn't wearing the symbol of the dreaded Blacksword.

He straightened and said, "I suppose, if we ever meet again, one of us will have to kill the other." It sounded almost as if he regretted the predestiny of that outcome.

Without thinking, her thoughts clouded by pain, she shrugged and said, "Perhaps not."

He didn't react to that, but turned away from her and hesitated for a moment over her discarded chest plate. Then he limped across the platform to the tracks, paused and looked both ways. He turned right and disappeared down the tunnel. The sound of her imploding reactor pack buzzing, hissing and crackling wasn't enough to drown out the sound of his boots clattering on some sort of creaky, metal structure.

Only then did she realize she had spoken her last words to him in Kelk, and he probably hadn't understood her; neertha kaaschmot, *perhaps not*. She thought it a shame that they'd never meet again, that he'd never know the true meaning of her words.

Pain sent her to the edge of consciousness. With the complete failure of her reactor pack and armor, she no longer had a suit computer to analyze her injuries and apply the appropriate pain killers, and she found it impossible to put two coherent thoughts together.

She heard a noise in the corridor that led to the platform, then a harshly uttered command spoken in the Kelk language. She took a deep breath to shout out to her comrades, but that made the burns on her back and ribs ignite with blistering pain. She managed to grunt out. "It's clear. He's gone."

Several seconds passed, then four Kelk soldiers sprinted out of the corridor and onto the platform. They spread out into a semicircle about her, dropped to one knee and shouldered their rifles, aiming them outward.

One of them shouted, "Clear."

Four more soldiers ran out of the corridor past their comrades. They split up, and while the first four covered them, they quickly swept the subway platform.

Geltkarl leaned over her, took one look at her and shouted, "Medic."

A medic knelt down beside her and pressed a small instrument to the side of her head. It tapped into her implants, and in a fraction of a second the medic had a full analysis of Nikaela's injuries. He rifled through his kit, then pressed another instrument to the side of her throat. "This will ease the pain," he said.

A blessed stillness settled into her chest as a combination of drugs and pain-blockage through her implants ended the gnawing agony of the burns and the throb in her missing foot. She leaned her head back against the concrete of the wall and closed her eyes. She could finally think clearly again.

Geltkarl said, "Mistress, how many were there?"

Nikaela wished she had seen the young man's face. She had gotten his name from the stencil on his chest plate—Mathius—but it would be nice to have something more by which to remember the Commonwealth soldier who had saved her life. And that set of coordinates he'd given her, a most curious thing to do. Had it been a warning from one comrade to another?

"Just one," she said, opening her eyes and pointing with a shaky finger. "He dropped down onto the subway tracks and disappeared into the tunnel."

Geltkarl barked orders at the soldiers under her command, telling them to search the tunnel in both directions.

Nikaela shook her head. "No need. I saw him go. I know which way."

She had seen him go right. Badly wounded, her people would catch up with him in short order. And after the casualties he had inflicted on them, they would show no quarter. With nothing more than his sidearm to fight with, the young man would not stand a chance.

Private Mathius had told her he was done with murder, and he had saved her from burning alive inside her own armor. One simple act from her, and he and she would be battle-kin, a rare thing indeed. "He went left," she said, hoping her face didn't betray the lie in her words. "Don't waste your time going right."

23

When Reality Intervenes

JOHN STRUGGLED TO put one foot in front of the other and staggered along the grav tracks in an unsteady shuffle. He looked over his shoulder repeatedly, expecting to see Kelk soldiers rounding the last turn in the subway tunnel. With nothing but a sidearm against assault rifles, and waves of pain slowing his reflexes, he would be easy fodder, but for some reason that didn't happen. After about a kilometer he stopped to rest and could hardly stand. He leaned against the wall of the tunnel to keep from falling over.

A kilometer? No, in his present condition it was probably more like half that, though he felt like he'd just run a five kilometer race. But still, the Kelk soldiers should have caught up with him by now and finished the job. He looked back down the dark subway tracks and saw no sign of pursuit.

He staggered on, and after what felt like another kilometer he spotted bright lights up ahead. With his grav pistol in hand, he moved forward cautiously and came to another subway station. He hesitated in the darkness of the tunnel listening for any sounds of life. After a few minutes he had heard nothing so he crouched down and moved forward, staying on the tracks and keeping well below the level of the platform. Then he straightened until his eyes were level with the concrete floor and scanned the station. It appeared deserted.

Like the station where he'd had his little dance with two Kelk and a micro-nuke, it had short catwalks that ran a few meters down the tunnel and ended at a ladder. He needed to get back to the surface, recalibrate his mapping system and figure out his location.

He gripped the ladder with his right hand and climbed upward. But half way up a wave of dizziness washed through him and he fell, landing on the tracks in a horrendously loud clatter of plast on plast. He lay there for a moment to catch his breath, and it occurred to him he might not be able to get up again.

"Computer," he said. "Maximum dose combat kikker, execute now."

As the drugs flooded his system and his heart threatened to pound its way out of his chest, he gasped and sat up. He struggled to his feet and stood there breathing heavily, then tried the ladder again. This time he made it without incident and stepped out onto the platform.

He found an inoperative escalator and staggered up it to the next level. There he followed a passageway with a slight but steady upward slope. Exit signs led him to concrete steps, at the top of which he saw a large opening, and a star-filled night sky. He climbed upward slowly and emerged onto the sidewalk next to a large city park. He felt horribly exposed, so he crossed the street and slipped into the shadows of the buildings there.

The steel monolith he'd ranged on earlier stood at the north end of the park, and when he recalibrated his mapping system, to his relief he learned he only had about two kilometers to go to the embassy grounds.

He keyed his com. "This is Mathius, third squad, *Defiant*. I'm two kilometers out and inbound."

He checked the time, was surprised to see that only about four hours had passed since their drop boat had spit his platoon out, and smeared them all over the late afternoon sky of Reisenar.

●●●●

The medic could do so much more than the medical systems in Nikaela's suit. While they waited for a grav stretcher he sprayed temporary synthetic skin over the burns on her back and ribs, and by the time the stretcher arrived, she felt clear-headed and more or less normal again. Geltkarl proved to be almost motherly as they bundled Nikaela onto the stretcher, then guided it up through the passageways beneath the city to street level. Twenty minutes later they deposited her in a bed in their temporary headquarters.

As Geltkarl turned to leave, Nikaela stopped her by saying, "I need to speak with Command Superior Thordahl."

"Rest now," the older woman said.

"Oberseergent," Nikaela said, using the formality of rank to get the woman's attention. "I have important information. It is extremely urgent that I speak with him as soon as possible."

Geltkarl's eyes narrowed and she considered Nikaela for a moment. Then she nodded and said, "I will tell him that right away, and urge him to come see you."

Her platoon mates helped the medic remove the remnants of her armor, then he went to work on the stump of her ankle. She felt nothing as he trimmed away the jagged stub of shattered bone and shredded skin. He spoke as he worked, "We won't be able to grow you a new foot, or even fit you with a descent prosthetic, until we get you back to *Reguskalde*."

He smiled at her. "But I know a few tricks, Command Boss."

She leaned back and rested while he worked. The coordinates young Private Mathius had given her nagged at her to do something about them. Why had he divulged that information? It had seemed like a strange peace offering, and what did it mean?

The medic fitted her right leg with a brace, and gave her a single-cell reactor pack to wear. Then he made some adjustments and said, "You can stand now."

"Stand?" she asked him, unable to hide the surprise in her voice.

"It's a temporary stump fix," he said. "The brace on your right leg has a grav generator built into it, which the reactor pack can power."

He helped her get to her feet—foot, she reminded herself. But she could stand on both legs again, the stump of her right leg levitated off the ground by about twenty centimeters of invisible gravity field.

"Stand up straight," he said, then stepped back and looked her over carefully. "It's a little off balance; looks like the gravity field is too long. I can fix that."

He knelt down and made an adjustment in the grav generator. As he worked he said, "You don't have a foot with heel and toe and an ankle joint. It's just a gravity field, the equivalent of a simple plast extension. But it'll work fine."

At that moment Thordahl entered the room, followed by Brynjar and Geltkarl. Nikaela and the medic snapped to attention.

"Ease," Thordahl said impatiently. "As you were."

He stopped in front of Nikaela, looked down at the invisible grav field beneath the stump of her right leg. He glanced at the medic and said, "Good work."

To Nikaela he said, "Now, Command Boss, Oberseergent Geltkarl tells me you have some urgent information to report."

Nikaela wasn't sure how she could explain her encounter with young Mathius, so she decided to blunder ahead. "The Commonwealth soldier we were tracking. He thought we attacked them, said we embushed them, said it wasn't the Commonwealth who started this."

Brynjar looked at her with distrust and asked, "How did you come to have words with an enemy combatant?"

"He saved my life," Nikaela said. She explained how the micro-nuke he'd thrown had damaged her reactor pack, and how its failsafes had failed. "I would have burned alive in my armor if he hadn't helped me. I was unarmed and he was armed. We talked briefly, and he gave me a set of coordinates, a building about three hundred meters from here, said we should investigate it and warned me that we should go armed and ready for trouble."

Thordahl's look of distrust mirrored that on Brynjar's face. "And you believe him?"

Nikaela nodded. "Yes, I do, maestra."

"Why?" he demanded flatly. "Why should I believe it's not some sort of trap?"

There it was, the question she had known would come. And the only answer she could give would reveal all to them. "We are battle-kin, he and I."

••••

John's hand and fingers throbbed with unremitting agony. Each step closer to the embassy sent a sharp lance of pain through the thigh wound, and he couldn't take a deep breath without a stabbing sensation from the plast splinters in his side. He struggled to prevent the pain from clouding his judgement, tried to remain diligent, to move cautiously using shadows to his advantage the way he'd done on Novalis III. But the pain overwhelmed him, and he found himself staggering down the middle of a street with no recollection of how he'd gotten there.

He came to his senses and moved quickly into the shadows of a nearby structure to take stock of his situation.

He had less than a kilometer to go to get to the embassy grounds. Approaching the outskirts of the city, the buildings had thinned out a bit with no structures taller than two stories, and the streets had narrowed considerably. He had more than enough reactor pack reserves, but if he got into a fight he'd be limited to his sidearm, grenades and a few remaining micro-nukes.

He pulled up an overlay map of the surrounding area. He'd stumbled into a residential neighborhood, with a small park not far in front of him.

He keyed his com. "This is Mathius. I'm less than a kilometer out."

Parma came online immediately. "We're still not getting any telemetry from you, Mathius. And you don't sound good."

John gave the sergeant a quick summary of his injuries and the damage to his suit. The sergeant asked, "Where are you?"

"East, northeast," he said. "Eight hundred meters from the embassy perimeter, bearing seventy-four degrees."

"Stay put," Parma said. "I'm sending a team out for you. Any landmarks we can key on?"

"There's a small park near here," he said. "I'll be waiting near the northeast corner."

"That'll work. Sit tight. We'll be there in ten."

John signed off, then headed for the park. He moved from the shadow of a tree, to a parked car, then skirted along a row of low bushes, always trying to maintain some sort of cover. A piece of him thought he might be a bit paranoid, but another piece reminded him that his caution had kept him alive so far. At the northeast corner of the park, he couldn't stand any longer, so he sat down beneath a tree to rest . . .

"Mathius."

Someone shook him awake and he realized he must have passed out. Six Com-SecCorps troopers stood in a protective semi-circle around him, their rifles aimed outward. A corporal stood over him, though he couldn't make out the name stenciled on the noncom's chest plate. A medic knelt beside him, plugging a telemetry line into a port on his reactor pack.

The medic looked at an instrument connected to the other end of the telemetry line, then said, "Shit! You're a fucking mess. What the hell happened to you?"

"Long story," John said. "Had a little party with a micro-nuke and a couple of Kelk."

The corporal standing over him spoke in a woman's voice. "Yah, we heard it was the Kelk. Fucking assholes."

"Not the Kelk," he said, thinking of the brief conversation he'd had with the young female officer.

The corporal asked, "It wasn't the Kelk did this to you?"

"No," he said. "It was the Kelk, but they're not the ones we should be worrying about."

"We don't have time for this," she said. "Not here, not now. Let's get back to the perimeter. We can worry about this shit later."

The medic juiced John up nicely, and triggered special pain-block software in his implants. John breathed easier as the pain receded.

"You'll be able to walk," the medic said. "So we won't have to carry you, but no strenuous exertion. All the crap you've been doing has aggravated the class-three in your side to a class-two. If any shit goes down, you just get low and hug dirt while we take care of it."

John could walk but he quickly ran out of breath and was forced to pause for several seconds at about two-hundred-meter intervals. He learned that his new comrades were a squad from *Wicked Fury*. He wanted to ask about Hey-You, but at that moment he couldn't remember her real name, and if he used her nick name he'd have to explain it. They probably already knew the story, but he kept silent anyway.

When they reached the perimeter some of his own platoon mates helped him cross the grounds to the embassy building, a large, two-story mansion. They half carried him to a temporary field hospital they had set up in one wing of the place. They laid him down on a portable cot and started stripping off his armor. A medic leaned over him and said, "We're going to induce stim sleep, now. Happy dreams, soldier."

John said, "But I got important int . . ."

••••

With the injuries Nikaela had sustained, her superiors wouldn't let her participate actively in the foray to investigate the coordinates young Mathius had given her. But she claimed battle-kin right, which forced them to at least allow her to observe. Her armor was beyond repair, but they did cobble together the equivalent of light body armor for her.

The sortie would be led by Command Superior Brynjar who had taken charge of her platoon. Nikaela would accompany them as excess baggage. She had reiterated Mathius's warning to go armed, and that he didn't think they would find friendlies there. With that in mind, they assumed it would be a difficult assault.

Thordahl had been quite upset to hear that someone had been keeping them under surveillance from higher ground. Without being obvious about it, their own lookouts on the roof carefully surveyed the structures between them and their target, including dimensions and heights. With that information, they had then mapped out two routes of approach that would keep them out of sight of their goal. Leaving two squads behind, they split the rest of the platoon into two assault teams, which would allow them to approach their target from opposite directions.

They slipped out of their building in groups of four on the downhill side where they couldn't be seen by their opponents. Nikaela snuck out with Brynjar in one of the first groups to leave. They assembled Assault Team One two blocks due north of their HQ, out of sight of the suspect building, while Assault Team Two assembled two blocks to the south. Brynjar sent a squad east to scout the way and ensure that they remained unobserved. Nikaela would have dearly loved to lead that squad, and chaffed at being forced to join the rear guard where she was doomed to see no action.

They worked their way slowly uphill. At one point, heavy construction blocked their designated route, something not visible from the roof of their temporary headquarters. They detoured a block out of the way, careful to stay out of sight of the target. A half hour after leaving their HQ they formed up behind a building next to their objective.

Nikaela monitored the command circuit as Brynjar said, "Team Two, what's your status?"

The answer came back quickly, "Forming up now, Command Superior. Last actives are still about five minutes out."

Nikaela tried not to show her impatience as she waited, something that would have been much easier done with her face hidden behind the visor of full combat armor.

Brynjar turned to her and retracted his visor. He gave her an angry look as he said, "Command Boss, you will not join the assault teams. That is a direct order. Is that clear?"

She nodded and said, "Yes, maestra."

He gave her an unpleasant grin. "And Oberseergent Geltkarl here—" He nodded past Nikaela. She glanced over her shoulder to find the older woman standing behind her in full combat armor. Brynjar continued. "Should your recent injuries cause an excusable lapse in your memory regarding those orders, Oberseergent Geltkarl has orders to restrain you physically if necessary."

His grin broadened even further, something she wouldn't have thought possible.

The command circuit came to life. "This is Team Two. We're in place."

Brynjar closed his visor and turned away from Nikaela. He walked to the corner of the building that hid them from view, leaned out slightly and looked up the street. Then he said, "This is Brynjar. Both teams, execute. Move out."

The squads of Team One split into two sub-teams, and double-timed it around both sides of the building concealing them. Team Two would be doing the same, and in that way they could hit their target from all four sides.

Nikaela stepped forward, intent on peering around the corner of the building to watch, but Geltkarl stepped in her way. "I'm sorry, mistress. I have my orders."

Nikaela heard the pop of supersonic rounds, then the crack and zing as they ricocheted off armor and the tarmac of the street. Their enemy had spotted them, and fired down upon them from the roof above.

"I just want to look," Nikaela said. "I won't go anywhere."

Geltkarl shook her head slowly from side to side. "I'm sorry, mistress. That makeshift armor we put together for you is just not good enough. We'll wait here until it's over."

Nikaela paced back and forth, listening to the muffled sounds of gunfire and explosions inside the three story building. It only lasted for about twenty minutes, then all went silent. Monitoring the command circuit she heard someone say, "Floor one clear." A few moments later, "Floor three clear."

A brief round of gunfire followed, then a muffled explosion, and a few seconds later someone else said, "Floor two clear."

She waited, then heard, "We've got the roof. The building is clear. Command Superior Brynjar, you should come up here."

Nikaela didn't wait for permission and marched out onto the sidewalk with Geltkarl on her heels. They crossed the street to the target building.

They'd blown the front entrance of the building, and Nikaela crossed a lobby littered with broken glass. She hesitated for a moment when her left foot crunched on the shards, while the invisible right foot of the gravity field made no sound at all. High velocity rounds had punched holes through a receptionist's desk in the lobby, and blackish-gray explosive residue stained the walls behind it. They'd blown the elevator as well and a guard stood in her way at the stairwell.

Someone must have told Brynjar she was coming because at that moment he spoke over the command circuit. "Allow Mistress Vreekande to proceed up to the roof."

The two flights of stairs up to the third floor winded her, reminding her that she had only just begun to recover from her wounds. She paused on the third floor for a few seconds to catch her breath, then climbed a ladder up through a hatch onto the roof.

Brynjar waited there with six prisoners, all on their knees in front of him and wearing light combat armor that had been no match for the more heavily armored Kelk. They knelt there with their hands cuffed behind their backs, a ring of armed Kelk troopers surrounding them. As she approached them Brynjar turned to her.

"Your Commonwealth battle-kin," he said. "That was good information he gave you." He nodded toward the six prisoners. "Mercenaries," he said. "They haven't yet told us who they are working for, but they will soon."

He looked at the troopers surrounding the prisoners. "Bring them with us back to headquarters. And don't harm them." He looked at the prisoners. "At least not yet."

One of them said in Lingua, "You don't have to hurt us. We got nothing to hide."

Brynjar retracted his visor and looked Nikaela in the eyes. "I must assume they have much to hide. But mercenaries have allegiance only to their next employer, or to the person holding a gun to their head. We'll know their secrets soon enough."

••••

For the return to their temporary HQ, Brynjar insisted they maintain combat discipline, and operate under the assumption they were traversing hostile territory. They split the prisoners up with one or two mercenaries assigned to each squad, and kept a close eye on them, even though none of them seemed inclined to bolt. Twenty minutes later Thordahl met them inside the building's main entrance. He had removed his helmet, and his head seemed small protruding from the neck seal of his combat armor.

"Come," he said to Nikaela and Brynjar. "And remove your helmets."

The helmet of Nikaela's light armor didn't conceal her face the way Brynjar's full armor did. She pulled it off now and shook her hair out. As Thordahl led them down a corridor, Brynjar removed his helmet as well, shaking out hair even longer than Nikaela's. Thordahl stopped at a door without opening it and turned to Nikaela. "Inside this room, I want you to be silent and allow me to conduct this interview."

"Yes, maestra," she said.

He offered no further explanation, but opened the door and held it for Nikaela and Brynjar.

Inside the room a middle-aged local woman sat at a table wringing her hands. Like many of the locals she had molded her hair into a stiff coif atop her head that moved rigidly when she turned to look at them, almost as if she wore some sort of helmet. She stared at them with wide and fearful eyes, somewhat obscured by an excess of makeup.

Thordahl spoke in Lingua, his words colored by an abundance of politeness and understanding. "Mistress Dandays, may I introduce Command Boss Vreekande, and Command Superior Brynjar."

The woman stammered as she spoke. "You have . . . women . . . soldiers?"

Nikaela had heard that the residents of Reisenar lived in a strict patriarchal society, with a rather provincial view of the role for women.

Thordahl turned to Nikaela and Brynjar. "Mistress Dandays has served Prime Minister Benkamil quite loyally for many years now. She is his trusted confidential secretary. And deservedly so. She is very trustworthy."

"Yes," the woman said, speaking in a breathless rush. "He is a great man, a wonderful man we all love."

Nikaela now realized why Thordahl had asked them to remove their helmets. The anonymity of armor and visors hid the foreign nature of their blood-red pupils and their grayish hair. The woman sat facing three Kelk monsters with blueish-white skin and demon-red eyes, and she proved quite willing to talk. Thordahl didn't have to question her, merely guide her a bit here and there. They quickly learned that Benkamil's relationship with the other factions on Reisenar was not as bad as he had led them to believe, was in fact quite good. They also learned the location of a secret residence he maintained.

When Thordahl appeared to have learned all he needed, he ushered Nikaela and Brynjar out of the room, leaving the woman there alone. After closing the door, he said, "I want you two to bring Benkamil to me—now, tonight."

He held out his hand, palm up, and slowly curled his fingers into a fist, as if wrapping them around some object he feared might escape his grasp. "I won't be happy until I have that man here, under my control, so he can address some doubts I've begun to have about his veracity."

24

That Kelk Woman

PRIME MINISTER BENKAMIL had come from a province more than a thousand kilometers from Helmanport. He had run for election on a platform of austerity, so his official residence near Parliament House reflected a somewhat somber lifestyle. While Nikaela and Brynjar assaulted the mercenary observation post, Thordahl had sent a small team to the official residence, but they had found the place deserted. At that point he had retrieved Benkamil's secretary from her office in Parliament House,

They learned from her that Benkamil maintained a private residence on the edge of the city. Further questioning revealed that he preferred opulence to austerity, and had outfitted the place quite extravagantly, with considerable attention to luxury and comfort. A cellar of fine wines and spirits—only the best—a kitchen staff ready to prepare sumptuous meals on a moment's notice, Benkamil lived quite well there, and spent only the occasional night at the official residence in the city. But allowing the public to see him leading such a lifestyle might bode ill for his further tenure as Prime Minister, so he had kept the existence of the private residence a secret, something not meant for the public eye. A secret residence would be an ideal place to hide during a troublesome incident that might start an interstellar war between the Supremacy and the Commonwealth.

They didn't have time to move their troops to the Prime Minister's secret estate on foot, and heavy combat armor took up a lot of room, so they were forced to limit their assault team to fifteen troopers. But a small number of heavily armed soldiers in full armor could dish out a lot of hurt, if need be.

Using the commandeered grav cars and grav truck, they shuttled Nikaela, Brynjar and the team to a rendezvous point a hundred meters from Benkamil's secret estate. The property measured about a hundred paces on each side, with a high wall surrounding carefully manicured grounds, and a two story house that could only be called a mansion. A heavy metal gate barred entrance to the common public, but when Brynjar barked over the command circuit, "Move out, soldiers," Nikaela's armored comrades simply keyed their gravity fields and floated over the wall with ease. A short hop like that didn't eat up too much of their reactor pack reserves, but it allowed them the advantage of quick, silent entry, and hopefully the element of surprise. Again, Nikaela was forced to wait with Geltkarl while others did the real work.

After ten minutes, and no sounds of gunfire or explosions, she began to wonder. And then the front gates creaked open on hinges powered by some hidden mechanism. Before they had opened fully, Brynjar walked out.

He retracted his visor and said, "The place is almost deserted. No one present but a housekeeper and a couple of servants."

Nikaela said, "The secretary. Do you think she lied?"

He shook his head. "No. She's too frightened of blue-skinned, demon Kelk monsters."

He pondered that for a moment, then said, "Let's go back to headquarters. It may be time for you to have another talk with your battle-kin. I believe you said he is named Mathius."

••••

During stim sleep the thalamus and cortex of the brain were carefully controlled to prevent inappropriate dreams. It could be counterproductive to have a patient's heart rate badly elevated by the fear and emotions of a nightmare, or, for that matter, a pleasant dream that included the thrill of an exciting sexual encounter. Medical technicians also carefully controlled the waking process, and John drifted back to consciousness in a pleasant state where he felt no pain, a marked improvement over recent events.

Carla sat on a stool near his cot, with Hey-You standing next to her, and Leeze standing behind them. All three had removed their helmets and held them tucked under one arm, but were otherwise encased from neck to toes in armor. Carla grinned and said, "Had a pretty exciting night so far, huh?"

Hey-You said, "I think he's just trying to build up the tough-guy image."

Leeze said, "Works for me, makes me all hot and bothered."

"Yah," Carla said. "Hardened, experienced combat veteran, and all that stuff."

Hey-You cocked her head slightly to one side and frowned, as if considering that. She gave John a leering grin and said, "Come to think of it, it's working for me too. He's just making my imagination run away with all sorts of inappropriate thoughts."

Matching the look on Hey-You's face, Carla frowned. "You know, I think it's working for me too. But it's going to be kind of difficult with all this armor in the way."

She glanced up at Hey-You and they shared a conspiratorial look. Carla said, "You know, we could cooperate and—"

John said, "Enough." The last thing he wanted was for the two of them to become friends.

He sat up, moving cautiously, and raised his bandaged left hand to look at it. Earlier, the little finger had been completely gone, with the two fingers next to it reduced to foreshortened stumps. Now the stumps had been removed as well, along with a good portion of his hand.

As if reading his mind, Carla said, "Medic told me to tell you the bone in the two stumps was badly splintered, and there was some serious damage to the hand. He repaired what damage he could, said they'll grow you new fingers and maybe a whole new hand when we get back to *Defiant*."

He looked at his thigh. Hey-You said, "They cleaned that up too, removed a couple flechettes, and stopped the bleeding."

With his right hand he probed gingerly at the wound in his side. Leeze said, "They removed the splinters and stitched you up."

Carla stood, and the three of them loomed over him. Carla said, "They've got you loaded up with regrowth and speed-healing stuff."

Hey-You said, "You were pretty fucked up."

He queried his implants and learned midnight was not far off. A lot had happened in just seven hours.

Carla demanded, "What the fuck happened?"

He shook his head. "It started with the boat. After the pilot ejected us, it came around again and slammed into me. Got my harness snagged on a hinge, would have gone down with the boat if another rocket hadn't hit it. Then everything went downhill from there. When we've got more time I'll tell you about it."

John swung his legs off the cot and planted his boots on the floor. "Am I allowed to get up?"

Hey-You shrugged. "Medic didn't say you couldn't."

John stood, didn't feel dizzy or anything like that.

"We've patched your armor," Carla said. "Parma says to get back into it right away. But be careful of the left gauntlet. It's going to be a weak spot until we replace it with a new one."

John asked, "Is Roark okay?"

She smiled and nodded. "He's here, and he's unhurt. That slob is too stupid to get killed."

"I need to talk to Parma," John said. "Right away. I think I picked up some important intel."

"First things first," Leeze said. "Back into your armor. Then we worry about the other stuff."

Roark, Carla, Leeze and Hey-You helped John don his damaged and repaired armor. When he got the helmet in place he was pleased to see they had replaced the cracked visor. He ran the armor through a full systems check, and with the exception of the impaired left gauntlet it checked out nicely.

"Okay," he said. "Now let's go see Parma."

Carla said, "Follow me."

As the four of them led John through the building, his blackened and scorched plast made him stand out among his comrades, who clearly had not seen the kind of action he had experienced. They found Parma conversing with a senior NCO from *Wicked Fury* named Iskaar, a woman of average height with short-cropped brown hair. Both had removed their helmets.

When Parma saw them approaching, he turned and looked John up and down, then said, "The Kelk messed you up pretty bad, huh?"

"Yah, Sergeant," he said. "It was the Kelk, but I don't think it's Kelk we gotta worry about."

Iskaar had already turned away, but at his words she hesitated and turned back to listen.

Parma frowned unhappily. "Explain, soldier."

John told them how he'd climbed to the roof of a taller building to reconnoiter. He was half-way though explaining how he had spotted the observation posts that didn't appear to be either Kelk or Commonwealth, when their CO, Lieutenant Katherine Komisky, marched into the room, her face clouded with anger.

John, Carla, Hey-You, Leeze and Roark snapped to attention as she stopped in front of John, then leaned forward the way the DIs had when they were really pissed off. "What the hell have you been up to, Mathius?"

"I don't understand, ma'am," John said. "I—"

"Just shut up and come with me," she snarled. She turned to the two NCOs. "You'd both better come too."

••••

Komisky led John and the two NCOs up to the second floor of the building, then into a room where a com tech sat at a bank of instruments. The CO of *Wicked Fury*'s marines, a male lieutenant named Marques, stood behind the com tech. Off to one side stood a female ComSec Lieutenant Colonel. She and the com tech were the only ones not wearing armor. She had chin-length dark-red hair, a figure like Carla's with lots of curves, stood average height and wore a Blacksword patch on her sleeve. She watched John follow Komisky across the room, and never took her eyes off him.

Komisky pointed to a spot next to the com tech and said to John, "Stand right there and don't move."

The lieutenant colonel crossed the room to a door that appeared to lead to an adjoining room, opened it, stuck her head into the other room and said, "Ambassador, he's here. Would you care to join us?"

She held the door for an older man who stepped into the room, a short fellow with close cropped gray hair. From his briefings, John recognized Martin Starkman, the Commonwealth ambassador to Reisenar. The old fellow crossed the room and stopped in front of John. John stood a couple of hand-spans taller than the ambassador, and he had to look down to meet the man's eyes.

"Well now, young man," Starkman said. "You've created quite a bit of excitement here."

John couldn't imagine why having a brawl with a couple of Kelk in a subway station would create a lot of excitement. He said, "I'm sorry, sir, I don't understand."

Starkman spoke in a kindly tone. "No, it is we who don't understand."

He turned to the com tech and said, "Please proceed."

The com tech hit a switch on the bank of instruments, then said, "We're back on line."

A female voice John recognized answered him. "Is this more shit-of-bull you give me? Where got Private Mathius? I said I talk him only."

The com tech said to John, "Just speak and she'll hear you."

John worked hard not to stammer as he said, "This is Mathius."

The com in front of him said, "Hello, Mathius breschkada. This is shit-of-bull Kelk woman you killed."

She paused and John heard a sudden flurry of whispers. Then she said, "Sorry. Need to practice Lingua for better. You *tried* killed. Not did killed. Glad you were smart enough I live. You still there?"

"Yes," John said, "I'm still here."

"Good. We liked coordinates you given me. Found merkineries there."

John said, "Do you mean mercenaries?"

"Yes, mercenaries. And guess who they working for."

The com went silent. Apparently, it hadn't been a rhetorical question and John was actually supposed to guess. He thought about it carefully, and if the mercenaries weren't working for the Commonwealth or the Kelk, that left only one answer.

He said, "They're working for one of the factions in the local government, aren't they?"

"Working for all factions," she said. "Even working for shit-of-bull Benkamil. And what think factions want, Mathius breschkada?"

John hesitated for only an instant. "War," he said, surprised at how easy the answer had come to him. "They want the Supremacy and the Commonwealth at war."

"I knew you smart guy. You give me coordinates, smart thing to do. You save my life, even smarter thing to do."

John had a sudden thought. "Maybe we should talk to Benkamil."

"We tried. Not at official residence, not at secret palace place either. Hiding somewhere we can't find him."

Someone put a hand on John's shoulder and he started. He turned to find that the Blacksword lieutenant colonel had approached him. Up close she stood taller than he had originally thought, could almost stand eye-to-eye with him. She looked toward the com and spoke so the Kelk could hear her. "This is Lieutenant Colonel Primatov. We're going to go offline for a few seconds to confer."

"Go. Talk. We wait."

The com tech hit a switch and nodded to Primatov. She looked pointedly at John, one eyebrow raised unhappily. "What kind of coordinates did you give her?"

He said, "I . . . uh . . ."

Everyone in the room waited silently for him to say something, all eyes focused on him. It had all seemed so clear, at least at the time, but when he thought about how to explain it to them, anything he might say now sounded like a self-indictment for treason.

She spoke calmly as if interrogating a child. "Take your time, Private. Think about it, and walk us through it carefully."

John said, "My suit was damaged, no telemetry feed, no GPS downlink. So I climbed to the top of a building to see if I could do a dead-reckoning reset on my mapping system. I spotted the Kelk on top of their HQ, but I also spotted what looked like observation posts on the top of other buildings, several of them. And they weren't Kelk or Commonwealth. One of them was there to keep an eye on the Kelk, and paying a lot of attention to them."

She said, "And I take it you gave the coordinates of that one to this young Kelk officer."

"Yes," he said, nodding eagerly and hoping she understood.

"Why?"

"I . . ." he said, again at a loss. "She told me the Kelk didn't ambush us, that the warships up there are fake Kelk. And since we didn't ambush them, it just seemed to me there might be a third party playing us one against the other."

She smiled and nodded as if she approved. "So you gave her those coordinates so they could learn that for themselves."

He hadn't thought it through that clearly at the time. "I guess that's why I did it."

She said, "They wouldn't have believed you otherwise. You did record the coordinates of the other observation posts, didn't you?"

"Yes," he said. "Of course."

"Of course." She looked at Parma. "Be sure to get those other coordinates from him. We'll want to question some of those mercenaries ourselves."

She turned away from John to address everyone in the room. "The Blacksword has had a select group of people on the ground here for some time keeping an eye on things. Besides the official residence, Benkamil maintains a secret estate on the outskirts of Helmanport—I assume that's what the young woman meant when she said *secret palace*. But right now he's not at either place, so I'm not surprised they came up empty handed."

Ambassador Starkman said, "And do you know where he is at this moment, Colonel?"

Primatov kept a straight face as she said, "We have a small team that's been watching him day and night for some months. At this moment he's hiding at his mistress's place, an apartment not far from here. If he leaves and goes elsewhere, I'll know about it immediately. I suggest we scoop him up, then propose to our Kelk colleagues that we work together."

"No," Komisky said, slashing a hand through the air like a knife. "We don't work with fucking Kelk. We—"

Clearly, she had forgotten to whom she was talking, and realized it now. She shut up and took a step back.

The ambassador gave Komisky an unpleasant look and said, "I concur with Colonel Primatov."

To Primatov he said, "Please tell our Kelk colleagues we'll collect Benkamil, then we'd like to meet with them. But only give them what information you absolutely must. No sense in giving away the store."

The com tech put them back on line and Primatov said, "This is Lieutenant Colonel Primatov again. We know where Benkamil is hiding. We're going to take him into protective custody. After that, we propose that you and we meet to compare what we've both learned."

A male voice came out of the com speaker, and spoke with very little accent. "This is Senior Command Superior Thordahl. Get hold of Benkamil, then we'll figure out a place to meet."

The com tech hit a switch and the instruments went silent.

The ambassador said, "Very good. I'll leave the details to you, Colonel." He left the room, using the same doorway through which he had entered.

Komisky marched up to John and pointed a shaking finger at him, holding it only a few centimeters from his nose. "You had a Kelk officer in your sights and you didn't kill her. You saved her fucking life? I'm putting you on report. And I'm going to bust you back to buck private."

She spun away from him and marched out of the room, slamming the door behind her. The two NCOs and Lieutenant Marquis looked at each other uncomfortably. John just stood there, unsure of what to say or do.

Primatov took him by the arm and said to the others, "I'd like to have a private word with this young man."

John tensed. If a lowly lieutenant wanted to bust him back to buck private, he couldn't imagine what a Blacksword lieutenant colonel had in mind for him.

Lieutenant Marques said, "We'll wait out in the hall, Colonel."

The two NCOs and the lieutenant walked out of the room, leaving John with the com tech and the Blacksword officer. The com tech looked up from his instruments and said, "Colonel, I'm sorry, but I'm not allowed to leave my post."

She smiled pleasantly and said. "I wouldn't dream of asking you to."

Still holding onto John's arm, she escorted him across the room, and turned to face him with her back to the com tech. She spoke softly, barely above a whisper. "Much that you've heard here in this room, and much that you're about to hear tonight, is highly classified. So be cautious about what you say to your friends, and see to it that it remains that way." She was actually quite pretty, but at that moment she turned a really impressive bitch-face on him.

He said, "Yes, ma'am."

He thought she would now dress him down, but she said, "That young Kelk officer, she called you 'Mathius breschkada' at least twice. Did you really save her life?"

"Yes, ma'am," John said. "I suppose I did. I'm sorry if I did something wrong."

"Explain, please."

John told her of his desperate rush down into the maze of passageways in the subway system, how he'd nearly killed the Kelk woman with the micro-nuke, and how he'd helped her out of her armor, rather that watch it cook her alive inside it.

When he finished, she said, "Do you know what the term 'breschkada' means to the Kelk?"

He shook his head. "No, ma'am."

She nodded and said, "It translates into something like *battle-kin*. To be breschkada, two mortal enemies, in the midst of combat, recognize that there is something more at stake than simply defeating the enemy. They save each other's lives and are therefore bound to each other as comrades-in-arms, of a sort. But they have to do so without committing treason, without betraying their comrades, oaths, loyalties or missions. It's kind of hard to do when their oaths, loyalties and missions are in direct opposition, so breschkada are rather rare. Does that sound like the events that occurred between you and this young Kelk woman?"

John tried to recall everything that had happened on that subway platform, and on the street beforehand. He said, "Everything but her saving my life. We sure tried to kill each other, and came pretty close to doing it, messed up both of us pretty bad. But I don't recall her saving me."

"Well, she must have," Primatov said, "probably in some way of which you are not aware. I should add that the bond between battle-kin is considered especially tight if they came close to killing each other first."

John had a sudden thought. "Do you speak Kelk?"

She shrugged and scrunched her nose. "A little. Why?"

John recalled his last words with the young Kelk officer. When he had said to her, "I suppose, if we ever meet again, one of us will have to kill the other," she had replied in Kelk.

He asked Primatov, "Do you know what 'neertha kaaschmot' means?"

"Sure," she said. "Common expression. Translates to something like 'perhaps not,' or 'maybe not'. Why do you ask?"

He said, "I heard her say it. Thought it might be important, but it isn't." He hoped she didn't detect the lie in his words, hoped she didn't interrogate him further on the matter.

She didn't.

John tried again and again to recall the events on that subway platform, and couldn't remember anything that strange Kelk woman might have done to save his life.

25

Hey-You

PRIMATOV TOOK COMMAND of everything. As the ranking Commonwealth line officer on Reisenar, she had that right, and as a high-ranking Blacksword she clearly intimidated just about everyone who wore a uniform. Ambassador Starkman appeared to be the only one immune to that.

John returned to his squad, again conscious of how his blackened and scorched plast made him stand out among his comrades. Parma immediately cornered him. "I need the coordinates of those mercenary observation posts."

While John had been unconscious, along with patching his armor, they had tried to repair his telemetry link. They had managed to restore some functions like his GPS down-link, but others still operated sporadically. That forced John to pull up the coordinates of the three mercenary observation posts in his implants and recite them verbally to Parma.

Parma gave him a new assault rifle, scavenged from a soldier too badly wounded to remain on the actives list. With only a thumb and forefinger remaining on his left hand, it felt odd to heft it, but the pain suppression software in his implants worked so well he thought he could function as a combatant without being a liability to his squad mates.

"You're not really on the actives list," Parma said. "But if some really bad shit goes down I want everyone armed. Now go get something to eat."

John hadn't had time to think of food, but once Parma mentioned it, his stomach growled and he thought longingly of a good meal. They had provisioned a large banquet room as a temporary mess hall where they served something a little better than ration packs, but not much. John, Carla, Leeze, Hey-You and Roark sat down at a table with trays of something in front of them. Sidewinder and two other senior troopers saw them, crossed the room and sat down without asking permission, one of the prerogatives of seniority.

One of Sidewinder's friends said, "Had a shit time of it, huh, kid?"

John grimaced. "Yah, it started out bad and got worse from there."

Sidewinder reached out and lifted John's left hand so his missing fingers were visible to all. He turned to his friend. "Don't call him kid no more. He earned better than that."

His friend nodded. "Yah, you got a point there."

Sidewinder released John's hand, toyed with the food in front of him, then said, "Took out some Kelk, I hear?"

John nodded. "Yah, a couple. And they almost took me out."

Sidewinder grinned. "Heard about that too. Also heard it ain't the Kelk we need to worry about. But we want to hear it from you."

John's friends and the older troopers waited silently for him to say something, but he wasn't one for storytelling, and he kept recalling Primatov's warning about blabbing classified information. He gave them an abbreviated version of what he had seen from the roof of that building, and of the action on the subway platform. He finished with, "She thought we ambushed them. That's when I figured things didn't add up."

Sidewinder's friend said, "Sounds like things did add up, only it's a different story than we thought."

Sidewinder said, "Parma says we're going to go get some of them mercs for ourselves."

One thing kept gnawing at John. "Where are *Defiant* and *Wicked Fury*? Why aren't we getting fire support from them?"

Sidewinder said, "Sarge told me we've been in contact with them, but they're outgunned by those two Kelk ships." He frowned and looked at John pointedly. "But that Kelk officer said they ain't Kelk ships, right?"

John said, "She called them fake Kelk."

"Well Kelk or not," Sidewinder said, "they've got our ships outgunned. *Defiant* and *Fury* can't fully engage without taking some bad hurt. They're just trying to keep 'em busy, keep 'em from shelling us."

Parma walked into the mess hall, spotted them, crossed the room and stopped at their table. "Mathius," he said. "That Blacksword colonel wants you upstairs. But she said no hurry, you can finish eating first."

Sidewinder stood and faced the sergeant. "Sarge," he said. "Komisky is spitting nails about our man here, completely blew a gasket, says she's gonna bust him back to buck."

Carla's, Roark's, Leeze's and Hey-You's eyes widened.

Sidewinder continued, "She's got some sort of private grudge against them Kelk, and it ain't right she takes it out on the kid here."

John decided not to point out to Sidewinder that he had just violated his own prohibition against calling him *kid*.

Parma grimaced as if he'd just chewed on a nail sandwich. "I'll work it out with the lieutenant. Leave it to me." He turned and walked out of the mess hall.

John finished eating, then climbed the stairs to the second floor. He returned to the room where the com tech sat at his instruments. The tech told him that Primatov, the officers and NCOs were all next door with the ambassador in some sort of big powwow. John put his helmet down on a nearby table then sat down to wait. He had long ago come to realize that learning to wait had been one of the most important lessons in his training. He dozed off sitting there.

••••

The hand that shook John awake was quite gentle, especially when he realized it belonged to Colonel Primatov. He jumped to his feet and tried to snap to attention all in one motion, but she'd been leaning over him and he almost knocked her over in doing so. She staggered back a step and he reached out to steady her, but then he realized he was reaching out to grab a Blacksword colonel, and he froze.

She recovered without his help and said, "Calm down, private."

"Sorry, ma'am," he said. "You startled me."

She shook her head and straightened her uniform. "No harm done."

She looked him over carefully. "You've had a tough night."

He nodded. "A long night, ma'am."

She smiled sympathetically. "Well it's not over yet. And since you're not on Sergeant Parma's actives list, I've asked that you be assigned to me as an observer."

"What—" he said, but clamped his mouth shut. Asking a colonel an uninvited question was one way to learn how much volume she could generate while discussing his ancestry, his complete lack of intelligence, and why he should be removed from the gene pool.

She raised an eyebrow in question, but when he didn't respond she said, "You were about to ask what we're going to do."

She then explained that they were sending two teams from the embassy, and two teams from one of the Blacksword platoons, to hit four targets: the three observation posts John had spotted, and Benkamil's love nest.

She grinned unpleasantly. "You and I are going to join the Blacksword team that's going after Benkamil."

At that point he decided to take a chance and ask one question. "Why me, ma'am?"

She looked at him carefully as if his question perplexed her. "Private Mathius," she said, like a mother teaching a young child. "There isn't one ComSec soldier in ten thousand who would have thought to give those coordinates to that Kelk officer. Most would have simply killed her and walked away."

John said, "Forgive me for being blunt, ma'am, but it seemed obvious . . . to me."

"Yes, Private, and here we are cooperating with them. Do you know what that means?"

He tried not to sound stupid as he said, "Uh, no, ma'am."

She stepped back and regarded him for a moment. "We've been confronting the Kelk now for a hundred and fifty years, and either we aim guns at each other and agree to back away and not kill each other, or we aim guns at each other and start shooting. Not once have we ever cooperated with them on anything. They'll work with independent systems, but not with the Commonwealth, and especially not with the Blacksword."

"Why?" he asked.

Her eyes narrowed in thought. "It's hard to say. We don't know a lot about the Kelk, haven't really tried to learn much about them either. I think our mutual animosity gets in the way. It's been a passion of mine to learn what I can, I suppose, because no one else is willing to try. With the exception of a few isolated scholars, I probably know more than most. We think they see us as a threat, and we certainly see them as a threat."

She let that hang for a moment, then continued, "And here we are, about to cooperate with them . . . all because of you. So I'm quite curious about you, Private Mathius."

She dismissed him and told him to meet her down in the embassy garage in twenty minutes.

••••

Primatov showed up in the garage in full combat armor. She and John boarded a small grav boat with three other Blackswords. One of them piloted the boat, holding it about four meters above the street as they skimmed just over the tops of abandoned and parked vehicles. The smaller boat didn't have internal gravity compensation, so they felt every bump and turn as they headed deeper into the city, the buildings on either side of them flashing past.

The pilot set the boat down in front of a four story structure that looked like a bank. Four more Blackswords climbed into the boat, another boat joined them, and they lifted off together.

A female soldier seated next to John said, "Heard you're the one had a little dance with a couple of Kelk and a micro-nuke."

John lifted his left hand with the missing fingers. "It was my own micro-nuke. I kind of did it to myself."

She asked, "Hurt them more than it hurt you?"

John recalled the Kelk soldier who lay unmoving, the young officer's burns and her missing foot. He simply said, "Yah, I think so."

The Blacksword nodded. "There you have it, kid. Shit's always going to happen. You just gotta make sure more shit happens to them than you."

They didn't speak after that. John glanced around surreptitiously. One of the soldiers seemed larger and a little more imposing than the rest, but for the most part they appeared kind of normal, just like that Major Teal in Brightlaw's office.

Primatov's voice came over the command circuit. "Mathius, you stay with me. Benkamil keeps his girlfriend tucked away in a penthouse apartment. The other boat's going in from the ground floor and coming up, we're going up to the roof and coming down."

John's stomach lurched as the boat lifted upward. At the same time the hatch in the side of the boat hissed open, and lighted apartment windows skimmed past just outside of it. The boat cleared the roof line, sliced sideways and came to a stop.

The pilot said, "Zoned for drop."

An NCO bellowed, "Go, people, go, go, go."

John's seat position made him the last one out of the boat. He joined Primatov on the roof just in time to see soldiers jump over the edge and disappear from sight, descending on their gravity fields.

Someone yelled, "Fire in the hole," and a metal hatch in a far corner of the roof popped open with a flash and bang. Soldiers rushed down through the hatch, leaving John and Primatov the only two remaining on the roof, his heart beating rapidly. He heard breaking glass and a woman screamed, but other than that John heard no gunfire or explosions, and the night went silent.

Monitoring the command circuit, John heard, "Building is secure. Rat's in the cage, though he's not happy about it."

"Private Mathius," Primatov said calmly. "Let's go have a chat with Prime Minister Benkamil."

John and Primatov descended to the top floor of the building through the hatch in the roof. They were walking down a hallway and approaching the penthouse apartment when they heard a man shout, "I know Commonwealth law. You can't make me tell you anything I don't want to."

Primatov paused and turned to John. She retracted her visor and he saw a sour look on her face. "Unfortunately, he's right. Our superiors frown on torture, though one is always tempted, isn't one?"

John decided the question was rhetorical and kept his mouth shut.

The standard briefing for all ComSecCorps soldiers included a picture of the Prime Minister, but when John stepped into the apartment he would have recognized him without that, because he was the only man in the room not wearing armor.

Benkamil stood in the middle of the apartment confronting a Blacksword lieutenant. He wore pajamas made of some silky looking material, his black hair in disarray. Behind him stood a much younger woman clutching at the neck of a long robe, her hair also a mess, tears tracing lines of dark makeup down her cheeks, the points of her nipples protruding quite visibly through the material of the robe. She glanced back and forth rapidly between Benkamil and the lieutenant. Four armed troopers stood in a ring surrounding the three of them.

Benkamil lifted a hand and pointed a finger at the lieutenant. He opened his mouth to say something, but then he spotted Primatov. His eyes flashed, he lowered the hand and started toward her. John stepped in front of her, his rifle held in front of him, but two Blackswords blocked the Prime Minister's path before he took two steps. He struggled with them, but they refused to allow him to pass, though John noticed they were careful not to harm him.

"You have no right," he shouted, waving a hand between the two troopers at Primatov.

Primatov spoke softly. "Private Mathius, thank you for your concern, but please step aside."

John did so.

She walked past him and stopped one pace from Benkamil. "Prime Minister Benkamil," she said. "Some of our people have been badly injured, and others killed. I'm not happy about that. So tonight, I decide what rights I have."

She snapped orders at the lieutenant. "Bring him, and the woman, but don't harm them."

•••

On their way back to the embassy Benkamil voiced a continuous stream of complaints regarding everything Blacksword. Seated in the small boat with the troopers, the Prime Minister and his mistress, John managed to ignore most of it, though he found it interesting when Benkamil said, "It's those Kelk demons you should be after, not an innocent man like me. They're the ones who attacked you." John thought it likely that if the Kelk had taken Benkamil into custody, he'd be spewing something like, "It's those Commonwealth bastards you should be after . . ."

When John climbed out of the boat in the embassy garage, Primatov said to him, "You can return to your squad. We'll let you know when we need you again."

She and her Blackswords led the Prime Minister and his woman away.

John wasn't sure why Primatov had chosen to have him accompany them. After all, he'd been completely superfluous. She probably had some sort of lesson in mind, something she wanted to teach him, but for the life of him he couldn't fathom what. He slung his rifle over his shoulder, removed his helmet, tucked it under his arm, and took a deep breath of the night air.

As John stepped out of the embassy garage, he met Carla, Leeze and Roark coming his way. "You have to come with us," Carla said, worry and fear clouding her features. "Now."

"What's wrong?" he asked.

"Hey-You," Roark said.

Carla said, "She was assigned to a team that went after one of those merc observation posts. It went bad—really bad."

They led him to the temporary field hospital where earlier he'd been treated. The medics had laid Hey-You on a table, stripped off most of her armor, and two of them were working on her, their attention focused on her abdomen and chest. Her eyes were open, blinking rapidly and trying to focus, blood everywhere. One of the medics looked at John and said, "Who are you?"

Leeze said, "They're kind of close."

The medic went back to work.

John stripped off his right gauntlet, and took Hey-You's hand in his. She clutched at his hand with a desperate, vice-like grip, looked into his eyes and appeared to focus for a moment, her mouth opening slightly and quivering as if she wanted to say something, but couldn't.

John asked the medics, "How bad?"

One of them shook his head slightly from side to side, an almost imperceptible gesture. He said, "If we had the full facilities of a ship . . ."

He didn't finish the thought.

John clutched desperately at Hey-You's hand while she looked into his eyes, her jaw quivering with unspoken words. He recalled sitting next to Phillan's cot and holding the young boy's hand as he slowly died. He tried not to think of that, tried to reject the superstitious fear that in reliving those memories he condemned Hey-You to the same fate as the boy.

When the light left her eyes and her life fluttered away, he knew that he would always remember that single instant in time. Her vice-like grip slackened, her breathing went silent, her eyes stopped blinking and her jaw stopped quivering. The two medics froze.

John held her hand and wished that he had gotten there a little earlier, so he could have heard the last words she kept trying to say to him. He didn't recall the medics walking away, or Carla, Leeze and Roark leaving him alone with her. Some unknown length of time later he came back to his senses, standing there alone still clutching Hey-You's hand, tears streaming down his cheeks.

　　　　　　　　　　J. L. Doty

Again, time passed in a seeming instant, and someone now stood on the other side of the table. He looked up into Primatov's face. She had taken hold of Hey-You's other hand.

He said, "Her name was Tamith."

She said, "I know, John."

The two of them stood there for several seconds without saying anything. Then Primatov spoke. "Take all the time you need, John. But when you're ready, come up stairs and help me find out who is responsible for this." He looked into her eyes, and it occurred to him that he really wouldn't want this woman to ever be angry with him, not with the kind of anger he saw in that moment.

She looked sadly at Hey-You's lifeless body for several seconds, then turned and walked away.

John checked the time. It was still only a couple of hours after midnight, and he thought it truly amazing that life could change so much in such a short and frightening period of time.

26

Difficult Cooperation

THE KELK ASSAULT on the building at the coordinates John had given them had alerted the other merc outposts that the game had changed. They increased their surveillance of the Kelk HQ, and added extra combatants to the outposts in the vicinity. The Commonwealth teams that assaulted them ran into stiff resistance, and Hey-You had triggered a booby trap. But again, the light combat armor the mercs wore proved no match against heavy armor, and they hadn't expected Commonwealth troops to assault them, apparently thinking only the Kelk were on to them. ComSecCorps captured more than twenty mercenaries. Rumor had it that among them a high-ranking officer had surrendered as well.

John again received orders to report to the com room on the second floor of the embassy. When he opened the door and stepped into the room, the brass were in the midst of some sort of conference that involved the ambassador, all of the ComSecCorps officers and senior NCOs, plus a couple of other civilians, one of whom he recognized as the vice consul. John put his back against the wall and tried to remain unobtrusive.

Primatov was speaking as he did so, but her eyes flashed his way briefly, and she gave him a slight nod. "He claims the rank of major," she said, "but I'll not dignify Borschek with any rank. He refuses to talk, but I've warned him that since we're not in a war zone, and since he is a Commonwealth citizen, he could face long imprisonment, or even execution. He clearly sees the advantages to bargaining for some clemency, and has hinted that there are certain powerful Commonwealth interests backing this play. He warned me that I don't realize whom I'm dealing with, and I don't like the sound of that."

Primatov looked very unhappy, down-right pissed, in fact.

Ambassador Starkman asked, "What about Benkamil?"

She shook her head. "He remains completely intransigent. As a foreign national he knows our hands are all but tied."

The meeting ended with that, and Primatov called John forward. "Private Mathius, please join us. It's time to contact our Kelk allies."

John had never before heard a Commonwealth officer refer to the Kelk as allies, and that surprised him.

The com tech established radio contact with the strange Kelk woman and her superiors. Both sides agreed to meet in person and bring their captives, but they had some difficulty agreeing upon a rendezvous location. The Kelk HQ inside the city was much too dangerous—too many mercs about, too easy for them to set up an ambush. The embassy grounds were ideal because they were situated on the outskirts of the city, and the mercs would have a difficult time sneaking up on them, but the Kelk had a little trust issue with that.

Ambassador Starkman came up with an idea. "The property next door is vacant, and of a similar size to the embassy grounds. Can we make use of that?"

Thordahl said, "Perhaps."

Primatov said, "We won't touch it, and you can establish your own perimeter there. Then we can meet as equals on the boundary between the two properties."

Thordahl added, "Those of us who meet at the boundary—only light armor and sidearms."

Primatov said, "But our backup troops behind us stay in heavy armor. We've still got mercs out there."

The young Kelk woman spoke, "Mathius breschkada, can we trust you?"

She had just asked John to vouch for Primatov's honesty, even if only indirectly, and he didn't know what to say. His knee-jerk reaction was to tell them that, of course they could trust her, but did this breschkada thing bestow upon him some greater responsibility? He wasn't about to contradict a Blacksword light colonel.

Primatov rescued him. She put a hand on his shoulder, smiled kindly, and spoke loud enough for the Kelk to hear. "Private Mathius, you have my word that if they do not draw weapons on us, we will not draw on them."

John also spoke loud enough for the Kelk to hear. "You heard her. She wouldn't lie."

"Good," the young Kelk woman said.

Thordahl said, "Colonel Primatov, when we meet please be sure to bring Private Mathius."

She said, "Of course."

At a sign from her, the com tech killed the signal.

Primatov looked at John and smiled like a predator. "I would never have considered not bringing you, Private Mathius."

••••

For the parley with the Kelk they needed to cobble together light combat armor. Primatov commandeered the armor of the staff embassy guards and authorized all attendees to draw from that supply, but it had been customized for each wearer and allowed for only minimal adjustment. John became the center of a flurry of activity as his squad mates tested various pieces on him, then tried to pull and stretch and make them fit. At least he ended up with a reasonably decent helmet and com gear, and of course he carried his own sidearm, but much of the rest fit him only marginally. Without the plast armor to cover him fully, the bandages on his thigh, chest, left hand and forearm made him stand out more than had the blackened and scorched heavy armor.

Standing beside Primatov on a second floor balcony of the embassy building, John focused a pair of binoculars on the adjacent property. Like the embassy, its grounds were open with no wall surrounding it. John watched the Kelk sweep in from the city in a couple of police grav cars and a heavy grav truck. The truck put down on the neighboring property, unloaded combatants in heavy armor, then disappeared back into the city. The two cars hovered over the property and swooped around it for a good half hour, obviously covering the troops on the ground while they secured the building and the grounds. The truck made a total of four trips from the city, ferrying more combatants and equipment each time. About three hours before dawn the activity on the property next door came to a standstill.

Primatov lowered her own binoculars and said, "Looks like they decided to move their HQ out of the city. That's probably wise."

A short time later the Kelk signaled that they were ready to meet.

The Commonwealth group consisted of Komisky and Parma, their counterparts from *Wicked Fury*, Primatov, the ambassador, the vice consul, Benkamil, and the mercenary officer Borschek, a man with a hard look not unlike that Cranach and Mercier had exhibited. Borschek's hands had been cuffed behind his back, and both he and Benkamil were accompanied by, and sandwiched between, two Blackswords each. John almost forgot to include himself in his tally of the group. After all, he had nothing to contribute to this and was simply excess baggage.

Primatov led them as they slowly crossed the carefully manicured embassy grounds to its perimeter. They stopped about ten paces short of the boundary and waited in silence. A few minutes later the Kelk contingent approached and stopped facing them, about twenty paces away.

Primatov walked forward and stopped at the boundary. A Kelk senior command superior came forward to meet her—that must be Thordahl. In the group of Kelk behind him, John thought he recognized the young Kelk officer he had nearly killed, and who had nearly killed him. It wasn't hard to spot her; like him, the bandages on her torso stood out rather dramatically, and the stump of her right leg appeared to float about twenty centimeters off the ground. And she didn't have curves as pronounced as Carla, but she had curves of her own and was clearly female.

Thordahl and Primatov spoke briefly, then the Kelk officer turned about and spoke to the group behind him in Kelk. Primatov looked over her shoulder and called out, "Private Mathius, please come forward."

Primatov had warned them all that under the circumstances, sudden movements would not be a good idea, and she had suspended normal military etiquette for this parley. So John didn't do what he would normally do when a colonel called him forward; he didn't rush forward and snap to attention. Instead he walked calmly and stopped beside her. The young Kelk woman came forward with an imposing older woman following protectively behind her, and they stopped facing him. John couldn't recall all his lessons regarding Kelk rank, but he thought the older woman wore the insignia of a senior NCO.

The younger woman lifted her right hand and held it rigidly flat and level just above her left breast. It took John a moment to realize she was extending to him the courtesy of a salute. He snapped to attention, raised his right hand to his forehead and returned her salute in the Commonwealth fashion. She relaxed, looked down at his left hand and said, "Sorry bout fiengers."

He said, "They'll grow me new ones." He looked down at the stump of her right leg hovering above the ground on an invisible gravity field. "Sorry about the foot."

She said, "They grow me new one."

Primatov said, "I think I've just witnessed an historic moment in interstellar diplomacy."

Thordahl said, "Private Mathius, again we thank you for the coordinates you gave Mistress Vreekande."

John almost flinched at finally learning the young woman's last name.

Thordahl continued. "It may have averted a terrible misunderstanding."

John's thoughts momentarily flashed to Hey-You, and a flood of anger washed through him. "Not a misunderstanding, sir. More like a lie perpetrated by some assholes I want to kill."

The Vreekande women grinned aggressively and nodded as if she agreed with him.

Primatov spoke kindly and said, "Private, the proper form of address for a male Kelk officer is maestra, not sir."

John nodded politely and tried to roll the r when he said, "Maestra, my apologies."

Thordahl said, "No offense taken. What are the words you used: assholes. Yes, those are good words for the people who did this. We've both lost good people."

He asked Primatov, "You have Benkamil?"

"Yes," she said. "We do. But he's not being terribly cooperative. We also have a mercenary officer named Borschek, and he's more cooperative. He's hinting that there are some powerful interests behind some sort of plot."

Thordahl nodded. "We too have a captive mercenary officer, and he has said some powerful Kelk players are involved."

Primatov stiffened and frowned. "Kelk? Our mercenary is saying powerful Commonwealth players."

Thordahl frowned much the way Primatov had. "You think maybe both?"

Primatov nodded her agreement. "I'm beginning to suspect that there's no maybe about it. Do you think it possible we're not the first Commonwealth and Kelk parties to cooperate?"

Thordahl considered her for a long thoughtful moment. "We do have our own . . . disagreements within the Supremacy. Factions, I believe you call them."

She said, "We have various factions within the Commonwealth as well."

"About Benkamil," Thordahl said. "I have an idea, perhaps a way to make the Prime Minister more cooperative. Please bring him forward."

Primatov said, "I can't allow you to physically harm him." She had put some emphasis on the word *physically*.

Thordahl shook his head. "We won't touch him."

Primatov called over her shoulder again. "Ambassador Starkman, please come forward." She barked a couple of names John didn't recognize. "You two bring Benkamil forward."

Thordahl turned about and called two more Kelk forward, then said something to Vreekande in Kelk. She grinned unpleasantly and said, "Mathius breschkada, we go to side standing."

John looked to Primatov for approval and she said, "Go ahead."

John and the young Kelk woman stepped about ten paces to one side, though the older NCO who seemed so protective of her remained with Thordahl. Starkman came forward, followed by two Blackswords escorting Benkamil held between them. The Prime Minister stiffened and became clearly uncomfortable as he approached the Kelk. The Vreekande woman said, "Watch this, Mathius friend. This will be fun."

John ignored her because he had a question that had been nagging at his thoughts. "On that subway platform, did you save my life in some way?"

She gave him a knowing, superior smile. "You saved mine life, why not save yours? Can't be breschkada-se without. And I think you make good breschkada-sa for me."

"You didn't answer my question."

The superior smile turned into a predatory grin. "We Kelk . . . we like not different races be relationship. But one exception okay: breschkada is okay. No one criticize breschkada relationship."

John wasn't sure what she meant by relationship. Did she mean something platonic, or something more intimate? His old Novalis III reflexes surfaced and he grew hot and flushed.

"Don't worry, Mathius breschkada. We have no debt between us."

"I know the word breschkada," he said. "But you said breschkada-sa. What is that?"

She squinted, and scrunched her face up in thought. "That means you are girl-type breschkada. Girl-type. You are girl-type guy."

He wasn't sure what that meant. Maybe she had the wrong idea about him. He asked, "And breschkada-se?"

"That means I am boy-type breschkada. I am boy-type woman."

And maybe he had the wrong idea about her.

A scream from Benkamil drew their attention. "No, you can't."

He struggled between the two Blackswords, but they held him in place. "No, he screamed. No, please no." He would have dropped to his knees, but the two troopers held him up by his armpits. "I'll tell you anything you want."

John turned to Vreekande, wondering if he'd ever learn her first name. "What are they doing to the Prime Minister?"

She let out a quiet laugh. "These Reisenar peoples, they believes stories about Kelk crazy peoples, thinks we eats childs. You don't thinks we eats childs, do you?"

"No," he said. "Those are stupid stories." He didn't tell her that not too long ago he had believed such tales.

She nodded, again laughing at something. "Your command hawk, she threatened give him to us. He thinks we cook him and eat him. Then maybe cook his childs and eat them too."

John couldn't help but laugh a little along with her.

Vreekande said, "Why you ships not give fire support? We could end this quick with fire support."

John said, "They're outgunned by those two fake Kelk."

"Outgunned," she asked, her eyes narrowing, "What is word outgunned?"

"The fake Kelk have more guns than our two ships."

She raised one eyebrow, again a very human gesture. "How bad outgunned?"

"Bad enough that all they can do is try to keep the fake Kelk too busy to provide fire support against us."

She spun away from him and marched toward Thordahl and Primatov. John followed her, and as the two of them approached the small group, the two Blackswords dragged a spluttering, sobbing Benkamil away. Vreekande said something to Thordahl in Kelk, speaking with a breathless urgency. The two of them stepped away from the group and put their heads together, rapidly firing words back and forth and keeping their voices low.

Primatov asked John, "What's going on, Private?"

He shook his head and said, "I don't know, ma'am. Something about our ships."

The two Kelk rejoined the group and Thordahl said to Vreekande, "Your idea, you tell them."

She beamed a big, white-toothed smile and said, "Would help from heavy cruiser make difference for your ships?"

Primatov answered cautiously. "Yes, it would."

Command Boss Vreekande's smile broadened even further, and at that moment John found her quite attractive. She said, "We have ship name *Reguskalde*. We work together here on ground." She hooked a thumb up toward the night sky. "We work together there."

••••

Nikaela watched the Commonwealth people walk away, paying particular attention to young Private Mathius. Something about him bothered her, though not in a fearful or suspicious way. Perhaps she had seen him before somewhere and now his face struck the chord of a distant memory. But that could not be; only once before had she ever faced any Commonwealth soldier, and that had been earlier in the night on that subway platform when he had nearly killed her, then saved her life, and then all she had seen of him was the faceless visor of his armor.

She and he were clearly of a similar age, though in many ways he seemed far younger than that, and in other ways far older. He had a kind face in which she saw both the naiveté of a child, and the haunted eyes of a hardened combat veteran. As she thought of his face she realized she considered him reasonably good-looking, at least for a common-face.

"Mistress Vreekande." Thordahl's words brought her out of her reverie. "Don't dally. We have much to do in a short period of time."

Nikaela looked one last time at the receding back of that young Commonwealth soldier, and turned to join her comrades.

27

Reluctant Cooperation

FOR SOME REASON that John didn't understand, Primatov kept him close at hand. They returned to the room with the com tech, the fellow fired up the transition com, and established contact with both *Defiant* and *Wicked Fury*. Their running battle with the two fake Kelk had taken them several hundred light-hours outside of the Vischas system. To get the commanding officers of the two ships to agree that they wouldn't fire on a third Kelk ship when it appeared on their screens, Primatov did quite a lot of explaining, and a fair amount of convincing. John finally got a glimpse of what he'd gotten himself into when the CO of *Wicked Fury* said, "A fucking private with a single stripe on his sleeve decided to establish diplomatic relations with the fucking enemy? If he's one of mine, I'm venting the little shit to space, and we'll let him breathe vacuum for a while."

Primatov gave John an uncomfortably sympathetic look, and it occurred to him that she was keeping him close at hand just to keep him alive. John's instructors had told them that the Commonwealth was not at war with the Kelk, that the strange humans with red eyes were not the enemy. He decided now was not the time to mention that.

Primatov managed to calm the *Fury*'s CO somewhat, but just barely. They finally agreed that they wouldn't fire upon *Reguskalde* if the Kelk warship immediately fired on the two fake Kelk as soon as she could range on them. Primatov then contacted Thordahl and explained the situation, though she said nothing about the ire of the *Fury*'s CO. The Kelk officer seemed to understand the delicacy of the situation, and John thought the fellow might be dealing with similar issues at his end. He said, "I have had to speak at some length with *Reguskalde*'s captain. She is somewhat . . . skeptical of the situation. I'll tell her to approach the fake Kelk warships from the opposite direction of your ships. She can then range on them and fire on them before your ships can range on her."

Primatov said, "Perhaps it's best if she *never* gets within range of our ships."

Thordahl said, "Good idea. I'll mention that." He signed off.

It bothered John that Primatov didn't make any attempt to get the CO of *Wicked Fury* to agree he wouldn't vent John. But the colonel probably had more important things on her mind than the survival of a lowly private first class. At least John wouldn't be under the man's command, though it occurred to him he couldn't be certain the CO of *Defiant* didn't feel the same.

Primatov had been correct when she had surmised that the Kelk had relocated their headquarters to the property adjacent to the embassy. They had set up a command post inside the two story mansion in the middle of the estate. And since Benkamil had reacted in such a dramatic way to the demon Kelk monsters, she decided that interrogating him there would give him extra incentive to speak freely. With an escort of several Blackswords, all in light armor and sidearms, they dragged a screaming, crying, sobbing, kicking, spluttering Benkamil to the new Kelk headquarters.

As a child John had taken the stories of Kelk atrocities at face value. But many of the excesses attributed to them were physically impossible, and as a teenager he had begun to suspect the veracity of those tales. He had now seen for himself that the wildly strange physical characteristics attributed to them in those stories were unquestionably false. Mistress Vreekande and her comrades were clearly very human, though he hadn't yet confirmed that her tongue wasn't forked. He didn't really need to. He was certain it wasn't.

He asked Primatov about Benkamil's overreaction and his belief in tales that were clearly false. She shrugged, grimaced and said, "We see that in some of the more isolated systems. They sometimes exist in their own self-contained environment, and percolate their insularity the way a scientist grows bacteria in a culture. Sometimes it feeds on itself."

A senior Kelk NCO led them to a room on the ground floor in the new Kelk HQ, where Thordahl and two Kelk officers waited. A simple chair had been placed in the middle of the floor, the only piece of furniture present. They sat Benkamil down in the chair, and before anyone asked a single question, he took one look at the Kelk, and started spilling his guts about powerful Commonwealth corporations cooperating with similar Kelk interests to start a war that would benefit them all.

Primatov said to a young Blacksword officer, "You wait here with me."

To John and the rest of them she said, "I think it would be best if you waited outside."

Benkamil continued to blather conspiracy stories as John and the Blackswords stepped out of the room into the hallway. Primatov paused in the doorway and said, "You didn't hear that, John. Remember, classified."

"Yes, ma'am," he said.

Her eyes scanned the Blackswords standing next to him, and she gave each of them a hard look. An NCO said, "We know the drill, ma'am."

She smiled, nodded, and closed the door.

One of the Blackswords standing there with John said, "You sure opened some can of shit, kid. What did you do?"

John grimaced and said, "You heard her. I don't think I'm supposed to say anything."

The NCO said, "Leave the kid alone."

"Come," a young Kelk officer said. The look on his face implied he'd been given the responsibility of performing some sort of exceedingly distasteful task. "Command Superior Thordahl told me to treat you well. Follow me."

He turned and marched down the hall. John and the Blackswords followed. The Kelk officer led them to a make-shift mess hall. "Would you like something to eat or drink?"

Intending to ask for some water, John opened his mouth and said, "I wouldn't mind—"

The Blacksword NCO silenced him with a look, leaned close to him and said, "We don't take anything from them. Who knows what they put in it?"

John and the Blackswords sat down at an empty table to wait. Kelk troopers wandered in and out of the mess hall, most with the helmet of their armor tucked under one arm. To John's surprise, their hair wasn't coarse and animalistic, was instead quite normal. A few wore ropey dreadlocks, while most let it simply hang straight down to their shoulders. But all of them had paid some attention to their appearance, though like most soldiers, they kept it simple.

John heard her before he saw her, though since she spoke Kelk he recognized only one word: breschkada. The Vreekande woman walked into the mess hall. "Ah," she said, "Mathius friend."

At the word friend, one of the Blackswords gave John an ugly look.

She marched up to their table. "We are breschkada, so I must know your name. I am Nikaela Vreekande."

John stood and stuck out his hand. "I'm John Mathius."

She looked at his extended hand with a frown. "What is this, John Mathius? Why push your hand at me?"

He withdrew the hand. "Nothing," he said. "Nothing."

••••

Lieutenant Colonel Katrine Primatov decided the Kelk effect on Benkamil might be enhanced if he forgot the presence of what he considered *humans*, and faced only the dreaded Kelk monsters. Once they sat Benkamil in the chair, and she dismissed young Mathius and the others, she got the attention of the young Blacksword officer accompanying her, and with a nod of her head he joined her at the back of the room behind the Prime Minister, and out of sight. He'd have to turn about completely to see anyone but the blue-skinned demons.

She spoke softly and said, "We'll wait here in silence, let them handle it."

He nodded and didn't say a word.

The three Kelk stood in front of the seated Prime Minister and loomed over him. Katrine did not need to ask a single question. She and her subordinate simply stood in the background and watched Thordahl guide the whimpering Prime Minister from one topic to the next. Benkamil told an interesting story of how a faction in the Commonwealth who hated the Kelk and wanted only war, had joined with a faction who had corporate interests that would benefit financially from such a war. They contacted Benkamil, and he introduced them to similar factions in the Supremacy. Once everyone realized they had certain mutual interests that could be satisfied by the same outcome, even though they despised one another, they found it rather easy to work together. Benkamil acted as liaison, coordinated activities with the factions on Reisenar, and stood to benefit quite handsomely from the arrangement.

Katrine thought it might be best for all concerned if the Prime Minister had an accident. Perhaps something in which a mechanical failure dropped a grav transport out of the sky. Benkamil's constituents could mourn the loss of their beloved Prime Minister, and they could replace him with someone less inclined to pad his personal coffers through the use of interstellar war. She decided to make that recommendation to her superiors.

When the Kelk had wrung every bit of information they could out of the poor fellow, he sat in the chair sobbing quietly. Katrine crossed the room to Thordahl and said, "May I have a private word with you, maestra?"

He said, "Certainly, Colonel."

They stepped out into the hallway where they could speak without being heard. Katrine handed him a small piece of paper, a very old fashioned way of communicating, but one that didn't leave any electronic footprint lying about.

He raised an eyebrow in question.

She said, "The name and contact information on that piece of paper is a merchant on Norandyne. If you ever wish to contact me in a discreet way, he can facilitate such communication. Though once you've memorized the information, do destroy that piece of paper."

He looked at her and met her eyes for a long moment, then smiled. "After the excitement here dies down, I'll contact him and let you know how you can contact me in a similar fashion."

She didn't offer to shake his hand. The Kelk didn't do that.

••••

The Blacksword officer who had remained with Primatov walked into the mess hall, led by a Kelk NCO. John and the Blackswords at the table stood. "Come, people," the officer said. "The Prime Minister has been most informative, and we're done here."

Mistress Vreekande accompanied them as the Kelk NCO led them to the front of the mansion and outside, where Primatov, Thordahl and the other Kelk waited for them. Two Kelk held a whimpering Benkamil supported between them and turned him over to the Blackswords. At the look on John's face, Primatov said, "Didn't have to lay a hand on him, John. We merely questioned him in a perfectly legal fashion."

She said to Thordahl, "Thank you for your help, Command Superior."

He said, "It has been mutually beneficial, Colonel."

Primatov spun on her heel and walked out across the lawn. With Benkamil in tow, the Blackswords followed her.

John took one last look at Nikaela, smiled, and for some reason he thought the strange Kelk woman looked quite appealing. But he shrugged that thought off and turned toward the embassy.

Nikaela caught his arm and spun him to face her. She leaned close to him and said, "I saw look you had on me. If we meet again, maybe I take you as lover."

John said, "I . . . Uhhh!"

He backed away from her, turned and followed quickly after his comrades.

••••

When *Reguskalde* fired the first rounds at the fake Kelk, realizing the odds had tipped against them, they turned and ran. And by the time the sun rose that morning, the city had calmed considerably, though its residents remained huddled in their homes.

Defiant and *Wicked Fury* returned to close orbit around Reisenar, and from that vantage had full command of the planet's airspace. One group of mercenaries tried to escape to the countryside in a grav boat, but the calm of a clear morning was broken by the ear-splitting crack of *Defiant*'s transition batteries, and the boat tumbled out of the sky in fiery pieces. After that, the Blackswords corralled the remaining mercenaries with little resistance.

Primatov sat John down and explained exactly what he could discuss with his comrades. He was to completely forget that he'd heard anything about the involvement of powerful Kelk and Commonwealth interests. If anyone asked, he didn't know anything, but had heard rumors it had been a plot orchestrated solely by Benkamil and his coconspirators in the other Reisenar factions. She warned him that if he said anything to the contrary, he'd face a court-martial and many years at hard labor. Above all, he was to say nothing about his breschkada status with Mistress Vreekande. Yes, they had nearly killed each other. And yes, he had given her the coordinates. And yes, that had resulted in very limited cooperation between them that foiled a plot by Reisenar's factions. But no breschkada.

She added, "Keep your mouth shut, your head down, and you'll probably make it to corporal."

John said, "May I ask a question about Mistress Vreekande?"

"Certainly," she said. "Though I may not know the answer."

"When she and I were standing off to the side, when we first met them, she called me breschkada-sa, and she called herself breschkada-se. I asked her what that meant, but I think we had some language difficulty."

Her eyebrows rose and her eyes widened. "Breschkada-sa is the one who first saved the other's life. Breschkada-se is the one who returned the favor. That at least confirms the sequence of events. By the way, breschkada-sa is considered a higher honor. Did you learn how she saved your life?"

"No," he said. "She said something else. When I asked her, she said Breschkada-sa meant I was a . . . girl-type guy?"

Primatov laughed quietly. "Yes, most definitely a language difficulty. I think what she meant is that Breschkada-sa is the feminine form of address, while Breschkada-se is the masculine. Many of their words have gender-specific forms or variations. Are you aware that Kelk society is highly matriarchal?"

"No," he said. "What does that mean?"

"For one thing, you'll frequently see more women in positions of authority than men. And feminine forms of address are dominant."

"Oh," John said. Now he thought he understood what Mistress Vreekande had been trying to tell him.

He shrugged and said, "Sorry to waste your time."

She shook her head. "John, you have not wasted my time."

The job of protecting the embassy turned into the milk run it should have been all along. However, as a seriously wounded combatant, they evacuated John with the other wounded two days after the end of the hostilities. John spent a tenday in sickbay. They cultured him a new hand, amputated the damaged one and replaced it.

Twenty-three days after they had made the disastrous drop to the surface of Reisenar, *Defiant* lined up on a collision course with the star Vischas. They buried their dead in space by venting them in vac-sealed body bags, then transited out of the system. *Wicked Fury* would follow the next day, and while it might take a month or two, Hey-You and the comrades they had lost, would eventually become the stuff of stars.

Komisky never did bust John back to buck private. In fact, two months after they left Reisenar, he received a promotion to corporal. She gave it to him with a sour look on her face, and after that went out of her way to make his life unpleasant. Sidewinder and Parma tried to help, and often shielded him from the worst of it. But she was the marine CO, and some days proved to be quite difficult.

A few months after leaving the Vischas system, John came across an article in the news feeds. Prime Minister Benkamil had died in a transport accident. The authorities on Reisenar were still investigating, but preliminary results pointed to a mechanical failure in his private grav ship. The citizens of Reisenar mourned their beloved prime minister, and laid him to rest with considerable ceremony.

When John's year of active duty ended, he returned to Miriteen for Command School.

••••

After the fake Kelk turned tail and ran, the two Commonwealth ships had *Reguskalde* seriously outgunned. Her captain didn't want to take the chance that old antagonisms might end the fragile cooperation between the two powers, so she parked her ship near the edge of the Vischas system, rigged for silent running and disappeared from everyone's screens. *Reguskalde* remained there until the Commonwealth ships transited out of the system, then she fired up her drive and parked in a close orbit around Reisenar. Because of her wounds Nikaela was one of the first evacuated.

After *Reguskalde* up-transited out of the Vischas system, Nikaela quickly grew bored in sickbay waiting for them to regrow her new ankle and foot, and culture new skin to repair the burns on her back and ribs. With an excess of time on her hands on the return journey, she thought a lot about her interactions with the strange Commonwealth common-faces. Time and again she recalled the way her breschkada's face had triggered in her some sort of vague memory, but when she tried to recall it she came up with nothing.

They attached the new ankle and foot about half way back to Viktorkinde, and she spent the rest of the journey in physical therapy getting used to it. The burns took a little longer than the ankle, but by the time she stepped onto the docks at Viktorkinde Prime, the medical people had repaired all the scarring, and she looked and felt as good as new. Still, she had trouble sorting out those memories of her breschkada's face.

To her disappointment they wanted her to exercise and recuperate further, so they gave her a desk job on the military docks on the big satellite. Regrettably, she said good bye to Thordahl and Geltkarl.

28

Duty Abandoned

AFTER A YEAR away, it felt strange to return to Miriteen along with the rest of his training battalion, almost as if they had never left. But John had left, and come back a very different person. He thought it quite probable that many of his comrades had changed as well. And some didn't come back at all, like Hey-You. He thought about her a lot.

John couldn't help but be self-conscious about his new corporal's stripes. Carla teased him mercilessly. "Man with a future," she said. "I just may have to get you under the sheets. You know"—she wiggled her chest at him—"keep the chain of command happy."

Leeze wiggled her chest at him too, but she didn't have the assets of a Carla, though she did have nice assets. She elbowed Carla. "Think he can handle a threesome?"

It wasn't the first time Carla had hinted at a closer relationship with John. The rest of the platoon took it as playful teasing, but comments she had voiced when they were alone had made it quite clear she was willing to take it farther than that. For him, it was too soon after he'd lost Hey-You, but he didn't say that.

John noticed DeLeon staring at him, his eyes hard and angry. A year without DeLeon had been a welcome relief, but nothing between them had really changed; another thing where time felt as if it had stood still. Roark must have noticed it too, because he said to Carla, "Cut it out. You're just pissing DeLeon off."

Carla gave Roark a nasty look and tilted her head to one side. "I really don't care what DeLeon thinks."

"Wake up," Roark said. "It's not you he's pissed at."

She glanced toward DeLeon and saw the sneer he directed at John. "Oh shit! Sorry, John!"

John shrugged. "He'd be pissed off at me anyway. I got an extra stripe before him, and he doesn't like that."

Their return to Miriteen after a year of active duty had a very specific purpose. Command School would not be more of the same. According to their instructors, they'd go through a series of exercises in which they would all have multiple opportunities to command a unit. The structure and size of a unit for any given exercise, the circumstances, everything would vary, all with the intent of maximizing their potential for leadership roles.

DeLeon had a more cynical and calculating view of Command School. "When they're done with us here, we'll all be pegged exactly where they think we fit: enlisted, NCO, officer, senior officer. And once they've made up their minds on you, you're never going beyond that. So you'd better look good now, or your career is going to be shit."

John asked Omuglu about that, and she said, "I suppose that happens in some officer's minds. But I know what's in your files, and there's nothing like that in there, nor will there be. And twenty years from now, whether you get a promotion or not, the decision will likely be made on all the stuff you do between now and then."

She gave John a pat on the back. "Just work hard, soldier, do your best, and try to ignore DeLeon."

Half way through their six-month stint at Command School, Carla and DeLeon both got an extra stripe, and DeLeon strutted around proudly displaying his. John hoped that now that he no longer outranked the fellow, DeLeon's jealousy would abate and there'd be less tension between them. Then it occurred to him that if Corporal DeLeon got another stripe, he'd outrank John, which would probably be even more unpleasant. But John didn't have to worry because a month later, he got his first sergeant's stripe. DeLeon's puckered, angry stare returned with a vengeance.

They finished Command School with a series of exercises in which all of them were given the opportunity to put their newly learned skills to use. During each exercise several of them were given temporarily elevated rank and placed in low-level positions of command. Macus DeLeon outranked him in one of the early exercises, and to John's surprise he didn't take advantage of the situation to make John's life unpleasant. In the last exercise, they placed John in command of third platoon, Echo Company, with DeLeon in charge of one of the squads reporting to him, and Carla in charge of another.

••••

John had tapped into an external camera in the large drop boat's nose, and he watched the terrain sweeping by beneath it on the inside of the helmet visor in his light combat armor. The boat's pilot skimmed the treetops as they descended into a shallow valley, dark smoke rising from the high ground in the distance. The forest beneath them thinned out as they crossed the valley and approached the hill they must defend, though John noted the underbrush remained thick and heavy. Fox Company had taken a pounding from First Battalion, and Echo would now reinforce and relieve them.

The dropmaster's voice sounded eerily calm as he said, "One minute to DZ."

John started to check his equipment. But he'd done that a dozen times already so he took a deep breath to calm his nerves, and just sat there.

He noted that the hill they approached had deep ravines cut into the side of it, probably put there by heavy seasonal rains. Gullies like that would provide good cover for an attacking force trying to storm the hill.

"Outboard personnel," the dropmaster said, "stand up."

John killed the feed to his visor and stood along with half his platoon mates.

"Inboard personnel, stand up."

The rest of them stood.

The drop boat's internal grav fields compensated for all motion, so John felt nothing as it descended into the drop zone. Standing at the rear of the craft, he would be one of the first out of the boat, leading Third Platoon, with Fourth to follow.

He heard the hum of motors and the whine of hydraulics, then a slit of sunlight appeared as the big cargo hatch in the aft belly of the boat descended. As it slowly opened it revealed a terrain of tents, bunkers, dirt, dust and smoke. The skin of the boat muffled the familiar pop of gunfire in the distance, but the smell of the smoke had the characteristic tang of expended ordinance. John checked the map displayed on the inside of his visor, which overlaid his view of the terrain about him. A red blip marked the east side of the hill, his destination.

The end of the cargo hatch touched the ground, providing a disembarking ramp. The dropmaster slapped John on the back of his shoulder and shouted, "Go."

John double-timed it down the ramp and took a sharp left. He came face-to-face with a female lieutenant.

"Third platoon," he said. "Echo company. We've been assigned the east perimeter."

John noted a line of stretchers with wounded to be evacuated. He had to forcefully recall that the blood and wounds he saw were merely simulations fed directly into his cerebral cortex through his implants. They all wore skin-tight sim-suits beneath their uniforms. If the combat simulation computers decided that a blank shot in the exercise would have produced a wound in a soldier in real combat, the soldier felt the pain of the wound as if it were real, and all of them saw virtual blood that didn't really flow. It provided an unreal sense of reality, and while the pain and blood could be switched off in an instant, the memory of it remained. It felt too much like Reisenar.

The drop turned out to be rather anticlimactic. The lieutenant gave John directions, which coincided with what he saw on the inside of his visor, though she warned

                    J. L. Doty

him about a ridge line where they could accidentally expose themselves to enemy snip-er fire, something not obvious on the terrain map. Staying low and moving in a crouch, they worked their way through the brush to an earthen redoubt on the eastern perimeter. They joined the platoon already covering that flank, and spent about an hour while the Fox Company soldiers briefed them on the situation.

John learned that First Battalion liked to attack at dawn. There were two ravines they had to watch closely because, as John had suspected, they provided good ave-nues of approach for the attacking forces. John assigned DeLeon's squad to cover the gully on their far right flank, and he gave Carla's squad the task of watching over the other ravine. During what remained of the day they carefully reconnoitered the terrain just outside the perimeter, then ate a lukewarm meal from ration packs, and hunkered down for the night. Nothing happened that first night, and boredom set in.

••••

It started with nothing more than the snap of a twig about an hour before dawn on their second night on the hill. Seated behind a bulwark of earthen-filled bags, John had drifted in and out of a light sleep, more through boredom than any real fatigue. At first he ignored that single, solitary sound. Their briefings had warned them that small de-sert predators weighing about twenty kilos prowled the nighttime forest hunting for smaller prey. John assumed that even the stealthiest animal would make some little sounds here and there. But when the leaves of a nearby tree rustled softly as if dis-turbed by a faint breeze, he froze and listened carefully.

There had been a light breeze drifting over their hill around midnight, more of a soft sigh to disturb the night air. But it had died a few hours earlier, leaving the dark-ness still and silent.

Sitting next to him behind the bulwark, Roark leaned toward him and said, "You know—"

John's hand shot out almost without thought and covered Roark's mouth. He raised a finger to his lips and shook his head silently, then tapped the finger to his ear. Roark nodded, acknowledging John's unspoken commands, so John lowered his hand.

They waited and listened. He thought he heard what could be the crunch of boots on gravel, but so feint he couldn't be certain he wasn't allowing his imagina-tion to go into overtime. Then silence for an untold number of heartbeats. Then an-other twig snap, and again silence. The crunch of boots on gravel, the snap of a twig, the rustle of leaves in a breeze that didn't exist, all convinced him that their enemy had snuck up to their redoubt using the cover of darkness. He couldn't be certain, but he thought several of their adversaries had approached to within about thirty paces of their position.

Miriteen had a small moon that generated tidal activity, but with a low reflectivity it produced almost no light at night, even in full aspect. Flood lights aimed outward from the perimeter illuminated the thin forest and brush for about thirty paces, but beyond that the darkness hung heavy and complete all around them. The perimeter lights left John and his comrades in dark shadow, and his helmet masked any infrared he might emit, so he didn't have to fear taking a head shot if he moved cautiously. He lowered his visor and rose slowly on his haunches, stopping when he could just see over the bulwark. His visor would spot any infrared signatures, but he saw nothing beyond the glare of the lamps, which confirmed his suspicions. If some sort of animal had been prowling about beyond the perimeter, he would have picked it up on IR.

He crouched back down behind the bulwark, keyed his implants to the command circuit and subvocalized, "Mathius here, third platoon on the east perimeter. I think we've got hostiles outside the bulwark, but no visual confirmation."

Up and down the line of the perimeter his platoon mates got off their butts and crouched behind the bulwark, weapons ready; they had been monitoring the command circuit. John keyed his implants to the platoon circuit. "Grenadiers, set your cartridges to fragment at three meters off the ground, and at a range of thirty meters."

The response from the command center came back immediately. "Sentry scans indicate we've got nothing on infrared, but they can stealth that." The voice paused. "The timing isn't right. They usually like dawn. Stand by."

John wondered if he'd have to argue with his commanding officer, but only a few seconds passed before the command center came back at him.

"We're going to light it up. You have permission to engage anyone outside the perimeter."

John's gut tightened with fear as he said over the platoon circuit, "You heard the man."

He slowly rose up again and rested his rifle on the top of the earthwork. A moment later the thump of a mortar shattered the silence of the night, and overhead a new sun appeared just above the treetops. It caught several shadows moving through the brush, but they froze. John fired a short burst at one of the shadows, and that triggered a response from everyone. The dull thumps of the grenade launchers were followed by the flash-bang of the fragmentation cartridges shredding the forest canopy. The night lit up with tracers slicing through the air, and the high-pitched whine of a rotary ground at his ears. More flares lit up the night sky and mortar rounds punched into the surrounding forest. Bullets thumped into the earthworks all around them. One of John's female platoon mates grunted and fell away from the wall, landing on her back, a round hole in the middle of her visor with a starburst of cracks radiating outward from it.

John reminded himself that almost all the violence he saw and heard were virtual sights and sounds fed to him through his implants. The soldier had taken a death wound, so her implants and sim suit had dropped her to the ground unconscious. She'd awake in their barracks with no ill effects, other than perhaps an unpleasant memory or two. He had to keep reminding himself of that.

The initial firefight must have taken its toll on the attackers from First Battalion, but it didn't slow their assault. When one of John's subordinates took a wound, the soldier appeared as a blip on the terrain map on the inside of his visor, color coded and iconized to indicate the severity of the wound. Losses piled up on both sides, and that night John learned that most of the rounds he fired were aimed blindly with no specific target, guided more by fear than skill. He'd done the same on Novalis III, and had thought all this training would make him better than that stupid kid he'd left behind.

The fight continued without letup and more and more blips appeared on his visor, coded as dead or no longer able to function as active combatants. But third platoon held the perimeter, held it well, and John felt a welling of pride for his comrades.

As dawn broke he thought they might repel the assault without taking heavy losses. But their far right flank suddenly collapsed, and several soldiers in his platoon died one after the other in quick succession. His visor defaulted to showing only the dead and wounded. He keyed it now to display the locations of his entire platoon, and saw DeLeon's squad moving out to the right, leaving the ravine unguarded and fully exposing their flank.

He keyed his implants into the platoon circuit. "DeLeon, what the hell are you doing?"

"Got a stroke of luck," DeLeon answered, "can't pass it up."

"Negative," John shouted. "Negative. Hold your position. Hold your position."

DeLeon chose not to answer him.

John rose up into a crouch and ran that way. "Myclos," he shouted into his implants, calling one of the other squad leaders, "with me, your squad, now."

Corporal Myclos and his squad spilled away from the bulwark and filed in behind John. But as they approached the ravine DeLeon's squad should be covering, hostile fire forced them to hug dirt. They returned fire, but were badly exposed, and bullets zinging around them forced them to retreat. They left half of Myclos's squad behind, dead.

They found some minimal cover behind a bend in the perimeter bulwark. John keyed into the command circuit. "The wall's been breached, far right flank of the eastern perimeter. Taking heavy losses."

John called in another squad to back them up, but they were badly outnumbered and retreated under fire, leaving more dead behind. The firefight turned into a battle of attrition as they slowly gave ground, and by the time Fourth Platoon reinforced them, John had lost over forty soldiers from his platoon.

Fourth Platoon repelled the First Battalion soldiers who had breached the perimeter, and the fight ended.

29

Harsh Retribution

AS JOHN STOOD looking over the line of stretchers, he noted that Leeze Caputto lay among them, her eyes unseeing. He again reminded himself that the wounds he saw weren't real, but it felt so real. When command killed the feed from the sim suits, his platoon mates would rise from the dead, forty-three of them in all. That didn't lessen the anger that churned at his gut.

Standing beside him, Carla demanded, "What the fuck happened?"

Her words snapped him out of his reverie. "Our right flank collapsed."

"Shit!" she said, but then she frowned and appeared to look more closely at the line of stretchers. "I don't see anyone from DeLeon's squad. They were covering that ravine on our right flank, weren't they? Why didn't they call for help? And why don't I see some of them here with the dead?"

John didn't answer her. During the battle she had probably left her visor keyed to see only the dead and wounded, and didn't know DeLeon's squad had abandoned the ravine.

She cocked her head to one side, and John watched her thinking it through. "If they were overwhelmed, there should be some of them here among the dead, maybe even all of them."

She turned to John, her brow wrinkled in thought. "Why . . ."

Clearly, she didn't know what question to ask, couldn't imagine that DeLeon would abandon their flank.

John said, "DeLeon and his squad weren't covering that ravine, and I'm going to find out why."

Her eyes widened for a moment, then her face hardened into sharp planes of fury. "I'm coming with you."

He'd never before seen her that angry. "No," he said. Right now the last thing he needed was a furious Carla ready to commit murder. "Go back to your squad. I'll handle this."

"No, I'm coming with you."

"No, you're not. Go back to your squad, and that's an order."

For an instant he thought she might refuse the order, but then she turned and marched away from him, her boots raising puffs of dust as she took each angry step.

First Battalion could attack again at any time, so all actives remained on the perimeter. They ate at their posts from ration packs, though individuals were allowed to take a latrine break when necessary. Carrying his rifle, John returned to the east perimeter and checked with the remnants of his platoon. Then he walked carefully toward the ravine on their far right flank.

DeLeon had three of his squad watching the ravine closely to give warning if the enemy attempted a daylight foray. The rest of his people sat in small groups, eating breakfast, or playing cards, or just talking.

DeLeon and Paul Ackrov sat at a small fire pit, DeLeon eating from a ration pack. Ackrov sat next to him, using a stick to stir the ashes in the fire. When John approached, DeLeon looked up, while Ackrov continued to stir the ashes, a distant, contemplative look on his face. DeLeon didn't acknowledge John's presence.

"Corporal DeLeon," John said, pulling rank on him. "A word with you please."

DeLeon stopped eating with a fork of food half way to his mouth. He considered John for a moment, and made it clear by the look on his face that he didn't approve of what he saw.

"Sure," he said. "Why not?"

He made a show of carefully putting the ration pack down near the fire, then stood and faced John.

Standing about five paces from DeLeon, John hooked a thumb over his shoulder and said, "Let's speak in private."

DeLeon shook his head. "No, Mathius. If you've got something to say, you can say it in front of my people."

For the first time Ackrov looked away from the fire and said to DeLeon, "I told you we shouldn't have done that."

"Do what," John asked, "abandon your post during a battle?"

Ackrov grimaced and returned his gaze to the fire.

DeLeon spit words in John's face. "We didn't abandon our post. We had a tactical opportunity to hurt the enemy, and we took it."

John asked, "What opportunity?"

DeLeon put his hands on his hips, and spoke as if lecturing a child. "Three squads from First Battalion tried to flank us. They didn't use the ravine as an approach, probably thought we'd be so focused on that we wouldn't spot them."

He hooked a thumb at his own chest. "But I was smart. I had one of my people covering the hillside approach above the ravine, and when he told me they were coming, we were able to ambush them."

He gave John a big, cheesy, satisfied grin. "Twenty-two confirmed kills, Mathius. That's what I've got to show for the night's work. And a good night's work it was. What have you got to show? You held the perimeter. That's all."

John had hoped to hear something about being overwhelmed by superior forces. Even then, holding their position and calling for reinforcements would have been the right thing to do. Had they been overrun in that way, abandoning their post without ensuring that the right flank was covered would have simply been bad judgement. John had wanted to hear anything but that DeLeon had sacrificed his platoon mates in an egotistical quest for personal glory.

John's anger dissipated, and quiet determination took its place. He surprised himself at how calm he sounded when he spoke. "No, Corporal, I have forty-three confirmed kills to show for the night's work."

DeLeon frowned uncertainly.

John continued. "Forty-three of *our* people died last night." He put hard emphasis on the word *our*. "Forty-three of our people died because you abandoned your post, and I'm not even counting the wounded."

DeLeon shook his head. "The only person you've got to blame for that is yourself. You were our platoon leader, you . . ."

John stopped listening. Standing there, holding his rifle carefully aimed at the ground and listening to DeLeon rant at him, he didn't really consider his actions. He simply raised the barrel of his rifle, and shot DeLeon in the knee.

DeLeon screamed and collapsed in the dirt, clutching at his knee and crying out in pain. Ackrov and the rest of his squad jumped to their feet, their eyes wide with disbelief. John walked forward as DeLeon screamed in agony. "You fucking maniac. What did you do that for?"

John stopped when he got to DeLeon, aimed his rifle and shot the asshole in the chest. DeLeon's sim suit determined that that round had been a kill shot, and he lost consciousness as a bright blossom of blood pooled in the center of his torso.

John looked to Ackrov. "You're now in charge of this squad."

He turned his back on them and began walking, tried to do so contemptuously, wanted them to understand that he didn't care if one of them decided to shoot him in the back. But about ten paces in front of him the air shimmered above the open ground, and Sergeant Omuglu appeared as if coalescing out of the air itself.

It took John only an instant to figure out how she'd appeared that way. Stealth suits worked best when combined with any reasonable cover like brush or shadows. They could nicely mimic a mottled or confusing background. But out in the open in broad daylight, the suit produced an obvious telltale shimmer in the air, easily raising one's suspicions even of one didn't know what to look for. John realized then that their NCOs and instructors had been walking freely among them throughout the entire exercise. They had probably inserted a bit of code in their implants to mask that shimmer, which made them truly invisible. And the only reason Omuglu would choose to reveal herself now was to let DeLeon's squad know that there were witnesses present, which meant there had been plenty of witnesses who saw John shoot DeLeon.

He thought about it for a moment, and realized that had he known beforehand that his superiors were walking among them, he still might have shot the son-of-a-bitch anyway.

••••

Had anyone asked John, he would have sworn that no one could shout louder or longer than a DI. But when the exercise ended the day after John shot DeLeon, Colonel Brightlaw proved him wrong on both counts.

Standing at attention in the middle of the Colonel's office, his arms braced at his sides, his back rigid and straight, with Hershman and Omuglu looking on, John prayed that they wouldn't court-martial him and throw him out of the corps. Succeeding in this ill-advised venture had come to mean something quite important to him.

Brightlaw marched back and forth in front of him waving his arms, his face a brilliant red, his voice growing hoarse. He stopped and faced John, leaning forward and putting his nose a fraction of an inch from John's. Tiny drops of spittle spattered John's face as Brightlaw said, "You blazing, fucking idiot. What were you thinking?"

"Sir," John said at the top of his lungs. "I was pissed off at Corporal DeLeon, sir. He abandoned—"

Brightlaw interrupted him. "Wrong answer, Sergeant."

"Sir, sorry, sir."

Brightlaw didn't let up. "You bet your ass you're sorry. You're the sorriest piece of shit I've ever seen. Now what's the right answer, moron?"

John took a guess at what the Colonel wanted to hear. "Sir, no excuse, sir."

"That's better," Brightlaw screamed, though apparently the correct response didn't appease his ire enough to get him to lower the volume. "And you don't get a pass just because you knew you wouldn't really kill him, that it was all sim suits and virtualization."

That took John by surprise, because at the time he'd shot DeLeon, he wasn't sure if he had really considered that. At that moment, with Brightlaw screaming in his face, he tried to recall if he had decided then that he could shoot DeLeon because it wouldn't really kill him, and he couldn't resurrect such a memory. Surely, that must have been part of his thinking. Surely, he hadn't really intended to kill the shit-head.

Brightlaw continued to rant. "I should court-martial you, throw you completely out of the corps. But I'm not going to be that nice to you. No, you're signed on for the duration, and I'm going to keep you in the corps so I can make your life the epitome of absolute misery. Do you understand me?"

"Sir, yes, sir."

Brightlaw marched circles around John, detailing all the horrendous tasks he would make him perform for years to come. Some John thought were actually impossible, like being stuffed into a vac suit, then towed behind a ComSec cruiser at the end of a long plast tether and keelhauled in and out of transition a few times. He made a mental note to look that one up, just in case.

Brightlaw finally wound down, finished by pointing to his office door and shouting, "Get out. Now. I don't want to ever see your ugly face again except when I go to the latrine. Because you're going to spend the rest of your military career on permanent latrine duty. You're going to be digging field latrines and cleaning them out with a teaspoon. Now get out."

John saluted.

Brightlaw didn't return the salute, but ignored him and looked past John at Omuglu. "Sergeant Omuglu—rocks. Start him with picking up rocks. We'll let him do that for a couple of years."

To John, he simply said, "Get out."

John completed the salute, executed a parade-ground about face, and marched past Omuglu and Hershman through the door, closing it carefully behind him.

••••

After the door closed, Stephen Brightlaw had trouble keeping a straight face. Hershman couldn't hold it in and laughed quietly. Omuglu's face remained impassive, though she did crack a slight smile.

Hershman said, "I liked the bit about the teaspoon."

Brightlaw raised an eyebrow, grinned and said, "Think I scared the shit out of him?"

Hershman grinned and nodded. "I think we came close to seeing a live demonstration of Sergeant Major Prescott's shit lecture."

Brightlaw felt rather proud of himself. "He was close to blowing brown, wasn't he?"

Omuglu sobered. "Sir, is he going to lose a stripe?"

Hershman stopped laughing and asked, "He didn't hesitate when he shot him, huh?"

Omuglu said, "Not a nanosecond, sir."

Hershman cocked his head to one side and appeared thoughtful. "I might have shot that moron myself."

"Sir," Omuglu said, "may I speak frankly."

Brightlaw couldn't hide his impatience. "By all means, Master Sergeant. You've more than earned the right."

Her lips curled upward in a faint smile, a rare occurrence for the woman. "I must confess, sir, that I was sorely tempted to shoot the son-of-a-bitch myself."

Brightlaw gave her a broad grin. "I'm glad I wasn't there, because I don't think I could have shown the same admirable restraint."

She raised an eyebrow and the faint smile disappeared.

Brightlaw killed the grin on his face and said to Omuglu, "Bring DeLeon in next. If you think I ripped Mathius a new asshole, wait 'till you see what I do to that idiot. After that, for the next tenday, I want both of them doing every shit job you can come up with; the shittier the better. And I want everyone to see them doing it side-by-side. But I need to deliver a clear message to the entire training regiment. DeLeon loses a stripe. Mathius doesn't."

Omuglu said, "DeLeon will hold that against him too, sir."

"Will he, now?" Brightlaw asked.

She nodded. "Yes, sir, he will."

That saddened Brightlaw; he knew DeLeon's parents. They washed out plenty of soldiers as a matter of course, but every year they lost one or two that he wished they could have saved. "Is Mr. DeLeon turning out to be a hard case?"

Omuglu shrugged. "More like a glory hound, sir. He thinks that'll get him into the Blacksword."

Hershman said, "I'm curious to see how our darkhorse will handle the glory hound." He looked pointedly at Omuglu. "We do have to let him handle it if he chooses to, don't you agree?"

Omuglu shrugged. "I'll be sure to look the other way when the time comes, sir."

Brightlaw said what they were all thinking. "If one of them kills the other, we'll have to hang the one who's still alive."

••••

John bent down, picked up another rock and tossed it into the bed of the autonomous grav truck. He picked up another, and another, and he followed the truck as it matched his pace. If he stopped to pick up several rocks in one place, it too stopped and waited for him, then started up again as soon as he marched on.

It had been an hour since Brightlaw had kicked John out of his office, and he hadn't yet made much progress in the rock department. Dusk wasn't far off when he spotted two people coming his way across the parade ground: Omuglu walking casually, and DeLeon stiffly marching to her orders. DeLeon had a hole torn in each of his sleeves just below his shoulders where his corporal's strips had been. It appeared that someone had forcibly cut them away, and not been gentle about it.

John didn't know what to make of that. He'd assumed they'd get around to taking away his stripes after he'd spent a couple of hours on rock patrol. But it appeared they'd cut away DeLeon's stripes immediately, right there in Brightlaw's office. And since they hadn't done that to John, did that mean they weren't going to take his stripes? And if so, did that mean DeLeon would hold that against him as well?

"Private," Omuglu said to DeLeon, making no attempt to hide her anger, "get to work."

DeLeon glared at John with hard, angry eyes as he joined John behind the rock truck.

John bent down to pick up a rock. DeLeon bent down beside him and whispered, "Mathius, you're going to pay for—"

Omuglu shouted, "Shut up, Private."

John and DeLeon walked side-by-side, picked up rocks and tossed them into the bed of the grav truck, with Omuglu following them. They worked in silence, the only sounds to be heard the whine of the truck's grav fields, the crunch of boots on the parade ground gravel, and the plink of the rocks as they landed in the bed of the truck.

About an hour after dusk Omuglu halted them and said, "It's chow time so I'm leaving you now. You'll both work until midnight, and don't either of you leave a second before that. Then report to me at oh-five-hundred sharp tomorrow morning. You're going to spend a tenday on shit detail, and if you want to stay in the corps, you'll perform every crap job I come up with as if it is the most important job you've ever had. Because it is. And trust me, I am going to get as inventive as I can for you two morons. Now get back to work."

She turned around and walked away.

John returned to picking up rocks. DeLeon remained still for a moment watching him, then joined him. They worked in silence for about ten minutes, then DeLeon said, "You cost me my stripes."

John didn't say anything.

"Answer me, Mathius."

John knew he couldn't make DeLeon understand that he had only himself to blame for his demotion, and he felt weary as he said, "Was there a question there I didn't hear?"

"You cost me my stripes, and we're going to settle this once and for all."

John straightened, stopped and turned to face DeLeon. "Not here, not now, unless you want to get drummed completely out of the corps."

DeLeon's eyes narrowed, and for a moment John thought he would start a fight then and there. But then a calculating look crossed his face and he said, "When the tenday of shit duty is over, and we're both free, then you and me, alone, no instructors, no officers, no witnesses. You and me, hand-to-hand, in private, the hard way."

John had learned his lessons well, and during the last two years had demonstrated proficiency at everything the corps had thrown at them. But DeLeon had trained in martial arts for a couple of years before joining the corps, and had proven time and again that he could best anyone in Second Battalion at hand-to-hand fighting. They both knew John didn't stand a chance against him, not if he played by DeLeon's rules. John closed his eyes and breathed a tired sigh. "The hard way it is."

He didn't think DeLeon really understood what the *hard way* would be like. John intended to teach him—the hard way.

30

The Hard Way

MASTER SERGEANT OMUGLU proved to be every bit as good as her word. The woman turned out to be incredibly inventive, though John reminded himself that he shouldn't be surprised at that. After all, she was an instructor, and they had all learned long ago how DIs had an unparalleled ability to take true evil to the limits of sanity. The first morning of their ten-day shit duty, she had John and DeLeon clean a fourteen tonne grav lift. But to do it, she gave them each a tiny little brush and a metal cup, then parked the grav lift out at the edge of the parade ground, with the nearest source of water two-hundred meters distant.

"You've got the whole day," she told them, "at the end of which this thing had better sparkle like it's brand new."

John had no idea what the grav lift had been used for recently, but dried mud and brown dirt caked its skids, grav plates, and hoist. Both John and DeLeon learned to sprint on their way to get the water, but if they didn't walk carefully back to the grav lift, there'd be little or no water left in the metal cup with which to clean the damn thing. Omuglu placed a small chair in the shade of the building near the water spigot, sat down and watched them work.

About ten minutes after she sat down, another instructor joined her carrying a chair and two beers. He handed her one of the beers, placed his chair beside hers, and sat down to enjoy the show. They clinked beer bottles and took a sip. A short time later another instructor joined them. Within an hour more than a dozen instructors sat on comfortable chairs in the shade. Someone had floated a grav stretcher out with a couple of coolers on it. Someone else fired up a field stove and they cooked synth steaks on it, and washed them down with plenty of beer. John's mouth watered as the wonderful smells wafted past him.

John and DeLeon spent the entire day on the grav lift, and never did get it even close to clean.

The second day she had them follow the autonomous grav truck around the parade ground. They started out in the morning with its bed filled with the rocks they had picked up a few days earlier. She tasked them with taking each rock out of the bed of the truck and carefully placing it on the parade ground, demanding that they spread them out evenly so they sparsely dotted the entire open area. They weren't allowed to simply drop a rock, not even by so much as a centimeter. Omuglu demanded that they bend over and carefully place each on the ground. And they were allowed to take only one rock at a time out of the bed of the truck, never a hand full. The next day she put them to work following the grav truck around, picking the rocks up off the ground and tossing them back into the bed of the truck. John and DeLeon could agree on almost nothing, but they did agree that the woman possessed a capacity for evilness beyond anything imaginable.

She occupied every spare moment they had, but she didn't let them use their assignment to punishment detail as an excuse to skip their academic studies and other training responsibilities. She made them attend every one of their classes, and if they happened to be covered in mud and shit at the time, she did let them wash their face and hands beforehand. Everyone in the regiment looked forward to the day when they didn't have to endure John and DeLeon's stink.

For breakfast, lunch and dinner, she brought them field rations and gave them ten minutes to wolf down their meal, though she let them drink all the water they wanted at any time. Latrine breaks were allowed every two hours, and if they couldn't get it out in a couple of minutes, they'd just have to hold it until the next break, or piss in their pants, which they were forced to do a couple of times. She gave them one minute to shower when their day ended each night at midnight. Then John toweled off, crawled into his bunk and fell into a deep and sound sleep, though he always recalled Omuglu's words standing in the dark that first night. She had said ". . . if you want to stay in the corps . . . ," and John did want that very much. Remembering those words, he took great care to always set an alarm in his implants for a few minutes before oh-five-hundred hours. When it woke him, he staggered out of his bunk each morning, hurriedly dressed, and reported to her on time.

John and DeLeon cleaned the barracks latrines with the same little brushes and tin cups they had used on the big grav lift. However, before they started on the latrine in a particular barracks, Omuglu turned off the water in that building, forcing them to go to a barracks next door to fill their tin cups. Again, they were forced to always walk back carefully to ensure some water remained in the little metal cups.

One day she dumped a couple thousand liters of water onto the middle of the parade ground. Then she handed them shovels, and made their barracks mates watch as they tried to dig a hole in the muddy quagmire she had created. The hot sun tended to dry out the mud, so she occasionally sprayed them with a fire hose just to keep things really mucky. And she told their barracks mates that if they didn't heckle John and DeLeon, they would have to join them digging in the mud. John tried not to fault his friends for the enthusiasm of their shouts, but they did seem to enjoy themselves a little too much.

One night after his shower near the end of the ten days, John toweled off, pulled on his shorts, and he found Carla and Roark waiting for him outside the showers.

"You okay?" Carla asked.

John said, "I'll survive."

Roark asked, "Pretty rough, huh?"

John raised an eyebrow and shrugged. "They have to make sure everyone understands what I did was wrong."

Carla asked, "Was it?"

John hadn't had time to really consider that, but he took a moment to do so, and he could only answer with, "Yah, it was."

Carla said, "Not as wrong as what DeLeon did."

John shook his head sadly. "No, but still wrong."

Roark's lips tightened into a scowl. "Would you do it again?"

That, John didn't need to think about. "Yah, I would."

Carla asked, "Even if it was for real?"

She didn't need to elaborate. She meant: if it had been real combat, real lives lost, no sim suits, and DeLeon truly dead after John shot him, would he still do it? That, John *did* need to think about for a moment, and then he said, "Yah, I think I might."

••••

Master Sergeant Omuglu proved to be true to her evil nature to the very last. John could not have imagined the things she came up with. But the ten days of shit detail did finally come to an end. On the eleventh day John awoke at a normal hour and returned to his training classes. When he walked into the first one that morning and he wasn't covered with dirt, sweat and mud, and he didn't stink, everyone stood, including the instructors. They all cheered and gave him a rousing round of applause. The instructor informed him that he was now named *shit-stink*, and told everyone to address John that way when in class.

John and DeLeon didn't cross paths much that day, and when they did they were never alone. If DeLeon just dropped the matter and they didn't have to settle the score between them, John wasn't sure if he'd be happy about that. DeLeon needed to pay for abandoning his post, for abandoning his comrades, and if DeLeon decided not to push the matter, John thought he might have to do the pushing. But as John returned to the barracks late that day carrying a load of laundry, he encountered DeLeon just outside the door, with no one else present. It didn't seem like a coincidence, and he thought it likely DeLeon had been watching for him.

"You're a coward," DeLeon said. "You're afraid to fight me."

John shrugged and cocked his head to one side. "Believe whatever you choose."

"You're afraid. Admit it."

John thought about that for a moment and realized that DeLeon couldn't understand what he did fear. "To be honest, Macus, I'm more afraid of what I'll do to you if we do fight."

DeLeon frowned with uncertainty, then he scoffed at John. "You're afraid and you're a coward."

John considered DeLeon for a moment, and realized that he could not get on with whatever career he might have in ComSecCorps until he put the matter to rest.

"Tonight," DeLeon said, "Right after lights-out. The gym will be empty. We'll have it to ourselves."

Resigned to the fact that he had no choice, John said, "Tonight, lights-out, I'll be there."

DeLeon smiled pleasantly and walked away.

••••

John had several hours to think about what he needed to do. It wouldn't be good if he or DeLeon came out of their fight unscathed. It must be clear to everyone that they had settled their differences, and that John had bested DeLeon, though that would surprise them all. But John also needed to make DeLeon understand a few very fundamental facts, and he could do that only with a very brutal lesson; the hard way, as DeLeon had put it.

At evening mess, Leeze said, "You look like you need to get laid."

Carla said, "What's got you so preoccupied?"

"Yah, shit-stink," Roark said. "You haven't said a word."

"Just thinking about us," John lied. "We're going to be done here in another tenday, and they'll give us our new duty assignments."

Carla said, "You gentlemen going to miss me?"

Roark said, "Of course I'll miss you, sweetheart, but I've never had any gentlemanly thoughts about you."

She wrinkled her nose. "Just nasty ones, eh?"

He gave her an evil grin. "Only the nastiest."

"Details," Leeze said. "Come on Checkov. I want to hear details, the nastier the better."

Their words were typical banter for the three of them, and John suspected that at some point Carla and Roark had taken it a lot further than just banter. But if so, it hadn't lasted, and he was glad it hadn't gotten in the way of their friendship.

Carla, seated across the table from John, leaned forward and whispered, "Don't look now, John, but DeLeon's seated three tables behind you, and he hasn't taken his eyes off your back all evening. If looks could kill . . ." She left that hanging.

"Yah," John said. "I guess I'm going to have to do something about him."

Carla, Leeze and Roark nodded their agreement, but John knew that they couldn't really understand what he meant.

After dinner John cleaned his gear and secured his bunk area and locker. Then he spent the rest of the evening with his barracks mates studying, though he had trouble concentrating. With exams approaching, the normally strict lights-out requirements had been relaxed somewhat, especially if someone wanted to do some last minute cramming at a library terminal. Their instructors had set aside special study rooms for that purpose.

As lights-out approached, John told Carla, Leeze and Roark, "I need to do a little cramming."

Roark said, "You want me to help?"

"Nah," John said. "I just gotta catch up on some reading I missed during shit-detail."

He took a small library terminal with him to make it look good, and walked toward the building that contained the study rooms. But once alone, he slipped into a shadow and headed in a different direction. He found DeLeon waiting for him just outside the gym.

"You showed up," DeLeon said. "I didn't think you would."

John gave him a pained smile. "I wouldn't miss it for the world."

DeLeon had already picked out a small exercise room. It had an open floor covered with mats, and no windows. He flicked on the lights, and they both stripped down to the waist. DeLeon warmed up, shadow sparring with the confidence of a man who knew with utmost certainty he would win. John warmed up as well, but with none of the flare DeLeon exhibited. Watching him, DeLeon's confidence appeared to swell even further. John could only hope that might give him an edge.

They squared off in the center of the room, both dancing lightly on the balls of their feet. DeLeon opened with a straight front kick. John back-stepped and evaded it easily. Then DeLeon stepped in and threw a left jab at his face, which John recognized as a fake preceding a side kick. John took the kick on his shoulder, which hurt some, but nothing like it would have had he taken it in the ribs. John threw a quick round kick, but DeLeon blocked it, throwing John off balance, then back-fisted him in the cheek. As they separated John got in a quick pick-up kick to DeLeon's ribs.

They squared off again, John's cheek throbbing, a small trickle of blood dripping down to his chin. He hoped DeLeon's ribs hurt, even if just a little.

They engaged again, a fast series of kick, block, counter-kick and jab. Then again they separated and squared off.

John did better than he had expected, but for every three blows in which DeLeon hurt him, John only returned the pain with one or two. After half an hour of fighting, both of them were winded, sore and bleeding from several injuries. Tomorrow, when they climbed out of their bunks, they'd be unable to hide some very visible cuts, bruises and swelling. Satisfied that he had accomplished his goal, John decided it was time to end it. He hoped he could.

DeLeon assumed that they would fight by the rigid rules of a sparring contest. Of course, he wouldn't hesitate to change those rules if necessary to win, but with his more extensive training, he shouldn't need to. And he knew that John would play by the rules, because John always did. What DeLeon didn't understand was that he had changed the rules when he'd ordered his squad to abandon their post.

John had enough skill to give the asshole some hurt, but more importantly he had enough skill to get within his guard. And John had another advantage: he was willing to take hurt to give hurt.

DeLeon came in with a waist-high round kick. John stepped into it, took it in the ribs and kicked the son-of-a-bitch in the knee. DeLeon cried out and staggered backward, clutching at his knee and limping badly. "What the fuck!"

John charged in and tackled him, picked him up and slammed him on his back to the mat, landing on top of him and putting his shoulder into the asshole's gut as they hit the floor. He heard DeLeon woof as he knocked the wind out of him.

With DeLeon dazed and gasping for air, John rose up and put one knee on his chest, then punched him squarely in the nose, breaking it the way Cranoch had broken his, and spattering blood across the mats. He followed that with a right hook to the bastard's cheek, opening up a large gash there. Then he jabbed him in the ribs several times, so that everyone would see the bruises the next time DeLeon showered. He didn't think he broke any of the asshole's ribs, though if he did, he could live with that. John finished with a few more punches to DeLeon's face to add more cuts and make sure the swelling would be severe.

John hurt everywhere as he climbed to his feet and stood over Macus DeLeon. He gingerly touched his face to see how much damage he'd taken, and realized that in a few hours his upper lip and cheek would be badly swollen, and he'd have a black eye, or maybe two. But DeLeon looked a lot worse than him, and would have trouble opening either eye as the swelling progressed.

DeLeon groaned, and when he spoke, because of the broken nose he sounded like a child with a bad cold. "You cheated. You broke the rules."

John shook his head slowly. "You don't get to pick and choose when we obey the rules. I'm not going to let you force me to obey your rules when it's convenient for you, then watch you break them when it's not. You set our rules when you abandoned your post, and now the only rule that governs you and me is that there are no rules between us. And what I just did was obey that rule to the letter."

DeLeon raised a hand to test the damage to his own face. "Why?"

John decided that above all else, he needed to make DeLeon understand how far he would go. "A man once told me cheaters always win. He was trying to teach me to cheat. He always cheated, so I killed him."

DeLeon froze and one eye opened wide. The other wouldn't open at all.

John leaned down and said, "I want you to remember one thing: cheaters never win. When we're out there and it's real, if you ever go for the glory shot again, and it costs anyone their life, if the corps doesn't execute you, I'll cross the breadth of the entire Commonwealth if I have to, and I'll find you, and I'll execute you myself."

DeLeon managed to get the other eye open a little, and he spoke like a child pleading for mercy. "You'd kill me? You'd actually kill me?"

John grinned, which hurt. "Without blinking an eye."

DeLeon stared at him for several seconds, and as he clearly came to the realization that John meant every word, the look on his face slowly turned to stark and naked fear.

"Come on," John said. He bent down and helped him to his feet. "Let's get you to medical. They may have to do something about that knee, and they're certainly going to have to do something about that nose."

With one of DeLeon's arms wrapped around John's shoulders so he didn't have to put weight on the damaged knee, they made their way to the entrance to the gym building, John limping almost as much as DeLeon. When they stepped out of the building, he found Carla, Leeze and Roark waiting for them.

Carla took one look at them and said, "Shit!"

Roark said, "Thought so. How bad is he?"

With DeLeon still leaning on him, John said, "Broken nose, maybe some torn ligaments in the knee. I don't think I broke any of his ribs."

Leeze looked DeLeon over in the dim lights of the nighttime camp. "Can't say you didn't deserve it, shit head."

Roark stepped in, lifted DeLeon's arm off John's shoulders and put it around his own. "We'll take Mr. DeLeon to the infirmary. Wouldn't look good if you showed up with him, not the way you look."

Carla took DeLeon's other arm and wrapped it around her shoulders. She said, "If you try to cop a feel, asshole, I'll take out the other knee."

The three of them staggered away, leaving John there with Leeze. She looked him over carefully. "There's blood all over you. Bet you left a mess in there. I'll go clean it up."

John limped back to the barracks and found Omuglu waiting for him just outside the door.

She looked him over carefully before saying, "Did you kill him?"

John shook his head. "No, though medical is going to have to fix him up a bit."

"Good," she said. "Did he learn anything?"

John considered her question for a moment. "Probably not what he needed to learn."

She gave him an unhappy frown. "Then what did he learn?"

Omuglu had access to his records, so she had to know he had come from Novalis III. John shrugged. "That he won't ever do that again. Not if he wants to stay alive."

Her lips curled up in a pained smile. "Well I guess that'll have to do."

31

The Few

AT REVEILLE THE next morning, knowing he'd be given no mercy by Omuglu, John climbed out of his bunk like an old man after a long illness. He couldn't open one eye, and with an upper lip swollen so badly it impeded the air flow through his nostrils, his words sounded mushy and included a lot of funny sibilants. He noticed that the bruises on his torso had turned an ugly bluish-yellow. Everyone else in the platoon noticed that too, and they apparently concluded he had lost badly to DeLeon, which he didn't mind. DeLeon was the only person to whom he needed to deliver a clear message, so the rest could believe what they wished. But as they assembled, Carla marched his way, and threw him a big high-five. He had no choice but to reach up and meet it, and that hurt like hell.

As she slapped his hand, she said, "Kicked the shit out of that mother-fucker, didn't you?"

That put a frown on a lot of faces.

None of his platoon mates missed the fact that DeLeon hadn't slept in his bunk, nor that John looked like he had been hit by a big grav truck, and the usual morning banter remained subdued. When they assembled for morning inspection, standing at attention at his bunk in his underwear, John noticed several of them taking surreptitious glances his way.

Omuglu walked down the line of young soldiers going through the normal routine as if nothing had happened the previous night. She stopped in front of John and said, "What happened to you, soldier?"

Since she knew exactly what had happened, he assumed she didn't want him to tell the truth in front of the entire platoon. "I fell down, Sergeant."

She pursed her lips and said, "Took a nasty fall, huh?"

"Yes, Sergeant."

"Hmmm!" she said. "Mr. DeLeon took a nasty fall last night as well. Is there some hazard here on the base that we should report? I wouldn't want other soldiers to take a nasty fall."

"No, I took care of it, Sergeant."

She grinned and looked up and down the line of soldiers, and finished by addressing John. "Private DeLeon's fall was much worse than yours. He's going to spend a couple of days in the infirmary while they grow some new ligaments in his knee and patch up his face. He's got a couple of broken ribs as well. It was a really bad fall, might have killed him. I'm glad you took care of whatever that hazard was, soldier. It's good to know you're proactive about such things. But do report to the infirmary and have those cuts and bruises looked at."

"Yes, Sergeant."

Again she looked up and down the line of soldiers. "Hopefully, it won't happen again."

The infirmary patched John up nicely. When they asked what had happened to him, he winced and said, "I fell down."

The medic gave him a dubious look. John had decided to stick to that ridiculous story no matter how much they pressed him, but all the fellow did was nod and say, "Nasty fall, huh?"

No one on the medical staff questioned him further, and John suspected that Omuglu had dropped a hint or two to let it slide. Thankfully, he had six days to recuperate before their exams.

••••

After a two-day absence, DeLeon returned to the barracks, exhibiting a faint limp, bruises blackening both eyes, his lips and cheeks swollen worse than John's. John tensed when DeLeon first appeared, and as he walked down the aisle that ran the length of the room between the rows of bunks, John feared that now he'd have to deal with some sort of unpleasant confrontation. But DeLeon had only taken a few steps when Leeze stepped out into the aisle walking the opposite direction. She bumped into him, their shoulders colliding briefly, causing both of them to stagger a little. They both ignored the accident and continued walking.

Another of their platoon mates stepped out into the aisle, walking the opposite direction, and they too collided in the same way. By the time DeLeon reached his bunk, he had suffered eight more similar collisions with eight more platoon mates. Upon careful consideration, John recalled that all ten soldiers who had stepped out into the aisle and shoulder-butted DeLeon were among those who had been *killed* during that last exercise.

DeLeon no longer openly glared at John, but looked at him now with obvious doubt, bordering on fear. Nor did he attempt to gather his friends around him like a sycophantic retinue. In any case, Paul Ackrov and a few others appeared to have had second thoughts about their friendship, and DeLeon seemed to have lost the charismatic draw that had originally attracted them. Forty-three soldiers had *died* during the last exercise because their right flank had been abandoned. They didn't openly deride DeLeon, but they made it quite clear they disapproved of his actions that day. And as a majority of the platoon, they formed a critical mass that influenced the opinions of everyone.

In the showers, John noticed that the medical people hadn't healed all the bruising to DeLeon's torso. Omuglu must have dropped a few hints to them about that as well.

Their exams lasted eight days, a series of grueling and intense assessments of the physical and academic skills they had acquired. They all knew that no one would fail the exams and get washed out; their basic training had taken care of that. But their performance on the exams would be a strong factor in their assignments. When the regiment posted the results, DeLeon came in at the top of the class, and John just squeaked into the top thirty percent.

During their first year at Miriteen, and now during Command School, whenever they got leave, those without family nearby had returned to the cheap hotels on the edge of town, but the partying had never been as raucous as the celebrations at the end of basic. And now, with Command School complete, the regiment granted them a ten-day leave, and many of them returned there one last time. To save money, John, and Roark shared a room, and Carla and Leeze shared another. Roark had a date, so he tossed his kit on one of the beds and left immediately, and as usual Leeze went out to party. Carla left a few minutes later, while John stayed and took time to unpack. His thoughts kept drifting back to that strange, young Kelk woman, and he thought of Hey-You, and of Carla.

John had no trouble finding a party where he met a young woman who kept giving him an inviting smile. But as he chatted with her he couldn't find the desire within him to take it a step further, so he excused himself and left. She didn't seem too disappointed that he walked away from her, so he had probably been wrong about the invitation in her smile.

John drifted through several parties, and noticed that the reverie in all of them remained considerably subdued. They would all be going to different assignments, and with more than twenty systems in the Commonwealth, many of them would never see each other again. Seated on a long bench seat at a table in a cheap bar, he thought again about Hey-You, and of Nikaela Vreekande, and of Carla, Leeze, and Roark, and a few others.

Without warning Carla plopped down onto the bench seat next to him. "Why so long in the face, hot shot?"

John shrugged. "Just thinking."

"What about?"

He shrugged again. "Nothing in particular."

She gave him that grin that meant she would now go into her teasing routine. "Why is it Roark thinks nasty thoughts about me, and you don't?"

He looked at her carefully, the pretty girl with all the curves who could kick the shit out of half of them, and attitude the shit out of the rest. Like all of them, after basic, she had allowed her dark-brown hair to grow out, though she'd kept it neatly trimmed at chin length. And he'd always thought she had light-brown eyes, but he now realized they were actually hazel. On impulse he leaned close to her and stopped with his lips a finger's breadth from hers. He said, "But I do."

She frowned uncertainly. "Do what?"

His lips brushed hers as he said, "Think about you."

She smiled and asked, "Nasty thoughts?"

"You'll just have to figure that out for yourself."

She looked into his eyes and said, "Are you trying to kiss me?"

He smiled, and barely making contact, he again brushed his lips across hers. "Yes."

Her eyes narrowed with suspicion. "Why now, after all this time? I think I've made it pretty clear I was willing, and you never took me up on it. So why now?"

He really didn't want to explain himself, but he had no choice. "Because, if I ever touched you—in that way—every time we got in the showers with everyone else, it would be kind of embarrassing. But now that we're going our separate ways . . ."

Her frown deepened. "Embarrassing? How? You—"

Her eyes widened and she said, "Oh!" Her lips curled upward in a broad grin. "You wouldn't be able to control yourself, would you?"

Her tongue wetted her lips, almost touching his lips. "So you'd be walking around in the showers with your flag at full-mast, huh? Well, there wouldn't be any flag involved, would there, but the mast would be up for all—"

He kissed her, didn't wait for permission, just kissed her, though she made it clear he had permission in the way she kissed him back. Her tongue explored his mouth, and the kiss lasted for quite a while. When they parted, she spoke breathlessly, "Should I get you a flag for that mast?"

He shut her up with another kiss.

"Get a room."

They both started at the sound of Roark's voice, and looked up to find him standing over their table.

Carla said, "I . . . uh . . ."

Roark sneered at her. "It's about time. It's been excruciatingly painful watching the two of you want to, and neither willing to do anything about it."

"Neither of us?" Carla demanded. "I was always—"

"Bullshit!" Roark said. "And you don't need to get a room because you've already got one. So go make use of it. And don't worry, I won't be returning there tonight. I'm going to be having my own fun elsewhere."

He turned and marched away.

John and Carla found it exceedingly difficult to make it back to their room. They kept finding it necessary to stop and kiss, and touch a little here and there. But they eventually made it, and had a thoroughly wonderful night.

Carla and Leeze had requested assignments to Naval Ops. When they returned to the ComSecCorps base, they learned they had both been assigned to the heavy cruiser *Fearless*, which was nice since the two of them had become inseparable friends. John didn't have an assignment yet, and he wondered if he'd really messed things up on Reisenar, or maybe *killing* DeLeon would now come back to haunt him, or perhaps beating the crap out of that shit would be his downfall. He thought again of that strangely appealing Kelk woman.

••••

Six months after returning to Viktorkinde, Nikaela had grown exceedingly bored with the desk job. She had taken a berth in bachelor officers' quarters on the big station, and her working hours were spent reviewing manifests and expediting repairs and supplies for outbound warships. To alleviate the boredom and occupy some of her free hours she took a lover, a handsome young command boss, senior rank, who worked in one of the other departments. Occasionally, when they made love, she thought of young Private Mathius, and the frightened look he had given her when she had threatened to take him as a lover the next time they met. It was joke, a tease, and she didn't really mean it. She was certain of that.

One night while she and her lover were in the throes of passion, she recalled that frightened look and couldn't suppress a tiny laugh. Her lover froze.

"Are you laughing at me?" he asked.

"No, darling," she said, "not at all. It only sounded like a laugh. It was a gasp . . . of pleasure."

They returned to their love making, and he did give her pleasure.

She applied repeatedly for a transfer to an assignment more challenging, and told herself she just had to be patient, though she did worry that the Novalis tragedy would forever remain a blot on her record. Then one afternoon she received a summons to report at her earliest convenience to the office of Brigadier Skalde Kristdokar on Hyerdride Military Base, the largest facility on Viktorkinde. She sent a reply that the earliest she could be there would be late the next morning, but that she would do everything possible to expedite her journey. She received an immediate response from Kristdokar's secretary, and was told that that would be sufficient.

She took a shuttle down from Viktorkinde Prime, and arrived at Hyerdride at mid-morning. She made her way immediately to Kristdokar's office, and the skalde's secretary told her to have a seat and wait. She sat there and tried not to fidget nervously. An hour later the secretary said, "Skalde Kristdokar will see you now."

Nikaela stepped into the skalde's office, went through the formalities of announcing herself along with the customary salute.

"Ease, Mistress Vreekande," Kristdokar said. She waved a hand toward a chair in front of her desk. "Sit down. Relax. I want to talk to you."

Nikaela sat down, placed her hands carefully in her lap and said, "What may I do for you, mistress?"

The skalde leaned back in her seat and smiled pleasantly. "I've been reviewing your record. I'm glad we managed to put that nasty business on Novalis III behind you. And you did well on Reisenar under very unusual circumstances."

"Thank you, mistress," she said.

"I spoke personally with Thordahl, and I wish to know more about this breschkada of yours."

"Whatever I can tell you, mistress."

"He is a lowly private, yes? And he is breschkada-sa?"

"Yes, mistress, on both counts."

"Please tell me more about the incident on the subway platform."

It had been quite some time and Nikaela had to think carefully to recall the details. She described the events of that night as well as she could. She finished by saying, "It has been more than six months, so I fear my memory may be somewhat cloudy."

Kristdokar dismissed her concerns with a casual wave of her hand. "I understand that, but you have filled in a number of blanks that aren't in the report."

Nikaela asked, "May I ask why I am here, mistress?"

Kristdokar said, "We're putting together a team to see how we might . . . exploit the opportunity you and he created, and I'd like you to join my staff."

Nikaela made no attempt to hide her excitement. "I'd be most pleased to join your staff, Brigadier Skalde."

Kristdokar nodded happily. "Then it's done. I'll cut the orders this afternoon. Take whatever time you need to get your gear down here from Prime. We won't have the team fully assembled for another tenday."

The skalde stood. Nikaela stood with her. The skalde leaned forward on her desk and turned serious. "Keep one thing in mind. This is all highly classified, if for no other reason than that there are factions within the Supremacy who will oppose us, the same factions who tried to start that little war. Right now they are not concerned with you, because you're quite junior and you simply stumbled into something, and thwarted them only by accident. It might not be good for you if they knew we were working actively to thwart them again."

The skalde's words didn't really bother Nikaela, and that night she decided to avoid her lover and sleep alone; she had grown bored with him anyway. She climbed into bed too excited to sleep. She had been glad to hear from the skalde's own lips that she had put the Novalis III business behind her, and now she had something thrilling and challenging to look forward to.

Novalis III. She thought again of that night on that subway platform. Describing the events to the skalde had returned those memories to the forefront of her thoughts. John Mathius had admitted to unnecessarily killing someone once, long ago, and when she pressed him on the matter, he had simply said, "Novalis III."

She sat up and gasped. Novalis III. The young boys she'd seen from the window in that dilapidated mansion in the rebel stronghold. She hadn't recognized him because he had gained some weight, had filled out and lost the look of gaunt emaciation. His eyes had been red and puffy from crying that day, and perhaps now she knew why.

••••

When the Blacksword major asked to meet privately with Stephen Brightlaw, the colonel's curiosity, already aroused, blossomed ten-fold. He had done a lot of reading-between-the-lines lately.

Colonel, his implants said. *Major Teal is here to see you.*

"Send him right in. And ask Master Sergeant Omuglu to make herself available. I may need her to join us."

Certainly, sir.

When Teal entered the office, Brightlaw stood and stepped around his desk, extending his hand. "Major Teal, good to see you again."

Teal smiled and shook his hand. "Thank you for making time for me, Colonel."

The colonel offered him a drink, which he declined, then they went through the formality of a brief bit of small talk. But Brightlaw saw that like him, the major wanted to get down to business and his heart wasn't in it.

Teal finally said, "I'm sure you're wondering why I asked to see you."

Brightlaw decided to cut the bullshit. "Does it have something to do with our darkhorse?"

"I'm curious," Teal said. "How did he do in Command School?"

"Finished in the top thirty percent. Nearly killed DeLeon in the process."

Teal nodded. "Yes, I did hear about that. Did Mr. DeLeon learn anything?"

Brightlaw shrugged. "Only time will tell."

He decided to see if he could get a reaction out of the major. "Tell me, Major, does this have something to do with Reisenar?"

Teal didn't blink, and Brightlaw marveled at how unassuming the Blacksword major could be. "Why would you ask that, Colonel?"

Brightlaw shook his head sadly. "Major, I've been doing this for a long time. I read the reports on that incident. I've also carefully reviewed the entries made into Mr. Mathius's file regarding that incident. Individually, there is something to be read between the lines in each, but when I consider both together, it's clear there's a whole mountain of shit that isn't there."

Teal took a deep breath and let out a long sigh. "Touché, Colonel."

Brightlaw said, "Sergeant Omuglu, whom I believe you have met, is also aware of that mountain of shit. I'd like her to join us."

Teal said, "Were you aware we offered her the Blacksword?"

"No, I was not."

"She turned it down."

"I'm not surprised. If she had accepted, she couldn't continue as a DI and instructor. She's one of the best, prides herself on producing the best for us."

Teal nodded. "By all means, have her join us."

Brightlaw spoke through his implants. "Is Sergeant Omuglu available?"

Yes, sir. She's waiting right here.

"Please have her join us."

A few seconds later Omuglu stepped into the room. Brightlaw pointed to a chair near Teal and said. "Relax and sit down, Sergeant."

Once she had gotten comfortable, Brightlaw said, "Major Teal and I were discussing Mr. Mathius, much as you and I discussed him when he returned from Reisenar."

Her face remained expressionless.

"So, Major," Brightlaw said to Teal, "what can you tell us?"

Teal sat in silence for several seconds, his eyes focused at some distant point. Then he said, "Your darkhorse did a most unusual thing. Where anyone else might have simply killed a Kelk officer, instead he saved her life, and gave her a piece of information that, for all intents and purposes, averted interstellar war between the Commonwealth and the Supremacy."

Brightlaw hadn't expected that. He leaned back in his chair and said, "Holy shit!"

Teal said, "Exactly, Colonel. Tell me, is he officer material?"

Brightlaw didn't have to think about that. "Yes. Why do you ask?"

Again, Teal appeared to consider carefully what he could divulge. "It might be beneficial for all concerned if he shared a similar rank to that of a certain young Kelk officer. If he must interact with her in the future, we'd like it to be as one equal to another."

Brightlaw didn't hesitate. "I would have no reservations about recommending him for O-School."

Teal leaned forward in his chair and said, "If I might make a suggestion, Colonel, don't merely recommend. Actively encourage. It will be good for the young man if you guide him down the right path."

••••

When John reported to Brightlaw's office, after his most recent interaction with the colonel, which had been at something close to ninety decibels, he entered the room with a certain amount of trepidation. He snapped smartly to attention in front of Brightlaw's desk and said, "Sergeant Mathius reporting as ordered, sir."

Brightlaw returned his salute with a casual wave of his hand. The colonel never did anything casually, and John's fears ratcheted up a notch.

"At ease, John," Brightlaw said. "Relax, sit down."

John's fears ratcheted up two notches.

"Sergeant Omuglu, get Mr. Mathius a drink."

Brightlaw had a glass on the desk in front of him containing an amber liquid. John glanced over his shoulder. Omuglu sat in a comfortable chair, a glass in one hand also containing amber liquid, a pleasant smile on her face.

Three notches.

Omuglu stood and crossed the room to a small table containing a bottle of amber liquid and a few empty glasses. She poured a couple of centimeters of the liquid into a glass, then carried it to John and handed it to him.

Four notches.

As Omuglu handed John the glass, she leaned close to him and whispered. "Don't worry, John. This is going to be okay."

Brightlaw came around from behind his desk and the three of them sat down in comfortable chairs. John then listened to the colonel talk quite convincingly about O-School and of how he was eminently qualified to be an officer, and how he could make a greater contribution to the good of the Commonwealth by accepting such an appointment and training hard. He recalled the sergeant in the recruiting office—back then he hadn't known how to read the chevrons of rank insignia. The fellow had told him that he had brains, and John remembered his words exactly, ". . . which, by the way, disqualifies you from ever being an officer."

John understood that he'd grown up quite a bit since that day when he'd left the boy Mathius behind to become the recruit John Mathius, and then the soldier John Mathius.

"So," Brightlaw said. "Are you willing to give it a try?"

John looked a question at Omuglu. She smiled and gave a slight nod of her head. More than anything, John knew that Omuglu wouldn't actively encourage him to do anything that wasn't right for him. "Yes, sir," he said, "I am."

Brightlaw stood. "Excellent! By the way, there's someone else who wants to speak with you? You remember Major Teal, don't you?"

Brightlaw opened the door to his office and in walked the nondescript, soft-spoken Blacksword major. John stood, and Omuglu stood with him. The major handed him a small envelope, saying, "We feel you have earned the right, and so we'd like to offer you the opportunity, to wear these."

John looked in the envelope. In it he saw two cloth patches that contained a background of silver thread surrounding a black sword.

A Comparison of Rank Equivalents

ComSec infantry rank is modeled after that of the United States Army. ComSec navel rank is modeled after that of the US Navy. Kelk rank is based on that of the Kelk Supremacy in effect at the time of this writing. A comparison of officer rank equivalents is provided below:

ComSec Infantry	ComSec Naval	Kelk
Lieutenant 2nd Class	Ensign	Command Boss J. R.
Lieutenant 1st Class	Lieutenant J. G.	Command Boss S. R.
Captain	Lieutenant	Command Superior
Major	Lt Commander	Senior Command Superior
Lieutenant Colonel	Commander	Command Hawk
Colonel	Captain	Command Eagle
Brigadier General	Rear Admiral Lower Half	Brigadier Skalde
Major General	Rear Admiral	Major Skalde
Lieutenant General	Vice Admiral	Vice Skalde
Chief of Staff of the Corp	Chief of Naval Operations	Skalde of the Supremacy
General of the Corp	Fleet Admiral	Skalde Supreme

Acknowledgements

I'D LIKE TO thank Clyde, Tory and Dave for fixing all my dotted t's and crossed i's, and for their invaluable insight, criticism and advice, Karen for both supporting my dream and being my most valuable critic, and Steve Himes, and the whole team at Telemachus, for getting a quality product out the door.

Books by J. L. Doty

Series: The Treasons Cycle
Of Treasons Born
A Choice of Treasons

Stand Alone Novel
The Thirteenth Man

Series: The Gods Within
Child of the Sword
The SteelMaster of Indwallin
The Heart of the Sands
The Name of the Sword

Series: The Dead Among Us
When Dead Ain't Dead Enough
Still Not Dead Enough
Never Dead Enough

Series: The Blacksword Regiment
A Hymn for the Dying
A Dirge for the Damned
A Prayer for the Fallen
A Requiem for the Forsaken

Series: Commonwealth Re-contact Novellas
Tranquility Lost

About the Author

JIM IS A full-time SF&F writer, scientist and laser geek (Ph.D. Electrical Engineering, specialty laser physics), and former running-dog-lackey for the bourgeois capitalist establishment. He's been writing for over 30 years, with 15 published books. His first success came through self-publishing when his books went word-of-mouth viral, and sold enough that he was able to quit his day-job, start working for himself and write full time—his new boss is a real jerk. That led to contracts with traditional publishers like Open Road Media and Harper Collins Voyager, and his books are now a mix of traditional and self-published.

The four novels in his new hard science fiction series, *The Blacksword Regiment*, were released in July 2020. Right now he's fleshing out ideas for the next book in *The Dead Among Us*, he's writing another episode in *The Treasons Cycle*, and he's working on a new fantasy series *The Deck of Chaos*.

Jim was born in Seattle, but he's lived most of his life in California, though he did live on the east coast and in Europe for a while. He now resides in Arizona with his wife Karen and three little beings who claim to be cats: Tilda, Julia and Natasha. But Jim is certain they're really extra-terrestrial aliens in disguise.

Visit the author's website at http://www.jldoty.com
Contact the author at jld@jldoty.com